BEN'S

Sammy Levitt

To order additional copies of this book, contact:
Xlibris
844-714-8691
www.Xlibris.com
Orders@Xlibris.com
825264

This book is dedicated to my mother,
Claudette Pantarelli Levitt, a teacher who worked in
the Philadelphia public school system for 60 years.

CONTENTS

BOOK III
Caesar's Palace

BOOK IV
Answer

PROLOGUE

There is no afterlife.
You create your own
heaven and hell right
here on earth.

BOOK I

Logan

CHAPTER 1

Philadelphia, June 1978

Fifteen-year-old eleventh-grader Tobias "Lil' Rock" Alston ventured to the men's room on the third floor. It was the final day of class before summer vacation at Cooke Junior High School at Broad and Louden Streets in the Logan section of North Philadelphia. At the moment, the students were between the third and fourth period, around eleven o'clock.

'Ventured' was probably the best word, too. The bathrooms at certain public schools in Philadelphia had become adventurous at best and death traps at worse. It wasn't a joke. In fact, if you asked the white students, who made up less than 5 percent of the overall number of youths there, they probably would say that in their entire public school careers, they only used the bathrooms once or twice. Many white kids couldn't even imagine what those men's rooms looked like. They could look like little chapels for all they knew.

Black and with a build that put you in mind of a seven-ounce Joe Frazier, Lil' Rock possessed no such fear. He wore dungarees and a white Adidas T-shirt. He wasn't afraid of the men's room or much of anything else for that matter. He was, after all, a member of the mighty Logan Nation gang, which was one of only two gangs of any significance at Cooke. The other outfit was the Nicetown gang. Nicetown was a section of the city just south of Logan. For the past two years, Logan Nation and Nicetown had been involved in a small but bloody gang war. Fights had occurred outside the school just about every afternoon. But for whatever reasons, these junior high schoolers rarely acted up inside the school itself. Overall, in the twenty-one months that the two gangs had feuded, five youngsters had already been killed. Seven others were doing life sentences at the moment for those murders, and more convictions were pending and expected. Philadelphia needed to overcome in its struggle to unsaddle a certain negative and minor league image that existed nationwide. As for the juvenile-violence specifically, the Logan Nation-Nicetown war was just a subset and throwback to the overall big picture. The police force with a special "gang control" division, the Catholic Church, the Police Athletic League, and other city agencies, as well as many volunteers, had, for the most part, gotten on top of the embarrassing situation. In recent years, there hadn't been nearly as much violence. Except for the Logan Nation-Nicetown fight, the death toll had declined greatly in recent years. However, in the prime years of this type of violence between 1973 and 1975, an average of forty-five to fifty-five were killed every year, mostly all by other youths in street-gang warfare city-wide, most of it coming during the school year months. It wasn't until this stretch (1973 to 1975) that the story received the publicity and attention it deserved. Yet, the statistics show that, from 1968 to 1972, there was an average of forty deaths every year.

In 1970, the Philadelphia police force formed a special "gang control" unit to deal with this problem. That same year, City Council allocated $400,000 for gang workers. The man who was mayor at the time, who was at the end of his term, held back these funds, and eventually they went to sanitation workers in what some called a political maneuver.

From the mid-sixties to the mid-seventies, gang violence had been a key political hot potato in Philadelphia. When the current mayor, Jimmy Cerrone was campaigning, he promised to wipe out the problem, but couldn't. *Philadelphia Magazine* wrote of it: *"The problem is not unimportant to him but it is clearly beyond his capacity to fully appreciate it or solve it."*

Lil' Rock urinated in the stall furthest to the right. He didn't mind school because of his popularity with his friends and with girls, too. His brother Pete was a "warlord," a type of leader in the Logan Nation gang. His next older brother would become a warlord next and eventually he would be one also, and everybody knew it. That was how it worked. It was similar to the Phantom comic strip. First, there was the Phantom, then there was his son, who became the Phantom, then his grandson became the Phantom, and so forth. Lil' Rock liked his next class, which was shop, in particular. During the past several weeks he had been carefully constructing the perfect zip gun. He was now in the process of putting the finishing touches on it. This popular type of homemade weapon was trendy like spinning tops once were, or the gigantic afro combs in the back of one or two pockets were, or mini-bikes were for a while. The zip gun would become obsolete shortly. It could only discharge one round at a time, which was one of its drawbacks, along with a lack of distance and accuracy. A door lock was employed as a type of barrel. Two pipes were used including one copper pipe which was reinforced with glue. Lil' Rock also used rubber bands, nails, and wood. He learned from his brother, an ex-convict from Holmesburg Prison, how to make a zip gun. Despite its flaws, the zip gun had proved to be surprisingly effective and certainly deadly. The zip gun had become sort of a symbol of the "juvenile gang war" era in Philadelphia.

During the short time between classes, the bathroom was always crowded and noisy. There were toilets flushing. Water was gushing in the sinks. The noisy paper towel dispensers were making that "clack-clack" sound. Groups of three or four gathered together to catch a quick smoke and talk about pussy and imagined conquests. As Lil Rock turned to leave after washing his hands, the place suddenly became eerily silent and very lonely. Everything had taken a moment or two longer than it should have. As he tried to exit the bathroom, he heard A fire engine rushing up Thirteenth Street outside the window toward his left. He turned that way to look out of the window. When he turned back to his right to leave, he was then startled by the presence of three young black males who seemed to grow from behind the first stall in the men's room. The one in the center of the black wall, the shortest and darkest of the three spoke.

"Where you from?" The words came like a demand or a statement, anything but a question. It was the last thing he wanted to hear. Like, "Let me hold a dime" these were, Lil Rock knew these primary precursors to this type of violence. Bad things happened when you heard one or the other of those questions. Lil Rock understood he was about to be "moved on."

Lil' Rock was familiar with the one speaking. His last name he thought was Bell. He didn't know his first name, but everybody just called him "Snake." Snake and the one to his right were both from Nicetown. Nicetown, according to gang experts, had an estimated 225 members. On the other hand, Logan Nation only had 100 to 150 members, but Logan Nation had more fire power they always contended. They had as many guns in fact, as some of the biggest gangs in the city such as The Moon from West Philly or the famed Valley gang from North Philly (according to 'gang control' files).

Lil' Rock noted Snake's gold chain with an "N" and a "T" crisscrossing, hanging on his neck, resting on a blue and white Adidas shirt. He wore a red Jeff. Physically Lil Rock and Snake were mirror images, both built like small linebackers. Height-wise Lil Rock was surprised to see now that they were eyeball to eyeball. He thought he was several inches taller than Snake. Snake's boys, the ones from Nicetown, always seemed to be tall and thin, like members of a basketball camp. Snake was always dwarfed by these guys, so he seemed smaller than he really was.

Yet, despite being shorter it always seemed to Lil Rock that Snake was a type of leader in the Nicetown gang. He seemed to be highly regarded by his taller peers. He always dressed nice too. In the winter Snake always wore the long-length, Shaft-like leather coat. Snake was similar to Lil' Rock in that each possessed a wild, fearless streak. The whispers were that Snake had planted two or three men already in his early life. Lil Rock caught Snake's act two weeks ago.

Lil Rock was with a girl at the Toddle House Restaurant, a small, mostly take-out place at Broad and Belfield Street, right on the Mason-Dixon Line dividing Logan and Nicetown. The couple was seated at a booth when Snake came in by himself. He had a take-out order of some hamburgers, French fries, onion rings, and even pecan pie. At 2:30 a.m. the place was crowded as usual because the bars emptied at two o'clock. When the food came, Snake grabbed the bag, turned around, then didn't run, didn't walk, but sort of trotted out onto Broad Street without paying. Twenty minutes later, as Lil Rock and his girlfriend got up to leave, they saw the mischievous Snake, his face pressed to the window, stuffing his face with French fries, laughing and taunting the staff. The staff, of course, having no bonds to Toddle House, really didn't care. Some, Lil Rock noted, suppressed smiles, some didn't even do that.

Lil Rock, despite being aware of Snake's reputation, was disturbed and worried about something else. He was concerned not primarily with Snake, a Nicetown boy, of course, or the other taller one to Snake's left, also from Nicetown. What troubled him immediately was the presence of the one to Snake's right. He had seen him around. They called him Chops, and he had a cousin or something in Logan. The two would occasionally be together playing basketball in the Logan school yard, which was the primarily home for Logan Nation. Lil Rock never knew his gang affiliation, if he had any. But today he was wearing a baseball cap with the bill facing backwards. That was disturbing, in Philadelphia in the seventies that meant North Philly. If Nicetown was somehow tied in with a corner from North Philly, even a small corner, it was all over because they could pull so many other corners and gangs, maybe even the notorious "valley" gang in north Philly and Logan Nation, with as much heart as they had, certainly didn't want them as an enemy.

"Where you from?" Snake asked again. Lil' Rock tried to think of a good answer.

"You from Logan Nation," the other tall one from Nicetown said. It was response time Lil' Rock knew. There simply would be no more questions or accusations. Lil' Rock, despite his very precarious situation, managed to keep a dignified posture and look. If there was fear in him, he didn't show it.

"No, man. I'm from Smedley Valley." The Smedley Valley gang was only a block away from Logan school yard. It was sort of a junior Logan Nation, a type of farm system for Logan Nation – not as big or powerful. There was thought behind that response from Lil' Rock. His adversaries already knew he was from Logan somewhere. Saying that he was from Smedley Valley, he hoped, would be a satisfying alternative to just saying he was from Logan Nation. At the same time, the answer allowed him to hold onto some macho bullshit dignity which he would think about right up until the very end. Also 'Smedley Valley' although they were small in numbers was in the 'Valley' network. It meant they could pull other Valley gangs or corners such as 24 and Burks Valley, or 16 and Oxford Valley or 15 and Venango Valley all of which were in North Philly. Lil' Rock believed it could save him and he didn't come off all pathetic and just say, "No, man, I'm not from any corner." That, he figured, would be an insult to their intelligence and ultimately wouldn't do him any good anyway, and would probably only be counterproductive. At that point, three kids from Nicetown were already dead and two from Logan nation. The score was about to be tied up.

"No man, you from Logan Nation," Snake said for the final time.

Lil' Rock's strategy didn't work out. Then Lil' Rock felt it. It came like a punch, a sharp pain and a dull blow. Then there were a few more. They came rapidly, several more punches each preceded by a sharp pain. The third one sent him forward off his feet. Snake held the increasingly limp youngster upright in his muscular arms. Lil' Rock felt at least two more sharp pricks and simultaneously felt a thud in his back. He was suddenly conscious of more Nicetown boys in the room than he originally thought there were. They started scampering out of the bathroom now. There were five or six in all. One had spray painted on the bathroom walls the words *"The town fucks up."* Lil' Rock grew weaker and weaker by the second. Snake allowed him to slowly descend to the floor in an almost caring fashion. The apathetic look on Lil' Rock's face never changed. This was precisely how a warrior was to go out. This was how a champion was supposed to go out, like Joe Louis did, on his back.

Snake wore nice dress pants and managed to lower Lil' Rock all the way to the floor while keeping his legs and pants and shoes at a safe distance, avoiding the blood as best as he could which now covered Lil' Rock from top to bottom in the back. Finally, Snake was the last to run out of the bathroom. Lil' Rock managed to twist himself around so that he lay prone on the floor. His face rested on the cool bathroom tile now. Somewhere in the distance the school bell went off, indicating it was time for the next class. His mind was still going as life continued to spill from his body. Lil' Rock thought about the last time he'd been laid, which was also the first time he'd been laid. It was only a week or so ago at the "swamp." That was a type of Lover's Lane in the furthermost part of West Logan in an abandoned former Yellow Cab garage. The sparkle left his eyes around then. If he wasn't what they call clinically dead at this point, at least death was in the room with him, on the floor with him now. If there was any hint of a look on his face, machismo or fright, or anything, it had long since vanished. His mind continued to process, however. He imagined that he was alone in an Olympic sized swimming pool, a luxury few people, and none that he knew, would ever experience. And in this post-conscious state, he imagined himself stretched out in the pool. Snake had his arms, and the one with the baseball cap backwards, Chops, had his feet. He was being pulled through the water at about 40 miles an hour. He could feel the water getting increasingly colder as it rushed down his back and ass and legs. It was also rushing with increasing speed underneath him, his belly, and his legs. He was being pulled faster and faster through the water, and then finally there was nothing…just darkness.

CHAPTER 2

Captain Harry Quinn headed the 53rd Police District which oversaw the Logan Section of North Philadelphia. Although Logan was north, it was really much further north than the areas most people in Philadelphia referred to when they said "North Philly." People from Logan, too, whether it was in the thirties, fifties, or now in the seventies, were always quick and sure to make that clear. Logan was a distinct neighborhood with its own look and character and set of problems. Quinn had begun as a street cop twenty-three years ago and with political help had obtained the rank of captain ten years ago. During his tenure as top cop in the District, he had withstood some heavy scandals and problems. In fact, his survival skills were pretty amazing considering police captains didn't ordinarily have a long shelf life. It turned out that police captains were very often convenient scapegoats when the heat was on. Their title made them sound just important enough that, whenever a captain was fired, it tended to satisfy whoever it was at that moment that had a crusade against the police, whether it be the media, the state, or the community.

On the other hand, captains were just powerless enough to not be able to fight it or do anything about it, and the top guys could remain insulated and protected, the status quo intact. By design, police captains for this reason possessed no power but were built up to appear powerful.

Quinn understood this. He knew he had done a good job here at the 53rd, but that really wasn't what mattered. What mattered was who exactly it was who was holding your strings. He didn't kid himself about that. He obviously had some big pull and he knew exactly who it was. He had worked hard as a young cop with the man who was currently the police commissioner, who was his Irish "paisano" and an appointee of Mayor Jimmy Cerrone himself.

Given his favorable position, Quinn didn't worry much about anything. The problem was that now Jimmy Cerrone was nearing the end of his second term as mayor. He won by a landslide in 1971, then four years later, another landslide victory in the '75 elections. According to a long-standing city charter, the mayor was held to a two-term limit. Now Cerrone's people were trying to change the charter in a special election in November. Then Cerrone, the idea was, would run for a third term in 1979. Just yesterday, Quinn attended a meeting downtown held by the Change the Charter committee. Unlike Cerrone's earlier victories, this election promised to be extremely close.

Cerrone had been the police commissioner in the turbulent sixties. He was seen as a tough law and order man, and that image carried over to today. In the 1960s when many other cities on the East Coast burned down and/or were significantly damaged, Philadelphia had sustained only very minor violence. And all of the violence or damage was done in the black community. Whites saw Cerrone now, as then, as the man who would keep their communities relatively crime-free. Inner-city whites loved Cerrone for this reason and voted enthusiastically for him every time. They loved his big 8,000-man police force who Cerrone once said could "invade a small country."

Cerrone had that loyal inner-city white vote and didn't worry about the minor black vote, and that was his winning formula. However, by this point in the late 1970s, the city had almost as many black residents as whites, and blacks had generally been in disagreement with Cerrone's policies over the years. The black community was much more unified in its opinion and stance regarding Cerrone. It was nearly 90 percent against him. The white community, on the other hand, was more evenly divided. Many whites, particularly many liberals and some other smaller groups, were against him. Despite all that, and in spite of the fact that the media would surely line up against Cerrone in this fight as well, Cerrone's people thought they had a good chance. The thing was, in Philadelphia, the black-vote-turnout was very low. Many black residents were not even registered to vote. Therefore, registration was going to be the most important issue in this election ... no question.

At the meeting, Quinn was informed that a registration drive mounted by the enemy was already underway and "Stop Cerrone" registration booths would be on every other block in Center City that summer. The Dagos talked down to Quinn at the meeting. They informed him that Logan with its racial mix could go either way. They said that Logan was a key neighborhood and reminded him that it was precisely those types of fringe neighborhoods that proved to be so flammable in the 1960s. They talked in particular about the Logan Nation Gang. They were counting on Quinn to keep Logan peaceful and quiet this summer. Historically, Cerrone enjoyed an unusual amount of popularity in Logan, even among the blacks. He had always taken care of Logan, paying attention to the trees, the parks, and the streets, as generally speaking, the mayor prided himself on the attention he paid to wildlife and flora in the city. That was a strong suit of his, whether you liked him or not.

The media kept an eye on Logan because there had always been a type of city-wide curiosity about the place. There were a few reasons for this. One thing was the near incredible beauty that the regular, working class neighborhood featured. From its parks, to its tree-lined streets, to the jewel of its crown - the beautiful Holy Child Catholic Church with its 80-foot steeple and stained glass. Labeled "The Cathedral of the North" by local historians, certainly the Holy Child Church, which was built in the 1920s, added to the mystique of the neighborhood. Residents took real pride in their community and the small lawns were nicely maintained with carefully pruned bushes. Many of the twins and row houses had cozy front porches with fresh painted furniture and pots of colorful flowers. In Philadelphia, a city that prided itself on diversity, Logan was the undisputed melting pot.

From 1880-1920 when the two major immigrant groups came to the United States (Irish and Italian) they, in general terms, went separate ways when they got to Philadelphia. The Italians went south and the Irish went north. Logan was mostly Irish, at least on the west side of Broad Street. On the east side of Broad Street (the main north-south artery which ran through the entire city and divided east from west) was a large Jewish community with several synagogues. During the course of the twentieth century, various immigrant groups settled in and embraced Logan. At one point or another, Jews, Ukrainians, Portuguese, Filipinos, and Koreans had populated Logan more than any other section of the city. In East Logan there was Birney grade School which was labeled "The School of All Nations."

Adding to the reputation of the neighborhood was the problem that it had with many of its homes, now called the "Sinking Homes" of Logan. Parts of Logan, especially in the southeast corner, were built inexpensively on a cinder and ash foundation over what possibly was a river that ran under the neighborhood. The homes slanted and leaned into each other like drunken sailors since the thirties and forties, but only recently had some serious drainage problems there developed which promised to only get worse. The "Sinking Homes" were visible to the motorists who drove by on the Roosevelt Boulevard heading home to the popular northeast and who pointed and laughed at the odd-looking houses.

Despite the problems, which included the 53rd District having the highest crime rate in the city...mostly of the misdemeanor sort, Logan was still a relatively safe neighborhood. Even in the mid-seventies when the juvenile gang war problems reached their peak, Logan had been fairly quiet.

This followed a rocky time in the late sixties to early seventies when Logan was in a racial transition and hostilities between the whites and blacks came to a boiling point. Logan at that time had become an area where the practice of blockbusting was rampant. This was the sinister operation of real estate agents scaring the hell out of white homeowners to get them to sell their houses cheaply. One of the tactics they would use would be to circulate flyers into a neighborhood or on a block saying that a record number of houses in the immediate neighborhood had been sold recently and that there were many anxious buyers waiting. The message was pretty clear. "The blacks are coming. Get out while your house is still worth something." The result of this was that both the whites who didn't sell and found that their houses were rapidly decreasing in value, as well as the blacks who were paying high interest rates in a deteriorating neighborhood each felt that they had been victimized or ripped off and a great deal of hostility and animosity flourished. The racial tension of the country resulting from civil rights battles, an unpopular war with an unfair draft, and other dramatic events, the centerpiece of which was the assassination of Martin Luther King Jr. were also reflected in this small changing community.

By 1970, a black juvenile/young adult gang, Logan Nation was the biggest gang in Logan, and they occupied the west side of Broad Street. There were three major white corners or gangs (Dunn's, Ben's and 1-5-D or Fifteenth and Duncannon) in Logan and all three of them had crossed swords at one time or another with Logan Nation. However, over the years, the only white gang left in Logan was "Ben's" (named after a candy store) on the east side of Broad Street. Gang control experts said that the current version of Ben's started sometime in the sixties, although the reality was that corner boys had hung there for generations. Four years ago there were as many as one hundred juveniles or young adults hanging there. The city's gang control experts, as well as social workers, worked hard in Logan resulting in the blacks and whites there eventually making peace in 1972. An uneasy co-existence lasted for about a year.

Then, on a little street named Albanus in the west part of Logan, a black youth called Fat Eddie was shot while riding his mini-bike. The shot had come from a rifle from one of the homes on that street.

A disheveled white boy unaffiliated with any gang was arrested for the crime. They took him out of his house in handcuffs, wearing dungarees and no shirt. He claimed that he had been sleeping in his living room at the time. The police didn't believe him. The black neighbors around there did believe him. They also believed that the shot came from another house on that block. It was never proven, but they believed that a boy named Frenchie, who lived on that street and was from Ben's, was somehow involved with the shooting.

New violence began between Logan Nation and Ben's that summer. Quinn, worried about a large-scale race riot, had put a police presence on the east side of Broad Street where Ben's hung. The gang control arm of the Philadelphia Police Department had sent Quinn a gang control expert who had been working with gang trouble spots in both North and South Philadelphia. His name was Ken Washington, and he was an expert in working with youngsters and young gangs in particular. Washington, Quinn remembered, was studying at that point to be a criminal psychologist. He was working on a master's degree from Temple University and was functioning as a sort of combination cop and social worker. He had been very valuable that summer keeping any young blood from getting worked up and preventing any further violence. By the time the winter came, Logan was peaceful again, but Washington stayed in the 53rd District mainly because Quinn was happy with the work he had done there.

About that time there was another scandal in Philadelphia. There were a series of allegations of police brutality, including one case where a suspect was coerced into confessing to a fire bombing of a house that killed a family of Latinos in the Feltonville section of North Philadelphia, only ten blocks south of Logan. That specific case led to the firing of eight detectives and the district attorney, and another appointee of Cerrone lost his next election bid. The upset was directly due to the events in Feltonville which made national news.

The Philadelphia Police Department by the mid-seventies had earned a sort of nation-wide notoriety. It was in 1974 that even Johnny Carson got into the act. It happened after his monologue one night and before he introduced his first guest. He had held up a picture of a group of policemen surrounding a man lying on the ground. It was actually in England. You could tell by the strange hats that the police wore. The police were brandishing nightclubs and Carson said, "This is a picture of a Philadelphian being arrested for jaywalking."

A few of the police brutality accusations occurred right in the 53rd District. This included one lawsuit brought by the family of a Hungarian immigrant who had been arrested after drinking too much in a Fifth Street bar, then getting arrested and later found hanging in a jail cell in the 53rd District. Another big case was the successful lawsuit brought by a fifteen-year-old youth who had been crossing the railroad tracks one night on his way home. The boy, a redhead called Torch, was ambushed by the police and taken off the tracks peacefully, but he broke away and made a run for it. He was harshly subdued by the police and taken then to the 53rd District.

At the time, a liberal Philadelphia magazine called *Brotherly Love Magazine* was there doing a report on police corruption and brutality. They had taken photos of Torch's face and neck, which looked a lot worse than it really was. The youth was originally booked for assault but was eventually cleared of all the charges against him, except for the misdemeanor of trespassing. He sued the city for injuries, and he also sued the railroad. The pictures came in handy at the boy's trial. Ken Washington had been present and was the officer of record. Given the political pressure from both local and state police brass just then, Quinn had no choice but to dismiss Washington from the 53rd District. He was transferred to North Philadelphia where the gang problem was at its worse.

The truth of the matter was that the Logan Nation-Nicetown war didn't really bother Quinn at the moment. It was summer now, and in that particular gang war, violence mostly seemed to occur during the school year, no doubt due to a power struggle at Cooke junior High School. On the other hand, it was sort of a tradition in Logan that whites and blacks went at it more in the summer than in the winter, and that was what worried him at the time moment.

Despite the fact that gang violence and gang killings had decreased significantly in Philadelphia the past three years, the black community was never pleased from the start about the way the juvenile violence was handled by the Cerrone administration. And after all, the black community had much more stock in the problem.

Nevertheless, politically speaking, at least from the viewpoint of Mayor Cerrone or Commissioner Burns or Captain Quinn, it didn't matter very much if blacks were pleased with the way the Philadelphia police handled the problem or how they reacted. As far as Quinn and the others were concerned, they didn't expect many blacks to vote for Cerrone anyway.

Therefore, to them it would be much more disastrous for another round of fighting between white Ben's and black Logan Nation to occur. This, of course, was especially true for Quinn. He was responsible for Logan, and he understood that even his relationship with the commissioner wouldn't save him. Quinn thought the decrease in reports of black-white gang violence in recent years in Logan was due to the fact that Ben's, like Dunn's and 1-5-D, had almost entirely disappeared. They either just got older or simply moved out of the neighborhood. He hadn't heard much of them at all the past few years which was fine with him. Yesterday however he received a report about a burglary right next to the Ben's Candy Store on Windrim Avenue. The victim of the burglary was an appliance store, Nate's Reliable. The report claimed that eighty TV sets had been stolen, a number which may or may not have been inflated somewhat for insurance reasons. (In fact, less than fifty TV sets were stolen). To the untrained eye, this was just a burglary that could be attributed to anybody. But certain clues led Quinn to believe that Ben's was responsible.

In addition to this burglary and much more important than this burglary was another incident in February that was really troubling Quinn and he couldn't get a line on it. It was a small robbery in East Logan by a group of pirates who were ripping off drug dealers and other illegal enterprises. They struck in Logan at the home of a small pot dealer that police knew as either Danny Partridge or Danny Parker. The troublesome thing was that these thieves identified themselves as plain clothes cops. At the time, Danny Parker had two

Ben's boys living at his house. One was named Frenchie (the alleged Albanus Street sniper) and the other was named Felix, who had most recently been laid off from nearby Fleer's bubblegum factory. At the time, there was also a visitor, a thirty-two-year-old former drug addict named Reds, whose brother Shine was also from Ben's.

The victims of the burglary were handcuffed face down, the shades drawn, and the telephone wire was cut. The group seemed to be experienced and well drilled. It appeared that they knew exactly what they were doing, only they chose the wrong victim. Danny Parker didn't have much cash or drugs in the house at that time or really at any other time. For no apparent reason, right in the middle of the robbery, a .32 caliber gun was put behind Red's ear, and he was shot and killed with one bullet. Apparently, this same group, always claiming to be off-duty police, had ripped off dealers before in addition to doing other things. Most recently this same creative bunch had been suspected of raiding a "cock fight" (fighting roosters) in North Philadelphia.

A juvenile race war and/or corrupt police officers were two big stories that the media would love to sink its teeth into which would be terrible press for Mayor Jimmy Cerrone, especially since for one thing, anything seen as anti-cop was also seen as anti-Cerrone.

When Quinn heard about the murder of Lil Rock, he hoped that this might be a good place for the Nicetown-Logan Nation war to end, at least for the summer. At the same time, he saw all this activity with Ben's letting him know that they were still around, and it troubled him because he didn't want to see them start fighting with Logan Nation just then. In other words, it was Ken Washington time again.

There was no doubt that the charter change proposal had to pass or it would be unemployment time for them all. Quinn personally could walk away with no regrets, but he had a twenty-five-year-old son who was already a supervisor down at traffic court and was going to marry a municipal judge's daughter. The boy had pull up the ass and a knack for politics. The sky was the limit for the kid.

Quinn's friendship with the commissioner could be helpful. That was contingent, of course, on them both being in office.

A knock came on Quinn's office door just then. Officer Bobby Shannon came in before he was told to. Shannon wasn't the most gracious guy in the world, nor was he Miss Manners or anything like that. He was a young maverick, cock-strong street cop who was both new and unhappy with being Quinn's secretary. Quinn had Shannon taken off the street because, in his three years on the force, he had exhibited a bit of a trigger finger. Worse, he also liked to drink in the bars on Fifth Street after work. Quinn personally caught his act a few times with him coming out of the Huddle, a cop bar on Fifth Street with his shirttail hanging out and the whole bit. Shannon had a pair of blue eyes that looked wild and glassy even when he wasn't drinking. He worried Quinn more than a little, so in these stressful times, Quinn had him pulled off the street. It gave him a little peace of mind, clipping his wings like that.

Shannon said that Ken Washington was there to see him and said he had an appointment. As Shannon said this, he had a strange look on his face, as if asking the question, "What the hell is he doing here?"

Quinn didn't respond to that. Shannon still had to learn to mind his own business which was probably the most important function of this job.

As Shannon went to get Washington, Quinn rose from his desk and straightened the plaque on the wall with an inscription on it. The plaque had been given to Quinn by Washington himself when he left his first tour of duty in the 53rd. At first the quote didn't quite resonate with Quinn. After a few times reading it though, the quote had a tendency to somehow almost hypnotize him. Quinn thought it was the perfect symbol for what they (the Criminal Justice System) ultimately tried to accomplish. The message was about accountability, self-preservation, selfresponsibility, all that modern-age stuff. Quinn believed the inscription made him appear more modern and hip:

*"Power at its best is love
Implementing the demands
Of justice. Justice at its
Best is love correcting
Everything that stands against love."*

Martin Luther King, Jr., 1968
<u>Where do we go from here; Chaos or community?</u>

Then Quinn walked across the room to the coffee pot. He caught a sideways look at himself in the mirror. He had aged dramatically in the past five years. For one thing, his hair loss had been significant during that span. It had actually started waving bye-bye about four years ago. He figured he looked a little silly in his police uniform these days. It reminded him of what a comedian said on Johnny Carson the other night. The guy was joking about baseball managers wearing their uniforms, just like the players, instead of wearing suits like the basketball coaches did. He was making fun of the baseball managers.

"That would be like Don Shula on the sidelines with his clipboard wearing a Dolphins helmet and shoulder pads," the comedian said.

Quinn grew up in Norristown, a section just outside of Philadelphia, with a kid named Tommy Lasorda. And the truth be known, Quinn was the better athlete of the two. Yet, it was Lasorda who got to play major league baseball in the fifties. Now Lasorda was famous as the manager of the defending National League Champion Dodgers. At times, Quinn was a little jealous of the really nice way Lasorda's life turned out. After all, LaSorda was the manager of the team of the stars who hobnobbed around with guys like Bob Hope and Frank Sinatra. Quinn hadn't remained friends with his old childhood friend over the years, but he had followed Lasorda's career. When the Dodgers were in town to play the Phillies last fall in the playoffs, Quinn had gone to see them a few times. He got a perverse pleasure out of seeing Lasorda in that tight uniform with that pear-shaped body, looking a little silly. Then again, after the game, which the Dodgers always won, Lasorda would again look like an ass bouncing out of the dugout, hugging and kissing his millionaire players, looking ridiculous in that ill-fitting costume.

Quinn was at the stage where people probably saw him wearing his uniform as equally funny. It was very strange that two kids whose lives had taken very different paths both wound up the same way... looking silly in these odd blue uniforms, Lasorda in the Dodger blue, and Quinn in the police uniform blues.

Quinn loved ex-President Richard Nixon who used to use sports analogies saying things like, "The ball's on the two yard line and I'm the fullback."

Quinn never used similar analogies but now it seemed appropriate. He was in fact the manager of the 53rd District, the captain of the crew, the Tommy Lasorda of the 53rd, and he looked at it like this. It was the bottom of the ninth inning and the opposition was mounting a threat, and he had to call in the ace relief pitcher, the best he had, "The closer"

"to put out the fire...Ken Washington."

CHAPTER 3

In a living room ten blocks south of the 53rd District in West Logan, nineteen-year-old Louis "Torch" Agre sat on the blue and white sofa watching a *Sanford and Son* rerun on TV. The house belonged to his girlfriend, Maria Flores. Torch had been given that nickname by his gym teacher at Logan Elementary School. Although his hair was now reddish-brown, Louis had bright red hair as a kid. He wasn't much of an athlete overall, except he could "run like hell," in the words of the gym teacher who remarked that when Louis ran past, all you could see was that flaming red hair like a torch going by. He got in the habit of calling Louis "Torch" and the nickname stuck.

Torch's reddish brown hair and blue eyes belied his lineage. He, his sister, a Philadelphia public school teacher, and his brother Charlie Tuna, a Vietnam War Veteran now a bartender in Germantown, a section just west of Logan, were the products of the union of a Jewish father and an Italian mother. A supervisor at Torch's job, upon learning of this combination said of Torch, that he could "bowl and keep score." Torch looked like, or at least he liked to think he looked like his favorite boxer, Danny "Little Red" Lopez, the featherweight champ. Each possessed the same red hair and freckle-face.

On an entirely different level, Torch looked similar to Danny Lopez, because they were built in a similar manner. This wasn't to say Torch was built like a boxer really because neither was Danny Lopez.

On the cover of a *Sports Illustrated* magazine in the late seventies, Danny "Little Red" Lopez was displayed prominently. He was wearing his boxer shorts with boxing gloves and sneakers, sitting with his arms and legs crossed. He was wearing the featherweight championship belt and an Indian-style headdress. On the top of the page was the inscription: Little Red on the Warpath. Then at the bottom of the page it said, "Featherweight Champ, Danny Lopez." The article was titled *"You can't keep a good man down."* It went on to say *"At least not featherweight champion Danny 'Little Red' Lopez who rises up to go on the warpath and deck the man who dropped him."*

The article was written by SI sportswriter Bruce Newman who described Lopez as follows: *"The first thing you look for on the kid is a bulge or a bump or something that might vaguely look like a muscle. What you find instead is a body built like a mailman's arches. The guy doesn't even have knobby KNEES, and the only thing skinnier than his legs are his arms."* It states later in the article that *"Lopez looks less like an Indian than the guy the cavalry sent out to scout for Indians."*

Maria, at the moment, was serving coffee on the Formica kitchen table coffee in the kitchen. She brought out a metal sugar bowl and a stainless-steel creamer that looked suspiciously like the one from the diner where she worked. From the window of the bright tidy room, you could see the railroad tracks which ran parallel to her street just about 30 feet behind her house, close enough so the entire house shook whenever a freight train passed. You could look out onto a small fenced-in backyard with tomato plants and flowers. Coffee seemed to be a recurring calling card in their relationship. It was, first of all, the reason they came together to begin with. She had worked and still did work at the North Star Diner on Ogontz Avenue, near Dunn's candy store, across from Logan's school yard, and right next to the Northwest Division of the Philadelphia Probation Department. The diner stayed open all night on weekends, catering to drunks that spilled out of the local bars at 2 or 3 a.m. Torch had kept Maria company at the diner on a few of those overnight shifts, drinking tons of coffee. This was to the displeasure of the many cops who would drop in during the night, who were also trying to get into Maria's pants. Torch believed Maria possessed this look which attracted men, not beauty exactly but something less than beauty, which worked as an even greater turn-on generally speaking. It was an "every woman's" type of look which had the tendency to put every man in mind of a girl that he had had at some time in the past. She had a very positive demeanor and was generally a pleasure to be around. She had the ability to get into a conversation on just about any subject whether it was boxing (especially local boxing) or horse racing or football or country music. She even had a favorite boxer, middle-weight Benny Briscoe from North Philadelphia, whom she had seen many times. Maria's father, Pedro, had been involved in horse racing at El Comandante Racetrack in Puerto Rico. At first, he had been a groom or hot walker, and then he got into the training side of the business. He was, from what Maria said, a trainer of some note in Puerto Rico. What Torch knew for sure was that Maria really understood horse racing and handicapping. She could read the racing form far better than he could, and she knew about such things as weight, class, breeding, and distance. Her interest in the sport of racing was unusual for a girl, in Torch's experience.

Then it was coffee again, all night long in the hospital, when they'd stay up all night to be with her son, Lee-Oskar, in Einstein Hospital. He had a history of breathing problems - asthma - not life-threatening, but it got pretty bad at times for him.

Maria seemed much taller than Torch. First of all, she was slightly heavier. Secondly, it was curiosity in life, but a truth, that women appeared to tower over men of the same exact height, like Diane Keaton over Al Pacino or Woody Allen. As for Maria and Torch, whenever they were together, she just seemed to overwhelm his skinny ass. Though they were the same height, he still seemed short while she seemed tall. At first Torch felt overmatched here. He gained confidence though because of her, he thought. Early on, she once said to him, "After my first husband, I didn't think I could ever fall for another man." When she said that Torch nearly looked behind him, thinking somebody else had just walked in the room. Nobody ever said anything close to that before.

Her hair was dark, continuing an exotic look which began with her opal eyes. In the winter, her complexion was purely Irish, and in the summer, her tan could come up fast and dark, but it was always shortlived. Within a few days, her fair and delicate complexion would return. Her overall personality seemed to light a fire in cops. Maybe it was a type of challenge she brought to their considerable machismo, and it gave a rise to something in them. But ultimately, Torch, suspected that it was Maria's remarkable tits that just seemed to defy gravity, which attracted cops from three districts to the North Star Diner. The Irish genes from her mother were strong in their family. Maria had two older brothers, one who looked Spanish and one who looked Irish. She also had one younger brother who also looked completely Irish, as did her son Lee Oskar, who was, in fact, 75 percent Irish.

In ways other than just physically, Maria also seemed more advanced than Torch. It was, after all, entirely her house, while Torch on the other hand, although he stayed with her often, continued to live with his parents. Maria allowed him to do his "work" from her house. Torch's parents, in Maria's words, had "bailed out" to the Northeast. Maria, unlike Torch, had previously been married. Her husband, whose name was David, had split like a thief in the night, screwing her all together on child support. In fairness to him, he probably knew Maria could take care of herself and would land on her feet, which she did. Torch never knew David, and since he wasn't from Dunn's or Ben's, he really never cared to know him. Torch's best friend, Jackie, once told him that he knew David, but Torch could never remember anybody else, including Maria's family mentioning the guy's name. The son, Lee-Oskar, was a result of that relationship. The boy's real first name was Lee. His middle name was Oskar, but as per the father's wishes, everybody called the boy "Lee-Oskar" after Lee-Oskar the world-famous harmonica player from the seventies R&B group War, which was his favorite (this accounted also for the unusual spelling). Torch didn't know what happened, and he didn't care; he was just happy that David was gone. Maria was the perfect girl to have at that young age and was really the first girlfriend he ever loved. He had seen her around Logan schoolyard several times when they were kids in the sixties or early seventies.

She was a tomboy. He remembered a "fair one" that she had with another girl. It was a catfight over some guy. It was a bithin', bitein', scratchin' hair-pullin' affair in Logan schoolyard. At least fifty kids had witnessed some or all of the fight. It would have been hard to say since it lasted so long, especially since the fight was stopped and restarted two or three times. The first time the battle was stopped, the girls were separated then brought together to shake hands. Then, at the last moment, Maria sucker-punched her opponent busting her upside her head. The war went on for so long, some kids went home to eat dinner, then came back, and the girls were still fighting. Finally, an adult woman, a mother of one of the other kids, broke it up. The other girl was a Russian who was from Torch's block on Seventeenth named Valentina, who eventually had her first name legally changed to "Logan."

Valentina or "Logan" spent the first thirteen or fourteen years of her life in Logan and never fully got it out of her system. She lived in several other towns and states during the rest of her childhood and as an adult and currently lives in Maryland. She said she never saw another "one size fits all" type of place like Logan was. And she was more sensitive of it because, of course, she was an immigrant. In this melting pot being unusual was usual. It was that way for everybody here.

Torch's only other, earlier, limited, awkward sexual experiences had been in a secluded lovers' lane in West Logan. Then a friend from the Police Administration Building, Jimmy had fixed him up with his girlfriend's best friend, Jeanette from South Philadelphia. For a while Torch carried on affairs with both girls. They were nice, but they didn't lasted very long. Then the romance with Jeanette ended badly for him, and Maria was there to pick up the pieces. This added to Torch's almost reverent view of Maria.

The union of a half-Puerto Rican and half-Irish girl, with a halfJewish and half-Italian man was bizarre even by Logan's standards. That she was bigger compounded this oddness. They were like a poor man's Sonny and Cher; only in this case, it was he, not she, who possessed a very Cher-esque nose. It was in that way (in the nose) that Torch did look very much like his hero Danny "Little Red" Lopez.

Given their differences, Torch was really an odd choice for Maria. She had gone out with a cop for a long time, and after their break-up, cops treated her, or, at least she thought cops were treating her, like she was damaged goods or something. She thought it was a type of code that they had in their fraternity. Some still wanted to screw her, but nothing more serious than that. Perhaps a small part of her enjoyed the fact that she chose Torch over them, and now they were probably scratching their heads saying when they left the diner together, "What's she see in that little punk?" At least, she hoped that.

Surely, he was no John Travolta or 007 or anybody like that. He was respectful, though, and loyal. She admired the way he had put himself into a position where money was gravitating toward him in spite of his lackadaisical attitude. "Bah-Bah" and those other gangsters seemed to like him and trust him, and she thought they would always be able to look over him.

Maria had grown up fast. She was proud of herself, too, the way she had stepped into adulthood like that. Yet, a part of her still wanted to be a kid. Going out with a cop or marrying was not just something adult, but rather something reflective of middle age. Torch, on the other hand, was the "anti-cop." He was one of the kids. She grew up with them, her brothers, Lil Rock and his older brothers, all of those guys. In her brief time as an adult, Maria had already suffered a few sad chapters. There was something about the way that Torch didn't seem to take life very seriously that was the key to her wanting to be around him. Maybe she saw him as a symbol, a representative of all those schoolyard kids and games she once had known, loved, and then lost too quickly.

From the time he graduated from high school until six months ago, Torch had worked at the Roundhouse, the Police Administration Building, doing some inconsequential clerical work. It was not a particularly challenging job, but Torch had always liked the idea of working for the city's judicial system. He also liked the atmosphere of the place and the people who worked there. Working for the city made him feel like he lived in a small town in the South where everybody worked for the local jelly factory. Although he was surrounded by higher level workers, such as probation officers and lawyers, he never really aspired to a more demanding job.

His mother and her sister were both Philadelphia public school teachers, and during his high school years, Torch wanted someday to be a writer like Jimmy Breslin in New York or a sportswriter at the *Philadelphia Daily News* like Jack Kiser. But when the city job came along Torch didn't hesitate taking it. There was never any second guessing on his part that he would be better off, financially or otherwise elsewhere. It was the place where he worked ... period. It was a good attitude to have, an attitude that could gracefully sustain a person through a career. He was a committed city employee. He wasn't religious nor was religion stressed in his home. Therefore, city work had become almost a religion to him. To Torch, City Hall, the centerpiece of city government, was no less a cathedral than the Holy Child Church. He viewed the judges in their robes as almost like bishops or cardinals.

Torch's father also worked for the courts in Philadelphia. When Torch was younger, his father was a building inspector who had the use of a black municipal car. Torch thought that was a big deal, and his goal was to one day have one of those city cars. It was strange, but Torch came to believe almost as if City Work was his calling in life-that he was supposed to be working there. Frankly working for the city was similar to hanging in Logan schoolyard and maybe Torch used the job the way Maria used him, to reach back and, at least, try to delay middle age.

Torch had an average intelligence and a less than average drive, but he displayed a very good memory. But apart from helping him in the numbers business at certain times, this skill only manifested itself in areas that did him no good. He could tell you what year the Skyliners sang "Since I Don't Have You" or when Frankie Avalon sang "Venus" or when Tommy Edwards sang, "All in the Game." Torch could rattle off the rotation of every pitching staff in the American League, or tell you what Larry Bowa batted in 1974. It was everybody's hope that this would, in some way, lead him to a satisfying job or maybe a career. This, of course, never happened, and since Torch showed very little enthusiasm at all where work was concerned, his father was just happy to see him gainfully employed. Of Torch, his father once said, quoting the Phillies manager Danny Ozark, who said the same thing of a bench warming outfielder, "His limitations are limitless."

After accepting the job, Torch found that he liked it a lot more than he thought he would. But he began to see that better jobs were being given to others with less experience or ability. Maybe it was because of political connections, or maybe it had something to do with his winning a lawsuit against the city a few years earlier.

Torch began to believe that the suit would always be held against him. So when a friend of his, Bah-Bah, offered him the job he had now, he accepted it with some reluctance. He had expected to work for the city for twenty or thirty years and leave with a pension. But Bah-Bah's offer looked good, and when Torch did leave the city job to write numbers, he never looked back nor did he ever regret his decision.

Maria was singing along with the radio in the kitchen. It was her favorite singer Teddy Pendergrass, from Philadelphia, now into his solo career, though he once was the lead singer of Harold Melvin & the Blue Notes also from Philly. In addition to everything else, Maria could really sing well, and her voice blended in now like an expert. Mystical to Torch on many levels was Maria.

Close the door let me give you what you been waiting for
Baby I got so much love to give and
I want to give it all to you
Close the door
No need to worry no more
Let's bring this pleasant day to an end
Girl, it's me and you now

The phone rang just about then. It was Harold, who worked as a type of porter at a bar, Oscar's, down on Sansom Street in Center City. For the last week or so, Harold had been in Graduate Hospital, just a few blocks away. Oscar's was also near the police administration building and where Torch met Gino and Alex.

Torch went to work now in the living room at his desk which was more like a tray you served kids a TV dinner on. Then he took out the master sheet with the current count of approximately sixty customers, mostly small numbers players and a few horse betters. Harold, at the moment, was stuck $38. He told Torch to wait a minute and then started talking to somebody else in the hospital room, apparently a nurse or a doctor. Torch remained silent and held on the line for about 30 seconds. Then he said to Maria, "How about this Mau-Mau? He has me on hold."

Maria said, "Mau-Mau?" Then she started singing again with the Teddy Bear.

> *Close the door*
> *Let me rub your back where you say it's sore.*
> *Come on get closer*
> *So close to me*
> *let's get lost in each other*
> *Come here, Baaabahh*

Harold came back on the line and talked to Torch for a moment. Then Torch wrote as he talked and he said, "You have two-one-five and seven-six-nine every night through Sunday. That is eight units, all right. All straight for a fish, that makes a total of $46."

"All right," Torch laughed at something Harold said. Harold wanted to settle up with him and told Torch he was in room 215 at Graduate Hospital, and said Torch could come there to settle up. Torch looked over at Maria who was now reading *The Daily News*, still seated at the kitchen table, singing.

"How about this guy, Maria? Getting money from him is always like pulling teeth. You have to catch him on pay day and even then it's tricky. One time Alex told me he used to catch him sneaking out the back door at five o'clock on Friday. He always pays, but you can grow whiskers waiting sometimes. But now he's all urgent and shit. Wants me to visit him in the hospital, so he can pay me … you know why?" Maria lifted her head as if to say, "G'head," although she was anxious to get back to the paper.

"Because he thinks he's going to die. See, I knew this guy in the newspaper and magazine business. He told me these old blacks think, if they die owing money, they'll go directly to hell. That's what I think is going on here. And I know that death is on his mind because he played 769, you know that's the death number. What a business."

"Is that what it is … a business?" Maria said, raising her eyebrows, and then she got up from the table. She brought the paper to him and pointed out an item in it. "Your boys are in the paper," she said. The *Daily News* story was under the heading of "*Olney Man released from Hospital after being shot.*"

"*An 18-year-old Olney man was released from Einstein Hospital after being shot by a former Philadelphia police officer.*" Police gave this account: "*Eighteen-year-old Joe Snyder was apparently confronted by four men from the Inky Gang named for Incarnation Church and Parrish in Olney. The gang had been feuding for several years with the Ben's Gang from the neighboring Logan section of North Philadelphia. Snyder claimed that he wasn't from any gang, nevertheless a fight broke out. A retired Philadelphia police officer saw the commotion in front of his house and tried to break it up before it escalated. He went inside his house and retrieved his police issued pistol and shot one of the men. The victim Joe McCracken, also 18, was released from Einstein Hospital with minor injuries last night.*"

Incarnation Catholic School and Church were on Fifth Street in Olney, just east of Logan. Corners from Logan and Holy Child Parrish had feuded with Incarnation for decades. However, it wasn't like they were fighting with each other recently as the story in the paper suggested. The last round of this on-going feud was three years ago in 1975. It all happened during a celebration for the Philadelphia Flyers, who had just, that afternoon, won the Stanley Cup. A few (two or three) Ben's boys visited the emergency room at Einstein that night, including Efrem, who looked like a young Clint Eastwood and had been stabbed then suffered a collapsed lung, as well as this boy Snyder.

The two neighborhoods were not very different and, in fact, were similar in many ways. An old theory about the rivalry between the two neighborhoods or parishes goes back to, at least, the 1930s. In those days, Logan, at least, East of Eleventh Street was largely Jewish, especially around Seventh and Eighth streets where the infamous "Sinking Homes" were now. Olney was largely German then. The two groups disliked each other to begin with. Then in 1936 the Nazis paraded up Olney's main thoroughfare ... Fifth Street. It was just a few blocks from a Jewish enclave. It didn't make much sense to think that that hostility would carry over all these years given that so many transformations, different races, and religions would go through those places. But in the seventies, there were still a few old–timers remaining that said that was how the rivalry started.

This latest incident had nothing to do with Nazis or 1936, of course. It probably was just an old beef, most likely having to do with the massacre on Fifth Street. Torch hadn't seen Snyder in a few weeks. He had moved out of Logan a few years ago but was one of those who always came back, always around the other side of Broad Street where they hung ... Ben's, The Warnock Tavern, Caesar's Palace where he sometimes "*crashed.*" Caesar's Palace wasn't a palace; it was an abandoned house there in East Logan where they hung a block from their other main spot, The Warnock Tavern. Several of Torch's boys lived there or stayed there. It was a place where they hung out, played cards, drank beer or wine, and basically used as a clubhouse.

It was funny and strange seeing that name -*Ben's*- in the newspaper like that as if they had some notoriety. Nobody before had seen that in the paper or heard it on the news.

Maria was saying that her brother was taking Lee Oskar to the Phillies game that night. It was the third or fourth time already this season that he took the boy there.

"That's nice, ya' know, that he does that," Torch said.

"Why didn't you ever take him? At least, my brothers show interest in Lee Oskar."

"They should. Lee Oskar is their nephew. I'm sayin', that's nice." Then addressing the slight accusation, Torch replied, "I'm not the boy's father, Maria."

The boy just missed his real father that was the bottom line. He never really liked Torch and the feeling was mutual. This odd relationship wasn't bad enough though for Torch to end what he had with Maria.

"I don't know. I just don't like going down there. I'd rather watch baseball on TV. You can see the strike zone. That's the most important thing I think."

Torch only liked baseball from a gambling standpoint in any case; he explained that before. Torch said the game was complex, and he was convinced you could find ways to beat the bookies, if you had a formula and stuck to it. Torch worked all during the past two seasons to discover this pot of gold. Maria thought it was pathetic, like a bald guy developing a hair-growing formula in his sink. He said he couldn't really get into any sport as a fan, unless there was betting involved. He had this hard-boiled attitude after just recently having his heart broken by the 76ers and Phillies in a five-month span. It just wasn't worth it he said.

At least, he spared her the usual indictment on Veterans Stadium in South Philly where the Phillies played and how he preferred going to the Connie Mack Stadium in North Philly where they played when he was a kid until 1971. Torch would go on and on about the Connie Mack Stadium. They would take the subway down to the heart of North Philly, and then walk west to 24th Street. There were apparently all these factories there in those days, and you would go through all this dirt, grime, and black smoke.

"Then you would get inside, push your way through the turnstiles and see that beautiful, manicured lawn which was nicer even than Yankee Stadium or Dodger Stadium, and it was like that scene in *The Wizard of Oz* when everything goes from black and white to color."

And Torch would talk about how all the seats were right on top of the field and you could smell the grass and all that bullshit.

"At the vet, you're so far from the field, ya' know? I see these guys yelling about balls and strikes from 500 feet away, and they don't have a nickel on the game. I never understood that."

The phone was ringing, and Torch took his time answering as he completed his speech. He turned off the TV, which was now displaying the afternoon news.

"Turn up the radio, will ya?" Torch said to Maria. Then he answered the phone.

"Hello, Regina, right, we're even right now."

"Okay six-eight-six straight a fish. Nine-two-zero straight a fish. Nine-seven-five, three over a fish."

"Slow down, Regina. If you want five-eight-five, say it that way. Don't say 'five-eighty-five,' you know what I mean? That's how you make mistakes."

Alex, Torch's mentor, had told him to write numbers in that fashion. The older man had written numbers for twenty years until his death last year and had given Torch advice based on his years of experience. Alex had been a bartender in Center City for many years until he retired from that job and started writing numbers for Gino, who was running a gambling operation. In addition to overseeing the numbers activity in both Center City and South Philadelphia, Gino had a few sports books as well, but his biggest thing, by far was loan-sharking. For twenty years, Gino had operated with no problem from anybody. It wasn't that he had muscle; at least, none that anybody really knew of. But in Center City, Gino, because he was from South Philadelphia and had the ear of Constantine (the local organized crime boss), he never needed any muscle. Nobody tried to rip him off for whatever reasons, and he never did anything to dissuade the idea that he was somewhat connected, even though he was really completely independent. Everybody liked him in Center City, and for years, he conducted his business on nothing more than the strength of a handshake.

Gino allegedly had $300,000 lent out on the street. A lot of this was small but high-interest loans to waitresses, bartenders, and other restaurant workers. Bartenders all over the city knew Gino, and many had borrowed from him over the years. Everything was fine for Gino as he was also well respected in South Philadelphia and, therefore, was able to conduct his business on his own and didn't have to pay any tribute for protection to anybody. However, with the advent of the recent referendum, which would grant nearby Atlantic City the right to install gambling casinos, the stakes were drastically heightened. Now a younger, local mob, probably with the backing of one of the big New York families, had started to take control of the Philadelphia rackets. Systematically, one by one, the members of the long-existing mob family in Philadelphia were turning up dead. This all started with the murder of the long-time boss Angelo Constantine, who was slain, shot-gunned in his car outside of his row house in South Philadelphia. Eventually Gino himself was approached and was read the riot act. He would have to pay a street tax or "elbow" which was what they called this type of extortion. Gino, paranoid and frightened all the time, even under the best circumstances, was now hysterical. In a year, he had suffered two heart attacks. He died shortly after Alex did. Officially he died from natural causes, but everybody knew that the turmoil he went through the past two years had accelerated his death.

After he died, Gino's sons and the son of Gino's best friend took over the operation, specifically Gino's best friend's son; Joey "Bah-Bah" Sylvestri now oversaw and ran Gino's numbers and gambling. Bah-Bah had also run a newsstand in Center City. When Torch worked in Center City, he routinely purchased the *Daily News* and *The Daily Racing Form* from Bah-Bah two or three times a week. Bah-Bah knew Torch had, for a short time, booked sports for Gino. Because Gino knew Torch and had apparently trusted him, at least, as much as Gino could trust anybody. He (Torch) was elected to fill in Alex's post when he took over Gino's business.

At first, Torch refused Bah-Bah's proposition to take over Alex's post. Honestly, Torch wasn't sure how secure the position was these days. Overall, Torch had always felt safe in Center City and never worried about anybody, including police bothering him. Flying under Gino's wing had always been more than good enough. Things in Philadelphia were changing though, and Torch was highly concerned about the near-future. Bah-Bah told him not to worry about it and that he was protected by one of Constantine's chief lieutenants, "Chickadee," who Bah-Bah's father had known very well and who, for many years, ran Constantine's gambling side of the overall operation. Chickadee, following Constantine's assassination, was essentially the current boss of the Philadelphia crime family. Torch nevertheless still had reservations about the whole deal. What concerned him most was the type of thing that happened to a small-time numbers writer who operated in a black section of South Philadelphia. He had been approached by a new type of "Black Mafia" that was spreading throughout the city. This outfit said that they wanted $500 a week from him. The man contended that, if he was to pay that type of street tax and pay off his hits every week, it didn't really pay for him to stay in business. He said he would just have to quit. They said he couldn't quit; if he did, he would die. Torch's only worry was that he would be caught one day in that type of trap, and that was exactly why he was reluctant to take on Bah-Bah's offer. However, Torch knew that Alex had been happy with the job, and he thought he'd give it a try. In the six months or so that he'd been doing it, the job had been an overall nice experience, but the numbers were starting to get to him. Alex, he assumed, must have really been a rock. Torch certainly had a greater appreciation now for Alex than he did while he was alive. Writing numbers really could become monotonous, and Torch couldn't understand or imagine anybody doing it for twenty years. Some nights Torch would dream about numbers. In the morning, he would wake up, and it seemed like he had worked all night writing numbers. Then he'd see a number come out on the TV set at night, and he'd wonder if somebody really played that with him or if he'd just dreamt about writing that particular number. That type of thing didn't bother Alex, or maybe he was just used to it. It wore on his eyes though,

Alex said, after so many years of doing it. Those old numbers guys wrote so small. They would put hundreds of numbers on one small sheet of paper. Alex was so goddamn cheap he probably wrote so small to save money on paper. He was the cheapest son of a bitch Torch had ever met. It must have been painful to use a dime to call Gino's bank to get the number three times every day. It must have pained him, too, when they would have coffee at Dunkin' Donuts and Alex left that fifty cent tip.

But Torch, now that he thought about it, thought he understood Alex better. Every coin or handful of change meant something to Alex.

He didn't see a quarter or fifty-cent piece the way others looked at them. Fifty cents or even a quarter was enough to put somebody in action. They could hit a number off that, resulting in a small score for Alex. Then they could take that $250 hit and play a number for five or ten dollars, resulting in a bigger score, and it all grew from that original 25 or 50 cent bet/play. And even if the customer didn't hit the number, that river of nickels, dimes and quarters all strung together, thousands and thousands over the years built up to his weekly ribbons. Therefore, to Alex, the coins weren't simply coins to be taken at face value. Those coins were symbols; they were the keys to his success. It had to be that, and it was why Alex threw those dimes and quarters around like so many manhole covers.

Then Maria dropped a bombshell on Torch and said it in such a matter-of-fact manner.

"Guess who was in the diner yesterday? Ken Washington. He asked about you."

Torch's look told Maria that she had clearly touched a nerve, like whenever Washington's name came up. Maria knew there were stories behind that look, stories which she wished she knew about. "Washington? Are you sure?" It was a ridiculous question, as though Maria could have made a mistake.

"He had breakfast there. Him and some other cop that looked like Lil' Abner."

"Lil' Abner?" Torch said.

"Right. The comic strip guy, you know."

"Were they in uniform?"

"Washington wasn't. The other guy was. Washington said he's starting back in the 53rd in a day or two. I have a feeling it has something to do with Lil' Rock. That's what I think."

Torch, now that he thought about it, figured Maria was probably right.

"Turn down that radio, will ya?" Suddenly, out of nowhere there was this seriousness in his tone.

"What's the matter, Torch? What is it with you and Washington anyway?"

"What did he say?"

"Well, to tell you the truth, he said that you were in over your head, and he didn't know everything you did, but you were going to get yourself jammed up. The other guy said the same thing. They were going to come down on your friends. 'Ben's' was actually what they said. Washington, you know, was always nice to me, and he always seems to like you. He always spoke well of you to me but not this time. He said something like, "I could pull Torch's hole card anytime I want." That's exactly what he said. "I could pull Torch's hole card. Torch thinks he's slick, but I know Torch better than he knows himself.""

"What about the other guy with him? Lil' Abner?" The question was designed to get off the track with Washington, but it didn't work. "I said that, 'whatever Torch is doing, it's probably small stuff.'"

"What did he say then?" Torch said.

"Then he said, 'What about murder? Is that small stuff?'"

That was below the belt, Torch thought. By digging up old issues and dragging Maria into it besides, that was unnecessary.

Then Maria said, "What did he mean by that, Torch?"

"I don't know. All right, I do know. I'll tell you. All right, because it's better that you hear it from me rather than somebody else. See, there was this guy; he was a faggot, is what he was. But in addition to that, he was also into getting spit on and kicked and stuff like that. And he would pay people to do this service for him. Boys, you know, would spit on him and stuff like that, and he would pay them. His name was Base. He got that name because when we used to play baseball, he would be second base and, you know, we would slide into him and kick him, and that's what he liked."

"That's terrible," Maria said. "And he paid you?"

"Right," Torch said. "We never got philosophical or thought much about what we were doing. To us, it never was really a big deal. Then one day we were cutting school up on the tracks. It was me, Jackie, Felix, and this other kid you don't know. Maybe you do know him, Teddy."

"Of course, I knew him. We were in the same grade at Holy Child. He was a nut."

"You ain't lying," Torch said. "All of a sudden, John Base comes over up on the railroad tracks. Teddy and Base went into this utility shack up there. We were waiting outside. Then 30 seconds later, Teddy comes flying out of this shack and starts running by us, and he was carrying Base's wallet. So we took off, too. He never told us what happened exactly, but we divided the money which was about $150. I still don't know exactly what happened in there, but the bottom line was that Teddy hit him over the head with a pipe, and he just didn't hit him; he killed him. That's what happened."

"And nobody knows this?"

"Well, nobody really cares, put it that way. They know about it, but see, Teddy's father was a cop in the northeast, and because of that and because John Base was, well, John Base, they had decided to let us slide, I guess. Washington was on the beat in those days. Of course, within a few hours, he knew who was involved in it and everything else. I was like a zombie. I was so scared. I walked home, and I didn't come out of the house for about four days. I never saw Teddy again. That night the father learned about what happened. He moved his family out of Logan the next day. I heard somewhere that they were in Pittsburgh. I guess that was part of a deal. A few days later, Jackie and Felix, they said that it was all right finally to come out because the cops apparently didn't care about it. I never heard another word about, except, once in a while, Washington would bring it up, like now. Washington, see, he won't leave it alone. He sees me as a weak link, and he knows I was scared. He thinks that I can tell him things about drugs and stuff like that, and he's holding this incident over my head."

"Well, he sounded pissed off. And the other guy said that some appliance store, Nate's Reliable, was robbed of eighty TV sets, and that you and your friends had something to do with.

"I don't know anything about TV sets," Torch lied, "and I don't care. I'm just concerned about that other matter."

"Washington was always good to you, right? So Jackie and them are probably right. He's probably just trying to scare you now, but it's a dead issue. If not probably most likely something would have happened by now. Think about it. Washington can't all of a sudden say that Torch and them committed this murder and he knew about it all along because it would only make him look bad. How long ago was it?" "About three or four years," Torch said.

"See what I mean?" Maria said. She made sense. Torch hadn't thought of it like that. Then again, Torch hadn't thought about it at all for a long time. He'd successfully put it out of his mind. It was a dead issue. "What happened with Washington and that lawsuit? That's what I'd like to know," Maria said.

"See. That is what Washington is mad about. He thinks I stabbed him in the back, but the truth is, he got jammed up because of me. He really hadn't done anything wrong. Originally, I had really helped Washington out, all of my friends did. He's studying to become a clinical psychologist, you know that, right?" Maria nodded her head and Torch continued. "He would get all my friends together, and he would interview us. He was doing this survey, this study, and we were helping him out. We used to go up to the 53rd District with him or even sometimes to his house. He lived up in Mt. Airy. I knew his wife from work. Her name was Esther Washington. She was a probation officer. The truth was, Washington let me slide for little stuff on a couple of occasions. I guess that's why he thinks I stabbed him in the back, and that's why he's so pissed off."

"But what exactly happened? How did you get that money, $50,000?

That's what I want to know."

"All right. I'll tell you what happened. Apparently, there were some kids playing on the tracks one afternoon and they broke into a 'control shack,' which is like a control center with all the switches and everything. They were fooling around with these switches. They were probably just playing around, but it could've been dangerous.

"Later that night, I was coming home and crossing the tracks, like I did every night. The railroad detectives and some of the cops from the 53rd District at the time were staking the shack out, looking for further vandalism. I walked right through there, and I was surrounded. I didn't resist or anything until they brought me off the tracks. Then I made a break for it, but they ran me down. I tried to escape again, but I got roughed up a little. At the time, the city cops were under investigation for a series of police brutality charges. *Brotherly Love Magazine* was at the 53rd shortly after they brought me in. They took pictures of my face, which was all swollen, and I had a black eye. A few months later, we had the hearing, and the case went to court about a year after that. I had the pictures from that night, and I wound up winning the case. My lawyer got $30,000 from the railroad and $30,000 from the city; I ended up with slightly less than $50,000. Washington never laid a hand on me, to be honest. But I refused to indicate specifically who the cops were that were involved. I just said I wasn't sure. Between the detectives and the regular cops, there were about four or five overall. I think Washington was the officer of record, though, and he was the one that got in trouble for what happened. That's why he's so pissed at me now." "That's some story," Maria said.

Torch was not happy at all to learn that Washington was back. Washington, the TV sets, Inky, Logan Nation, and the rest of the 53rd cops. Like Captain Quinn of the 53rd District, Torch saw this summer shaping up to be an eventful one. It was probably safe to say that things, by the end of the summer in both Philadelphia in general and Logan in particular, were going to be very different than they were now.

CHAPTER 4

Police Officer Bobby Shannon led Ken Washington to the office of Captain Quinn. He did so in a manner that suggested Washington didn't know the exact location, although they had worked together there for almost two and a half years. Shannon knocked on the door, and then opened it for Washington. He then held the door open for him with his right hand, allowing for Washington to enter. Shannon remained in the doorway a moment longer than necessary before leaving. In that moment, Quinn caught the puzzling look on Shannon's face. It was a look that asked the questions: "What's going on? What's he doing back here?"

It occurred to Quinn, once again, that he must have a talk with Shannon. Unaccustomed as he was to this "white-out" detail or secretarial work, Shannon didn't yet understand the importance of minding his own business. Quinn had to explain to him that it was this characteristic — the ability to mind your own business — that was probably the most important ability needed to function adequately in a job such as this.

Washington, on this day, wore a navy-blue pin-striped suit. He carried a thin leather briefcase.

"Look at this guy," Quinn said to himself.

Washington's wearing a suit and his not wearing one caused him to reflect. Just that morning, he had been thinking that he had worn a police uniform his entire adult life with no prospect of wearing something classier.

Now here was Washington, and it was like he was saying, "No police uniform for me. I'm a famous gang control expert." Well, excuuuse me.

But it wasn't primarily the suit that irritated Quinn. More specifically, it was the high-collared starched white shirt that Washington wore. It was precisely the type of shirt that Cerrone himself favored. Quinn contemplated for a second, the uncomfortable idea that this spear-chucker could one day be his boss. The thought of that irritated him, but Quinn knew that he needed Washington's help and special skills now, so he had to be nice to him. He also was confident that Washington wouldn't let him down at this crucial time. Quinn rose to shake Washington's hand.

"You look great, Ken. Look at you. Have a seat."

Quinn gestured toward the chair across from him. He wore an artificial smile, and Washington realized that the captain was pouring on the bullshit. When they were seated across from each other, Quinn's smile vanished. He said, "You know, Ken; we've had our disagreements over the years. And I admit that the problems mainly generated from this end. I admit that, but I'm old, you know, set in my ways. I got twenty-three years in. Christ, I could be your father … in a manner of speaking."

An awkward second went by, and then both men laughed simultaneously. These men shared an unusual relationship. They shared an honesty, a knowledge about each other. They had never liked each other, but, at least, they both knew where the other stood, and that was all right, too.

"I'm not always right. In fact, I'm probably wrong most times, but I always did what I thought I should have. That always worked for me, and I could never gracefully grasp the concept of change. My mind never could go in that direction. With people like me, it gets worse, too, when you get old. Now everything is changing, the country, the city, the neighborhood, the world is changing. Quite frankly, in my eyes, I think you epitomize that change. Of course, it isn't your fault, but you must understand. It's a scary thing when you're old and you've been lucky and complacent for so many years. Then suddenly you see change happening all around you."

Washington originally thought Quinn was apologizing somehow for his dismissal from the 53rd District, but he soon came to realize that the captain was talking about something else as well.

"It's scary when you don't know where you'll be when the dust settles," Quinn said.

"You're talking about the charter change proposal maybe being turned down now. Is that it?"

"Cerrone is a high-ranking cop. Fundamentally, that's what he is, a cop. He isn't some wavering, pandering politician. We know he is in our corner for the long haul … regardless. The liberals want to make this into a racial divide type of thing. But we must recognize where our collective bread is buttered."

Washington honestly figured that he was in a no-lose situation, whether the charter was upheld or not. Quinn, purposely it seemed, kept using the word "we," and the word bounced around inside Washington's head. It made Washington think of that old story: *"The Lone Ranger and Tonto were surrounded by savage Indians. The Lone Ranger said to Tonto, 'Tonto, it looks like we are surrounded.' Then Tonto replied, 'What do you mean 'we,' paleface?"*

Whites had a monopoly on power in Philadelphia for 200 years. First the WASPS had it. Then the Irish had struggled it away. Now the Italians had the political power with an Irish-dominated police force. Yeah, Washington supposed, change was scary to all of them, but was he somehow supposed to feel sorry for them?

"The city is on the verge of falling apart. That's the issue. I'm not saying this because Cerrone is a cop, but he has been a good mayor for all the people, despite the media making him look foolish. For instance, here is a man who made fighting crime a priority, and the media turns it around, turns it against him."

Washington always had the feeling that his being called back to Logan had something to do with Cerrone, now he was certain of it.

"Cerrone is his worst enemy sometimes," Washington said.

"No question about that. He puts his foot in his mouth, and he makes for great copy with those foolish quotes of his. Still, the media takes advantage."

It got so bad a few years ago that Cerrone began an individual blackout of the media. Of course, that only made him look more foolish than anything he possibly could have said. How can a mayor of a major city black-out the media? It's not like Steve Carlton blacking out the media.

"I cringe when I see the guy on the news, and I just found out that he's going to be on national TV in a couple of weeks. Somebody is doing a segment on him. The footage, I understand, has already been shot, unfortunately."

"Is it a news show?"

"The show is called *Top Cop*, and they interview political leaders and police commissioners from various cities around the country. It's a news/TV magazine comparable to *60 Minutes*, I heard. I can see it now, that famous shot of Cerrone coming from a formal dinner in his tuxedo with the nightstick stuck in the cummerbund. It's funny but until that incident, I never knew what a cummerbund was. Anyway, you know they'll make him sound bad. The media always does. Speaking of which, listen to this. It's from *Brotherly Love Magazine* in the July issue."

Quinn began to read, "*The Cerrone administration has not been good for Philadelphia. Bit by bit, the agencies that have the job of providing services to Philadelphians have been taken over by Cerrone's drones in a ruthless quest for power. The city's coffers have been drained as he uses the money for his own political advantage while ignoring the good of the city and corruption is rampant.*"

Then the article touched on what might have been Cerrone's biggest political mistake. In 1976 Philadelphia planned to host a gigantic World's Fair-type of celebration commemorating the Bicentennial. Cerrone received information that thousands of protesters were going to invade Philadelphia and disrupt the party.

The mayor heard not only of the protesters coming, but also some proposed malicious acts of terrorism. Consequently, he requested the presence of 15,000 federal troops to come to Philadelphia during the Bicentennial Celebration. This served to not only scare the criminals away, but also it scared everybody else away. The summer in Philadelphia in 1976 was no less boring than any other summer in Philadelphia. The magazine article continued. Quinn read, *"The whole country watches with amazement and scorn. The request for federal troops, for example, made national headlines."*

Quinn continued to read aloud the last part of the article which talked about more incompetence and bad PR for the city. The article touched on "millions of dollars" from Washington that Philadelphia no longer received.

"Allow me to address a few of these points," Quinn said. "It's true that Cerrone calling in the federal troops was a disaster from a PR standpoint, but even that was done with Philadelphia's citizens in mind. This article doesn't talk about the plot, for example, to poison the reservoirs in 1976. Federal help was asked for because Cerrone genuinely loves Philadelphia. As far as incompetence and pay-offs in city government, I don't know about that. It wouldn't surprise me, but that institution has been in place long before Cerrone's administration. That's for sure, and as far as that goes, city work is city work. They would love to nail something concrete on Cerrone, but they can't do it, even though they've tried. They keep talking about Cerrone's lifestyle, but they can't point to anything illegal, anything specific. And it's true that he doesn't get as much money from Washington, 'millions of dollars,' as it says in the article, but that isn't his fault. It doesn't say that Cerrone was the first mayor from Philadelphia who could get 'millions of dollars' from Washington in the first place. Cerrone got along famously with Richard Nixon. Nixon really took care of Philadelphia; at least, that's my understanding of it. Then Nixon got in trouble, and President Carter now doesn't have that same relationship with Cerrone. In fact, it's probably true that Carter gives Cerrone and the City of Philadelphia the cold shoulder precisely because Cerrone was close to Nixon. Carter probably feels it's better to divorce himself from Cerrone. It's just politics. Most people in power, I'm sure, have some skeletons in their closets. That's politics, and if the end justifies the means, then ultimately nobody has anything to bitch about. With Cerrone, it is a little different. He has been held under a microscope by a hostile press who would like nothing more than to see him serve his next term in Allenwood prison."

Ken Washington always appreciated the way people got fired up, one way or the other, where Cerrone was concerned. This clearly wasn't simply a case of whites and blacks on opposite sides of the fence. There was a class struggle here among whites as well. To whites like Quinn, for instance, Cerrone could never do wrong. The middle-class whites, who were generally more educated and generally more liberal, often felt just as passionately, in a negative sense, about Cerrone. This splitting of the white vote would possibly leave the door open for a black candidate and mayor in the near future. This matter of whites not being politically on the same page was what would lead them to eventually lose their long-held grasp on the city. That was how Washington saw it; a kid could see it. All that was needed was a little foresight. There was a lack of passion in the black community where politics was concerned. The voter registration numbers were extremely low. So despite the fact that the city was almost fifty percent non-white, they would still have to wait for the whites to self-destruct and, amazingly, they were doing it.

Washington not only paid attention to politics, but he was astute about it. He was a child of the sixties, when politics seemed to have a more urgent tone, no doubt because of the Vietnam War, civil rights, and everything else. In the seventies, Washington felt that politics, in general, took on a lesser form with everybody only caring about their own ass and feathering their own nest. His parents were educated, and his mother was active in the Civil Rights Movement. He particularly remembered the '68 presidential primaries. People still talked a lot about the Democratic Primary of '68 and the infamous riots in Chicago that occurred there. Washington remembered the passion on the faces of those white boys protesting the war. That had been really inspiring to him, and it had left an impression. He never once saw that passion again. But it was the Republican Convention of 1968, which Washington always pointed to as what initially got him interested in politics. He remembered the big names at that convention, not only Richard Nixon but also Nelson Rockefeller and another big name which he thought might have been Barry Goldwater. He remembered the balloons and the red, white, and blue banners, and the individual states with their speakers with them big voices "… and the great state of Massachusetts, home of the remarkable American League Champion Boston Red Sox, casts 485 votes for the next president of the United States, Richard Nixon." It probably wasn't entirely coincidental that directly because of that convention, Washington became a lifelong Republican. At that time, young Washington was just a student at Germantown High School, not far from Logan. But he was fascinated by the convention and the election that followed.

"See, the press is powerful," Quinn was saying. "It's one thing for Johnny Carson to say negative things about the city. That by itself doesn't hurt anybody, but when you have a little here and a little more there, then finally you have like what I saw on 'Barney Miller' the other night."

Washington nodded, acknowledging he knew what Quinn was talking about.

"Did you see it?" Quinn asked.

"I heard about it. What did he say? Something about cops I heard."

"Right, this guy apparently owned a store in the neighborhood, and he said he was there to pay the captain. And then Barney Miller says, 'What are you talking about? You don't have to pay me or my men to protect your store.' The other guy says, 'Look, I know how these things work, so just tell me how much. Then Barney Miller says, 'Wait. Did anybody from the precinct confront you about payment to us?' And the other guy says, 'No, I just moved to the neighborhood.' And Barney says, 'Where are you from?' And the store owner says, 'Philadelphia.' It was of those times when you thought he would say that, but then when he really did say it, you still couldn't believe it. I mean, where did that come from, you know?

"So I guess you can put together why you're back here. Then there is that guy Reds getting killed. By itself, that isn't something I would ordinarily be worried about. The thing is, there has been a series of holdups by a group pretending to be cops. They are the people that killed him. Obviously that is something that worries me, especially if they were 53rd cops, and I can't get a line on them, nothing. I'm hopeful that you can overturn some rocks. I know you still have people in Logan, contacts. By the way, did you know Reds?"

"I must have known him. I just can't picture him. He had a drug problem, I know that. And I know he was originally from Dunn's."

Dunn's was a candy store right across the street from Logan schoolyard in West Logan. In the sixties, Dunn's was one of the biggest drug corners in the city. As the neighborhood changed and Dunn's only had a few youngsters hanging there, they eventually joined up with Ben's. Actually they had no choice. Ben's came over there, including Felix and his brother Johnny, and they essentially just said, *"Hey, Dunn's! Give us your buns or go get your guns."*

"I knew his brother, Shine," Washington said. "He was from Ben's.

In fact, I tested him."

"Right, I remember Shine, too. A scary guy, how could I forget him?"

"He is harmless, really. It's just that he's so big." "In fact," Quinn said, "I arrested him myself once." "Was it car theft?" Washington said.

"No, this was a burglary of a delicatessen in Logan. The look-out guy, the getaway driver, fell asleep in his car. His name was Brian."

"Right … right, I remember that. That was Ben's. It sounds like them anyway," Washington said.

"You said you tested Shine. What do you mean by that?"

"At the time, I was testing young offenders, juvenile and young adults. It was for my psychology work. In fact, it was for my thesis at Temple."

"Oh, right. Are you still doing that work? How is that coming along?"

"Fine … fine. It's a tough field to break into, but at least, I got to use it in my work with gangs. As for now, I'm still just a cop. I always wanted to combine the two careers, police work and psychology. Sort of like a clinical psychologist, maybe at the Youth Study Center or something. Hopefully, that will happen one day, but for now, I'm a cop. A welldressed cop, but still a cop. Sort of like that black guy on Barney Miller."

"You know, he sort of reminds me of you that guy, Harris. I mean because he is well-dressed all the time and is an insightful guy." "I tested all kinds of juvenile gangs and juvenile corners." "What is the difference between them?" Quinn asked.

"Usually we label them a gang if they are big in number or if they are organized and traffic in some sort of illegal activity. I mean, if a group of five or six were committing burglaries, for example, we would call them a gang. Logan Nation isn't a criminal enterprise, but they are big enough, for sure, to be a gang. Dunn's was a gang because they sold drugs, even after they dropped in numbers. Ben's is only a corner both because they aren't organized and they are too small, at this point, to be called a gang. Gangs, or corners even, have a negative impact somewhere along the line and wanted to find out more about any 'long-term' damage and track these juveniles over several years. I wanted to know how vital the presence of a father in the house is, for instance, or how important work, religion, and education are, and mostly the role that the environment plays. I wrote a study called 'The Lineup' where I pointed too big families where the father has been incarcerated at some point. How likely is he to have a son in jail or in trouble, and how about the younger ones, you see? I did most of my work in black neighborhoods, North Philly, West Philly."

"That's interesting, but I'm curious. Why would you test Shine? For what purpose? I mean, he is white, isn't he?" Quinn couldn't resist that jab.

Washington smiled. "I suppose it's difficult to see how testing Shine could somehow result in any social redeeming value. But honestly, my survey was very telling. I did the whole project, to be quite honest, to better understand and better prepare black juveniles."

That figured, Quinn thought. Did Washington think all young white kids automatically had their shit together and never needed help, or did he just not care about them?

"And what did you conclude?" Quinn asked, not that he really cared.

"Well, when I first came to Logan, I tested thirty white kids from around Ben's. Then I tested thirty black kids from Logan Nation. Then I tested thirty white kids from the northeast in a section called Northwood. It is not a middle-class neighborhood, but it's a good working-class type of place. The family ties are strong there with a religious backbone. There is crime, but the neighborhood is clean and relatively drug-free. I used a test that I developed myself called 'The Criminal Aptitude Test.' It's designed to show how aware the subject is of the whole criminal culture. I figured that the more involved the kid was in the whole criminal society and the more he knew about it, the greater the chance he'd get into trouble with the law at some point. So in my test, the higher you score, the worse off you figure to be. What I found was that the white kids from Ben's had nearly the exact same high score as the black kids from Logan Nation while the white kids from Northwood scored much lower.

"This wasn't really surprising. For years, sociologists have contended that environment plays a big part in a child's development and the bad neighborhoods, all the factors such as the constant reinforcement of manhood by unlawful acts, the apathetic acceptance of drugs, booze, even cigarettes ... all are detrimental. So you can guess that kids from these neighborhoods are at greater risk. But — and this is my point — when I went back and looked at these kids four or five years later, there was a significant difference between the Logan Nation and Ben's. Most of the guys from Ben's are married or working regularly and have gotten on with their lives. With the exception of Reds, none have died. But with Logan Nation, of the thirty I surveyed, three are dead, and six are in jail doing juvenile life. Only one member from Ben's is in jail, a troubled car thief, and another was recently in the brig, and that's it.

"Don't you think it's odd that, despite the similar scoring which was done at a comparable age and in the same neighborhood, that there is such a drastic difference here?"

"I guess," Quinn said, in an uninterested fashion.

"You guess? You guess?" Washington's voice raised a notch. "The answer is yes. Everybody should turn out roughly the same, all things being equal. But it is not equal, see institutional racism exists all over. It is present from the public school system right up to us ... the criminal justice system. Do you see what I'm trying to say?"

"Yes ... yes ... a thousand times, yes!" Quinn said. "All of that is a mystery, I admit. But for right now, the important thing is to prevent more trouble. It's been peaceful in Logan the past three or four summers. When the whites controlled Logan, it was peaceful. Now blacks control Logan, and it's still peaceful. It was just that three or four-year period when we had the transition. That was when we had the trouble. So what I'm saying is, to be quite frank about it, it isn't the black end like Logan Nation that I'm concerned about. What worries me are the white boys ... Ben's. I thought they had vanished. I thought that was why there was no longer a problem. But now I see things and I hear reports, and it's troubling because I don't want another round of fighting between Ben's and Logan Nation right now. The timing is disastrous. First Reds gets killed in February, and then you have the burglary of the Penn Fruit two weeks later which you yourself said they probably committed. Now you have this burglary across the street from the Penn Fruit. What's it called?"

"Nate's Reliable. I heard about it."

"Right, Nate's Reliable. I have a report that eighty TVs were stolen."

"Right, I heard about that."

"How did you know about it?"

"Shannon told me," Washington said. "What about it?"

"Everything about it points to those guys, your friends ... Ben's. First of all, the location of the burglary was right behind the store on the railroad tracks. That leads me to suspect them."

"It sounds kind of big to me for them," Washington said.

"And I was never convinced they weren't into trafficking drugs."

"You always said that. You overestimate this group. There are only ten or twelve of them left."

"Also, the time of the burglary is interesting, too. It was on a Sunday night."

This was attached to an old, tired theory which Washington hotly disagreed with. With certain crimes, such as this burglary, it made no sense to commit the offence during the week. It made more sense to commit this crime on a Friday night or Saturday night. That way, when the crime was finally discovered on Monday morning, the trail would already be somewhat cold. White offenders, particularly young white offenders, however, committed this type of crime during the week or on a Sunday. The idea was that white offenders were more scared of jail, so they would commit their crime during the weekday so as to not be incarcerated for the entire weekend or part of the weekend. Committing the crime on a weekday night or a Sunday night would probably ensure that they would be processed and released the next day. This theory applies most specifically to white juveniles who were scared of the Youth Study Center which was in Center City and had less than 2 percent white residents. Blacks, on the other hand, weren't afraid of the Youth Study Center, and that was the difference.

This idea was as ridiculous as it sounded. It was one of the places where Washington and Quinn didn't see eye-to-eye. Quinn stubbornly held onto this pig-headed idea, and Washington never even felt like explaining how and why on a few levels this theory made no sense. Then there was the Penn Fruit burglary, if you wanted to call it a burglary. Penn Fruit was a supermarket that had gone out of business. It was right across the street from Ben's candy store. The market was vacant, but that didn't stop these perpetrators. They stole the shelving which hadn't yet been removed from the store. The ones involved, led by Frenchie, received a grand total of $400 for the work. It wasn't much divided by five ways, minus the cost of a U-Haul truck, which was used to haul the goods to New Jersey. There, a business that sells shelving, made the purchase of the hot goods. The shelving was actually worth a lot more; Frenchie and them just didn't know it. Anyway, the burglary coincidentally occurred on a Sunday night. When Quinn learned through Washington's information that white boys had committed the burglary, he was all proud, thinking he was such a smart detective n' shit.

"The burglary at Nat's Reliable, by itself, doesn't worry me. It's just the activity in general that I'm seeing, and like I said, the timing is kind of bad."

"Maybe, you know it's possible," Washington said. "Yeah, I'd even say it's probable. I went back on the tracks personally with Shannon and the way the act was committed had all the earmarks of amateurs like them."

"What do you mean 'earmarks'?" Quinn asked.

"Basically, it looks like they used sledgehammers and picks and knocked a hole through the wall in the back. That's something amateurs would do. They do it at a time when one of those long, slow, freight trains comes by, see, and the sound of the train drowns out any noise they might make.

"I vaguely remember a similar burglary of a beer distributor about a mile down the tracks from there. I don't think anybody was ever arrested for that one. I'm going to check it out. I'm pretty sure it was in 1973 or '74. I would bet anything that the same ones involved with the beer distributor burglary also had something to do with Nat's Reliable.

"But as far as them selling drugs, I never heard or saw any evidence of that. This group doesn't possess the type of temperament needed for something like that, and they are too small now to accomplish anything significant. At least they realized this, and as a result, they would never even think about something like that."

"Are they too small?" Quinn said. "What do you know about the Scorpions?"

"The motorcycle club?"

"Ralph Kramden and Ed Norton belonged to a club. The Scorpions are an outlaw motorcycle gang, the third biggest in the country behind the Hell's Angels in California and the Breed in Ohio." "What about them?" Washington said.

"Did you ever see a connection between Ben's and the Scorpions?" Quinn asked.

Washington laughed. "You think too highly of these people. These are really only kids."

"Didn't you tell me that some of the Scorpions were originally from Ben's?"

"There were a few; a guy named Mickey is one I tested. There also was a guy named Glenn, but he was before my time in Logan, and I never tested him. Neither is around anymore. I'm sure there is no connection."

"We have information of a methamphetamine laboratory run by the Scorpions which is in this two or three-block radius." Then Quinn pulled out a wall map of Logan that was behind his desk. He circled a two or three-block area on the map with his index finger. Then he said, "It's somewhere between 10th Street and 11th, and between Duncannon Avenue and Windrim Avenue. That's Ben's territory. That's why I can't see them not knowing something about it. It's pretty amazing how we learned of this laboratory. We had arrested a Colombian drug dealer who was an illegal immigrant at the time, and we were going to deport him. He told us about this lab, that he could smell it. He said he could smell the methamphetamine cooking but only on certain days, and he never really could pinpoint precisely where it was. He also told us, in no uncertain terms, that he was going to rob the place until he learned that it was run by the Scorpions, and he thought better of it. He also said that a big outlet for diet pills was right on that street … Windrim Avenue.

"Yet my main concern, as of right now, isn't meth or diet pills and certainly not those TV sets. I saw what happened here in Logan after that kid got shot on his mini-bike. Or rather I saw what didn't happen here in Logan, so I know what you can accomplish? Also, I have to find out about Reds. If Ben's has nothing to do with drugs, why was that house selected to rob in the first place? Maybe you're right and Ben's is insignificant, but they're in the middle of my worries at the moment. There is nobody who can help me out as well as you can right now."

"If I was so great, I keep wondering why I was transferred away from Logan in the first place."

"That was purely out of my hands. A transfer is not uncommon when there is a charge of brutality lodged against an offer, especially when a lawsuit is brought like the one against you."

"And you know I never laid a hand on that little faggot."

"It doesn't matter. You were the officer of record."

"I was the black kid that got caught holding the pocketbook. That's what I was. I was the scapegoat."

Quinn didn't respond, but his face registered some disapproval. He was thinking, *This guy is right. This guy is right.*

Finally, Quinn said, "Then I personally requested you to work with us again after I felt ample time went by to let the dust settle. That was primarily why you were back here last winter. It was because of me. But then you were requested to go back to North Philly as the gang wars started up again. Don't you think it was better considering everything that you did return to North Philly? I mean, look at what has happened. You have saved lives, and I'm happy to see you finally being acknowledged for your work. If you hadn't been sent to North Philly, then you would never have received this credit. The gang killings have almost stopped completely since you've been back there, and that is significantly more important than pounding the beat up here."

It was true that the decrease in juvenile gang-related violence had been dramatic in North Philly. It had been getting out of hand and much of the blame (not that it was justified) was laid on the police and Cerrone. It had gotten so bad down there that a rumor surfaced about how certain local undertakers were refusing to handle the viewing and funerals of slain gang members because they were afraid of further violence at their establishments.

Washington pointed out to Quinn that there were many other factors that contributed to the successful battle against gang violence. He talked about the Catholic church, the police athletic league, about funds from the city and volunteers from the community, as well as attention given to the problem by the public school system. But inside Washington always felt there was something else, something he couldn't put his finger on. It was something more powerful than all these factors combined. It was more powerful than all the therapy provided both for groups and individuals. Certainly catchy slogans hadn't helped. For instance, in 1974, there was a slogan: "No Gang War in '74." It turned out to be one of the most violent years. Then, in 1975, the slogan was "Keep Them Alive in '75." The number of gang war deaths increased, once again, in 1975. In 1976, the statistics suggested that the gang warring stopped. There was a dramatic decrease in gang war-related deaths. The reality of it, though, was that, despite Cerrone's promise to flood Philadelphia with federal troops for the Bicentennial celebration, the gang war violence was nearly as prevalent as it had been. It just so happened that there hadn't been many deaths that year. The mystery of the decrease in both deaths and the juvenile-gang violence in general over the next several years was solved by a large marijuana dealer in North Philly named Cookie Rojas. Washington personally had been in on the bust of Rojas following a twelve-month investigation.

In 1977, the gang warring stopped all together, and according to Rojas, the peacefulness was directly linked to a ton of marijuana dumped on Philadelphia. Rojas maintained that the marijuana, perhaps treated with something that made it stronger, had a lethargic effect on the young gang warriors. There was so much pot that, in a case of supply and demand, the prices for marijuana dropped dramatically. In 1977, pot only cost $40 an ounce. For five dollars, you could buy a bag containing thirteen joints, and we were talking white-boy joints now. And the stuff was dynamite — Panama Red ... Colombian Gold ... Decent. Rojas explained that one group of boys might be jonesing while another group of boys had plenty of reefer. That being the case, and everybody knowing that in a week or two the reverse could be true; the idea now was to get along with each other and share. The battle cry in 1977 could very well have been: *"A friend with weed is a friend indeed."*

The same situation seemed to exist in New York at that time. Comedian George Carlin, in one of his routines of that era, said that kids in public junior high schools had gone from making zip guns in shop to constructing marijuana pipes in shop.

Then briefly, in North Philadelphia in January of 1978, the gang wars began to flare up again. Washington couldn't figure out why, whether the marijuana supply dried up or what, but the violence there resembled the old violence from the early and mid-seventies, and Washington was credited, at least, partially for preventing the problem from getting out of hand.

"I know these guys, believe me; they aren't moving any quantity of drugs or anything like that. But I will admit they do sell a little bit, they do deal a little, if you want to call it that. Yes, they do sell drugs on a very small scale. See, what they do is, the ones that can do it anyway, they go to diet doctors for obesity. The doctors give them prescriptions then for diet pills. Then the hoodlums turn around and sell the diet pills for a dollar each."

"You're kidding me!" Quinn exclaimed.

"That's right. 'Schoobies' they called the diet pills. This is the quality of criminal you are dealing with. What am I supposed to do, lock up all of the fat ones? Because it's only the fat ones that can really get many Schoobies."

Quinn laughed at that and said, "The fat ones, I like that, the fat ones."

"See. It's funny, right? You're laughing, right? I'll look into all of this, but believe me; you won't find Goldfinger in this crew or anybody like that. This isn't exactly like busting the French Connection."

As often was the case, Quinn wondered how Washington knew so much about Ben's. He asked him once, ut Washington deflected the question. Clearly Washington had turned somebody. In other words, he caught somebody in a criminal act who was now giving

Washington information to save his ass. If Quinn asked Washington about it, which was unethical to begin with really, Washington would just tell him to mind his own business. He'd be in his rights to say that, too.

Washington was thinking about what they talked about earlier and how racism had an adverse effect on black lives. Sometimes, very often times, racism was so subtle that the white guys, like Quinn here, couldn't even see it.

"Something about this leaves a bad taste in my mouth," Washington said.

"What?" Quinn said.

"Well, you touched on something yourself just a minute ago. You maintain that white boys are afraid of the Youth Study Center and more afraid of jail in general. They think they'll be beaten up and possibly raped while they're in custody. That isn't necessarily true at all, but it's the perception that matters. As a result, these institutions are excellent deterrents to crime for white boys."

"That is good, right?" Quinn said.

"Well, it's good for white kids, but it doesn't do the black community any good. The Youth Study Center takes care of its residents who are virtually all black. Very often, in fact, the black kids are better off, at least, in the short term, in the Youth Study Center than they are at home. It is a little different; I mean, often they have corner boys, neighborhood acquaintances, possibly even a cousin or two is in there with them. In the final analysis, it doesn't help them because it doesn't serve as a deterrent to crime which the white kids benefit from."

Damn, Quinn was thinking. If the residents, who were virtually all black, were treated poorly by the whites who ran the Youth Study Center, then it would be racism. Instead, the residents of the Youth Study Center were treated very well, and it was *still* racism. He didn't want to say that and get into an impossible to win argument or debate with Washington who was as slick as any politician he ever knew and with as much bullshit, too. Politics, that was the ticket for Washington, Quinn was thinking to himself. Yeah, he could see Washington as a politician. The only problem was that big butt of his and those big teeth. Quinn smiled now, thinking for a moment of some cruel political cartoonist drawing up a caricature of Washington using those silly, exaggerated proportions they were famous for.

"That is purely unintentional." Quinn said, speaking of the Youth Study Center and it not helping the black community a great deal as Washington was suggesting.

"Let me tell you something about racism," Washington said. "There are two kinds of racism. One is intentional, and the other is unintentional.

Between the two, unintentional racism is worse."

Quinn didn't know what to say to that, so he didn't say anything.

"And look here ... look here," Washington said. "This is another example of what I'm talking about. You have a gang war between Logan Nation and Nicetown right in your backyard. In all, six black kids have died in that fight, yet you're more concerned about some hub-cap thieves. Besides, I heard Ben's is having their problems with Inky. I can't believe they're still around."

"Inky has been around for three generations. Their grandfathers, their fathers, and now they still hang on the same corner around 5th and Lindley, in Olney, around Incarnation Church ... Inky." "Are they into anything serious?" Washington said.

"If they are, they have been doing a fine job of keeping it quiet. They are like Ben's; they aren't into anything major that we know about, only that there are more of them than Ben's at this point because Olney is still mainly white. You should test them. I'm sure, if you did, you would find just as high a mortality rate as Logan Nation, and probably just as high an incarceration rate."

Washington said, "That isn't my point. I'm sure there are some places in the world where white kids are getting into as much trouble as black kids. I'm not saying that. All I'm maintaining is that, all things being equal, it's still worse off for blacks. But you're right. I did actually think of testing Inky about three or four year ago. It may have been interesting."

"I don't know about that," Quinn said. "I can't see anything with any … what did you call it … 'social redeeming value' coming out of Inky. Only two good things ever came out of Inky, and that's Tom Gola and Lindley Avenue." (Gola was a legendary basketball player who played at LaSalle before turning pro. He was one the best ever to come out of the city, right up there with Wilt Chamberlain. He was originally from Incarnation Parish.)

"But you see what I'm saying?" Washington said. "Look how much more concern there is here for Ben's as opposed to Logan Nation. That's not right."

"All right. I hear you there. That makes sense what you're saying, but you know, it's simply politics, baby." As Quinn said this, he hunched his shoulders, stretched his arms out to each side, then turned his palms upward and feigned an innocent look.

"There are enough black adults in the city right now to run it if they organized and voted."

Washington was sure Quinn here was accurate on this point. This was a guy who would know, a living, breathing poster boy for what politics can achieve. Washington himself was one -quarter Irish, and he was proud of that, proud to be the grandson of an Irishman. He admired them and the way they rose up. Quinn here, for example, he wasn't born with a loaf of bread under each arm. Shucks! His grandparents, maybe even one of his parents, were probably immigrants. They weren't much better off really than the so-called boat people, whoever the hell they were, who now inhabited Logan. He admired them, the Irish, for the way they supported each other and organized and for their political savvy. It worked for them, with their little beef and beers with the macaroni salad, 50-50 door prizes, bingo, and "basket of cheer" raffles. They rose rapidly and had political control over the city, led by an Irish mayor by the 1950s. By the early sixties, they even had an Irish Catholic lad in the White House. The Italians probably had more political power for the time being in Philadelphia with Cerrone at the top, and they had, too, done it the same way. Washington knew that, at least, the Irish still had their grasp on the mighty Philadelphia police department from the commissioner on down.

And now here was Quinn with this cake job, this appointed position. With his jelly doughnuts and *The Daily Racing Form*, Washington was sure, if you looked close enough, you could see the holes in the back of his neck where the strings were attached. The guy had it made, and it was because his ancestors had done the heavy lifting. All the years he had known Quinn, he never seemed worried at all. Washington would come in to talk shop, talk about police work, and Quinn would want to talk about the Phillies or when Billy Conn *almost* beat Joe Louis or tell another lie about him and Tommy Lasorda. Now he was all serious, though, concerned about his job; that's what it was. Now suddenly everything was all urgent and shit. Quinn was right on the money though. These white guys were shrewd when it came to money and jobs. It was politics to be sure, but it was capitalism, too. They understood that, in this system, there would be winners and losers. They acted like, the more losers there were, the greater chance they had of being successful and having these cushy jobs in city government. White people in power didn't reach down to help poor whites, so why should black people expect help from them?

It would never happen. Heck! Nobody helped the ethnics rise up. Jews, Italians, Irish, nobody helped them. This was what was at stake; this was the chance for the black community to organize right now. It boiled down to helping each other as well as their children, grandchildren. They had to overthrow this charter change drive and put their own people in charge in the near future. Cerrone inadvertently was making it possible since many whites were displeased with him. He was not exactly a uniting force. Now was the key time in the history of this city, the summer of 1978. This could be a dynasty. It was a divide and conquer thing right out of the play book of somebody like Malcolm X. Someday it could be Washington's son or grandson pulling those strings. On the other hand, if black people didn't organize and vote against this charter change, they might never gain control, never have this chance again. This was how it was in America, and if the black people of Philadelphia didn't want to play that white man's game, then they really shouldn't complain about certain political inequities that would surface.

"I hear what you're saying," Washington said. "Blacks traditionally don't vote in Philadelphia mayoral elections. But remember, in the past it was usually a Republican who was white, against a Democrat who was also white and possibly a third party candidate who was also white. But this election, the charter change, is a little different. See, blacks won't vote for things, but they will vote *against* things like this charter change proposal."

Talking to Washington was maddening because of all the riddles. What did that mean? "*Won't vote for things but will vote against things*"?

"It's like what happened in Atlanta in 1974," Washington continued. "There was a referendum to reform a welfare bill in Atlanta. The blacks saw that was a threat or an assault against them. They voted against it. It's the same thing here. He's going to get the black community fired up and politically active for the first time in Philadelphia, and it's going to open the door for a black mayor in the near future, maybe as early as '82."

"I think you are wrong about that," Quinn said. Absent a black candidate, he just couldn't see the black voters coming out. Besides that, Washington was full of crap. In both of Cerrone's victorious elections, a black candidate was on the ballot somewhere. It was just that neither received adequate support on Election Day, even in the black districts.

"You'll see," Washington said. "I was in Center City yesterday for court. I saw all these tables where people were registering to vote. Most of them, I'll bet, never voted in their lives and they were all black." "It remains to be seen if they actually will vote," Quinn said.

"You'll see," Washington said.

"Did you ever hear that joke about the two black guys from Philadelphia at a rally in Center City? It was at a square, sort of like a park, and a black preacher was making this speech about blacks not voting in Philadelphia.

"The preacher was addressing this black crowd that had gathered in the square, and these two black guys were in the back drinking a bottle of wine. Anyway, the preacher said, 'You know, brothers, we have a very poor voting record in the black community. The problems are, first of all, a lack of knowledge in the black community and an abundance of apathy in the black community.' Meanwhile, the two guys are in the back, and the one guy says to the other, 'What does he mean 'a lack of knowledge and an abundance of apathy'?' Then the other guy turns around and says, 'I don't know, and I don't care."

CHAPTER 5

It was 11:15 a.m. and Torch sat in the quiet house, drinking a second cup of coffee. Maria had already gone to work at the diner. Lee-Oskar was staying at Maria's parents' house as he often did. That always made Torch happy because, for some reason, Torch noticed that it was much easier to get laid when the boy wasn't there. Maria denied that was a factor one time, and Torch never brought it up again. When they dropped the boy off at Maria's mother's house the night before, the grandma said that she was going to put Lee-Oskar to B-E-D, the way you would say it in front of a little kid that you didn't want to know what you were saying. Then Maria said that was fine with her, and she was going to F-U-C-K. When she said that, Torch noticed the odd look that registered on the boy's face just then. Torch couldn't see how it was possible, but the boy seemed to know what his mother was talking about. There was a look of disappointment or jealousy or something on Lee-Oskar's face, but that was too bad … Torch had won this round.

As always, on weekdays, starting at eleven o'clock, Torch listened to the Solid Hour of Sinatra on WPEN. He also frequently listened to the Philadelphia Tradition, which consisted of Friday with Frank and Sunday with Sinatra, hosted by Sinatra enthusiast Sid Mark on WWDB, with the music entirely Sinatra for four hours each time.

The daily peacefulness of his present life was something Torch really valued. After all, it was America, and he liked the idea of calling his own shots. In this type job, he was rewarded by hustling and perhaps working harder than the week before as opposed to working for the city where he made exactly the same amount each week. The possibility of making more money was important to him in light of how monotonous the numbers job could get at times. There was an excitement about it, however, when Torch would check the sheet every night to see if any of his customers had "hit" the number that day. Torch never sat on any numbers. He called all his numbers in … straight numbers, parlays, leads, etc. The rule of thumb was that it didn't pay to sit on numbers unless you had a whole lot which would make it worthwhile. For it to be practical to sit on numbers, you needed a quantity of them so that you could overcome customers hitting the number and still make a profit. Torch was happy, just like Alex was, just to get his 25 percent of the losing action he called in. This was known as the "ribbon." Just on the ribbon, Torch made about $250 a week. In addition, when a customer hit the number, Torch got 20 percent. If a customer hit for $500 dollars, Bah-Bah gave Torch $600, and he (Torch) kept $100 as a type of commission. Also, the joyous lucky customer would usually give the numbers writer a tip for his being paid so quickly and efficiently with no problems.

A year earlier, in 1977, the Commonwealth of Pennsylvania started its own three-digit legal numbers game with a live drawing every night at seven o'clock. The day number, the illegal number or street number, on the other hand, came from the results of the racetracks in New York City, Aqueduct, or Belmont which raced alternately year around.

It probably was the original intention of the state to cut into the day number and, thereby, increase the handle on the legal night number. This didn't necessarily happen. The state number also paid 500 to 1 and was very popular and received more play every week. But if anything, the night number only increased the day number business, too. Many customers watched the live drawing on television and played their favorite number, for instance, 724, both day and night. Overall, the legal number simply got more people into playing numbers. It followed that the day number flourished when the legal night number started. However, Bah–Bah didn't take the night number. Torch's night number went to Jose or Mr. J., a Spanish ex-boxer and ex-bartender from South Philly who had been friendly with Gino. Gino had supposedly given Jose his start and now Mr. J. was an up and comer in the business.

There was a very good reason why Bah–Bah didn't want the night numbers. The district attorney of Philadelphia, who decades later would be the city's mayor, had Gino arrested one time. It was explained to Gino, at that time, that writing day numbers was all right with them. They really didn't care about the day numbers. On the other hand, they told Gino that writing the night number was an entirely different ball game because to write those numbers was to detract from the state revenue, and that was an entirely different issue. It was as if they were saying, "We don't care if you rip people off, just don't cut into our ripping people off." Gino reluctantly went along with that agreement since the day number had many built-in advantages to it and was still much more lucrative. First of all, the day number came out periodically in three sections all afternoon. This enticed people to play heavier. Say for example, 724 was someone's regular number, but he forgot to play it that day and a "7" was leading. People who played numbers were extremely superstitious, even more so than horse players or sports betters. That being the case, this customer would frantically play a $5 or $10 on a two-to-four back parlay as if to cut their losses. The night number, coming out all at once as it did, didn't have that advantage. Parlays were big in the day numbers game and nearly non-existent in the legal night game. Plus, the bookies paid better on parlays than the state did. Some customers played "leads" or individual numbers as opposed to two or all three numbers. The legal number booked by the state didn't offer this. Customers would play for example "$50 on the 8 up front" or "$40 on the7 on the end."

Gino had too much to lose by taking the night number and getting on the bad side of the district attorney. Mr. J. paid Torch 30 percent of everything he called in. That was a good deal, and Torch could have written day numbers for Mr. J. for that same bargain rate, which was slightly better than what Bah-Bah was giving him. Nevertheless, Torch just figured that, in the long run, he would be better off working for Bah-Bah. He (Bah-Bah) figured to last longer than Mr. J., who Torch didn't think had any muscle now that Gino was gone. At least Bah-Bah still had some pull, although it was certainly not as much as he acted like he had or thought he had.

Torch fielded six phone calls and wrote about twenty-five numbers which really wasn't as bad as it had been in the recent weeks, although it was far from acceptable. Alex warned him that business, like almost every other business in Center City, decreased in the summer.

Despite the decrease in work, Torch still had a lot of paperwork to do. He got his two notebooks out of an out-of-the-way drawer. One was a green notebook which was for the National League, and the other was red for the American League. He also had a three by five card devoted to every pitching staff. Maria told Torch that he was a compulsive gambler. She said gambling was a symbol of his "impaired personality" which was basically the same thing Washington once told him. Maria made remarks about the gambling, saying, "You are going to destroy all of that money" (which now was closer to $45,000 than $50,000).

Given how she felt, Torch took a little caution to keep his gambling quiet and avoided any conversation he really didn't need. He didn't see himself ever completely stopping. He couldn't imagine a summer without it, so he just tried to be careful about it.

He kept his betting small and realistic. He really didn't think of it as gambling. Washington had been right about him though. Torch had a severe inferiority complex. According to Washington, it was somehow manifested in his gambling. Torch once told Washington about his betting, and Washington jumped right on it. It was what Maria was talking about, too. Torch basically suffered from a lack of self-confidence and a personality like his, combined with gambling, was a recipe for disaster. But the booking, even on this small scale, gave Torch an insight and a different perspective on betting. Last year, during baseball season alone, he lost almost $2,500. It was crazy, and he didn't want to do that again. These days Torch thought of bookies and their customers as having a similar type of relationship to that of cops and criminals. Clearly you had to be on one side or the other … period. Like a policeman, Torch was happy and felt fortunate to be on the side that he was. He supposed, when he thought about it, that this type of work was positive since it somewhat decreased his own gambling which inside he realized was destructive.

A former supervisor of his from *The roundhouse* (the Police administration building), Kevin Reynolds, called him. Kevin liked to bet harness racing where the driver sat behind the horse in a "sulky" and which was hitting its prime years now in the 1970s. To Torch, it didn't seem to be as exciting as thoroughbred racing, and the pay-offs weren't as bountiful. It was generally a slower sport. Yet, it was preferred by the younger horse better, generally speaking. Naturally older betters preferred thoroughbreds because they had a lifelong connection to it; they had grown up on it. Harness racing, on the other hand, was conducted at night and with more of an emphasis on restaurants and other niceties unimportant to older players.

Kevin's family had originally been from a rural area just outside of Philadelphia near Brandywine (a harness track which was in nearby Delaware). His family had been in the standard-bred or harness business in a breeding and then training capacity. Kevin broke away from the successful family business and got involved in politics. One thing led to another, and now he was a supervisor in city administration. These days, Kevin liked to keep a hand in the business of his uncles and cousins. He bet on a few of the horses that he was familiar with. Usually the horses won, but they never went off at good odds and never really paid much.

Unlike the numbers, Torch sat on all of the horse racing action which he got from four or five customers during the week because he saw this as an easy way to make extra money. However, it was a two-way street. Two or three weeks earlier, he was set back considerably by two bombs who ran at Delaware Park, called in by a Center City bartender named Freddy Kelly which resulted in $1300 out of Torch's pocket. Kevin's bets, on the other hand, even if they won, couldn't really sting Torch, and he was grateful for the action. Booking these horses was what originally gave Torch an interest in this odd-looking sport. He liked following the harness racing in the paper, the entries, the results, and he got into it more and more. It was the colorful names that hooked him such as Gum Boots, Silk Stockings, Adios Vic, Roman Chief, Doe Liner, and Committeeman. Plus, he liked the *Philadelphia Daily News* coverage of the game led by sportswriter Jack Kiser. Three or four times a month, he went to the Liberty Bell Racetrack with Maria.

On this occasion, Kevin bet on a favorite of his. The horse's name was Mr. Joe Man. He was a hard-closing old veteran with Kevin's favorite driver Jack Smith, Jr. This old horse won a race the past winter at the age of fourteen. Kevin also bet on another horse by the name of Sunder Chief. It was ridden by Joe Scorsone. Kevin bet each horse for his standard $40 to win. Notwithstanding the two long shots that had recently been dropped on him, Torch usually made out considerably well booking horses. It was an advantage that Torch had over his predecessor Alex, who called in everything to his ribbon. As Gino once said, "Alex wouldn't sit on a 25 cent number." A drawback, however, was Torch's personal interest in betting on horses. Today, for example, Torch saw a horse running in the eighth race at Keystone (in the northeast). The horse was named Rico's Spy. He was just an old and relatively inexpensive claiming horse who appeared to Torch to simply overachieve when he got the right jockey and trainer. Today he was entered, perhaps somewhat optimistically, in a $25,000 allowance race. Torch had seen Rico's Spy win impressively last summer at Keystone against lighter company. Then the horse had an unsuccessful spring at the Garden State Racetrack in New Jersey. But Torch believed Rico's Spy, in those particular races, didn't have a jockey that suited his style. He tended to be a slow starter, a plodder. He clearly showed that he ran his best in the latter stages of every race. It followed, therefore, that Rico's Spy was adversely affected by not only the jockey maybe, but also by the short distances he had been entered in recently which were not conducive to his strong closing kick which he had displayed last summer. It was as though the trainer, having continually seen the horse fall back, had recently been entering the him in shorter races to increase his early speed and to give him a chance. Torch didn't think stamina was a problem at all for the veteran. Finally, today the horse was asked to go two turns at a mile and 70 yards. The fact that Rico's Spy was shooting high in this weekday feature race didn't deter Torch's enthusiasm. In horse racing, no matter where it was, there was always more integrity in betting a horse who was moving up in class as opposed to a horse who was moving down and would seemingly have a class advantage. This was especially true at Keystone Racetrack where drop-down horses historically had a terrible record. In fact, Torch's enthusiasm was heightened somewhat by his moving up because he knew the jump was enough to scare off a lot of betters. As a result, Rico's Spy would probably go off at fairly generous odds. Also, Torch liked this jockey whose name was Rochelle Lee and who was the first female jockey that Torch knew of. She was certainly the first female jockey of any note at Keystone Racetrack. Yet there seemed to be a little bias on behalf of the betters. She was slightly under bet because she was a female, which was an added bonus. Torch wound up betting $60 on Rico's Spy — $30 to win (first) and $30 to place (second). By one o'clock, Torch had called everything in and was sitting at the table drinking another of coffee. At that moment, he was listening to Bob Craig's 'Solid Hour of Sinatra' as he sang "Something Stupid." The phone rang. It was Felix. He said that he had something for Torch, and they were all going to meet in Ben's in about a half an hour. Torch could tell by Felix's voice that he'd sold a few of the TV sets.

Torch was wearing his official summer uniform of Dungarees, a muscle undershirt, or "wife beater", and his white high-top converse All Stars or Chuck Taylor's with the blue star on the side, also referred to as "Chucks." He left the house out the back way and just before squeezing through a hole in the fence, and onto the railroad tracks. He took a cursory look at Maria's vegetable garden. She grew tomatoes, and the plants were still green, of course, as it was early summer. Maria also grew cucumbers usually and peppers. But at this early stage, the only thing that was edible was the radishes. Radishes came up first every year. Those things, Torch was convinced, would grow in cement. They never had a bad year, sort of like Pete Rose. Then Torch proceeded up the hill and walked toward Logan Railroad Station. The tracks were like a poorly healed scar, that ran through Logan, connecting east and west, which was connected only by a railroad bridge that ran high above Broad Street. That is Philadelphia's main north-south artery, which runs through the entire city. Usually Torch crossed that bridge walking across a catwalk built there for the railroad workers. However, on this occasion, Torch exited the tracks like a normal railroad commuter through the piss-scented tunnel. Normally he would exit the tracks right behind the plumbing supply store, which was only a few doors east of Ben's. But this time, the idea was to avoid the violated Nate's Reliable. It was attached to something Torch once heard on a detective show about how the offending criminal usually, in one way or another, returns to the scene of the crime.

The day was damp and the tunnel smelled particularly vile. That was not the only reason he hadn't walked through the tunnel since he was a kid. The other reason was that it was a sort of death trap. At the moment, they weren't fighting with Logan Nation, but he got into the habit of moving around carefully. There was a ton of graffiti in the tunnel, including one red spray-painted message that said "Free Angela." Another sign in red spray paint read: "*Cornbread King of the Walls.*" There also was a sign in black spray paint: "*Lump of Logan.*" Then there was other graffiti that simply read "*Speed Kills.*"

Weather-wise, it was the kind of day where the Phillies who played in South Philly would be in a perpetual state of rain delay, while in Logan, the sun peeked out. Then in forty-five minutes or so, the reverse would be true. It would be sunny at Veterans Stadium and raining in Logan.

Torch exited the tunnel and approached Broad Street. No cars were coming south just then, so Torch crept out into the median strip. There were many wider streets in Philadelphia than Broad Street, but Broad Street was among the most difficult to cross because the lights had a tendency to change a little rapidly. Loganites and Philadelphians, in general, Torch supposed, knew when they crossed into advanced middle age when they started crossing Broad Street in sections. That was when you waited for a green light and crossed halfway to the median strip, then waited for the second green light to complete the journey.

Now Torch found himself in the middle of Broad Street standing on the unprotected median strip. Torch looked south on Broad Street which ran the length of the entire city. But it wasn't straight the way people thought of it as being. It was true that it generally went uphill from City Hall, which was downtown. But it went up and down in almost a roller coaster fashion. In North Philly, there tended to be a dip almost like a valley. In the summer, like today, you could see the smog and condensation gather in the valley of North Philly. From there, it seemed to continually rise up slightly and gradually up into Logan and points north. You could look straight into Center City and see city hall. It was the cornerstone of city government, where the courts were and where the mayor had his office. At the top of the city hall tower, the highest building in the city then, was a 37-foot bronze statue of William Penn, the Quaker who founded Pennsylvania, looking over this not-somighty-metropolis called Philadelphia. He had a secretary or lieutenant named James Logan, who this gave his name to the Logan section of north Philadelphia.

Half a block east of Broad Street, Torch made a left turn into Ben's, walking past some out-of-town newspapers which were outside. The door was closed as the air-conditioning was on. The door was green with a Canada Dry sign on it. Torch immediately smelled cigars. Both brothers Ben, 55, and Lou, 65, were in the store. Ben smoked big brown cigars and now was behind the counter to Torch's left. To his right, above and below him, were racks and racks of magazines, most of which were of the pornographic sort. Most of the time one or the other of the two brothers was at the store. This time, both happened to be present. Ben was the bigger of the two brothers and seemed to be more in charge of running the business.

Lou, on this day, as usual, was wearing a red shirt just large enough to accommodate his pot belly and just long enough to reach his pants, which were always black, and came up to a point below the crotch area. Unlike Ben, Lou smoked short, smelly, nasty black Italian stogies, the kind the Old Italian immigrants who fermented them in anisette preferred. Ben ate the same thing for lunch every day for thirty years. Italian salami on a roll with mustard.

Jackie Reilly, who was named after the first Catholic President, was at the pinball machine right now. The others, including Efrem, Tommy, Shine, Felix, and two of Jackie's six brothers and ten siblings, Jimmy and Leo, surrounded the machine. By the look in their eyes Torch could tell that something special was going on. Jackie was making an assault on the record high score. He already had hit the maximum three games and had 82,000 points but needed 5,000 more to break the record, which was 87,000.

The machine, like all pinball machines, had a name. This one was called Teacher's Pet. Torch remembered this model at Dunn's when he was younger. Torch could remember playing, standing on a wooden soda crate to play this same machine. It was a special model. You only needed 4,000 points to "hit" (win a free game), and there was a way to get 500 points when you shot any one of the five balls. It wasn't easy, but one time in Dunn's, Torch saw a chink kid named Jay make that shot four or five times.

Jackie's hair was in his face, which was a mask of concentration. His head was down. His eyes followed the silver ball, rolling and swinging back and forth across the board. His lit Marlboro burned on the glass of the machine, and he snuck a quick drag off it when he could. He slapped at the flippers but was overall gentler than he normally would be, only shaking the machine slightly knowing that this one was easy to "tilt."

When Torch first met Jackie, his hair was much blonder and lighter, and was cut in an almost Prince Valiant style. His hair got darker as the years went on and now was overall almost entirely gold, the color of one of Ben's Vanilla Cokes, and in certain spots, it looked light brown. Jackie wore a gold crucifix that rested on his chest, and on his arm was the tattoo of a boxer with black hair who looked like a little Rocky Marciano, and in the tattoo was the inscription *"Ben's."* The others cheered Jackie on as he shot his last ball, leaving only 4,000 to tie the record of 61,000. The old record was held by "the Professor," who was an English and Drama teacher at Central High School in West Logan near Dunn's. In fact, Torch knew him when he used to play pinball there frequently. "The Professor's" real name was Dave Rothman, and he was an expert magician specializing in card tricks. He was very mysterious looking with a devil type of goatee, and he usually wore dark clothes and often carried a cane. He liked to drink gin and allegedly was, at one time, a cocaine user. He was a regular, not only at Ben's store, but also at the Warnock Bar, and he also would stop over to Caesar's Palace every now and then. The Professor contended that playing pinball was excellent for hand-eye coordination, and pinball provided excellent practice for his elaborate card tricks and stunts.

The Professor was fifty-seven years old but still found it necessary to adhere to the timeless tradition of writing his name and high score on the pinball machine. "Teacher's Pet" was a special game. There was a way you could get 500 points right off the bat. There was a certain way you could shoot the ball (thumb it), and if you got it just right, it would go into the center slot. That would get you 500 points right there. It wasn't so easy, but one time, in Dunn's, Torch saw a chink kid named Jay make that shot four out of the five times. As they all watched Jackie play now, Felix gestured to Torch to come closer to him and shoved six fifty-dollar bills in Torch's hand. The short muscular Felix told him, "I sold five TV sets to a party on Fifth Street, the cleaners." Torch knew who he meant by that. "I tried to get $400 each, but I couldn't. I only got $300 each. He jewed me down."

Torch wasn't complaining. It was a big sale after all, and whoever brought that many goods deserved a sort of discount, he figured. They originally agreed to sell the TV sets for $400, but that was negotiable.

Felix was the one guy that Washington was most intrigued by. He and his brother Johnny or J.R.B, also from Ben's, had an intact family, but their parents couldn't control them. Consequently, the majority of their childhood was spent in foster homes or juvenile facilities. They both had been in the types of places where the recidivism rate hovered around the 100 percent mark. Washington was puzzled by Felix because he couldn't believe he was still around, frankly. Since he had been a habitual criminal since he was eleven, there was a ton of data on him. Back in the seventies, there was less crime and drugs. Cerrone's men ruled with an iron fist and whether it was during his tenure as police commissioner or as mayor, they had a toe hold on the crime problem, for the most part. The criminal justice system ran smoothly. Bench warrants were issued and scofflaws were perused and detained. Probation officers, court psychologists, and presentence investigators had much more time to write on each "customer." Felix's files, that was both his juvenile folder and his adult folder, were interesting to Washington.

As Jackie passed the 87,000 mark, everybody cheered, encouraging him. Torch walked back to the soda counter and asked Ben for a cherry Coke. He then took a porno magazine off the rack and thumbed through it. It was called *Cavalier*. Inside, Torch was looking at a sequence of shots depicting a guy in the movie theater being raped by two girls, one blonde and one brunette.

In the store, beyond the pinball machines, were about two hundred inexpensive old books stacked haphazardly on shelves and tables. There was a sign there that read "Lou's Lending Library." The only person that really paid attention to this library was Mac, who also hung with them. He read, he claimed, about one of these books every single day. Torch thought that Mac was the only customer that this library had ever had.

On the radio, which was playing softly in the background, was a love song called "You Take my Heart Away" from the *Rocky* soundtrack.

Torch returned the magazine and sat at the counter eating Mexican Hats and Red-hot Silver Dollars. Shine silently played the car racing machine with much less fanfare than Jackie had attracted. Shine loved to play that machine, and nobody could come close to his scores. He was the champion at that. Yet no matter how good you were at these games, you couldn't register a free play which didn't seem to matter to him. Shine was fascinated by the game. Torch supposed that Shine, on probation now for car theft, liked to drive any car as long as it wasn't his own. Shine wore a black shirt and blue overalls which, possibly, were borrowed from Haystacks Calhoun. The customer next to Torch at the counter was eating a dish of ice cream and drinking a glass of water Ben had set there for him. He was reading the *New York Daily News*, Jimmy Breslin's column. The article concerned the Son of Sam, whose trial would be held that summer. Felix came over to the counter and sat next to Torch and asked Ben for a glass of water.

"Felix is my best customer," Ben said. "First he asks for a pack of matches and now a glass of water." Ben put the glass in front of Felix and walked away.

Then Felix talked to Torch. "There were a bunch of 53rd cops at Caesar's Palace this morning. There were about five or six of them. Washington was the leader. He said he was looking for some TV sets. It was me and Doc there at the time. See, I told you that Caesar's Palace would be the first place they would look."

Originally Torch and some of the others thought they should hide the TV sets at Caesar's Palace. It was Felix's idea to keep them next door at Grant's house. As usual with matters such as this, Felix was right. "Washington?" Torch said.

"Right. Washington. And guess what he said? He said, 'The hotel is closed.' He said, 'This is private property.'"

To Torch and the others, there was no such thing as private city property. Anything that belonged to the city was theirs. It was public domain. It seemed that, in Philadelphia, all kids felt the same way. They seemed to come to believe that ripping off the city in any capacity was sort of a birthright, whether it was filing a faulty lawsuit or simply swiping some salt in the winter from a public park.

"They put a padlock on Caesar's Palace. I don't know what we'll do now."

Felix, Frenchy, and Doc and another kid, Billy, all lived at Caesar's Palace. Torch and the others only lost an office and a club house. These guys had lost their home. But surely even Felix and certainly Jackie and Torch were more concerned that Washington was back around than about anything else. After the murder of John Base, even though Teddy had basically admitted his guilt by fleeing Logan, they all would be forever bound in their common paranoia that something could, one day, link them to that murder, even though Washington seemed to be the only one that cared about it or even remembered it.

"Is that exactly what he said? The hotel is closed?" Torch asked.

"That's exactly what he said," Felix said.

A little Spanish kid who was about ten was picking over a large tray of penny candy. The tray included not only Mexican Hats and Red-Hot Silver Dollars, but also miniature Mary Janes and individual Peanut Chews, a Philadelphia delicacy. Ben said to the boy, "Can I help you with anything, Jose?" Then Ben, as Torch knew he would, slyly shifted his eyes over to see if Torch had gotten the little joke.

Felix led everybody out of the store. They had talked about going to the racetrack before Torch even got there, and they decided to go. Then Torch noticed that Jackie didn't seem to be in his usual happy-go-lucky mood. Torch guessed that Jackie was thinking about Washington; surely that had been on Torch's mind as well. Torch walked over to Jackie as they walked out of Ben's store and said, "I know what you're thinking. Don't worry about it. That's what you told me before, yourself. He can't bother us with that old stuff. Just try to have a good time at the track. It's been too long for him to bring up that old stuff anymore."

Jackie and Torch got into the back seat of Felix's car which was a black Electra Deuce-and-a-Quarter. Shine, of course, got in the front seat and Felix drove.

"Love Won't Let Me wait," a big Philly song from 1975 by Major Harris was playing on the radio just then. The car proceeded east on Wyoming Avenue which led into the Roosevelt Boulevard.

On Wyoming Avenue, they drove by Goldenberg's Peanut Chews Factory. At that Point, Felix said, "You know, when I was little, I used to live around here. It wasn't bad, but you know it used to stink. You know, see, chocolate stinks. It's not like everybody thinks. See, it's the peanuts and the syrup and the sugar and everything that smells good. But chocolate by itself really stinks. People don't realize that."

"Games People Play" by the Spinners was playing when they turned off the boulevard onto Street Road, which led them right to Keystone Racetrack. "Why do they call it Keystone Racetrack, anyway?" Shine asked.

"Because Pennsylvania is the Keystone State," Jackie said.

"Why? What's that mean? 'The Keystone State'?" somebody asked.

"I thought it was because maybe Pennsylvania was shaped like a keystone, but that isn't what it was."

Torch was saying that he learned from Mac that when the country was less than twenty-five or thirty years old, Pennsylvania was the *keystone* to the country because it bound the northern states such as New York and New Jersey with what was the South in those years. Essentially, the South was Maryland, Delaware, and Virginia, and maybe one or two other states. Pennsylvania served as a sort of keystone in a bridge. If you removed that stone from the structure, the entire bridge would crumble.

If you removed Pennsylvania at that time, then the whole union would have crumbled. That was why they called it the Keystone State. Mac was very well read and was particularly on top of anything that had to do with American or Irish history, especially Irish history.

Felix made a left turn off Street Road into Keystone. He paid the general parking fee. Once in the track, they headed straight for the refreshment stand. They each had a bowl of clam chowder, which Keystone was famous for. Then they went on the opposite side of the refreshment stand to the bar, which was perpendicular to the finish line. They stayed in that same area all afternoon. They didn't have a very good day betting, at least early on. They threatened to leave more than half of their recent windfall of money at these windows.

Finally the eighth race came around. They pooled their money, chipped in and bought a $10 Exacta Box using Rico's Spy, top and bottom with the rest of the field. They also used Rico's Spy in $10 late Daily Doubles, with a few assorted long-shots in the ninth race. Torch, even though he had bet the horse into his own book earlier, stepped on the gas and went further on him.

The horse seemed to break well and was right in the middle of the pack early on. As suspected, Kahoutec, who was clearly the class of the race took the early lead. He was displaying both his early speed and the confidence that he was the outstanding force in this field. A hopeless long-shot, a one dimensional speed ball by the name of Can-U-AffordMe, went right out with Kahoutec. Jack Lamar who was the voice of horse racing in Philadelphia said in his unique style,

"That's Kahoutec first to show. Can-U-Afford-Me, prompting the pace second. A length back on the rail that's sound of the El ... Another two lengths back on the outside is Ornithologist ... Pal Joey is on the inside with Rico's Spy between them, and then Danny Boy, and we still have a mile to run."

Rochelle Lee was exercising patience here as Torch had hoped. Kahoutec and Can-U-Afford-Me continued to slug it out up front, engaging in a suicidal speed duel. All day it seemed, at least in the races where Torch was paying attention that speed wasn't holding up. It had been horses that came from off the pace that were winning today. That was frequently the case at Keystone in the hot weather months. On the other hand, during the winter especially dry winters, providing there was no snow, the inside was frequently lightning fast. Horses that went to the rail early stayed there and often won easily on certain days. This race would turn out differently. Even though Rico's Spy was losing ground as he raced on the outside, Torch didn't think it was all that bad. It rained that morning, and there were a few thunder showers overnight.

Supposedly the rain drained toward the inside of the racetrack near the rail. That being the case, the inside tended to be deeper and somewhat sluggish on days such as this, and it slowed the horses down. Without question, the outside was the best place to be today.

Somewhere along the back stretch, Kahoutec finally shook Can-U-Afford-Me. Kahoutec increased his lead, but Can-U-Afford-Me, in those early fractions, took a lot out of Kahoutec. As they entered the top of the stretch, Kahoutec still had a sizable lead of our lengths, but Rico's Spy had now positioned himself outside in second place. As they made the turn into what Jack Lamar called "the furlong grounds," Rico's Spy lost a step or two when he tried to "change leads." Instead of moving further ahead, he seemed to go in almost a diagonal fashion, putting him further outside than he already was. Still, being on the outside probably was faster real estate than closer to the rail as Kahoutec was. It was at that point that Rochelle Lee seemed to take control of her horse, and she made a charge directly at Kahoutec. With fifty yards to go to the finish line, Rico's Spy brushed passed Kahoutec and won by two lengths. Kahoutec, with a very enthusiastic all-out ride by his jockey, managed to finish second. It was a strange race as a 60 to 1 long-shot finished third. Rico's Spy went off at 6-1 and paid $14. He combined with the favorite Kahoutec for a modest $50 Exacta, but they had it five times for $250. The boys celebrated at the bar with more beer, and each had a shot, too. During this jubilation, Torch noticed Felix's father out of the corner of his eye. Felix's father saw the boys at the same time, acted like he didn't see them, and headed in another direction. Torch had been the only one who had noticed Felix's father, and he didn't say anything. One time at Liberty Bell Racetrack a few years ago, Torch had seen him. Later that night at the Rockland, he had told Felix's brother Johnny that he had seen his father at the track. Then Johnny had mentioned to his mother that Torch said he had seen her husband at the track that night. That would have been alright except that he (the father) had told his wife that he had spent that evening bowling. After that incident, Felix's father always avoided Torch and the others whenever he saw them there, and Torch understood that. Torch hadn't even seen him at all at any track in about twelve months. He guessed that was what they meant when they said, "I'll see ya." And then the other guy would answer, "Not if I see you first."

Things got even better as one of the horses they hooked up in the Daily Double won the ninth race easily. His name was Yuessela, and like Rico's Spy, he went off at 6-1 odds and combined with Rico's Spy for a $60 Double. They had that also for $10 or five times which amounted to a $300 comeback. Shine had never been to the track; therefore he was elected to cash in the big ticket. They had another drink at the bar as the place thinned out.

As they drove home, Hy Lit was on the Oldies Station. He was the dean of disc jockeys in Philadelphia at that time. Hy Lit was, or at least he claimed to be, from Logan. At the moment he was playing "Right on the Tip of My Tongue" by Philadelphia's Brenda and the Tabulations. Then he played "Mixed Up, Shook Up Girl" by Camden's Patty and the Emblems. Torch mentioned that he saw something funny on *Saturday Night Live* the other night on TV at the Rockland Bar. He said it was him, Navy, Turkey, and Poodle Head. He said there was a skit in which these birds, like parrots, were dressed up and speaking. One, for example, had a dark tuxedo and was talking like Marlon Brando in the *Godfather*. Also somebody mentioned watching at the Rockland, Larry Holmes narrowly decisioning Ken Norton to win the heavyweight championship of the world. Just as they turned off the Boulevard onto C Street, which would lead them to Fisher and then a left to Logan, then 'Coolin' Out" by Jerry "The Iceman" Butler came on the radio. It was another underrated song that never charted around the country, but it was a big hit in Philadelphia and it seemed Logan in particular, especially at the Warnock Bar. Felix's car had good speakers in the back.

I'm just thinkin' 'bout coolin' out
I'm just thinkin' 'bout coolin' out
I'm just thinkin' 'bout coolin' out

When they got back to the steps of Caesar's Palace and they got out of the car, you could plainly see that there was, in fact, a padlock on the front door next to a pillar with an ornament in the form of a white cat nailed to it which the previous owner had put up.

Torch vaguely remembered that family. They had a daughter named Ginger. They were a white family and they only lived here for about one year. They had moved out unexpectedly, it seemed, in the middle of the night. That really wasn't uncommon in Logan. When the neighborhood was going through a racial transition, many white homeowners were embarrassed to be leaving. As a result, you would see moving vans at four o'clock in the morning. The neighborhood was mostly black already by the time Ginger's family had moved. Therefore, embarrassment or any fear of vandalism by angry white neighbors were not factors in that case at all, it just reminded Torch of those days.

Nevertheless, it was amazing how some homes would be occupied by the same family for three generations or more, while the house next door would be very transitory. Caesar's Palace fell into the latter category with all types of characters living there in the past ten years or so. Through it all, however, that cat had remained up there and in everyone's mind had become a symbol of the place. At night, when any of them were going to Caesar's Palace, they didn't look for the address or the door or anything like that; they looked for the cat.

Efrem, who worked at Marc's Beer Distributors, and Kevin who lived in nearby Olney, as well as Kevin's cousin Connell, who also worked at the beer distributor, were standing on the steps of Caesar's Palace. Connell, who was originally from Northern Ireland, had been the closest thing to a celebrity among them. He had apparently been suspected by being an I.R.A. member and was fortunate to escape with his life after serving a short time in an English prison. He was here in America as a political refugee, and he was a hero in this largely Irish neighborhood. In fact, last summer, they had had a parade downtown for him in which Mayor Cerrone participated.

Jackie then told a joke that went like this: "When does a Puerto Rican become Spanish? When he marries your sister."

Shortly thereafter, they broke up, and Torch walked back to his house. He was thinking he could watch some Gomer Pyle, which came on at five o'clock. Drunk with wealth, he didn't have a care in the world. He was walking between Caesar's Palace and Ben's store on Windrim Avenue when a car pulled up next to him. Before he looked, Torch knew it was the police because of the squeaky brakes.

You could always tell. The car hadn't even come to a stop it seemed when the passenger door opened and an athletically inclined cop, who had been sitting in the shotgun seat, was right on top of Torch, grabbing him by his neck and shoving him against a garage door. He put his hands in Torch's pocket and brought out the money that was there. Torch had some money, the fifties that Felix had given him earlier in one pocket and $200 or $300 he had from the racetrack in another pocket. The cop took both bundles out, put them together, shoved them back in Torch's pocket, and said, "Wise up, motherfucker." Then he walked back to the car. When the cop drove away, Torch was left with two thoughts. The first thing was, "What is it with these cops all of a sudden?" The other thought he had was, "Goddamn, he really does look like Lil Abner."

CHAPTER 6

Torch took *The PhiladelPhia inquirer* from the step at 8:30 a.m. The Phillies were out on the West Coast, and he had watched them play against the San Diego Padres last night until about 1:30 a.m. when he fell asleep.

Torch was busy on Saturdays. It would be a long day for him in Center City. Afterward, as usual, Torch would then drive to Bah-Bah's house and settle up with him. He would deliver his "ribbon" and take his cut. However, the week from gambling on baseball, which he also did with Bah-Bah, was separate. That was always taken care of on Thursday or Friday, at the latest. It was easier for both of them to keep the two amounts separate, rather than try to combine them. Last week, for instance, Torch only bet two games. He won one, and he lost one, and there was no need for them to settle up. As for his score on Rico's Spy, that would have to wait until next Thursday, if he didn't destroy everything by then.

On the front page of *the Inquirer*, it was reported that another highranking gangster from the older, long-standing, seemingly invincible mob had been found dead in a South Philadelphia alley. His name was Joe Miami, and his particular specialty was loansharking. Torch had heard that he was a type of "enforcer" as well. Torch's cousin told him that Joe Miami had personally tracked down the two actual killers of Constantine and murdered them both, dumping the bodies in a vacant lot in the Bronx in New York.

Bah-Bah, as always, was up and running early in the morning Torch didn't feel uncomfortable about calling him, even though it was only nine o'clock. Bah-Bah said that he had heard the news and wasn't too concerned about it. Nevertheless, Torch detected a certain little change in Bah-Bah's voice. It seemed like there was some uneasiness on his part for the first time.

Torch hung around to answer phones that morning and early afternoon, but hardly anybody called. Lee-Oskar had gone out at about eleven o'clock, and Maria was working breakfast at the diner. Torch normally didn't eat a big breakfast but this figured to be a long day for him, so he went to the North Star Diner for ham and eggs.

Torch had brought in the *Daily News* which was sold in the vestibule of the diner. He went directly to the story about Joe Miami. Famous for their big headlines and graphic pictures, the *Daily News* had become sort of the unofficial newspaper of the current mob war going on in Philadelphia, as well as the juvenile wars in the city. The article said that the war had to do with control of organized crime concerns in Atlantic City. It stated further that there were two different ideas about who was behind the murders. One theory was that a large New York crime family was behind the killings. The other theory was that this was all caused by a breakaway faction of Constantine's mob led by former loyalist Vito Moscariello. Then there was the usual recap of everybody who had been killed, starting with Constantine, who was shot outside his house. Philadelphians knew these names and the circumstances by heart. This one was killed, shot in a phone booth in Atlantic City. Another was found in the trunk of his gold Cadillac at Tenth and Mifflin. Still another one was found in a field out by the airport and so on.

Now there was Joe Miami. The *Daily News* had a picture of the street in South Philadelphia with an arrow pointing to the alley where Joe Miami was found. Torch read the quotes by the neighbors. Ever since Constantine had been killed, it had become sort of a South Philadelphia ritual for the neighbors to run out to be interviewed. They liked to look at the camera and then say, "I didn't see anything. I didn't hear anything," or "I don't know what you're talking about."

Torch turned toward the back of the *Daily News* and sought out the column by Jack Kiser, the harness racing-writer. In the entries at Liberty Bell Park, the harness track in the Northeast, Torch noticed a horse named Leroy Nickawampus. Torch had a customer in Center City named Sam the Blade, named so by Gino because of his job at a cutlery store, who bet on this horse every time he came to post. Blade had three or four horses that he called his "stable" that he would consistently bet. As for Leroy Nickawampus, Torch had seen him race his last time at Liberty Bell about ten days ago. On that night, Blade had bet $100 to win and place. Torch had noticed that Leroy Nickawampus had been blatantly and clearly interfered with at the top of the stretch. The infraction seemed to cause Leroy Nickawampus to break his momentum, lose his composure, and essentially lose all of his interest in winning the race. Nevertheless, Leroy Nickawampus, racing on the far outside and losing ground every step, still managed to finish fourth. Considering everything, it was an impressive effort given by Leroy Nickawampus. Certainly, Jack Kiser had seen the infraction even if the judges hadn't. s little comment next to Leroy Nickawampus read *"Brutal' hit' victim, last.* Perhaps with a little racing luck and an uninterrupted "trip" closer to the rail, Leroy Nickawampus would be a worthwhile bet tonight, Torch believed.

Torch knew from Bah-Bah that Sam the Blade, in addition to betting numbers and horses, was also a sports bettor currently on a downhill spiral. At the moment, Blade owed Torch over a hundred dollars and would, no doubt, want to bet Leroy Nickawampus tonight. Torch made a mental note to get the money up front from him or, at least, settle up before he allowed Blade to get again. Torch would be watching Blade and keeping him on a very short leash these days.

After Torch had another cup of coffee, he tried to reconstruct a dream that he had last night. The dream was vague, but he remembered it had something to do with the San Diego Chicken, who was the mascot of the San Diego Padres who he had watched last night.

Torch drove from the diner in Logan through Nicetown and got on the expressway which could take him right to Center City. Torch, instead, exited the expressway and took the scenic East River Drive. The Average White Band was playing on his 8-track player. The song just then was "Schoolboy Crush." It was a live concert performed in the midseventies at the Tower Theater right here in West Philly.

Saturdays were pleasant in Center City because all of the offices were closed, and it was generally quieter and much less hectic than during the weekdays. The important places were open though, specifically the bars and most of the restaurants. Many of the employees had been customers of Alex and now bet with Torch. The customers that hung around the bars all day on Saturday were generally an older group. Many of them were retired and a few of them had a lot of money. These older customers came around normally only on Saturdays, and all seemed to live by the same motto which was "It's better to live rich than to die rich." They liked to gamble all day long. They played heavily on the lead numbers and the parlays and bet the horses at Keystone Racetrack. In Eddie's Bar, they watched the cable program devoted to Keystone Racetrack. Torch would take action from them all day.

There were three bars on the little street that Alex and now Torch made the nerve center of their numbers business. The street was a little block called Samson between 15th and 16th, and between Walnut Street and Chestnut Street. The first bar was the Little Pub. Then there was Eddie's and finally Oscar's. Of the three, Torch preferred Eddie's and stayed in there most of the day. The nice thing about Eddie's was that it was small, unlike the other two, and didn't serve food. People went to Eddie's to gamble, not eat. Since it was so small, the air conditioning was very effective, and was traditionally the coldest spot in the city. The bar itself was a low white Formica-topped sort. The bartender usually was Mickey, a jittery nervous type who lived on black coffee, Courvoisier and cigarettes. He was a heavy numbers player who had once hit Alex for $30,000, and a few months ago hit Bah-Bah for $10,000. It was the biggest score Torch had ever made. He made $2,000 off the top, and Mickey gave him a $500 tip when Torch delivered a shoebox full of cash to him.

Another of Torch's best customers was Big Bobby who also bartended at Eddie's. Bobby, as Alex said, "Never came up for air," and was in constant action. A year or so ago, Bobby got in over his head with Alex and gave him a big gold chain instead of cash. Torch went with Alex to 8th and Samson, the jewelry district in Philadelphia, to pawn the chain which got Alex $800 and got Bobby out of the hole. Bobby was frequently also in debt to Gino for loans.

The mood in Eddie's on Saturdays was always festive and loud and smoky. It was so busy that, aside from Torch, there was usually another bookmaker there and sometimes two bookmakers. Bookies or numbers writers would "give each other a play." It was a professional courtesy. For example, one would play a number such as 135 for $50 straight, or box a six-way number for $10. It was like a bartender dropping in to see another and giving him a huge tip. The biggest bookmaker there almost every Saturday was Blue Eyes, who not only spread money around, buying the customers drinks, but also brought in loaves of pepperoni bread and sometimes stromboli.

Torch had learned from Gino that buying drinks was an excellent way to drum up business. Torch knew, for a fact, that Gino gave Alex extra money to buy drinks, even though Alex never did it once to his knowledge. "You gotta spray the infield every once in a while," Gino had told him.

On Saturdays, all kinds of characters would come in. This was especially true when Alex was still alive. Alex used his book to write his own ticket. He dealt with employees of stores who got things for him, and Alex gave them credit to play numbers and horses. In this way, Alex obtained hats, socks, clothes, and shoes. He got his nails done, got his hair cut, went to the movies, and got his shoes shined — all for free. One guy used to bring Alex gallons of homemade Italian wine. Another, a loyal cab driver that he knew, used to bring him cannoli from Isgro's Bakery in South Philadelphia. Alex also, at times, brought home takeout fried chicken or Chinese food. He would sometimes bring home batteries or miniature flashlights. Alex's wife never was sure what treasure or surprise he might bring home. When Torch first met Alex, it was during the winter. A customer of Alex's had gotten himself into a jam and had stolen a fine leather coat from the department store where he worked and had given it to Alex to get even. The only problem was, the coat was about five sizes too large for Alex, and Torch could still remember the image of him walking down the street, looking like he was swimming in that big brown coat. Anyway, it was safe to say that Alex was a firm believer in the barter system.

Oscar's was a bar/restaurant run by two brothers, Handsome Bobby and Joe, as well as an ex-boxer named Jackie, who had once fought Willie Pep. "I couldn't hit Willie Pep in the ass," Jackie once said of his encounter with the great featherweight. Many of the people who were employed at Oscar's were customers of Torch as were the employees of the Oyster House between Oscar's and Eddie's on Samson Street. As a result, Torch rarely left the block on Saturdays. The day number would always be a jewel for book-makers, and Sansom Street was a perfect model for why. On Saturdays customers playing 50 dollar leads and 50 dollar parleys were not unheard of. They might play 50 dollars across the board on a horse. Then at night, having destroyed themselves during the daytime, they would bet heavily on the night number (leads and parlays) to try to get even.

Unlike the weekdays, Torch called in all of the Saturday horse action.

Today was a particularly and exciting day on Sansom Street. Affirmed had won the Kentucky Derby and the Preakness and now was in a position to sweep the Triple Crown series if he won today's Belmont Stakes in New York.

Affirmed's main rival through the series was Alydar, who had been the favorite at the racetrack in the first two events. However, virtually all of Torch's customers had bet Affirmed all along. The thinking was that the horses were evenly matched, so Torch's bettors backed Affirmed in hopes of getting a small price. Therefore, Torch had to root for Alydar to beat Affirmed to help his ribbon. The truth was Torch liked Alydar from the beginning mainly because of his jockey, Jorge Velasquez, who was his all-time favorite.

The first time Torch went to Garden State Rack Track, Jorge Velasquez had three mounts. The track was sloppy that day, and Velasquez's three mounts were all heavily favored. Velazquez rode the heavily favored horses the way you were supposed to ride a superior horse, which was to say he went right out to the front and led all the way around. Velasquez didn't risk getting in traffic trouble or having his horse dislike getting mud kicked in his face.

When the eighth and feature race came around, Torch watched Velasquez closely in the post-parade before the race. Velasquez was the only jockey not to have mud splashed on him. His white silks were as smooth and white as Carnation Milk. He also had purple and yellow trim on his silks, making him look like some rare, exotic Latin-American bird. Velasquez was a hero to the many Hispanics who attended Garden State.

In the big race that day, Velasquez went right to the top. He didn't look back and went wire-to-wire again. The crowd was cheering for him, "Jorge! Jorge! Jorge!" Garden State was the opposite of Keystone Racetrack. It had roses all over the infield and shrubbery on the outside and inside of the track. It had a huge outside grandstand which Keystone didn't have. There was a certain class and pageantry at Garden State, which made Torch feel like he was at a bullfight or a very important event such as a world cup soccer match. Velasquez left such an impression on Torch that, no matter what, Torch would always think Velasquez was the greatest jockey in the world. It was similar to the way the older generations, such as the group in Eddie's, would always say Willie Shoemaker was the greatest jockey ever. They all said that, even Alex, who didn't know the first thing about horse racing.

At one point, Torch left Eddie's Bar and crossed the street to the phone booth. The lead number was a nine, and the second number was a six. Bobby, the bartender at Eddie's, had bet a $10 parlay of 0-6, which translated to a $660 comeback, which Torch had fortunately called in. Torch had the money right in his pocket and paid Bobby on the spot, since he was loaded just then as he planned to see Bah–Bah later. Torch had money from the TV sets and also from the Exacta and Daily Double that he had hit two days ago on Rico's Spy. He liked to pay off Bobby right on the spot. The rule of thumb for a bookmaker was to pay off the winning customer as soon as possible. It was another trick Torch learned from Alex.

In the middle of the block, outside Sherman's Shoe Store between Oscar's and Eddie's, Torch spotted Paco. Paco had originally been Constantine's heavy hitter in the old days. Along with Joe Miami, he had been the old mob's primary muscle. Paco seemed happy and carefree. He wore a short leather jacket borrowed perhaps from Geraldo Rivera. He was sixty years old but was still trim and in good shape. He was with girl young enough to be his daughter. Paco had sharp features like Lee Van Cleef in *The Good, the Bad, and the Ugly* and a helmet of gray hair.

At one time, the Philadelphia mob was run by five brothers. The mother was extremely religious and named all six of her boys after Popes. It was rumored that Paco single-handedly was responsible for the murders of three of the brothers. Paco, they said, had iron balls and was a notorious high-roller who had become a local celebrity in gambling circles. In 1974, he bet $50,000 on Muhammad Ali as an underdog when he upset George Foreman to take back his title. Ali was such an underdog in that fight that Paco made about $140,000, according to what Torch heard. Last February, he bet heavily on Leon Spinks in the big underdog role against champion Muhammad Ali. The rumor was that Paco, taking big odds on the fight, wiped out the local bookies for $100,000.

It turned out that the Kentucky Derby and Preakness were only warmups for the Belmont Stakes. Andrew Beyer, the horseracing writer from the *Washington Post*, wrote: *"The 1978 Belmont was universally regarded as one of the greatest races of all time. Again, Affirmed took the lead. Again Alydar drew abreast and fought him head and head through the stretch. But with the Triple Crown on the line, affirmed wouldn't let his rival go by, and he won another photo finish. The late trainer, Woody Stephens, called the colt's rivalry "the greatest act horseracing has ever seen."*

The race was held up for television coverage, and since the last digit of the number came directly from that eighth race at Belmont, Torch was still around Sansom Street at a quarter of six when the results from Belmont finally flashed. Torch called Maria at home and told her that he wouldn't be home and asked her to call Mr. J. with the night action. She was used to doing that as occasionally she had pinch hit for Torch in emergency situations before, although, in this case, hardly anybody would call, they both knew. Plus, she would only be answering the phone until about 6:20 at the latest. That gave them time to ensure that everything was called in by 6:30 to Mr. J. Some customers such as Bobby might play $20 straight on a number or "8-X-8, $10 run down." You had to give Mr. J., at least, a half an hour if not more so that he could hedge some of that off.

Torch got his car out of the parking garage and drove to Bah-Bah's house. His car was a '63 Buick, a classy car in its day, featuring the dashboard of the late fifties and early sixties with the chrome lighters and the big dials, making it seem almost like a spaceship.

He drove down Broad Street and made a left on Washington Avenue toward Bah-Bah's house. It took fifteen minutes in all, and Torch made a right turn onto Bah-Bah's street. He hated coming onto this block, especially in the summer when everybody was outside. It was one of those narrow streets in South Philly where everybody automatically knew you were a stranger just by the cautious way you drove down the narrow street. Torch parked across the street from Bah-Bah's house and approached the door and rang the bell. A Jimmy Cerrone poster which said VOTE YES TO CHARTER CHANGE was on the door.

Torch and Bah-Bah settled up, and Torch asked him if Joe Miami's death had frightened him at all. Bah-Bah said that gangsters like that could be killed for any number of reasons. It didn't necessarily have to do with "the Beast," Bah-Bah once told him. "That's who killed Constantine, the Beast." Bah-Bah told Torch that it really didn't concern him, and it certainly didn't concern Torch. He did, however, express his displeasure for booking in South Philadelphia where everybody minded everybody else's business. He said that his brother-in-law, "John Taggs" was a good friend and right-hand-man of an ex-U.S. Senator named Augie Sangiamino. Sangiamino from South Philadelphia had been sent up for some shady political activities, but he still had a lot of power, and he had the ear of Jimmy Cerrone. Through John Taggs, Bah-Bah was given the opportunity to purchase one of three buildings in various spots in North Philadelphia. The City of Philadelphia, at that time, was selling certain abandoned properties for only $1 to responsible families or businessmen who agreed to occupy the properties and fix them up. Bah-Bah had the idea that he would purchase one of these locations and use it as a type of office. Of course, he would still live in South Philadelphia, and only use this spot for his "work."

Torch mentioned that he had seen Paco today on Samson Street. That seemed to make Bah-Bah very interested. It occurred to Torch, just then, that Bah-Bah, despite how he acted, really must have been concerned about the Beast if he was thinking about moving his operations to North Philadelphia. Bah-Bah said one of the spots available was a storefront in West Oak Lane. Another was an office type of place in Olney, and the third was a house in Logan, which Bah-Bah said was near Torch.

After he left Bah-Bah, Torch stopped at a newsstand that was open twenty-four hours and bought an advanced edition of *The Daily Racing Form* in the off-chance he would be at Keystone the following day. He and his friends planned to go down the shore later that night for blue fishing in the resort town of Oceanwood, New Jersey. They'd be on a big party boat that was leaving about five in the morning with roughly twenty-five people, most of whom were from Leo's work. Torch slept at Jackie's house that night, and they all got up at about three in the morning. Torch, Leo, and Crunchy, another of Jackie's brothers, went in one car, and they met at a predestined spot, a diner outside of Oceanwood with Tommy Taimanglo, Billy, Efrem, and Chucky Reilly. Torch was told that Shine had stolen a car, an expensive MG, and had been spotted by the Oceanwood police who pursued him. Shine turned off the main street, and that was the last anybody saw of him. They assumed that Shine was in some half-assed jail in Oceanwood, and there was nothing anybody could do for him. It was a tough rap, not only because Shine was on probation, but also because, as everyone knew, Oceanwood cops were tough on kids from Philly, especially during the summer. The police in Oceanwood were notorious for gearing up for summer situations, and Shine fell right into their trap. The only thing that saved Shine from going to prison in the past was that there had never been any occurrences of violence on his record. As a result, his public defender, as well as his probation officer, had always gone to bat for him. In New Jersey, however, it would be completely different this time.

The sea was unruly that day, and at one point or another, both Tommy and Jamie had done some chumming in the ocean. This didn't deter their fishing. Although they were both seasick, they actually continued fishing by holding the pole in their hands while simultaneously laying on their backs. Amazingly, one of them had accidentally hooked an eel, which looked to Torch like some sort of sea serpent. At one point or another during the day, they noticed the Coast Guard boat out there in the middle of the ocean with them, but really didn't think anything about it just then. They also witnessed a giant sea turtle, about the size of a Volkswagen, swimming just a few feet below the surface. Torch won the pool for catching the biggest fish, which amounted to about $80. Both Jamie and Efrem flashed the INQUIRY AND OBJECTION signs. They claimed that the fish really wasn't caught by Torch, that one of them had actually caught it. They all had a great day on the boat, fishing and drinking and eating. On the way home, Torch and Leo and Crunchy ate an overpriced breakfast at a Jersey diner called Olga's. They came into Philly across the Tacony-Palmyra and headed south on the Boulevard making a right on C Street and then a left on Fisher Avenue, avoiding the construction in the sinking homes area. When they got to 10th Street, they stopped at a light. From the back seat, Torch could see across the street to the Warnock Tavern. A bartender, Ronnie, who worked at the Warnock was walking across the street toward his car which was a new green Chevy Caprice. There was something telling in the way Ronny walked across the street. The best way Torch could describe it was that Ronny was walking with the absence of any type of body language. He walked across the street like he was in a trance or something. That was a tip off that something unusual and bad had happened. Crunchy made a right turn, and they drove up to Jack's Variety Store. Jack was Tommy Taimanglo's brother, and their mother was working right now in the store. When Torch, Crunchy and Leo walked in, about five people started talking to them at once. Mrs. Taimanglo was plainly distraught and was crying. It was hard to sort everything out, but basically what they were saying was that Shine was dead. They thought that Tommy and maybe one or two of the others were also dead. They said that Shine was killed in some kind of car accident. Torch assured them that that wasn't the case. He said Shine was probably right now sitting in an Oceanwood jail cell, and he tried to assure Mrs. Taimanglo that Tommy was fine. In fact, he had just left him, and only two hours ago, Tommy had been laying his back fishing, and occasionally lifting his head over the rail and throwing up. Torch failed to convince them. Surely Torch didn't know what he was talking about because definitely Shine was dead, that much was certain. The Oceanwood police themselves had called back to the Philly police and reported the incident. Still, Torch couldn't help thinking that a mistake had been made ; least, he hoped that was the case.

What had happened was the police had found Tommy's van which was vacant and assumed that perhaps Tommy was in the car with Shine, who did, in fact, die in an accident. Still, this seemed bizarre to Torch. How could they not know who was in the car and who wasn't. When Torch got home, Billy's father called him. He kept saying the same thing, that he was afraid Billy was in the car with Shine. He kept say, "Now, Torch, be honest with me, boy. Billy was with Shine, wasn't he?"

"No," Torch kept saying. "Billy was with us out on the boat."

"Really, Torch," Billy's father kept saying. "You can be honest with me." Then Billy's father told Torch exactly what happened. After Shine turned off the main street in the stolen car, the police pursued him, but Shine didn't pull over. He tried to outrun the Oceanwood Police. In all, three or four cars were involved in chasing Shine. During the ten or fifteen-minute chase, Shine avoided traps and roadblocks that had been set up for him. Finally he made it to the causeway leading out of Oceanwood and into the next town, which was Stone Harbor.

The policeman who spoke with Billy's father said that he personally caught up to Shine's car and tried to bump him a couple times to get Shine to pull off the road. The cop said that he looked Shine right in the eye. That part Torch always questioned. If he pulled up next to Shine and actually looked in the car, he would have known that Shine was alone in the car, instead of getting everybody's families all nervous and upset. A drawbridge about one mile or so up on the causeway had its lights turned out. The drawbridge was opened halfway, about head level. Torch and the others would never know if Shine saw the bridge or not. They would never know if it was just that Shine didn't care or that he was too scared or what. In life Shine never made much of an impact on society. His life really wasn't worth that much except to his friends and his family. His death, on the other hand, would be highly unusual, if not extraordinary, and would raise questions. He had hit the bridge head first going an estimated 130 miles an hour.

CHAPTER 7

Life went on, and on Monday morning, Torch was back at work at Maria's house. Mondays were busy in the numbers business. Although he didn't receive the big action like on Fridays or Saturdays, the large amount of smaller players who called on the phone made to play their "steadies" for the week made Mondays very important for Torch.

The numbers business was fueled by the small players. There used to be a bookmaker in Center City named John who worked from the cover of a newsstand when Torch worked down there. John was Irish, with white hair and blue eyes, and he had booked horses and numbers since the thirties. He allegedly worked for Constantine, and he lived a long, prosperous life with a comfortable home in South Philadelphia. He also put four children through college, all from his "newsstand business." He was one of the biggest bookmakers in the city as far as horse betting was concerned; he told Torch once that, surprisingly enough, it was the "two dollar bettor that was the backbone of his business." John was arrested forty times from 1930 to 1978 for "illegal lottery." He had a very easygoing way about him. "Happy-go-lucky" was what his probation officer called him. John was right on the verge of retirement when Torch took over Alex's route, and he retired shortly thereafter, before Moscariello's people got around to shaking him down.

Even in the casino business, year in and year out, a 25 cent slot machine probably earned more revenue for the casino than a high-stakes crap table. And like a slot machine, to even greater extent, the numbers business preyed on the lower income population. This small army of little bettors was Torch's bread and butter. They were hard-core numbers players, most of whom were women. Torch believed that they played the birthdays or birth weight of their grandkids. They would usually play amounts such as 50 cents over 25 cents, or even 25 cents over 10 cents. Some of the bets on numbers came from dreams they may have had, but it was necessarily the exact number that they dreamt about. Each dream had objects in it or symbols in it. These objects or symbols usually translated to a number. There was a dream book sold at newsstands for a few dollars. Each object had a corresponding number. For example, if somebody had a dream in which birds appeared, then the corresponding number was 211. Why was it so? Because the dream book said it was so. Or people had their own magic numbers. One lady had called Torch and played an unusually high amount of money, 5 over 2 ($15) on the number 917. This particular woman said that she had had a dream in which she ate Chinese food. She said that, when she was a little girl, the most famous Chinese restaurant in Chinatown was at 917 Arch Street in Center City. She said there was a giant sign outside which flashed in red numbers simply 917. She always associated Chinese food and Chinatown with that particular number. Another customer, Harold, played 769 the other day because he was worried about dying and that was the death number in the dream book. A waitress from Oscar's named Kay, who was in fact Gino's girlfriend, called and said that she had had a dream the other night in which city workers were outside of her house for some reason drawing big zeroes in chalk. From the dream she extracted the number 000.

John also booked numbers, but they were never very important to him. His customers were mainly horse players. As for numbers, John offered his customers only 4-1, or "400 to 1" on each straight bet … a large rip-off. As if that wasn't bad enough, John had numerous "cut numbers." Cut numbers were numbers that, for whatever reason, the public played heavily, and the bookies would only pay off about half of what they should. In John's case, he would only pay out 200-1 on a cut number. An example of a cut number would be the shield number of a Philadelphia police officer who had been shot and whose photo was in the paper. Or it may be the number of a flight that crashed. These numbers would receive a high play. As for Gino, he only had two "cut numbers." In March the numbers 317 (St. Patrick's Birthday) and 319 (St. Joseph's Birthday) were cut down to 3-1 (300-1). Apparently one time, about five years ago, on St. Patrick's Day, 317 came out as straight as six o'clock. A weird type of "urban myth" grew out of that. Irish numbers players tended to play 317 or 319 like it was written in stone somewhere that it was going to come out.

Torch was embarrassed to tell his customers that those numbers were cut, but he understood why Bah–Bah had to do it. One of Torch's customers named Regina played the number 317 year around. In that case, Torch never mentioned that the number was cut. He would be embarrassed to tell this lady who played that number religiously all year that all of a sudden it was going to pay less than half of what it normally did. Torch didn't think that was right, and he told Bah–Bah about it. Bah–Bah explained to him that a cut number was a cut number. He didn't make the rules, and that was all there was to it. Torch assured Regina that he would pay her the full amount if her number ever came out, even during March. Torch would do that even if he had to make up the difference out of his own pocket. Regina was a good customer. Her mother was in the numbers business in North Philly. She would often call Torch to lay off numbers that her mother's book was over loaded with so he extended her that courtesy.

Keystone Racetrack was closed on Monday. so there were no horse players calling in. Still, Mondays were busier than the other days because customers called to put in their numbers for the week.

A hundred times in the past twenty-four hours, Torch thought about Shine, trying to understand those last few minutes. Was it just that Shine was so scared and just didn't care? Was it simply a glorified case of suicide? Could it ever simply be called that? Torch liked to think that Shine, a guy who always wanted to be a stunt driver in the movies, was simply in his mind, playing and winning a real-life game exactly like the one he used to play in Ben's Candy Store. Then he died instantly, never really foreseeing his doom, never knowing what hit him. Torch tried to leave it at that, but he couldn't. It was just too bizarre, and the circumstances surrounding it wouldn't allow for somebody to dismiss it so easily.

Ironically, only a few weeks ago, Torch heard a detective from the New York City Police Force on a late night radio talk show explaining the big controversy over police chases going on around that time. The debate had to do with chasing a suspect if it put the general public at risk. Torch understood that the chase through Oceanwood ran up and down streets crowded with pedestrians. Torch also heard that on, at least, two occasions, the police in Oceanwood had Shine trapped, but he got out of it. Torch wondered if they had intentionally let him get away knowing that Shine would eventually head for the bridge leading out of Oceanwood. Frankly, Torch wouldn't doubt it. He didn't blame the police for chasing Shine, but after all, it could have just as easily been some young kid that stole his daddy's car. Torch thought about the police in Oceanwood during the summer months, the ones with the pimples and long hair.

Torch drank a bottle of 7up and read the big story in *The Philadelphia Inquirer* which profiled Chickadee. Outside of South Philadelphia, Chick-a-dee had always been in the background. Everyone knew he always had been one of Constantine's two top lieutenants. Yet, unlike Constantine, most Philadelphians wouldn't even recognize him. The press and the police also had always acknowledged Constantine to be the boss and he was.

Yet it was Chick-a-dee, Bah-Bah had always said, who was the one out on the streets running things. He was forty-five years old, but he looked about sixty. The pictures of Chick-a-dee in *The Inquirer* were dated. He had a lot more and darker hair in these photos. Torch had personally seen Chick-a-dee only twice in his life. The first time was at the funeral for Gino's nephew who had died in an accident a couple years ago. The second time was at Gino's bocce club in South Philadelphia on a Super Bowl Sunday. The writer kept reminding everybody that Chick-a-dee was the last living powerful force in

Constantine's old gang. Torch sensed that the writer was skeptical about exactly how long that last remaining link would be around. It all read to Torch like a pre-death obituary.

Torch remembered the funeral on South Broad Street for Gino's nephew. He would never forget that experience. Constantine himself had stopped in, and Torch easily recognized him with his ever-present, thick, horn-rimmed black glasses. It was the only time he ever saw Constantine in person.

Normally, at those kinds of funerals or wakes, people would gather afterward and say nice things about the deceased party. In this case, everybody was saying nice things about Constantine: A.C. did this. A.C. did that. A.C. did this other thing. The people talked about Constantine like he was the answer to every little problem, and in a peculiar way, Torch thought they believed that, too.

Bah–Bah once explained to Torch, "You have to understand, those people literally don't know how to live without Constantine."

As for Bah–Bah personally, however, although he was no less enamored of A.C., his real idol, it seemed, was always Chickadee. For instance, Bah–Bah a few times told Torch about the time when he and Gino saw Sinatra at the Latin Casino in New Jersey. Bah–Bah said that Sinatra looked right at Gino and said, "Tell Chickadee I said hi."

Every time Bah–Bah told Torch that story, it was clear that he had been extremely impressed by that. Bah–Bah also said that Chickadee had "friends" in New York. Torch, on the other hand, was not so sure that either of those things were very important now, especially the part about Sinatra.

Sam the Blade called and played a steady number, 807, for one dollar. Blade reminded Torch that a harness horse he bet on Saturday night, Leroy Nickawampus, won and paid $12.80. Torch had called in the $100 bet into his book, which came to a $540 win for Blade. Unfortunately, Torch forgot to bet on the horse himself, which he had planned to do. It was just that he had been so busy with Affirmed. Now that he thought about it, if Affirmed had lost, had his arch rival Alydar beaten him, Torch would have made roughly $300 from the race. In addition, Bah-Bah would have been so happy; he probably would have given Torch an extra hundred dollars.

Torch called everything in to Bah-Bah, and around 1:30, he went out his back door, walked across the railroad bridge, and exited the tracks right behind Caesar's Place.

That day, it seemed liked everybody all around Logan — in Jack's candy store, the Warnock-tavern, Ben's or in Big Jim's Luncheonette on 10th Street where they met today — was talking about the incident. Big Jim's was normally closed by noon since it opened at five in the morning, catering to the early shift of Fleers bubblegum workers across the street. In fact, for many years, Torch never saw the place opened. It was a strange-looking place that you had to walk down steps to get into. Frenchie called it "the Dugout." Big Jim was the father of the Taimanglos. He was retired after a remarkable career in the navy that spanned three wars (World War Two, Korea, and Vietnam).

Everybody, it seemed, was still stunned from the incident and seemed to be walking around in a trance like that bartender Ronny Miller from the Warnock the other day.

A kid named Mouse, who lived on Shine's block and was standing outside the padlocked Caesar's Palace, talked about why it was probably so difficult for everyone to accept. "He was just so big," he said. To Mouse, Shine's very size had made him seem sort of invincible, and to a certain extent, Mouse was right. Because of his size, there had been a sense of strength surrounding him.

Torch thought not only about Shine's size but also his age. Shine was always big. Even as a young kid, he was bigger than all of the adults. Therefore, it didn't quite make sense to think of him being as young as he was — one week short of twenty-one. Another strange thing about it was that Shine was Red's brother. It was odd that both brothers had died tragically and somewhat mysteriously in just the past six months. Collectively, there was a frightening and angry feeling that one of them could be removed in such a malicious, vicious, and effortless way with no recourse. At least, if Shine had been black, somebody would have probably said, "The police killed him." Or somebody like Washington might have said, "Society killed him." A social worker could have said that Shine's previous actions, which were well-documented in the courts, signaled a cry for help, all of which went unheeded. They would say that this was obviously the only possible ending and speak of the injustice of it.

It wasn't exactly the same as a rank and file corner boy rolling a seven and leaving for good. In the case of it being Shine, there was a difference. Primarily it again had to do with how big he was. It was like a building, a landmark that you saw every day that was no longer there. A mobile building, that for a month afterward you still sort of expected to see when you turned the corner. Shine obviously was into cars. He was and had always been an auto mechanic. He never worked in or had his own shop, but he was always working on cars. He was a street mechanic. He changed oil or installed car stereos, ball joints, or motor mounts. He often had a customer's car which he rode around the streets like a madman. Everybody else got into the habit of looking out for him whether they were on foot or in a car, and that habit seemed to last for a month as well. Clearly, for several reasons he wouldn't soon be forgotten.

The circumstances surrounding it all wouldn't allow it.

"That's a day we won't forget for a long time," Efrem had said.

Ken Washington, on the other hand, was more simplistic about the whole matter. He had a way of reducing things like this to the lowest common denominator. The first time Torch and them ran into Washington after the incident he hadn't made a big deal at all about it. He simply shook his head and said something like "It was a byproduct of the way he lived, of the way you all live."

Most of Torch's friends had jobs, although they were not always steady jobs, with regular hours. So there were usually four of five of them around at any given time. Today, four of them were playing a game of pinochle on the steps of Caesar's Palace. Earth, Wind and Fire played on a radio while they shared a case of beer. They were not in a festive mood, and Torch left early. Maria was cooking the last of the blue fish they had caught. Torch couldn't wait. It was as if, as long as that fish, the taste, or even just the smell of it was in the air, the memory of that day would linger.

That night, Torch stayed in and listened to the baseball game on the radio. He bet the Twins with right-handed pitcher David Goltz at home against the Yankees as a pick. The game was fine; the Twins won, and Torch felt more relaxed.

The next day, Torch booked on the phone but again didn't feel like going into Center City. The number in Philadelphia on Tuesdays came out a little earlier than usual. Tuesdays traditionally were "dark" days for New York's racetracks. On Tuesdays, therefore, the Philadelphia street number came directly from Keystone Racetrack which had a slightly earlier post-time than New York. Torch booked a few numbers and hung around the house until about 1:30 which was about when the first number came out. It was a zero. That was the one number which negated virtually all of his chances for a big hit. Bah-Bah and all numbers backers loved it when a zero came out front. Few people played numbers, at least "straight" numbers that began with a zero for whatever reason.

On the other hand, when a '1' led, it was usually a disaster for a numbers backer. Alex told him one time that his book was so strong that, when a '1' led, at least one customer of his normally hit the number regardless of what other two numbers followed that '1'.

One of Torch's boys, Billy Young, called him from work. Billy was short and muscular like Felix but had blond hair. He had rough features and could remind somebody of a young Nick Nolte in *Rich Man/Poor Man*. He hadn't seen Billy since the day out on the boat and they talked about Shine. Torch told Billy that his father had called him on the phone that crazy afternoon. Billy had grown up going from foster home to foster home, but the majority of his childhood was spent living on the streets. He was originally from Germantown, and then Logan, on Torch's side of Broad Street. Eventually, he started hanging around Ben's somehow, and they sort of took him under their wing. Until the city padlocked Caesar's Palace, Billy had been living in the basement suite. Leo had gotten him a good union job, and he eventually married a girl from Inky. He played on Ben's football team in the winter. He was a real Ben's success story and a source of pride for them all, especially for Torch who had sort of founded him.

Torch left his house and crossed the tracks right by Ben's store. He drank a cherry Coke at the counter and read the *Daily News*. The first thing he looked for was Jack Kiser's column again and sought out two horses that Sam the Blade had bet. The one horse was named Farm Super. As Torch knew, Farm Super was a top-notched pacer sired by Super Bowl, who was one of the top sires in the East at that time, and he was ridden by Donald Dancer, the leading driver at Liberty Bell. Torch figured the horse would win but would pay so little that he didn't mind sitting on the bet. Jack Kiser had Farm Super picked on top with the line being even money on him. His comment was for him, *"A short price is better than a long face."*

The second horse that the Blade bet on was named Follow the Leader. Torch had never heard of the horse and called that bet in. He had three poor races in his last efforts according to Kiser, and the comment for Follow the Leader was *"aptly named hoss."*

Daily News columnist Peter Dexter wrote something that caught Torch's eye. The column had to do with a man called "Bird." Dexter said that he had been in the meat business, catering to bars mainly in South Philadelphia and Delaware County. Bird, according to Dexter, had also smuggled untaxed cigarettes up from South Carolina. He stocked vending machines with his cigarettes and sold them at high Pennsylvania prices. Bird told Dexter that Constantine had a virtual monopoly on the vending machine business in the area, especially where cigarettes were concerned. Bird said that he had gotten friendly with Constantine since many of the bars that he did business with were also controlled by Constantine. Constantine may or may not have gotten a gratuity of some sort from Bird for this privilege, but it didn't say anything about that. At least, according to Bird in this story, Constantine had allowed him to operate in that fashion. Dexter added that now Bird was out of business entirely.

"Bird had the ear of Constantine," Dexter had written. *"That was until somebody put a shotgun to the ear of Constantine and that changed everything."*

The story brought Torch's mind back to the turmoil in Bah-Bah's neck of the woods right now. As for himself, Torch knew that he was safe up here in Logan. There hadn't even been problems lately with the black kids around Caesar's Palace or Logan Nation over where he lived, or the white kids from Inky. Torch was mildly concerned about Center City. It wasn't enough to just stay up here and work on the phones. It was a necessity of his business to go into Center City, at least, a few times a week. It was a rush for Torch. Sansom Street was a stage, and the spotlight was on him. For certain people, bartenders, waiters, waitresses, barbers, people who shined shoes or parked cars or worked in Center City office buildings, numbers were like a drug, and Torch was the dealer. It was an addictive drug that helped them get through the day or, at least, the latter part of the day since the first number didn't usually come out until about 1:45.

For the time being, it seemed like Center City was still very safe. It didn't seem like, at least for the moment, that anybody was very interested in Center City. Torch suspected that the reason for this was there were so many police in Center City, including undercover police all over the place. These police had never really been hostile toward Constantine. Every year or so, Gino or John at the newsstand would have to stand for a pinch which usually was enough to satisfy the local police captain or judge or special prosecutor for another year or so.

They would actually arrange the arrest beforehand, and they would make a big show of it. They would tell John, for example, that they would lock him up outside of his newsstand at two o'clock in the afternoon. They would tell John to have "a few betting slips around." It would be just enough to prevent the suspect from ever possibly maintaining that he was an ordinary citizen being harassed. On the other hand, only a few slips were not enough to prosecute for being a numbers writer if the arrest ever came to court, which it never did anyway.

Torch remembered how Alex would make a big deal of speaking in a code. For example, if the four was leading, Alex would come around the bar and say to everybody that "he had to go over to Fourth Street to see his brother." If the second number was a seven, Alex would announce to everybody in the bar that "he had to go over to 47th and Pine to see his mother." If they were standing outside of Oscar's or someplace, Alex would sometimes take a slip he had on him and force it into a crack of a store window so that, if the police frisked him, he wouldn't have anything incriminating on him. The truth was that the police knew what Alex was doing, and they just didn't really care. Alex was too small, Torch believed for them to bother him. It just wouldn't be worth it. Alex knew this, of course, and his actions were more examples of his entertaining himself more than anything else.

Outside Caesar's Palace that day, the healing process had accelerated greatly it seemed. The mood was almost festive compared to the previous day. A case of Schmidt's, 16-ounce cans, was on the steps, and each one had a can in front of him. A bottle of Jameson's swung clockwise, and a joint circled counterclockwise up and around everybody on the steps, magically passing over the heads of the ones who traditionally didn't smoke pot. Grant, who now both owned and bartended at the Warnock Tavern two blocks away between 10th and 11th was there. He wore, as usual, a Phillies hat and sunglasses. He wore a loose white silk shirt with a pack of smokes in the top pocket. Since yesterday, the cat that was nailed to the pillar of Caesar's Palace had lost one of its two or three screws and had been hanging upside down. Grant now was banging with a hammer, fixing the cat so it stood upright. He put as much effort into maintenance for Caesar's Palace as he did with his own house. Grant was concerned that the city was apparently going to do something with the house. He always looked at having the boys there as sort of a 24-hour protection system. His paranoia had been heightened after the rash of burglaries, including the one at Harum-Scarum house in which Reds was killed by those bandits or unmarked police or whoever they were. That incident had troubled Grant more than a little bit. He was grateful that Felix, Frenchie, Doc, Billy, and whichever other temporary squatters were always at the house next door. It obviously worried Grant that the city would sell the house to a noisy neighbor.

Felix and Frenchie had moved back to set up housekeeping at Danny Parkers house. As for Billy and Doc, they probably would be on the street living in some abandoned car. There were usually three or four young men around who were temporarily "streeted" for one reason or another. Eventually, Billy and Doc and others would find another house to squat in.

Somebody somehow had obtained a newspaper from Oceanwood. There was a picture of a big crane lifting the GM that Shine had driven out of the bay. Seeing the picture of the destroyed car, with the water rushing off it brought that day back to Torch. Torch had just been getting it out of his mind, but now all thoughts came rushing back. The main thoughts were about any kind of death wish that Shine really must have had, and other about how the police would probably never be held accountable for what they did.

Grant, after finishing his task of nailing the cat to the pillar, called Felix aside and explained that he wanted those TVs out of his house. Grant talked to the group about the Phillies, who were still struggling offensively on the West Coast.

At about four o'clock, they all split up. Washington was going to be around soon. Torch had to leave anyway. He was going up to his mother's house in the northeast to get his suit for Shine's funeral. First he was going to see the barber at 7th and Rockland, who, in addition to cutting his hair, played a steady number with him and occasionally bet a horse race. As he sat in the shop, the Supremes were singing their last song with Diana Ross, "Someday, We'll Be Together." Torch was reading that day's *Daily News*. There was a story about a teenager killed in West Philly in a gang war. *Daily News* columnist John Chapman often wrote about the gang wars and was obviously very troubled by them.

Chapman was a fierce fighter for Civil Rights and had become a type of champion for the under-represented black population in Philadelphia. Just last week, he had written a column which spurred a rally that ultimately shut down the Gallery, a Center City shopping mall, because of a lack of minority hiring. For the past few months, Chapman had written a few times about the drive to register black voters and subsequently sustain the City Charter which would ultimately unseat Jimmy Cerrone. Over the years, about seventy-five black fugitives in Philadelphia had surrendered to Chapman to assure that they wouldn't be beaten by the police when in custody. Yet Chapman was odd compared to other Philadelphia blacks. With his flat-top gray hair, wingtipped shoes, and his ever-present bowtie, he was as dissimilar to them as Truman Capote must have been to the townspeople when he went out to Kansas to write *In Cold Blood*.

A few years later, Chapman would receive national headlines when he was called by the Governor of Pennsylvania in 1981 to intercede in a prison riot upstate where the prisoners had overtaken the jail and held six or eight guards as hostages. It was Chapman, who, during an all-night negotiation session, brought the very dangerous situation to a peaceful conclusion. Torch had read this story of the gang-war killing. The victim, it said, had been a member of the notorious Moon Gang from Osage Avenue in West Philly. Next to his column, Chapman printed a poem that he always printed whenever he was writing about youth-gang violence, or any other column that dealt with misguided youth and their consequences. Chapman printed this particular poem five or six times a year. In the past, whenever Torch read this poem, it made him think of the gang wars and the kids he knew from Parkway High School who had been killed. Until recently though, the poem seemed foreign to him. But given what he saw in Logan just so far this summer, the poem, from now on, reminded him of what had already transpired, specifically the murders of both Lil Rock and Shine. The poem seemed closer, more. It was about misguided youth and how they all, Ben's Logan Nation, all of them like those in the poem were inadvertently rushing to meet death or trouble. The poem had a strange name like 'eight at the Poolroom' or something like that, but was better known and easier found under its subtitle: "We Real Cool." The author of the poem was named Gwendolyn Brooks.

We real cool...we
Quit school...we
Lurk late...we
Shoot straight...we
Sling sin...we
Thin gin...we Jazz June...we Die soon.

After Torch left the barber shop, he got in his car and turned on the radio to the oldies station. 'Sally's Sayin' Something' by Philadelphia's Billy "The Percolator" Harner, was playing. Before Torch left, he glanced over and saw a Korean grocery store that made him think about something. The store itself, with all of its history and all the transformation it had undergone, made it sort of a symbol of the whole neighborhood. Long before Torch was born and maybe before Torch's father was born, the place was a bakery. That was in the twenties or thirties, during that time, which wasn't long after World War I, there was still a great deal of anti-German sentiment in America. That was particularly true in this part of Logan, now known as the Sinking Homes Area, which in those days was mainly Jewish. It didn't help matters, of course, that, in 1936, Nazis marched on Fifth Street, which was just two blocks away in Olney. Also, bakeries weren't just bakeries back them. They were sort of a symbol of Germany since Germans always did have the best baked goods, and that even included Italian baked goods. As a result, there was a series of German bakeries having their windows smashed, and not too unpredictably, that happened to this particular German bakery there at Seventh and Rockland. It was only in recent years that Torch put a face on the baker in his mind. To him, the baker looked like Ed Asner's character as the German baker in the seventies TV mini-series *Rich Man-Poor Man*. When Torch was little, the place had been a Kosher deli. Torch remembered the indistinguishable, indecipherable symbollike Hebrew letters on the sign outside. The Jews sold the store in 1974, and some American businessman owned it, operating a discount supply store there. They sold such things as sodas and cigarettes in quantity at reduced prices to retail stores all over North Philadelphia, including Ben's and Jack's. There were clubs consisting of graffiti artists in those days in Philadelphia. They included groups such as the H.C.S. (Hip City Swingers), W.W.A. (Wall Writers Anonymous), and K.C.D. (Klub City Decorators). It was one or two of these groups that vandalized this particular store front. Torch could remember the graffiti with the names of the vandals and the names of their club affiliations. Torch could remember the indecipherable writings and indistinguishable symbols spray painted on the wall. Now, all these years later, the store was a Korean grocer. And the store was covered with signs featuring indistinguishable and indecipherable Korean letters on the outside of it … Logan.

BOOK II

Bah-Bah

CHAPTER 8

The window at the front of the row house on Snyder Avenue in South Philadelphia rattled and shook violently. The house was owned by Rose Pantarelli, grandmother of Joe "Bah-Bah" Sylvestri. Out of eight grandchildren, "Giuseppe" had always been her favorite. He, after all, was the only one who had stayed in the neighborhood and, therefore, was closer to her.

When Joe was single, he used to spend a lot of time at this house. Basically the back room was his own room with all his stuff, clothes, a razor, cologne, et cetera. Even if he didn't stay overnight for two years, it still was always exactly the same way he'd left it the last time he was there. These nights, Joe was using the house to book baseball from. On most nights such as this one, Joe had the house entirely to himself. Rose, whom he called "Nana" and whom his friends called "Nana Bah-Bah," had dinner and was visiting with a friend who lived down the street and who was battling advanced cancer.

Joe's own house, also in South Philly, was ten blocks north of this one, just a half-block from the famous Pat's Steaks. His decision to conduct his affairs here at his grandmother's had to do with this corporate takeover of sorts that was being conducted by his new, younger mob that was in the process of throwing out the old order and operating all of the Philly rackets by themselves. What they didn't want to run, they, at least, wanted to help themselves to a steady "street tax" which was known as "the Elbow." Of course, it was unrealistic to think that Bah-Bah could keep his secret hidden for long, not anywhere in South Philly, where, unlike North Philly, people tended not to mind their own business. Surely people were watching him. They had closed in on Gino, and they had to figure that Bah-Bah, a life-long Gino loyalist, whose father had, after all, been Gino's best friend and partner, was no doubt running the business of that break-away faction of the old Philadelphia family. Bah-Bah thought, or at least he liked to think, that his booking out of Rose's house made it safer for his family. Certainly every little bit helped, although he knew that this was not a permanent solution by any means. It just made good sense during those turbulent days to work someplace other than in his own house. You couldn't trust anybody, and you didn't know who was a spy. For example, Bah-Bah's son might have brought a friend over to the house for one reason or another. The street smart little boy might have noticed rice paper laying around with figures written on it and with words such as "Yankees," "Dodgers," "Twins." This same boy might have mentioned this to his father, who then may turn around and tell somebody connected in an attempt to score points with the new boss.

On another level, Bah-Bah just always felt secure here. Rose kept the place like a cathedral with her chandelier in the middle of the living room, the plastic slipcovers (a South Philadelphia staple), and a clock that chimed "London Bridge Is Falling Down" every hour. Bah-Bah had had a warm association with this house since childhood. Every Christmas, Rose made a big deal out of having a big tree with not only lights and red and white balls, but also a very realistic-looking train set that went around the bottom of the tree. The train featured green passenger cars and very heavy black steam engines. Little miniature trees and bushes created a countryside facsimile. She even had the white powder to sprinkle on everything that made it look like it was snowing. Then there were pictures of relatives, most of whom were deceased now, looking down on him. This museum of pictures included one of his father and mother together, and one of Rose's husband Mike (Bah-Bah's grandfather). There were also pictures of Joe DiMaggio, Jimmy Cerrone, and J.F.K. The picture of J.F.K. had been taken right outside on Snyder

Avenue when he came through South Philly in 1960. In the picture, he was waving to everybody from his open-air limousine. Rose had taken the picture herself and had had it blown up and framed. "He looked right at me," Rose said. "He was even more handsome than on television. Did you know he had red hair? Not a twinge of red like I thought. It was red … red-red." She always said it just that way. There was also a picture of television news broadcaster John Facenda.

Like many Italian immigrants of her age group, Rose was distrustful of the media. She believed there was a definite anti-Italian bias which did not begin with Mario Puzo and *The Godfather*. In fact, it was much more severe in the first decades that Rose lived in America after coming here in 1919. So the Italian community in general liked John Facenda because they trusted him, as an Italian-American, to be fair. Although Rose was extremely patriotic and loyal to the country of her birth, her loyalty, Joe noticed, was very subdued and dignified. She may vote for any politician who had an Italian-sounding name or lean toward a jockey or trainer with an Italian surname at the racetrack, but she didn't make a big deal about it to strangers. She was afraid that would make her sound like a *cafone* (which simply meant "country") and was dialecticed into "Gavone," which basically was a type of hillbilly. Bah-Bah noticed that all of his relatives of that generation were the same way. There always was a certain dignity attached to their love of Italy. He couldn't imagine them, for example, wearing a shirt that said *"The Italian Stallion"* on it. They never had bumper stickers that read *"Mafia Staff car, Keep-a-you-hands -off."* Rose spoke Italian but did so only to her sister and a few of her paisani here in this Italian enclave. She never spoke the language uptown (Center City) or with other Italians in the Wanamaker's department store where she worked.

Rose despised anything that had to do with Italians involved in organized crime or anything like that. For example, Bah-Bah once asked her if she knew Constantine. Rose said she didn't know him and added that she really didn't care to know him. Bah-Bah didn't press her or question her about it since it was clear that Bah-Bah's just asking about Constantine somehow disappointed her. Bah-Bah didn't think much about it at the time, but he figured that it was virtually impossible for his grandmother to not know Constantine. After all, they lived right across the street from one another for forty years and attended the same church. Rose never watched *The Godfather* or any movies like that. She never found all that "leave the gun, take the cannoli" stuff charming at all. All those movies did was throw fuel on the fire and allow the media to tell more stories. In the off chance that she did watch one of those movies, she certainly wouldn't say that she somehow could identify with the female characters. For the record though, Rose really didn't know Constantine except from seeing him on the news. She vaguely knew Mrs. Constantine. They knew each other from bingo and Rose didn't care for her. Mrs. Constantine thought she should run the show there somehow because of who she was married to, and Rose disagreed with that idea. Unlike her husband who was so famously discreet, Mrs. Constantine was something of a *chiacchierone* (chatterbox). Once she claimed that her husband had an incredible amount of money, maybe $5 million, stashed someplace.

This comment was picked up, somehow, on a federal wiretap. At a subsequent rackets hearing, the feds were grilling Constantine on his business interests. However, due largely to his modest lifestyle and because he had planned ahead and made precautions, there really was nothing to nail him on. On paper, he was an employee at a local cigarette vending company. At the hearing Constantine invoked his Fifth Amendment right nineteen times.

The young, ambitious district attorney referred to the statement Mrs. Constantine had made a few years prior about this incredible sum of undeclared money. He wondered how a cigarette salesman could acquire $5 million dollars. It was only hearsay anyway, so Constantine didn't have to defend himself, but on this matter, against the wishes of his attorney, he spoke anyway. He said, "I'm a cigarette salesman and a damn good one."

The feds didn't think Constantine was so funny. They never viewed him as charming and classy like the local cops always did. For failing to cooperate here, he was given a two-year sentence. He was in his sixties by then and had emphysema. Due to his poor health, he only spent a year in prison.

Rose, like the feds, probably didn't think the comment was clever or witty. She was from an era when it was extremely difficult for Italian immigrants who didn't speak the language to assimilate to American life. Gangster movies and shows like *The Untouchables* weren't as hurtful now because everybody knows those gangsters only make up a very small percentage of Italians, just like Italians make up only a small number of gangsters and criminals. However, in the thirties and forties, those mafia tales and stereotypes were very hurtful and seriously impeded their overall progress. Italians eventually had their share of heroes, such as Rocky Marciano, Joe DiMaggio, Frank Sinatra, and, on a local level, Joey Giardello, middleweight champion from South Philadelphia. However, Rose was most proud of those Italians who had made it in the academic world such as doctors, lawyers, writers, and politicians. Nothing made her prouder than having two college-educated daughters, one of whom — Bah-Bah's mother — was a nurse, and the other was a public high school teacher.

John Facenda was a long-time Philadelphia news broadcaster. In Facenda, Italians in Philadelphia identified with somebody in the media for the first time. He broadcasted the news on radio and then on Channel 10 Television from 1948 until 1973. Despite the fact that Facenda had retired five years ago, Rose still watched Channel 10 news and would do so until she died twenty years later. Steven Martorano, a Philadelphia talk show host, spoke of John Facenda on the day of his death in 1984. He called John Facenda the "Walter Cronkite of South Philadelphia." Bah-Bah also liked the fact that he could always get a decent meal at Rose's. Living with his Irish wife constantly reminded him of a joke his uncle used to tell him that had something to do with the cooks in hell being Irish. It was ironic that Bah-Bah, a guy who put such a priority on food, would marry a girl who couldn't cook.

When Bah-Bah was a young man, he was on top of the world, thanks in large part to his solid position under Gino. He and his friend

Bobby Santoro had dated many girls. Most of these girls were Italian from the neighborhood who Bah–Bah quickly learned had faults of their own. Bah–Bah learned long ago that Italian girls weren't always "just like the girl that married dear old dad." It was strange, though, the way opposites attracted and how you couldn't foresee who you would marry or who was the right one for you. Sometimes it was like Rocky said in the movie — it had to do with gaps.

"I got gaps. She got gaps. Together we fill gaps."

Largely due to his mother, as well as Rose, Bah–Bah could speak Italian, and his dream was to, one day, marry an Italian girl ... from Italy.

Chrissie, the girl he did eventually marry, turned out to be the best one, despite her cooking. What broke the ice for them was that Chrissie originally lived in St. Thomas Parish, which was on the west side of Broad Street (both Bah–Bah and his grandmother lived east of Broad.) That meant her house was hooked up to cable TV. In the early days of cable in Philadelphia, around 1975 and 1976, only South Philly had this advantage and only the west side of Broad Street (which coincidentally or not so coincidentally was where Cerrone was from). Torch's friend Leo, said, around that time, that Cerrone was "taking care of his paisans." To Bah–Bah, this meant that he could watch the 76ers home games. It wasn't that he cared about the 76ers, but it meant that he could watch the 76ers play their arch rivals, the Boston Celtics.

Therefore, Chrissie had a built-in advantage over the other girls that Bah–Bah was seeing just then. The other thing was that St. Thomas Church was where Rocky himself had been married. That was where Bah–Bah's wedding ceremony was performed. Afterward, they had an outdoor wedding reception at Bah–Bah's mother's house. Junior Pirillo, Bobby Finizio, and their group — The Four Js from South Philly — were personal friends of Bah–Bah's and performed at the reception that day. Their assortment of songs included their two big hits — "Rock and Roll Age" and "Here am I."

In short, Bah–Bah loved Chrissie but probably not as much as he loved the idea of watching the Celtics in their road green on cable TV and getting married in the same church as Rocky. As for her cooking, it was improving. Chrissie made a few of his favorites, such as peppers and eggs and fried dough almost as well as his own mother made them.

The other night Rose had made Joe (she hated the name Bah-Bah) his favorite dish which was spizzare or spizzod as they pronounced it. It was a white chicken dish similar to Sicilian chicken in that it featured black olives, oil, peppers and garlic.

Rose always made more than enough and Bah-Bah that night ate the cold spizzare which he liked as much as hot spizzare. Bah-Bah called his office in the northeast and got the "line" for tonight's baseball games. Beside Bah-Bah's own book, two smaller bookmakers (one in South Philadelphia and one in Center City), called their action into the main office in the northeast. A Jewish kid named Joel manned the telephones in the northeast office. Bah-Bah was wearing a blue robe and had a towel wrapped around his wet hair. He walked to the window again and checked the street. He already had completed his pre-booking ritual which consisted of an hour of calisthenics while listening to music, usually disco music. The music, the exercises, and then the cold shower all served to energize him so that, when he got on the phone, he was flawless and alert. This deterred him from making any little mistakes which could turn out to be costly or create bad will. A tiny error such as not moving the line at the right time or writing down the word "over" instead of the word "under" could create a costly mistake. This was more important, of course, during the hectic football season than it was now.

Bah-Bah fielded a few calls. The first guy just asked about a few games, and the second customer asked for the entire slate of games. Usually a serious customer would get the line like these guys, hang up, then look at the games and call back a little later. It was unusual for a customer to call and bet on a game or games right on the spot.

Bah-Bah had the *Daily News* sports section laid out on the kitchen table in front of him. He looked at the results from yesterday's races at Keystone Racetrack. The horse who won the fifth race was named

Camden Snake. The horse paid a whopping $48.00. Five of Bah–Bah's customers, including two who had never even bet horses with him before, had laid it in on this particular horse. The suspicious thing was all of them were from South Philly. Bah–Bah smelled a rat. He didn't add it all up just then, but was sure he would pay out about $4,000. He smacked the table; he knew he should have gotten rid of the bets. He wasn't just upset about the money he had to pay out. This was a two-way street after all. It was more that he wasn't in on this. To the contrary, he had been played, or at least, that was how he looked at it. Ordinarily, he wouldn't mind it so much, rationalizing that he would eventually get all of this money back … and then some. Bah–Bah was raised in this business by his father and by Gino. A customer winning a lot of money, whether it was with a horse like this or a string of winning football bets or whatever, was actually beneficial to the bookmaker in the long run. A big score gave the customer confidence, kept him from being discouraged, kept him happy about his habit. It lulled him into a false sense of security and, in the long run, was actually counter-productive.

It was just that, for one thing, business had been slow. More importantly, Bah–Bah understood that there was a very real possibility that his operation would soon be out of business altogether. This $4,000 (or whatever it was going to be) was going to sting.

Bah–Bah contemplated the window again. On a Sunday night, three years ago in the fall of 1975, Bah–Bah had been at Rose's house when the same window rattled just like it had tonight. There had been an explosion that night at the Arco Oil Refinery, just a little south and west of where Rose lived. Fighting the blaze that ensued, six Philadelphia firemen had been killed. Mayor Cerrone, for some unexplained reason, was not only on the scene but had actually supervised the battling of the fire, and it had earned him a broken hip.

Bah–Bah had explained to Torch his theory of what was really going on in South Philly. According to him, it wasn't some big New York crime family that was causing the majority of the problems like some were saying. Bah–Bah agreed with the majority of newspaper accounts. He claimed that it all had to do with South Philly people terrorizing other South Philly people. The Beast was led after all by Vito "The Mosquito" Moscariello, who was a fallen angel in Constantine's old family. Constantine had sent the unmanageable Moscariello to Atlantic City as a type of banishment, a punishment for a spur-of-the-moment fight in a South Philly diner which resulted in the stabbing death of a sailor who was stationed at the South Philly Naval Base. Ten years later, when the gambling referendum was passed, Moscariello found himself in the Garden spot. He realized that he was in a powerful position. Atlantic City was his town. What he needed was a group of people to help him run Atlantic City and eventually Philadelphia who weren't affiliated with, loyal to, or afraid of Constantine. He found this group in the sons and nephews of the old mobsters, and they were the ones rebelling now. It was this younger, discontented group who thought it was their birthright to fill their ancestors' positions.

"Except," Bah-Bah told Torch, "in Philadelphia, it wasn't like New York in that it didn't automatically go from father to son ... not necessarily." Bah-Bah told Torch it wasn't like in *The Godfather*. It was just that they thought it should be like in *The Godfather*.

Daily News columnist Pete Dexter left the paper in the early eighties to wrote books. The first of which was a novel called *God's Pocket*, which was about a neighborhood in South Philadelphia. In one passage, he talked about a man named Vinnie, and he wrote this:

"Vinnie had been Like Angelo's right hand, but since the new people started running things that didn't count no more. Actually they wasn't new. They'd always been there, but nobody noticed. They was muscle or go-fers mostly. Sons and nephews of men with brains and experience and balls, who used that to come into the business but nobody ever took them serious. Angelo didn't, to him they was like children, in a hurry for everything, always pushin' — and look what it got him. The new people had discovered respect, and they was in a hurry for that, too.

Then, with Atlantic City legalizing gambling, New York probably supported the revolt. "To be sure," Bah-Bah said, "the hit on Constantine had to have gone through New York."

As much as Bah-Bah hated them, the truth was that a part of him could sympathize with this younger group to some extent. He had grown up in a similar environment, both inside and outside of the house.

Bah-Bah was doing fine, but what he had was little compared to what he could have in the next three year or so; it could happen that quickly. That being the case, this younger mob, "The Beast" as he often referred to them, many of whom Bah-Bah had been friendly with since childhood, couldn't understand why he never expressed a desire to join them. The difference was that Bah-Bah already had something going on his own; the other guys didn't. He had bookmaking, loan-sharking, numbers, and his newsstand. Bah-Bah didn't sell drugs, and the police, if they even knew of him at all, left him alone. He worked very hard to remain independent, the way Gino had done it. He was his own boss and was doing very well. He had remained old-school and didn't bother anybody. This group, on the other hand, was terrorizing their own people. They had beat up an old bookmaker, a venerable Constantine loyalist called Frankie Flowers for not paying the street tax. He was from near the Italian Market, only a few blocks away by the famous Pat's Steaks. When he still refused to pay "The Elbow," he was killed. They scared Gino to death. They said it was cancer, but the two heart attacks in the last ten months of his life didn't help him, and Gino had been like an uncle to Bah-Bah. These guys had extorted money from a weekly card game made up of old men who probably came over on the boat with their grandparents. In one case, Bah-Bah heard of a guy setting up his own father. Another time a man shot his own brother. Bah-Bah wanted no parts of them. His hope was that Chickadee, who still had friends in New York, along with maybe Paco here in Philly and others, would somehow withstand this onslaught going on now.

The newspapers, including a very popular Philadelphia Inquirer columnist named Steve Lopez, continually called this crew who was taking over now "wannabes" or "nobody's." They were wrong, however, when they often joked about how stupid this younger Philadelphia mob was. They underestimated them. In a short time, they would have their hands in union pension funds, as well as construction and other whitecollar endeavors. In one famous episode, they even shook down one of Philadelphia's leading developers for $500,000. Yet at the same time, they always found time to bother some little numbers writer, some kid selling football pools, or some old Italian immigrant who sold homemade wine from his cellar to make a few extra dollars.

Soon Bah-Bah would move his operation elsewhere. He hoped that running his businesses from somewhere in North Philadelphia would give him some peace of mind. He planned to return home every night. If anybody asked him, he would just say that he had a job up in the northeast somewhere or something like that. Torch was right. Nobody would bother him up there. To South Philadelphians, North Philadelphia was the jungle. It was the other side of the world. North Philadelphia, to them, was a great mystery. Since the young men who made up Moscariello's organization were mainly native South Philadelphians, they didn't know or understand North Philadelphia, and they really didn't want to. They knew this though — those kind of places had their own wise guys.

★ ★ ★

Booking was always slow during the summer. Baseball traditionally wasn't a very big betting sport. A few guys who Bah-Bah called a "cult" would bet baseball. Many baseball bettors also liked to bet horses. Generally speaking, however, baseball season was quiet. There were, after all, 162 games during the regular baseball season, so the same enthusiasm day in and day out just wasn't there for most fans and bettors. Plus, baseball differed from football and basketball because bookmakers offered odds as opposed to a simple point spread, which the majority of bettors seemed to prefer. In baseball, one had to consider the starting pitchers on both squads, as well as the parks and the effects those two had on the starting line-up, the relief pitchers, and several other factors. It amounted to a lot more effort, generally speaking. The odds, which invariably knocked your brains out, turned most of the betting public off to baseball.

During football season, Bah–Bah handled up to forty customers as opposed to having about eight hard–core baseball bettors. Basketball was a big betting sport, too, although not in the same league as football. Generally speaking, the basketball bettors were mainly a Jewish lot from the northeast. They were big bettors and good payers and Bah–Bah was always pleased to do business with them.

Sometimes during the summer, the phone rang so infrequently that Bah–Bah wondered what the hell he was doing there.

Again, Bah–Bah in his robe with his curly, wet hair and Rocky Marciano face went to the window to check the street. He saw no people or activity of any kind, except the trackless trolley rolling down Snyder Avenue.

★ ★ ★

On the opposite side of the city, way up north in Logan, Torch checked the sheet for any hits on the night number. He was sitting at his desk when he noticed a completed crossword puzzle Maria had done from *The Philadelphia Inquirer*. He had already read the sports page and selected one baseball game that he wanted to bet that night. The Sid Mark-Sinatra show, "Friday with Frank," was on the radio in the kitchen. The show that was "often imitated but never duplicated" could probably never be matched because of Sid Mark as much as of Sinatra himself. Sid Mark had a soothing voice that was strong and relaxing at the same time. It was the perfect voice for a Sunday morning when you were slightly hung over. It was the perfect voice for the long ride home from the shore on the Atlantic City Expressway on Sunday mornings during the summer. At the same time, the voice was perfect if you were home alone on Friday nights, all depressed, thinking about "The One Who Got Away."

He took a closer look at some of the questions Maria had answered. They were no match for her: 13 across, seven letters, 1975 John Denver hit ... CALYPSO ... 20 down, six letters, Sinatra's

1968 cinema wife ... REMICK ... 30 across, four letters, *West Side Story* co-star......WOOD ... 43 across, seven letters, 1967 Oscar Winner ... KENNEDY ... 63 across, 6 letters, Cassavetes in *The Dirty Dozen* ... FRANCO ... 73 down, six letters, cut man in *Requiem for a Heavyweight* ... Rooney.

At ten minutes after seven, Torch snubbed out his cigarette, walked to the phone in the kitchen, and called Bah-Bah. At the moment, he was wearing a 76ers T-shirt and a pair of boxer shorts and nothing else. His suit was upstairs on a hanger in anticipation of Shine's viewing that night in the neighborhood.

Torch thought about the baseball game he "liked." He was betting on the New York Mets as a home underdog against the Atlanta Braves. The Mets pitcher was a betting favorite of his, the underrated Craig Swan. Atlanta's pitcher was ace Phil Niekro. He was a future Hall of Fame pitcher but hadn't been doing so well in recent road efforts. Torch thought it was a strong play, the only stand-out game in the past few nights, and he'd betted $100 on the contest.

Sid Mark was playing a live album of Sinatra's on the kitchen radio. It was the Main Event concert from Madison Square Garden on October 13, 1974. First there was a drum roll; then trumpets were playing a song. Howard Cosell was doing the introduction. It was Cosell's shining hour.

"Live from New York, the city whose landmarks are famous all over the world. A world center for shipping, transportation, finance, fashion, and above all, entertainment. A city that pulsates always because of the millions of people who live here, work here, visit here. And in the heart of the metropolis, the great arena, Madison Square Garden, which has created and housed so many champions, and which is why tonight from the Garden, the most enduring champion of all, Frank Sinatra, comes to the entire western hemisphere live with the Main Event concert."

Torch had heard this introduction many times but had never thought about the song playing in the background. For the first time he, identified it as "It was a Very Good Year." The song was the perfect setting for the melancholy tone of the concert. *"But now the days are short. I'm in the autumn of the year."* That kind of thing.

Cosell continued, "*Madison Square Garden, October 13,1974. Jam Packed with 20,000 people, just people, people from all walks of life. People who are young and people who are old, here to see, hear, pay homage to a man who has bridged four generations and somehow never found a gap.*

"*Hello again, everybody. I'm Howard Cosell, and I've been here so many times, and in a curious way, this event, live with the king of entertainment carries with it the breathless anticipation of a heavyweight championship fight. Celebrities are here in profusion, one after another. Rex Harrison, Professor Higgins, if you will, Carol Channing "Hello, Dolly," Walter Cronkite, Mr. Believable, and of course, the great romantic hero Robert Redford.*

"*But here, coming through the same tunnel as so many champions have walked before, the great man, Frank Sinatra, who has the phrasing, who has the control, who understands the composers, who knows what losing means as so many of us have, who made the great comeback, who stands still, enduringly, on top of the entertainment world. Ladies and gentlemen, from here on in, it's Frank Sinatra.*"

Torch had seen this concert two or three times on public television. Therefore, it was easy for him to picture the scene now as Sinatra walked toward the stage, shaking a few hands along the way. He was wearing a black tuxedo. He reached the stage, walked to the center, took the mike, and went into his first song.

She gets too hungry
For dinner at eight …

Sinatra's voice was pretty much shot by this time. It was a lot more Johnny Cash than Johnny Mathis. That was for sure, but he pulled it off here. It was ironic that Cosell, in the introduction, compared Sinatra to a champion boxer because that was what he was like in this concert. He was like a cagey, old, veteran championship fighter who used every trick in the book. He, of course, still had the heavy guns behind him in the band. He had the best song writers. He did two Cole Porter songs and a poor version of a Stevie Wonder song. Despite the many years and miles on his throat, the Jack Daniels and smoke, the concert was a big success overall. His voice was a far cry from the pipes that belted out songs like "Come Fly with Me" in the 1950s. There was no ring-a-ding-ding here or anything like that.

But the voice he had right then fit ever better with certain sad songs such as "It was a Very Good Year" and especially "Angel Eyes." In the final analysis, Torch liked this concert as much as any of them, including the famous one from the Sands in Vegas with the Count Basie Orchestra that was produced by Quincy Jones.

He was still Sinatra here in this 1974 concert. He was Sinatra in the late seventies, just like he was in the early eighties, for that matter. As opposed to the nineties, when he did *Duets*, and really wasn't Sinatra at all.

Torch looked at his advance edition of *The Daily Racing Form*. Tomorrow the Atlantic City Racetrack would be running its premier race of the summer, the Matchmaker Stakes. This was a race that was run by three-year-old fillies. The winner would have the honor of having a very expensive rendezvous with the best colt or maybe second best colt in the country who would be either Affirmed or Alydar.

* * *

The phone rang again at Rose's house in South Philadelphia. This time, it was Joel calling from the office in the northeast, where he worked for Bah-Bah. He asked Bah-Bah if he'd heard the news.

"What news?" Bah-Bah said.

"Somebody just bombed Chickadee's house. They blew him up right on his porch."

"He's dead? Chickadee is dead?" Bah-Bah asked. Shock was the first emotion that hit him. The real sadness would come about an hour later.

"My mother just called me. My aunt lives on that block and a piece of the *payment* flew across the street and hit her window."

Joel was very intelligent. He was the point man in Bah-Bah's sports booking operation. It was his job, and he did it very well, matching up all of the bets that the overall "book" took in. Taking the bets and the odds into consideration, Joel had to take in just enough action on both sides to ensure that the book won, regardless of the outcome of the actual games. If he was overloaded on one side or another, it was Joel's job to hedge some of the money off. To do that type of job well, you had to have intelligence. Nevertheless, like many native Philadelphians, Joel used the word *payment* when he meant to say *pavement*. "Jesus Christ," Bah-Bah said. "When did this happen?" "About a half hour ago, I think," Joel said.

Bah-Bah stared at the window that had been shaking.

*   *   *

Torch learned of the big news at 7:15 when he changed the station to KYW All News Radio in Philadelphia. At a quarter of and a quarter after each hour, KYW ran down the sports scores. At 7:15, they recapped the entire racing card and the results from Keystone Racetrack. Before they got to the sports, as always, KYW ran through the weather and the top story. In this case, of course, the top story was the bombing and murder just about forty-five minutes ago of the notorious Philadelphia mob boss Michael "Chick-a-dee" Santucci. The first thing Torch thought of was how Bah-Bah would react.

After he listened to the results on the radio, Torch called Bah-Bah again. He was not surprised to know that he had already heard the news. Torch, respecting and understanding that Bah-Bah couldn't talk very long on the phone just then, said that he would talk to him later. Before Torch could hang up, however, Bah-Bah said, "Wait a second. I got to tell you something. I bought a house today. My brother-in-law hooked it up. It's just going to be like an office for me. It only cost me $1. Yeah, the place is up around you somewhere in Logan. It's on Windrim Avenue. I'm not sure of the address. Eleven-Twenty-Seven, I think it is. I rode by it earlier with my brother-in-law. It's a row house. It's got a reddish-brown door framed by two columns. The one column has a cat ornament nailed on it."

Goddamn, Torch thought to himself. He was talking about Caesar's Palace. Suddenly, in the story that was this wild summer, the plot had thickened dramatically, and it was still two weeks short of the all-star break.

CHAPTER 9

The question wasn't whether Chick-a-dee's murder would change things. The question was to what extent things would change.

No murder, not even that of the great Constantine, or the handful of gangland murders that ensued, figured to have as many ramifications. The incident was even immortalized in a Bruce Springsteen song called "Atlantic City" in the early 1980s. The killing essentially ended any hope that the old Philadelphia crime family, formerly headed by Constantine, would survive. After all, Chick-a-dee was probably the last one alive who had the power and reputation to possibly outfight Moscariello's group or recruit new troops if either of those things were ever even a consideration in the first place. These motherfuckers were terrorizing South Philadelphia, but there had been a glimmer of hope among those directly or indirectly affected that somehow Constantine's peaceful reign here could return. Chick-a-dee had been around a long time. He, at least allegedly, had pull in New York, and there was always a wishful thought that he could plead his case to them. Of course, it wasn't written in stone that a New York family wasn't in some way behind this takeover from the start.

Philadelphia's foremost "mob-watcher" was reporter George Anastasia of the *Philadelphia Inquirer* who once wrote of Moscariello: *"He was the antithesis of Constantine."*

Constantine had always run a low-key operation. He didn't flaunt his riches or dress in a flashy manner. He lived in a modest row home and never had elaborate Fourth of July parties with fireworks or gave away turkeys at Thanksgiving. Constantine and his men didn't live the kind of extravagant lives that kids wanted to emulate. Not only that but hardly any organized crime-related murders took place while he was boss. Things were quiet, and organized crime wasn't discussed much. As a result of all of this, the police were generally apathetic toward Constantine and his business interests. In Center City, Gino ran things the same way, meaning everything was in the shadows.

He (Constantine) had run organized crime in Philadelphia since the 1950s. Once in awhile, you'd hear about some drug dealer or some other underworld figure that was killed in the Philadelphia area but rarely was it ever connected to Constantine's people. That wasn't to say it never happened during his watch. Philadelphians, particularly South Philadelphians, in later years and decades, when speaking about Constantine in these nostalgic tones tended to talk about how peaceful it was then and how nobody ever got killed during that period. The truth was that it really did happen. There may have even been isolated incidents were certain illegal entrepreneurs had to pay a tribute to the Philadelphia family, but so rarely did it happen and so rarely did you hear about it that it just seemed like it never occurred. Even if /when it did happen, nobody cared since no innocent persons were hurt or at risk. On Constantine's watch, there were very few headlines and never anything like this.

Chick-a-dee's violent and reckless murder was different, unusual in Philadelphia. It wasn't like anything else Philadelphians had seen in decades. Frankly, Philadelphians weren't prepared or ready for that type of excitement. You'd hear, once in awhile, about a brazen type of murder in New York inside a barbershop, or on the outdoor deck of a restaurant, or a, t a clam house in Little Italy, but never anything like that in Philadelphia. Clearly, there was a new sheriff in town, and Moscariello's crew spent the next six or seven years years flexing their muscles.

"Chick-a-dee's murder opened the floodgates," Joe Halligan, the head of the local organized crime commission said many years later in a documentary about organized crime in Philadelphia and the impact casino gambling in Atlantic City had. "After that murder, there was no stopping them. It was their town now."

A dozen more of Constantine's associates were killed in the next six or seven years. Overall, forty gangland murders would occur in the Philadelphia and Atlantic City areas in the next twenty years. The majority of them were blamed one way or the other on Moscariello.

The bizarre method chosen to assassinate the head of the Philadelphia crime family obviously was designed to shock and send a message of terror. To that end, it was extremely successful. Yet the murder also brought tremendous, unwanted heat. For one thing, the bombingmurder resulted in a huge public outcry over organized crime for the first time in Philadelphia in decades. It didn't help matters that Chick-a-dee lived on one of the classiest blocks in the entire city. Nor did it help that the people in that neighborhood were among Jimmy Cerrone's most loyal, wealthiest, and powerful constituents, including two municipal court judges.

The murder mobilized federal prosecutors and judges who were now armed with the powerful R.I.C.O. organized crime laws. A handful of Philadelphia lawyers still maintain, to this day, that it was Chick-a-dee's infamous murder that resulted in having the R.I.C.O. laws enacted in Philadelphia the first place. That wasn't the case at all. The truth was that the Federal Government already had the R.I.C.O. laws. Ironically in fact, the government had just opened a R.I.C.O. case against Chicka-dee two or three days before he was killed. Over the next ten years, Philadelphians saw a series of trials which resulted in lengthy prison sentences for many of Moscariello's top men. In the final analysis, the murder simultaneously ended one enemy and brought forth another — the Federal Government.

As for Torch, the murder couldn't have shaken him up more had he lived next door to Chick-a-dee. It didn't help that he hadn't fully gotten over the shock of Shine's death. Shine's murder, of course, affected Torch in a more personal way, but it didn't impact his near future like Chicka-dee's did. This started Torch thinking about another line of work. He always knew that, eventually, he would address his future realistically, but he always figured that he would let fate guide him, so he never took an initiative.

He never really saw himself going anywhere or wanting necessarily to go anywhere in this business anyway. He wanted to be a professional gambler, like those guys from Las Vegas you saw during the football season. They were all about forty or fifty years old and looked half that age. They all had the same "top of the world" smile on their faces. Maybe he could become a sports writer like Jack Kiser from the *Daily News* or write books like Jimmy Breslin in New York.

Torch had the option of leaving this business, and he'd do so with no regrets. It had been fun, a pleasant experience while it lasted, waking up just in time for the "Solid Hour of Sinatra," then going into Center City a few times a week and right into the cast of *Guys And Dolls*. Surely nobody could blame him for leaving, given the recent turn of events. Bah-Bah, on the other hand, was, no doubt, more in a type of vise now. It seemed as though it was just a matter of time before he would be approached. He was the one who was in the precarious situation with a lot more to lose.

Bah-Bah would land on his feet, even if it meant returning exclusively to the newsstand business which he had built up … that wouldn't be too bad. At least Bah-Bah now was taking it all more seriously and was taking precautions, the centerpiece of which was his plan to relocate his business to Logan and Caesar's Palace. It was a move that, no doubt, would be interesting for everybody.

As usual, Torch went into Center City that Saturday. He stopped in Ben's first and bought the *Daily News* to read about the murder and look over the box scores on the way down. Unlike last week, he took the subway this Saturday so that he wouldn't look so much like a pussy when he called Bah-Bah to tell him that he couldn't come into South Philly to see him. It wasn't that Torch was crazy about going into Center City either, but he had a lot of work to do. Eleven of his customers had bet Affirmed last week in the Belmont Stakes. Torch had seen most of the bettors during the week and paid them off, but there were still a few retirees who came around only on Saturdays that Torch still had to see. Torch decided that as ruthless and aggressive as Moscariello's men were, there would be a grace period to allow things to cool down.

Torch had lost $100 the previous night on the Mets game which turned out to be a wild, extra-inning affair. He had come home early from playing cards at Caesar's Palace in order to listen to the game on the radio. However, on many nights, the New York Mets games, unlike the New York Yankees games, didn't come over clearly on the radio in his house. For some reason, the Mets games always came through better on the car radio. He would ride around the streets of Logan for almost two hours, listening to the game on the radio. First the Braves knocked Swan out of the box in the third inning and rushed out to a big lead. The Mets rallied back however, and it wasn't until 12:30 in the morning, following a rain delay that Atlanta pushed across what ultimately would be the winning run.

When Torch arrived in Center City at noon, it was already hot and sticky. This particular Saturday seemed more like a Sunday, which was to say the place was deserted. There was a very lonely, eerie feeling about it, and it was as though the whole city had run for cover in the aftermath of what had happened.

Torch had to man up somewhat and be more like Felix, Jackie, and those guys. They didn't seem to worry about anything. It was a characteristic of theirs that Torch always admired. Torch liked to act hard and invulnerable. He was a "Ben's Boy"; he was also full of shit. The truth was that he was just a skinny, frightened insecure, fuckin' kid when his boys weren't around.

His first stop in Center City was at Chock Full O' Nuts where he bought two large coffees to go. It was the V.S.O.P. of Center City coffee, and they brought them to the cutlery store where Sam the Blade worked.

Henkel's Cutlery was among the oldest retail stores in the city. It had a shop in the back with wet wheels, coarse wheels, and leather wheels for sharpening all types of scissors, knives, and other tools. They did sharpening for individual customers but also the scissors for every Center City barber, hair salon, and even for the mummers. They also sharpened knives for many local restaurants. The window display featured cutting boards, wooden blocks for storing kitchen knives, straight razors, sharpening straps, shaving mugs, shaving soaps, and sharpening steels. There was also a three or four-foot model of an elaborate Swiss army knife with the various blades, nail files, and scissors moving in and out of it.

Sam the Blade was about 5'10" with brown hair and was skinnier than even Torch. He wore a gold chain around his neck with a tiny straight razor charm which was sort of his trademark ... the Blade. He was about twelve years older than Torch, in his early thirties. Alex once told Torch that Blade had briefly helped Gino in the numbers business by working, for a short-time, under Gino's son. Alex also said Blade had been a hotshot pitcher at Germantown High School. Alex told Torch that Blade threw one no-hitter after the other. Blade had earned a baseball scholarship and was educated at a university in Florida. His college allowed him to sidestep the Vietnam draft then in the late sixties. He said that Blade was doing fine until he blew out his knee playing a schoolyard basketball game and never fully recovered. He now was not only no longer an athlete but also had a pronounced limped when he walked. The problems were not just physical apparently but mental, too. He lost his scholarship but finished up locally at Temple University in Philadelphia. Bah-Bah told Torch that he believed there was a certain self-destructiveness attached to Blade's gambling that stemmed from his injury. Bah-Bah said that, when the Blade's baseball career ended before it ever began, he became a regular visitor to "the snow man" and morphed into a Center City coke dealer himself. According to Alex, Blade made $,1000 a week selling drugs, and the cutlery store manager was simply a nice front that kept him connected to barbers, hair stylists, young manicurists, and restaurant workers who were among his best, steadiest customers. Blade's boss in the cutlery business owned harness horses, and Blade, at one point, co-owned three or four horses stabled at Liberty Bell Racetrack. He hadn't had much success as an owner. But one horse (Labuc) had done well locally and was even shipped up to the prestigious Meadowlands Racetrack built in the swamps of New Jersey. On paper, Labuc was overmatched in that race but finished second in a $100,000 event. Between the almost $25,000 they received from the purse for finishing second, plus the nearly $6,000 they won by using Labuc in a monster exacta, it was a score that almost got Blade and his partner even. Shortly after that Blade got his wings clipped, and he was currently on probation.

Getting arrested shook Blade up, but there were other reasons beside legal ones that kept him on the sidelines. He was like Torch. Both of them had started out during Constantine's laissez-faire era. Of course, it was different now. Blade was conscience and more than a bit afraid of "the elbow" (street tax). He had also been busted by cops that wanted to shake him down and put him on a payment plan. He received a letter which he believed they'd sent. The letter was sitting in his mailbox one day; it scared the shit out of him. The letter wasn't postmarked. That was the tip off that it wasn't on the level. There was an address, however, and Blade wrote a letter to them saying he was legit now and working and to please leave him alone. Even if he had ever entertained the thought of getting back into the business, the fantasy ended with a boom last night.

Blade's mentor in the cocaine business, another from Germantown named Eddie, explained to him that, once you were arrested, you were public domain, the cat was out of the bag, and you were vulnerable to all types of things like this. Blade's stint as a drug merchant was over. He lost just about everything he made betting on baseball games and horses anyway. He wasn't raking it in these days, but he didn't have the worries either. Even with the added hours two nights a week at Henkel's other store in the gallery, he still worked less overall. He wasn't making as much and no longer sat in an owner's box at Liberty Bell, but he didn't gamble and lose as much, and of course, he made fewer trips to the snowman himself these days.

The job at Henkel's wasn't simply a "front" now, but it was what he did. Instead of owning horses, he just bet on them. Instead of playing baseball, he was one of Bah-Bah's most enthusiastic baseball betters. Torch was very intrigued by Bah-Bah's claim that Blade's gambling was connected to some sort of self-destructiveness. After all, Washington had said the same thing about him, so did Maria, for that matter, but she was probably just repeating what she'd heard Washington say. Specifically, Washington had said that his gambling was attached to what they called in Gamblers Anonymous "the big shot syndrome." Washington added that this "syndrome" was the byproduct of Torch's being a little man both in the literal and figurative sense. Torch didn't understand but took for granted that both Washington and Bah-Bah were onto something, given they were both insightful individuals. Torch always looked to Blade for clues into his own personality. They were similar — the baseball and horses, movies, boxing, and they both liked Philadelphia boxing, Philadelphia music, and Philadelphia writers like *Daily News* columnists Larry McMullen and Pete Dexter, also New York's Jimmy Breslin. They had mutual acquaintances like Gino and Bah-Bah and Alex. They both had reason to hate the Beast and this ongoing takeover. Blade was from Germantown but knew both Logan and Ben's. He had even, for a time, been an old head from Dunn's. They had similar bloodlines, too; Blade was also a Hebbruzzi, both with Italian mothers. From strictly a character standpoint, you could even say that Torch used Blade as a type of mirror. This allowed him to examine his own personality. Maybe Torch could detect flaws that he believed may have existed but that he didn't understand by observing Blade. What specifically interested Torch was the bullshit about how compulsive gamblers were always looking to lose. It was the same concept James Caan struggled with in the movie *The Gambler.* What the hell was that anyway? Couldn't it be that a person gambled because it was fun or exciting? Weren't they all trying to string several wins together, roll it over, and ultimately make a score? Finally, what was this "self-destructive behavior" crap? In Blade, Torch saw what had to be a tortured soul, somebody who'd lost a real chance to have a big life. Was Blade a slightly older alter ego? Instead of the crippling injury, was Torch's inferiority complex encompassing him the same way? Blade lost his dream to play baseball and then lost a thriving cocaine business. He lost what amounted to a stable of racehorses, and then his old lady left him. It made Torch think of something Maria once said, "You're lucky to have me, Torch. If it wasn't for me, you wouldn't get any pussy at all."

Did Blade gamble to fulfill an empty spot in his life, in his soul? If so, was Torch doing the same thing? Washington once said that Torch had both an inferiority complex and a conniving personality. Again, here Torch didn't quite understand all that, but his behavior, the drinking, gambling, and smoking all could be labeled as self-destructive. At least part of it was probably connected to this bullshit image he had created to fit in with his boys and to impress Maria. It was or, at least, it was close to the "big shot syndrome" Washington talked about. Blade seemed to have a similar personality. They both had the ability to baffle you with so much bullshit; you didn't realize there was not much substance present. It was how Torch fit in with his men after all, and it was how he got Maria. Blade and Torch both threw up this smoke screen until the fog of it made you unable to see that there was really little there-there. Sam the Blade was educated but so what? He had no real skills; he was a retail clerk. When you got beyond the facade, the clothes, the chains, the rings, the manicured nails, his old, well-maintained '67 Cadillac, most shit he bought during his short nouveau riche period, that was all Blade was. Heck, Torch took home more every week and on a good week bought and sold him. Yet, Blade performed this magic act and when he started talking about this boxer and his contemporaries or that song, who performed it, the year it came out, he became something else, it seemed. They both left you thinking that there was something higher here, that they were somehow on top of things or destined for something; all of which was, in fact, untrue.

Blade wore white dress pants with a knit white and red shirt. He wore black shoes and white sweat socks. He wore a political button on his shirt that read "Vote YES to Charter Change." He was sitting on a stool alone in the store, eating from a bucket of fried clams when Torch entered the store. It was still roughly forty-five minutes until the first number was to come out. Blade had won $540 on his score on Leroy Nickawampus. Then he had lost some back on numbers and horses, so Torch had to give about $480.

Torch set the two coffees on the glass display case. Blade told Torch that he half-expected him not to show up after what happened last night. Torch shrugged it off like it was just an ordinary Saturday. Then Blade asked Torch where he'd parked when he came into town. Without going into a song and dance about it, Torch said he took the soul train that day but usually parked up the street between 16th and17th and Sansom. "It's only $$4.50 a day," Torch told him.

Blade said he'd parked across the street. Torch said it was a rip-off, only a block closer and they charged twice as much. Then Torch said, "Plus, I do a lot of business up the street from the guys who park the cars. The other place, they play numbers, too, like crazy, but always with Blue Eyes or Eddie. There is a phone on that corner. I use it two or three times a day … call the action in, ya know? That's maybe fifteen times a week, and every time one of them says, 'Hey, Torch! What's leading?' or "Hey, Torch! What's out?' So it isn't like they don't know me or what I do. But they never give me a play. It was the same thing with Alex."

"I saw an old friend of yours the other night in the Warnock, John Blocks." Torch said.

John Blocks went to high school with Torch although in a different section. Blocks had had classes with Parkway's most famous alumni … actor Kevin Bacon. Blocks and his brother Robby both hung at Ben's and, in fact, lived on Windrim Avenue, only four or five doors away from Caesar's Palace. Blocks worked at a passport photo place nearby here in Center City and photographed weddings on the weekends.

"He told me he has your wedding pictures."

"That was from three years ago. My wife left me. Now finally he has my pictures?"

"Well, anyway, he said to call him," Torch said.

"I been meaning to call him, but I lost my personal phone book. Well, I didn't really lose it. When I got busted, the cops stole it. They do that sometimes. I heard, if it's a dealer or gangster or bookie even, they steal the personal phone book. A cop will do that, especially a dirty one."

"I saw *The Godfather Part Two* last night," Blade said. "I like it more than even the first one. I mean the flashback parts with DeNiro. They were the best things in the whole saga to me."

Torch took a fried clam and licked his fingers. "I still like the original. When I first saw the sequel, I didn't like it. It was just that the first one was a tough act to follow, I guess. But as time goes on, there is no question — the second one was a great movie in its own right. The parts with DeNiro were great. I hear ya' but it was the other part of *The Godfather Part Two* that I liked. I mean the storyline regarding Pantangeli and all that with him going to see Mike in Vegas, then him nearly getting killed in the bar, then him testifying, and finally Duvall visiting him in prison, the best scene in the movie."

"Let's face it," Blade said. "It was probably the best scene in any goddamn movie. Also that scene when Pantangei is about to testify they and bring in his brother from Sicily. They knew he wouldn't drop a dime with his brother there."

"Right. It was a powerful scene."

"If you notice, the brother is wearing this red tie in that scene. The tie had these two little balls of cotton ... it looked like ... hanging on it.

They represented his testicles. It was a message to Pantangeli that they had him by the balls."

"That's deep. How do you know that?"

"I did business with these Sicilians. They owned the pizza place around the corner, Joe's Pizza. They also had a restaurant. We used to do their knives. They told me about that."

"Well, if the second one was better than the first one, it was because of that storyline, not the old parts with DeNiro, in my opinion," Torch said, sipping his coffee. "Do you know Pantangeli's bodyguard in that was the gangster from *Rocky*? I seen him in other movies, too."

"Joe Spinell," Blade said." He was in *The Seven-Ups* and Taxi Driver.

He was also in the original *The Godfather*, too. He was in many movies." "Did you like *Rocky*?" Torch asked Blade.

"It was all right. Burgess Meredith was fantastic."

"I liked the first half of it but not the second half. It came out around all those great movies, ya' know? *Chinatown, Dog Day Afternoon, One Flew over the Cuckoo's Nest, The Godfather Part Two, Jaws. Rocky* was good, but it couldn't hang with those others."

"It was the movie of the year."

"Any of those movies would have beaten it," Torch said. "It musta been a weak year."

"It beat four movies — *Taxi Driver, All the President's Men, Network,* and an independent film, a documentary, something like that. It wasn't a weak year," Blade said.

"I didn't like any of them, not even *Taxi Driver.* Like I said, to me, it was two different movies. Once Apollo Creed entered into it, it got a little silly. I didn't like Creed, I didn't like Burt Young's character either. The second half of the movie was a little phony. In the first half of the movie, the actors made it seem so real. I mean like, when Rocky and Mickey were yelling at each other in the gym, you actually felt like you were standing there. That was how good the acting was … and you're right. Burgess Meredith was great, so was Stallone."

"It was what it was," Blade said. "You're right. It wasn't a great movie in the classic sense maybe. Nobody ever said that. It wasn't *On the Waterfront.* Stallone isn't Marlon Brando. What it was, though, was the classic example of something small and insignificant becoming gigantic. I mean Rocky was a small-time hood. He was a boxer who fought in clubs, a nobody really and suddenly, because of these unforeseen circumstances, because he was from Philly and it is the bicentennial and he has this cool nickname and Creed has nobody else to fight just then, he gets to fight for the title. Then it turns out he can really fight. It was like that movie *Charley Varrick* with Walter Matthau. They were bank robbers that robbed only small banks in small towns. It wasn't big scores they wanted, just $10,000 or $15,000 at a time with little risk. Then they rob this one bank in the sticks like the others, and they net $300,000, and it turned out that this organized crime outfit was using this particular bank as a drop. It was Mafia money, so for the rest of the movie, they are being chased. It wasn't a great movie either, but it contained that winning formula. There was another flick, an old one from the forties maybe. It starred Richard Widmark. I think it was called *Pick up on South Street*. It was about these crooks that picked pockets on the subway. Nobody cared about them. Then they lift a wallet, and it turned out the victim was a spy, and the formula for the atom bomb was written on a piece of paper in his wallet. Suddenly the secret service and the F.B.I. and the K.G.B. are looking for them. They become these significant people, see? You see that in movies or literature all the time. Even *The Godfather* had that element in it to a certain extent. But never did that dynamic present itself or come through as clearly as it did in *Rocky*. That was why it was movie of the year. If you look at it that way, *Rocky* was an amazing movie. I heard Stallone on TV, talking about the soundtrack to *Rocky*. Nobody would say it was a memorable soundtrack. It wasn't exactly *Goldfinger* or *Easy Rider* or *Saturday Night Fever* or anything like that. But Stallone was talking about the composer Bill Conte's amazing job at putting such a 'grandiose' — that was the word he used — piece of music together for this one small man. Right there, Stallone was letting you know that he got precisely what he wanted and knew exactly what he was doing. Not only that but Stallone's personal story paralleled the movie. He was a nothing actor. I mean, what was his big movie up to then *The Lords of Flatbush*? It was an example of lightning striking, then something tiny becoming significant.

"It's like what is going on here in Philly right now. Constantine ran everything. They were rich; their power was unchallenged. Nobody even dreamed of fucking with them, big fish in a small pond. Then — boom! — they legalize gambling in Atlantic City, unforeseeable circumstances. Certain people want to run the rackets there, younger guys. 'The Young Turks,' the papers call them, want to bring in drugs maybe, and suddenly, because of the proximity to A.C., these people become very important. Now it isn't just Philly;

it's New Jersey, New York, a whole new ballgame. Constantine gets killed, then the others, and finally you have what we saw last night. They should write a screenplay about it."

"*You* should write a screenplay about it," Torch said. "You sound like Rex Reed or one of them. I don't know about all this Siskel and Ebert stuff. But I do know that the clock on the wall there dictates everything. I have to make my rounds."

Torch left the store just as a couple, a man and woman, were entering. He walked to Eddie's bar, then Oscar's, but nobody was around. The couple in the store looked around so much, and the man asked so many stupid questions that they were just leaving when Torch came back. Blade was behind the counter now cleaning pen knives in a display case. He was wiping down Swiss army knives, their gleaming tiny blades, scissors, nail files, all exposed for the customers to see.

"Can I use your phone? I have to call central. Only three guys can call central."

Torch called Bah–Bah's house. There was no such place as "central."

Bah–Bah told Torch that a "three" was leading. Torch hung up, turned to Blade, and said, "A tree grows in Brooklyn." Then Torch took out his pen and pad. "You want anything?" he asked in the same tone of voice he used all the time when it was starting out. It was a tone that said, "It's no big deal if you don't want anything." "I'm all right," Blade said.

"You been pretty lucky with them back parlays lately," Torch said with a bit more hopefulness attached to it.

This, Blade understood, was the start of an afternoon long quest to get money out of him. Torch was a nice kid when they were talking about Sinatra or Humphrey Bogart or the J.F.K. assassination or something like that, but he was a pain in the ass, too, a vulture. It was just like when Alex ran the show here for Gino. Blade had been through this dance with Alex one hundred times. They knew Blade was a compulsive gambler. They were both vultures with an unrelenting desire to avoid honest labor. Torch himself once admitted to Blade, "I'm not afraid of hard work, I will lay down right next to it".

"No numbers today, Torch. I have to get yesterday's bank deposit together. I never made it over there last night." This was a hint to Torch that he was overstaying his welcome. But instead of reacting to the hint, Torch threw another curveball up there.

"You want something in the matchmaker tonight?" Torch said. There was a hint of desperation now behind his voice.

"Nah, I'm okay," Blade replied, enjoying fouling off the pitches.

Then Torch came right out with it. "You have all that money in your pocket. You have to give me something."

"All right," Blade said, anxious to get rid of Torch for a while. "I want to bet a horse tomorrow night at Liberty Bell." He turned to Jack Kiser in the *Daily News*. The *News* didn't come out on Sunday, so Kiser put in the entries and comments for both Saturday and Sunday in the thin Saturday edition of the paper. The horse he was considering was named Moshannon Express.

Torch was remotely familiar with the horse. He was a hard closer but rarely got there. He had been away for a long time, but according to the advance program that Blade had, the horse had just won a relatively cheap race in the slop up at the Meadowlands. Torch looked at Blade's paper and at Kiser's comment which read, "*Crushed Big Swampers last.*"

Blade bet $40 to win and $40 to place on the horse, but Torch refused the $80 he tried to hand him. "This goes on next week. We'll settle up next Saturday," Torch said. This would give Torch an excuse to drop by the store next Saturday.

On the way back to Ed's, Torch, wearing sunglasses now, walked up the street flashing three raised fingers into all of the windows of the places where his customers worked — a restaurant, a shoe store, a barber, a blueprint shop. It was very slow all over, a major contrast to last Saturday when Affirmed and Alydar went at it in the Belmont Stakes. Even most of the old cigar-chomping retirees hadn't come around.

At about five in the afternoon, Bah-Bah came uptown (Center City), drove by Oscar's, and parked along the street. Torch saw the white Cadillac from the window in the bar, came outside, and got in the front seat. He delivered his ribbon, and Bah-Bah gave him his cut, which was only about $200. Torch didn't say anything about Chick-adee. He would leave it up to him if he wanted to talk about it. Bah-Bah *did* mention that he would start moving into the house up in Logan sometime next week.

★ ★ ★

That night at home, Torch felt the need to tell Maria about everything. Ordinarily, Torch kept that part of his life secret from her. For one thing, Maria never seemed very interested in what Torch did. The other thing was that Maria obviously was friendly with a lot of cops from the diner. Torch felt more comfortable knowing that she could never accidentally say anything that could somehow hurt him.

Torch told Maria the whole story — Moscariello, the street tax, Bah-Bah, and his plan now to move into Caesar's Palace. He explained everything, starting with the referendum to legalize gambling in Atlantic City to Chick-a-dee's murder last night. Afterwards, he wasn't sure why he had told her but he did.

On Sunday afternoon, Torch and Maria watched the Phillies and the San Francisco Giants on TV. The Giants pitcher was veteran left-hander Vida Blue. The Phillies, at that point, had the strongest offense in the national league and had a tremendous record against left-handers. Torch stepped on the gas here and bet $200 on the Phillies. He lost the bet to Bah-Bah when Blue, who the papers called "Ageless" Vida Blue, shut the Phillies out.

That night, Torch and Maria went to Liberty Bell Racetrack. Lee Oskar was over at his grandmother's. The two of them drove up early to Liberty Bell and had dinner in the clubhouse. Torch, aware that he was on a downhill spiral, bet very conservatively, only $5 or $10 each race. He was about even when the fifth race came up. It was the Moshanon Express race. The horse was hovering around

6-1 on the odds board, which was an overlay. Torch knew another horse in the race, BooLaRoo, who was a one-dimensional speed horse that figured to set honest fractions and set up the closing kick for Moshannon Express. On the basis of this logic, as well as the generous odds, Torch laid off the $50 win-place bet Blade gave him; plus he added another $60 to "win" for himself.

Torch and Maria stood in the clubhouse watching the race on a TV monitor from a vantage point that allowed them a view of the racetrack. Marv Bachrad, the race caller from Liberty Bell, called it this way: "It's Boo-La-Roo, showing the way. Sunderchief now second. Madbo Ernie and High Hope Benny juggling for third. Another length back, that's Chef of the Future, Jolly Roger, Stray Kitty and Moshannon Express has the best view."

It remained that same order until about the half-mile pole. Then the leaders started to tire. BooLaRoo was fading as usual up front. Moshannon Express made a big move from the back then. It was, at that point, that announcer Marv Bachrad said, "*... and here comes the Moshannon Express, whoop ... whoop ... whoop ... whoop*" (imitating the sound of a locomotive).

Moshannon Express came very wide and, for a moment, looked like he had caught the front-runner, but Sundechief, who happened to run the race of his life that night, held him off.

Torch just shook his head at Maria. "He went too wide. He went too far wide," Torch said to Maria.

"He was all over the racetrack," she said.

Torch made a mental note to bet Moshannon Express the next time out. With a decent trip, at least with a decent trip against this same company, he should win easily.

Torch was angry at himself for not backing the horse up and betting him first and second as Sam the Blade had. At those odds, it was worth a place bet. That was precisely the kind of amateur mistake that a traumatic thing like Chick-a-dee's murder, combined with a losing streak made somebody do. Torch wasn't thinking rationally. He wanted to get that $300 he'd just lost in baseball games back in one two–minute race. Nevertheless, Maria noticed that Torch was feeling a lot better when they got to the track.

On the way home, going down the boulevard, Maria told Torch that Lee Oscar was going to spend the night at her mother's. The previous night, they'd had a very uneventful time of love-making. Torch hadn't been that timid since the first time they'd ever made love two years ago. Tonight, they both knew, would be different. Losing at the racetrack, for some reason, always put Torch in a certain mood. It made him horny; it really did which was good, since like everybody else, he lost most times. Maybe it had something to do with him taking his frustrations out on her. Torch didn't know what it was. He could never gauge how much influence his gambling had on his personality, if any, but it did affect his sex drive somehow. Torch, sometimes, fantasized as he did tonight that he was a big stallion like Northern Dancer or Mr. Prospector. Maria, in Torch's fantasy, which he never told her about was a young filly who had just won the Matchmaker Stakes in Atlantic City, and he covered her, entering her, mounting her from behind.

In bed, they listened to the Sunday Night Oldies Show, another Philadelphia tradition. The disk jockey Harvey Holiday played music from "the golden decade" from the mid–fifties up until the Beatles in '63 or '64. It was The Crests, Frankie Lymon and the Juniors, Little Anthony and the Imperials, as well as many old Philly groups, including The Four Jays and Billy Carlucci and the Essentials, which were both from South Philly. At one point, they played Philly's Lee Andrews and the Hearts singing Maria's favorite song "Long and Lonely Nights."

"They should erect statues to the man," Maria said of Lee Andrews.

* * *

In West Philadelphia, *Daily News* columnist John Chapman turned on his TV set. Channel 6 was showing the debut of the nationwide show called Super Chief. The show was a program centering specifically on law enforcement leaders, such as police commissioners or wardens.

The media almost showed Cerrone in a negative light. Many people thought this show wouldn't be any different. The timing of the show was the tip-off. If this show really planned to be as successful, even remotely as popular as *60 Minutes* then surely, it would have its debut in the fall. This was strictly a political thing.

There was an overriding feeling that the show would contribute to sustaining the City Charter, which amounted to unseating Mayor Cerrone. This theory was widely held by row-house Philadelphians (the white ones anyway). The feeling was that there wouldn't be anything positive on Cerrone, such as his defusing potentially disastrous and costly riots twice in the 1960s or the improvements he made in the city or his tough stance on crime and his effective police force, which featured one of the best 911 systems in the country.

As for Chapman himself, being the spirited voice of the black community, he was no bystander in this battle against Cerrone. Blasting mayors had become Chapman's calling card. Not only did Cerrone take a bashing, but so would the next two mayors.

As for tonight's show, the footage was old. It showed Cerrone first as a Philadelphia police commissioner in the sixties. They talked about his 8,000-member police force. The footage showed Cerrone inspecting a new class of police recruits. And it showed Cerrone swinging his nightstick in what looked like the middle of a gang fight.

At least one of the two broadcasters, Chapman thought, was Canadian. Speaking of his police force, Cerrone said, "They could invade Cuba." Chapman, meanwhile, was scribbling in shorthand every little quote and looking for any little detail on the screen that he could use. Chapman was seated at a table in his living room, writing on a clipboard.

Cerrone, with his Romanesque face and dark brown eyes and baritone voice, filled the screen. It was the same way his presence filled a room when he walked into it. Cerrone's hair was shiny black like a seal's skin in the sunlight, freshly out of the water. Cerrone was very proud of that hair, sort of like ex-President JFK and his famous head of reddishbrown hair. Like JFK, nobody could remember Cerrone ever wearing a hat, even on the coldest days.

Cerrone was an ex-cop. He was anything but a polished politician, and he was proud of that. He said himself on numerous occasions, "I'm just a high-ranking cop who took on the politicians."

One of the broadcasters said, "The commissioner is a very pragmatic man. He has decided it is his job to maintain law and order while others are debating the Constitution's subtleties. Actually Cerrone considers himself a general whose 8,000 men are engaged in a holy war."

Cerrone took the bait and sounded even crazier than what they probably hoped for. Chapman, on the other hand, like all Philadelphians, was familiar with Cerrone's "pull-no-punches" style of speech. Therefore, nobody in the Philadelphia area was surprised when Cerrone said, "That's exactly what it is — a holy war, almost as severe as the war in Vietnam." Chapman now knew why they used this old footage. Now he knew why they kept this around for ten years. Already Chapman had the formation of a full column in his head. Cerrone was only getting warmed up, however.

"We ran a comparison a couple weekends in our city against the casualties in Vietnam, and surprisingly we had more homicides, deaths, and casualties than they did in Vietnam."

Chapman couldn't ask for more. He actually said out loud, "That's right, Jimmy. Do that. Say that, brother."

"Don't get me wrong," Cerrone said. "The streets in Philadelphia aren't bad. It's just the people in the streets that make them bad."
"Good one," Chapman said.

Then the broadcasters talked about the two-term mayor and his bid to change the City Charter and run again. They said, "There's no civilian review board in Philadelphia. The mayor of the city has given the police 'carte blanche' and uses the police force as something comparable to his own private army."

The truth was there was a half-assed civilian review board which was supposed to hold police accountable, but nobody in Philadelphia knew who they were or what exactly they did. In addition to that, Chapman himself wrote of the review board: "You always have to be skeptical when any organization does an investigation on itself, especially when it comes to government." Chapman also wrote: "It would be tantamount to a baseball owner managing his own team. If the team was failing and was disorganized with no leadership and a change was in order, would the owner then be expected to fire himself?"

The Canadian broadcaster threw more fuel on the fire by saying, "You have a very clear-cut opinion of what's right and what's wrong, don't you?"

Cerrone again sounded like a nut and said, "Absolutely. Everyone deserves a second chance, maybe even three chances. But we're talking about forgiving a crim'nal the eighth, ninth, tenth time. No, we're becoming ridiculous. We have crim'nals out there walking around who will not be rehabilitated, cannot be rehabilitated, and should be put in prison."

"Cerrone is popular with most Philadelphians," one of the broadcasters said, "for preventing the city's black ghettos from erupting and for taking a hard line on militant radicals."

On the subject of crime, the Canadian reminded everybody that Cerrone had said, "I'm going to make Attila the Hun look like a faggot."

Chapman wrote it down and said out loud, "Perfect." He then drove his Plymouth Fury with the radio turned off to the *Daily News* building. VCRs weren't around in those days, but the newsroom surely would have a videotape of the show. Chapman, in the car, was adding detail to the main quotes Cerrone had made for the column. By the time he reached the building on Broad Street, it was all in his head, just waiting for him to spill it out onto the paper. Chapman had never felt this good before. He was on the right side in this war. He was with the white liberals, the black community, the black clergy, and the media for sure. Chapman, with the vehicle that was his tri-weekly column, was at the center of it. This was his world. This was his city. It had always kind of bothered him that he didn't exactly fit with other blacks, particularly Philadelphia's poor blacks. But now it was this educated black man who was the spokesman for the people. He had been in Center City just the other day, and the spirit there reminded him of the Civil Rights rallies in the sixties. There were registration booths all over Center City. There was a registration booth every two blocks. These booths had signs calling them exactly what they were — "Dump Cerrone Stations." There was one lady he saw, a big, blonde, Amazon holding a sign that read "Impeach Cerrone." Chapman, until now, in an odd and sort of sad way, never really felt comfortable about his being educated. His education, in a way, had sort of alienated him from his people, at least many in the inner city that he cared most about. He was demonstrating how powerful an education could be, and that was the best part of his being. He was leading by example, and now it was directly because of that education that he was in the spotlight and why Cerrone and the other lame duck politicians in his administration feared him.

Chapman was the voice. He was the champion of the underrepresented black community. He was like Jackie Wilson ... Mr. Excitement ... Yeah, baby! His column that appeared on the Philadelphia streets the next day was its usual 800 words, but the title of the column, which was just two lines, said it all:

"Register and vote as if your life
Depends on it ... cuz it does."

CHAPTER 10

In 1978, South Philadelphia was a very old neighborhood, from its houses to its bakeries, candy stores, diners, and restaurants, many of which had been around so long they had earned "institution" status. Since South Philly was virtually devoid of tree or leaf, there wasn't a thing to remind you of newness, rebirth, spring, or anything like that. But the sense of oldness in the neighborhood was mostly due to the large number of senior citizens who lived there. Many of them had been a part of the vast immigration into this country in the early twentieth century. Although they were well into advanced age now, they still congregated en masse at the local recreation centers. They played pinochle and bocce. They talked about numbers that they had hit thirty years ago like it was yesterday, or they talked about the "Whiz Kids," the Phillies who won the pennant in 1950. Also, an unusually high number of Yankee fans lived in South Philadelphia because of the many great Yankee players of Italian descent. They included, not only Joe DiMaggio, but also people like Phil Rizzuto, Joe Pepitone, Yogi Berra or Billy Martin.

While most of the working inner-city whites in Philadelphia seemed to be actively pursuing the American dream, which was essentially to move to the gracious suburbs, it differed in South Philadelphia. There, the dream was to put a new front on your house or to make a gleaming second kitchen in your basement. If South Philadelphians moved at all, the upward mobility was to further south, past Snyder Avenue, maybe even south of Oregon

Avenue where the homes were newer and had small front lawns, driveways, and backyards with grills. It didn't matter how successful you became. South Philadelphia residents were South Philadelphia residents — period. Some of the best marble and brickwork in the city on the fronts of houses was found here, especially south of Snyder Avenue. The other upwardly mobile option was to go west to South Philadelphia's classy Girard Estates neighborhood where Chicka-dee had lived.

Every other year, the South Philadelphia boys had a reunion. They talked about the days when they had basketball and half-ball leagues and the struggles they had in the first few decades in this country. The reunion participants numbered in the hundreds, and people, including celebrities, came from all over the country. South Philadelphians were particularly proud of the many celebrities who grew up in their neighborhood. They would gladly drive you around to show you where Bobby Rydell, Frankie Avalon, Mario Lanza, or some other famous person once lived. They might show you where Joe the Boss, who ran the Philadelphia crime family before Constantine, had lived, or they might take you to "Cerrone Street," near Fifteenth, which was the local unofficial name for the narrow block on which the mayor had grown up.

It was a unique place where everybody knew the name of their block captain, congressman, and state senator. Everybody supported the police, their church, and the neighborhood. They had these old-world customs such as *La Serenada*, when local singers and musicians would serenade a young woman from outside her house on the eve of her wedding day. You could still find, at this point in this the late 1970s, an old Italian woman who could free you from "the horns" or *malocchio*, a type of curse an enemy put on you.

That was the South Philadelphia that Bah-Bah grew up in. Now, however, organized crime was disrupting all that niceness and old worldliness. Change was coming to the "eternal neighborhood." BahBah had lived here his entire life and had never even considered going anywhere else. Now he couldn't wait to leave.

Bah-Bah met Bobby Santore at Chief's Pool Room, a few blocks from Rose's house, that Monday morning. This was a well-known South Philadelphia establishment across from the famous Ambrose Diner. It was the spot where local pool hero Anthony Fusco upset the legendary Minnesota Fats. The place was given over to young hustlers and thieves at night, but during the day, it was a type of social club for senior citizens. A pinochle game was in progress as an old man called Cheech sat alone in a corner, his cheeks furiously working to resuscitate a dead cigar.

Constantine was instrumental in obtaining Bobby a sweet job as a judge's "personal." At least, Bah-Bah told Torch that Constantine was behind it somehow. He had booked sports at night for somebody connected to Constantine. Bobby said that his day-job with the city was just "too easy." Bobby said that city work was "where the work ethic goes to die." He wasn't raised that way, and after a while, it got to where he couldn't stand it anymore. He felt guilty thinking of his brick-laying, immigrant grandfather and his hard-working father who ran a grocery store. It bothered him that he was wasting, he believed, the good workexample passed on to him by his forefathers, as well as the strong work ethic instilled by both his parents. He was blessed, and he knew he had the potential to do better or, at least, do *more*. Eventually he parlayed his two incomes and now was the legit owner of one the better Italian restaurants in South Philly. He wore a suit. He did most days, even when he was off. He was a fitness guy, but still looked forty-five at thirty-five with specks of gray hair.

They left the poolroom together and walked across the street to Texas Weiner's for an early lunch. Bah-Bah ordered the surf and turf, which was a hot dog on a roll and a fish cake on another separate roll. Bobby ordered a "combo," which was a hot dog and fish cake on the same roll.

Bah-Bah explained to Bobby that he was closing up his office in the northeast. He told his people to call in as many outstanding debts as possible in the next few weeks, and then he was letting everybody go. The leases on the houses they used in both Center City and in the northeast ran through December. Nevertheless, Bah-Bah was prepared to accept any losses he might sustain from this move. It was just too risky given the recent turn of events. He explained to Bobby that he was going to move up to Logan. He was going to run a one-man booking and loan-sharking operation from there. Plus, he still was going to have Torch's numbers business in Center City, if Torch could ever get that rolling again.

"Logan?" Bobby asked. "That's up in North Philly, isn't it?"

"Way up there, yeah."

"That's all *tuttsoons*, isn't it?"

"That's the point. I figure nobody will bother me up there. As far as anybody else is going to know, I am an employee at an auto supply place up on State Road. I'm even on the books up there. The house I bought is a dynamite set up. Got the place for one dollar."

"Isn't that where the 'sinking homes' are?"

"That's only one section of Logan. The sinking homes start about five blocks from where this house is. Besides, like I said, I bought the house for a dollar, so I'm not really worried about that. The house has been abandoned for years. Torch is from up there, and he told me about it. He said the house is in good shape because four or five squatters live there and take care of it. These are Irish kids, Torch's friends. He said the house is sort of a hang-out or something. He told me a drug dealer lives next door, and in all those years, if the house needed any maintenance, he took care of it. I thought a lot about this move. If they can do what they did to Chick-a-dee, they wouldn't hesitate coming after me or anybody on my payroll."

Bah–Bah asked Bobby about Camden Snake and it turned out that Bobby was familiar with the horse as well as the race in question. Originally, Bah-Bah thought he had to pay off about $4,000. Actually, when he calculated everything, including money they'd bet on "place," it was closer to five grand. Bah-Bah said he thought the race was fixed. Bobby thought that claim was interesting. He had been at Keystone that day.

"It sure looked like a fixed race," Bobby said. "I mean, Camden Snake had a right to win, I guess. He has some early speed, but he is so cheap; I couldn't rationalize betting him in that spot. I mean, he had been struggling with rock-bottom claimers, and suddenly they moved him way up in class. That's why he paid so much. They brought in a girl jockey nobody ever heard of to ride the horse. That also helped his odds significantly. She sat behind the field, and the pace up front was extremely fast, as I remember. The race broke down, and she slipped Camden Snake along the inside and won easy. The rail was very fast that day, but in that particular race, the other jockeys didn't seem to want it. I'm not saying it was fixed, but it looked like it. Everything went in his favor. It was like they were air mailing him home. When he won at those whopping odds, I wanted to kick myself in the ass because, like I said, he showed speed in the past. He has talent but a heart the size of a pea, and when I took a second look at *The Racing Form*, I felt better. It's easy to say one thing after the race is over, but the truth is I never could have bet him against that group. I remember the race well. You don't think those ham-N-eggers could fix a race, do you?"

"No, of course not, but I think they heard something. They didn't tell me because they figured I'd lay the bets off at the track, and plus with betting it myself, it would hurt the odds. So they just kept it on ice. That wasn't right. Yeah, I would have bet on the horse, but I could have laid all of it off elsewhere. It wouldn't have hurt them to tell me."

If the race *was* fixed, it wouldn't be the first time at Keystone. The place was so shady even Las Vegas didn't take bets from there, and that wasn't common. It was on the up and up as much as mountain climbing, though compared to its neighbor and harness-racing counterpart Liberty Bell. The Bell was a racetrack awash in corruption. It eventually became a place that seemed to exist only for gangsters until it went out of business in the early eighties. Both had more food, the specialty, Texas-tommies. They featured this brown secret sauce and these specially made little rolls. Nobody ever went to Texas Wieners without eating a lot more than they originally planned to. Bah-Bah had been going there since the late fifties when they were down the street toward Broad, next to what used to be the Mario Lanza museum. Even with soft drinks, the bill was less than $20 for the whole shootin' match, and Bah-Bah gladly picked up the check.

He had been extremely cautious since that fateful Friday night. He knew it was only a matter of time until somebody found out that he was booking out of his grandmother's house. He would be out of South Philadelphia within a couple days, and until then, he wasn't taking any chances. This morning, on the way back from Chief's, he stopped at the newsstand at Broad and Snyder and bought the *Daily News, The Inquirer*, and two soft pretzels. It was a newsstand where *The Daily Racing Form* nearly outsold *The Philadelphia Inquirer*.

When he got back to Rose's, Bah-Bah read the Inquirer. By then, Chick-a-dee's funeral arrangements were disclosed. Gangsters in Philadelphia almost always were laid out in one of two places. Chicka-dee was going to the Luccia Brothers Funeral Home. It was the same funeral home where Constantine and Gino had had their funerals. The second of the two places was a few blocks further south on Broad Street. That particular funeral home was also run by two brothers, one of whom had been a regular at the Zigonette games at Bah-Bah's house when he was a kid. Luccia Brothers was the older of the two establishments, and the older gangsters went there, while the younger gangsters seemed to prefer the other place.

Bah-Bah was still deciding which one he wanted to go to.

The blast that killed Chick-a-dee, according to the paper, was apparently activated by a remote detonator. One article said that the bomb went off just as Chick-a-dee walked onto his porch. Apparently, the bomb was embedded in a small brick wall that was on his porch. It didn't say, but Bah-Bah wondered if the culprit rang the doorbell first, then blew up the porch just as Chick-a-dee went out to answer the door. It sounded like it, and somehow it fit. The whole thing sounded very strange to Bah-Bah. It all made him think of the "Land Shark" bit on *Saturday Night Live*. Chick-a-dee lived in a corner house, and the blast was so powerful that bricks, stones, and other debris landed in the park across the street. The house next to Chick-a-dee's had its front windows blown out. It wasn't very clear, but apparently, an elderly woman who lived in that house was asleep upstairs when it happened. A teenager on the block was questioned about the incident.

"These guys are into gambling. What's that, a little gambling, so what," he said. Then when asked about how terrible it was that innocent people were put in jeopardy, the kid replied, "Well, the person who was most at risk was the woman next door, and she was old."

The reporter asked if the boy was saying that it didn't matter if they were innocent victims because they were old.

"No, I'm not saying that," the kid replied. "I'm just saying, you know, they probably figured that, since the people next door were old, they wouldn't wake up or something."

As usual, when a gangland murder occurred, there were quotes from the same "local organized crime experts." George Anastasia was Philadelphia's foremost mob-watcher who would go on to write books and novels in the eighties centering primarily on Moscariello's mob. Today, as a reporter working for *the Inquirer*, he wrote, "The specter of organized crime hangs like a dark, menacing cloud over the casinogambling industry. This, despite the most stringent regulations in the world."

Even the governor of New Jersey was quoted in the piece. "It's naïve to think that organized crime won't try to move in on this bonanza." That statement by the governor seemed to be much milder than the statement he had made in 1977 immediately after the referendum passed to legalize gambling in Atlantic City. At that time, he had said, "I'm telling organized crime, 'Keep your greasy hands out of Atlantic City.'"

Anastasia quoted another expert mob-watcher as saying, "Gambling has historically attracted organized crime like sharks seeing blood on the water. The mob seeks to prey on the millions of dollars in cold hard cash that flows through the casinos." Then Anastasia added, "Right now, it looks like the sharks are fighting among themselves."

In another article related to this topic, another mob expert said, "The local mob is in pieces." He talked about the five or six mobsters who had died in the aftermath of Constantine's death the previous year, as well as a large labor union leader who was friendly with Constantine, who was killed at his Northeast Philadelphia home.

"Now it's just a matter of waiting to see which New York crime family moves in to pick up the pieces." That statement fit in with yet another story headlined: Next Boss Will Have New York Mailing Address.

Bah-Bah had his doubts about that. Within twenty-four hours of the incident, Bah-Bah heard who the guilty parties were, but he was skeptical of the information he received. The rumor was that the hit man was a local nineteen-year old whose father Bah-Bah had been friendly with. Bah-Bah had, in fact, even been to the boy's christening. This certainly wasn't the work of a high-level imported New York hit man. Yet, he couldn't believe that this nineteen-year old, who no one had ever heard of, was given such an important contract. This is who they picked to kill the under boss of the great Constantine and friend of Sinatra? A punk who played Doorbell Dixie and blew the Godfather sky high? BahBah couldn't believe it. It fit somehow, though, indicative of this overall craziness. The other thing was this clearly was the work of amateurs. It sounded more like the kind of brazen act the Scorpions might engineer.

Bah-Bah then ate his second breakfast of the day. It was a piece of cantaloupe with a slice of prosciutto across the top of it. South Philadelphia had the best prosciutto in the city. It featured a certain rough, salty texture to it, and the saltiness against the sweetness of the fruit was what made it another of Bah-Bah's favorites. His mother used to serve it to him and told Bah- Bah that they ate that particular dish at the JFK White House, but he didn't know about that.

He had a lot of paperwork to do every Monday. Mondays, of course, started a new week, so he not only had to do the previous day's work, but also had to consult his master sheet to determine each customer's final figure. He had to prepare the new master sheet with the name of each customer at the top, all separated with the help of a ruler. He also had to prepare his nightly "sheets" for the week. He had the *Daily News* open to the box scores. The *News* had the best box scores in the city for the simple fact that it came out later and had the scores from the West Coast which, of course, were necessary. During the baseball season, you had to see who the pitchers were since a few players from time to time would "specify" a certain pitcher. It was frequently necessary to see who the starters were to accurately determine how much a certain customer won or lost on a game.

After Bah–Bah completed his paperwork, he called his brother-in-law. He was told that he could pick up the deed to the abandoned house on Thursday from a notary public on North Broad Street up in Logan. The digital clock on Rose's kitchen cabinet indicated it was eleven o'clock.

★ ★ ★

Three blocks west of Rose's house, Police Officer Ed Kelly sat in his own car across from the Ambrose Diner. His partner, Jim Kelly, who Ed called "Jimbo," sat inside the diner, at the counter, drinking coffee. The two were called the "Kelly Brothers" often, although they weren't related at all. They simply shared Ireland's most common surname. They had been partners for many years, and since they looked similar, at least, in the respect that they each had blue eyes and sandy hair. Naturally they were often mistaken for brothers.

They had worked together originally five years ago on the security team at Keystone Racetrack and then joined the police force together. Following a short stint as partners in South Philadelphia, they were transferred up into Germantown's 14th District. Together, they transferred eighteen months ago back to South Philadelphia. The Kellys, along with another cop from South Philly and a few others in North Philadelphia, had shaken down drug rings, gambling operations, massage parlors, and other illegal activities. It was essentially a variation of Moscariello's "elbow." These types of extortions were similar, both Moscariello and the dirty cops conveniently preyed on victims who couldn't go to the police for help. It was all dirty money anyhow, so they saw nothing wrong with helping themselves to some of it. Together, the Kelly brothers had ripped off nearly $80,000. Ed was the more sinister of the two. He was five years older, and he was the senior partner. It was he who saw that there was easy money to be made from the monumental graft that was around. That was why they wanted to transfer to South Philadelphia. North Philly was small time. They had been reduced to raiding cock fights and crap games for Christ's sake! Jim Kelly didn't feel right about the whole cock-fight business. That was a cultural thing. He didn't want to bother the Puerto Rican bastards. Besides which, what the hell did Ed think they were going to get anyway? Jim Kelly didn't feel very comfortable busting some numbers joint either. This was Ed's idea, too. Jimbo thought it was best to stick to ripping off dealers; that was where they made their biggest scores, and by dealers, he didn't mean marijuana dealers. There were other projects on the horizon, including a Center City-based coke and meth dealer named Sam the Blade. He had money, was vulnerable, and was unconnected to anybody, at least, anybody significant. They tried to contact him by sending him a letter. They wanted to scare him a little. They certainly didn't want to frighten the Jew bastard so much that he would fold his hand. Their intention was to simply make contact and deal with him. They only wanted maybe $200 or $300 a week. Blade was a mouse; both Kelly's knew him from when they worked security at Keystone Racetrack. He wasn't a bad guy with all his baseball trivia questions and movie trivia. They would put it to him like it was a two-way business deal, like they were offering protection which, of course, they weren't.

At any rate, it was the "under-the-table" business, not police business, which brought them to the Ambrose Diner this morning.

Across the counter from Jim Kelly, polishing off a bacon-andegg breakfast was a twenty-two-year-old disco dancer named Rickie Pasquariello. He wore an orange "fly" shirt with an 8-ball on the front of it and a rack of pool balls on the back. He also wore, just like every other kid from South Philadelphia wore then, a gold dog tag with his name stenciled into it. The young man was doomed, and everybody in the neighborhood knew it. A few Saturday nights ago, the tattooed, mustachioed young man was in an alleged mob-run disco around the corner called "The Roman Gardens". It was a unique structure, originally a church that was transformed into the disco. On paper, The Roman Gardens was owned by local talented singer Sonny Rago. He was the premier Frank Sinatra sound-alike who performed his songs headlining mainly down Atlantic-City both before and after the casino boom. Frank Sinatra Jr. had performed there a few times which was saying something. The real owner of "The Roman Garden's" many said was Angelo Constantine.

Pasquariello and a friend of his got into a fight in the club over a woman. Or at least a girl was involved somehow. The details were sketchy, but a girl had been hit in the face during the brawl. Two Bouncers were on the scene and broke the fight up. Then Pasquariello pulled a gun and shot both employees of the club. One was seriously wounded and the other was mortally wounded, dying a few hours later in a South Philadelphia Hospital. Pasquariello and his friend fled the scene in a black Monte Carlo. The other man was heard to say something like "I'm glad you shot the s.o.b." Soon Pasquariello was arrested and was currently out on bail. From what everybody was saying, he would never make it to trial. The deceased bouncer was a connected guy under Constantine. Or at least he was a friend of Constantine and company and Pasquariello was a marked man because of some bullshit attached to how Constantine's men had to save face. It was like they were pretending this situation was important, which it really wasn't in light of more pressing problems that Constantine's family had at the moment. The Kelly Brothers saw this as an opening to get back into action. In the past six months, the entire unholy team had decided to lay low.

It was Ed Kelly who had to put Reds down in the house on Wellens Street up in Logan. It wasn't supposed to be that way at all. First of all, they had bad information. That guy up there, Danny Parker, was supposed to be a major pot guy, a "weight" guy. When Jimbo saw that cheap-ass scale and those tiny sandwich baggies, he knew they'd fucked up. Unfortunately, though, it was too late by then, things were in motion and they couldn't back out of it. They got no cash whatsoever and a grand total of one-and-a-half ounces of pot which was only worth about $60 and they gave it away to a hooker/snitch they had. For that, they had to lay low all this time. Reds had been a star basketball player at Cardinal Dougherty High School when Ed Kelly too started for North Catholic. Ed Kelly was only on the squad one year and only played Daugherty twice (home-away). Reds didn't seem to recognize Ed Kelly, but Ed Kelly recognized him and couldn't take a chance.

The whole situation up there in Logan and what happened up there that day, both saddened and embarrassed Ed Kelly. Ed Kelly worked hard on this type of thing, His partner, Jimbo, always admired Eddie for his attention to details. That was why he was the boss of this partnership. The truth was that Ed Kelly had stalked this Danny Parker character for weeks, both on and off duty. Danny was a sharp dresser of medium build and looked in the face to Kelly like a young version of Charles Manson. The two men even once had a conversation in the Warnock Bar. And it wasn't like the Kellys didn't know that there would be others in the house. They did know. It was just that Ed Kelly never got a close look at reds until that day and simply didn't recognize him until they were all in the living room. Other than this major fuck-up, the plan was going smoothly. Kelly thought he covered all the bases. On the morning of the move, there were two small customers supposed to make a buy. One was named Shine, who Kelly knew and another was called 'Torch' who he was also vaguely familiar with. Ed had these two intercepted on the way, locked up for a bogus and ridiculous 'suspicion of a purse snatching' charge. They were held at the 53rd district for a few hours. The idea was to prevent these two nobodies from arriving at the scene of the crime and messing up the whole thing. Now there was this situation...

Inside the diner at the counter wearing his regulation Philadelphia police uniform, Jim Kelly crossed his massive forearms with tattoos of serpents wrapped around them and watched Rickie Pasquarello eat. Jim Kelly, unlike Ed, was thinking more along the lines of a long-term payment plan in this case, rather than the cold-blooded rip-off that Ed Kelly preferred. Ed Kelly had convinced his younger partner that his long-term idea wasn't possible. This had to be a quick, one-shot deal. The business was numbers. Ed learned that Pasquariello worked in one of Constantine's big numbers banks in the area. He hoped to find the whereabouts of this bank and then rip them off. Ed was convinced that Constantine's business would soon be obsolete. That was why he was so certain that a one-shot rip-off was the way to go in this case.

Jim had plans for his future that didn't involve Philadelphia. He loved Denver and had family out there. He planned to steal enough money by the time he was thirty-five to retire to Denver. Then he would be courtside at the Denver Nuggets games, watching his favorite basketball player, David Thompson, the original sky walker.

The Ambrose was yet another South Philadelphia institution just like Chief's or Texas Wieners. It was a microcosm of the neighborhood, more so than even the other places. The customers never changed; the menu never changed. The teenagers liked to order by number, that was what the kool kids did. For instance, a bacon-cheeseburger was an "S-3". It was S-3 thirty years ago, and it was now, and it would still be that in the twenty-first century. Even the prices \ the menu hadn't changed very much. The waitresses didn't change either, and each one had a name-tag on their uniform with a star on it. Inside the star was a number indicating how many years they had worked there … eighteen years … twenty-two years … twenty-seven years. And the food was consistently good. Eating establishments in South Philly had to be good because they weren't only competing with other food joints but also everybody's mother and grandmother. At the counter, Jim Kelly, in his police uniform, drank his coffee and read *The Daily News*, turning to the story by John Chapman on Cerrone. Chapman, as usual, was bashing Jim Kelly's hero, but Kelly got a kick out of the way the man wrote.

"Can you call it progress when the city, founded by William Penn, ennobled by Ben Franklin, and enshrined by Thomas Jefferson, is now

governed by Jimmy Cerrone? Then Chapman talked about last night's televised show in which Cerrone appeared.

Rickie knew Kelly was watching him finish his breakfast. That was fine with Kelly. That was the plan. Once this cement head realized that submitting himself to police was his only shot, then it would be easier for the Kellys to do their thing. Ideally, after they befriended him, the young man would tell them things about the large numbers bank and the overall business. Of course, the boy didn't know that the long-range plan was to murder him, make it look like gangsters affiliated with Constantine were responsible, and then discard his body over in the Pinelands of New Jersey where his soul could mingle with that of the Jersey Devil.

Jim finished his coffee and walked out of the diner. He went across the street and got in the passenger side of his partner's new 1978 beige Coronet. The street was on the rim of the Ambrose parking lot. They kept their eyes on the vestibule of the diner. One could exit the Ambrose two ways. You could turn right onto Snyder Avenue or left onto Passyunk Avenue. Either way, you had to come into the vestibule. They couldn't miss him from their vantage point.

Ed was a music lover of a very diverse nature. His favorite group, by far, was the Rolling Stones, and he always talked about seeing them when they came to Philadelphia back in the sixties for the first time.

"Mick looked right at me," Ed always said. "'Jumpin' Jack Flash' was their first song."

Yet right now, as he did every weekday at eleven o'clock, Ed Kelly listened to Bob Craig's Solid Hour of Sinatra. He didn't start work that day until four o'clock and, at the moment, was dressed in blue Dungarees and a red, white, and blue Steve Mix 76ers Jersey.

"What's it look like in there?" Ed asked Jim when he sat next to him in the car.

"It looks like he doesn't have a care in the world. He's flipping through the songs on the jukebox and singing. He doesn't seem to be worried at all. You know, his father knows people. Maybe he got this all straightened out or something."

Ed shook his head. "His father is one of those guys who knows everybody and nobody."

Jim knew exactly what Ed was talking about. Ed grew up in South Philadelphia, and he explained the situation to Jimbo when they worked there before, "This neighborhood is full of people who think or act like they have connections. And they buy a Cadillac and play this part for so many years; they eventually really believe it themselves. His father is in the bar supply business, so he probably ran up against it over the years, but right now with all the craziness, it wasn't enough. I mean, from what I heard he tried, don't get me wrong, he tried.

"Everything is disorganized right now. Maybe if Constantine or even Chick-a-dee were around, then it could be worked out. But from what I understand, this is like a big important thing, not to let this guy slide as if anybody gives a shit about him. It's too bad, but to be honest with you, I haven't heard one positive thing about this kid. I mean, I get the impression he was never well liked to begin with. That might be part of it, too. Plus, maybe they think that Moscariello's people are waiting to see what happens here."

"You think so?" Jim asked.

"No, I don't think so at all. It's all dago, macho bullshit is what I think."

Sinatra sang "Street of Dreams."

Love laughs at a king
Kings don't mean a thing
On the street of dreams
Dreams broken in two Can be made like new
On the street of dreams

"This reminds me of Chick-a-dee, ya' know 'Kings don't mean a thing.' They don't mean a damn thing," Jimbo said.

"It always reminds me of the first time I saw Sinatra. I was with my father in Atlantic City. It wasn't a concert; it was a fundraiser put on by the democrats for Hubert Humphrey in '68. Sinatra was there. He sang three or four songs. This was one of them. But, yeah,

I can see where it would make you think of Chick or Constantine for that matter.

"Speaking of Chick-a-dee," Ed Kelly continued, "there was something funny about that murder. I have my doubts about this, but I heard that the Scorpions may have had something to do with it. And frankly, the way he was killed makes you wonder. The Scorpions have manufactured the meth around Philly since the sixties. They had this benevolent relationship with Constantine, and that was fine. They don't have that working relationship with Moscariello and never will. The theory is that the meth trade is up for grabs now or will be very soon anyway. The Scorpions hope to move Chick-a -dee and company out before Moscariello's mob does, and eventually the Scorpions can run it exclusively."

Jim Kelly looked at the handful of 8-track tapes that Ed had in the console between the seats. The 8-tracks included two Rolling Stones albums and *Positively Lou* by Lou Rawls, and *Aphrodisiac* by the Main Ingredient. There was also an 8-track by West Philadelphia's Trammps.

Jim had a very limited knowledge of music. He was a Philadelphia street musician (a mummer). His group, the Greater Kensington String Band, along with hundreds of other Mummers, marched up Broad Street every New Year's Day. To Jim Kelly, the Mummers were a religion. It was, in no particular order, the Mummers, Rocky, God, guts, guns, the Eagles, and Jimmy Cerrone. Jim Kelly's favorite song was probably a song like "Dem Golden Slippers." It was almost a religious hymn to Jimbo. His string bands spent $40,000 on their feathers and the outfits they wore — all to win a grand prize of $15,000. That was how the Mummers were, and they wouldn't change it for anything. It was a Philadelphia Tradition started here in South Philadelphia. In the early eighties, Greater Kensington would win the award for best string band. A few years ago, Jimbo himself won an award for the best original costume when he dressed as a vegetable garden, a rip-off of a contestant on the show *Let's Make a Deal* which Kelly saw in the 1960s.

"You know what Sinatra song I like?" Jim Kelly said. "'Something Stupid.' Do you know that one?"

"'Something Stupid' by Sinatra?" Ed said. "Let me see, Sinatra sang a lot of stupid songs. How about 'Old McDonald,' 'The French Foreign Legion,' 'Mac the Knife' or 'Mrs. Robinson,' or how about 'The Coffee Song'? That was pretty stupid."

"No, I mean 'Something Stupid' is the name of the song ... 'Something Stupid.'"

"I know the song, I'm only kiddin'. It's a duet with Nancy Sinatra. I used to have the 45. 'Sugar Town' was on the flip side, I think."

"Is that right?" Jim remarked although he was fairly sure he didn't remember "Sugar Town." "Sinatra sang 'Mrs. Robinson'?" Jim asked. "That's right. 'Mrs. Robinson,' the Simon and Garfunkel song.

Sinatra sang that song, too. He butchered it, but he sang it." "I never heard Sinatra sing that," Jim remarked.

"You aren't missing anything. Yeah, they play a live version of the song. At the end of it, Sinatra say, 'Keep those cards and letters coming.' I never knew what that meant. Then about two weeks ago, I was listening to 'Friday with Frank' with Sid Mark. Apparently Simon and Garfunkel had sent Sinatra a letter expressing their displeasure at Sinatra massacring their signature song. You know Sinatra could be a ball-breaker sometimes, and he didn't appreciate them doing that. That's what Sinatra meant when he said that."

"And I like 'The Coffee Song.'"

"Can you explain that to me?" asked Ed with mock concern. "You know I heard Sid Mark say that 'The Coffee Song" is one of the most requested songs on his show. I'll never understand that."

Then Ed started singing a few off-key lines from "The Coffee Song":

"Man they got some coffee
A whole lot of coffee
They got a gang of coffee
In Brazillllllllll"

Inside the diner, Rickie Pasquariello played some more songs on the miniature, individual jukebox on the counter and sipped another cup of coffee. A song of his screamed out. It was a disco anthem by Philadelphia's Sister Sledge:

(I wonder … wow)
he's the greatest dancer
(I wonder … won)
that I've ever seen.

When the song had ended, Pasquariello walked into the bathroom.

Across the street in the coronet, an uneasiness was setting in. It hit them both at the same moment that it was taking a long time for this idiot to finish his breakfast.

"Did you ever think about robbing this place?" Jim said.

"Are you crazy?" Ed answered.

"No, I wouldn't do it, but I'm just saying. On a Friday or Saturday night, all them rich Jewish and Italian kids, all high on 'lude's, all that jewelry. The place is a gold mine."

"Forget it. Believe me, you'd never get out of South Philly," Ed said. "From what I hear, between you and me, bent noses own this place."

Just as Ed said that, he who should have known better, was struck by a very unpleasant thought. He looked over at his partner who seemed to have the same notion.

"I should go back in there," Jimbo said.

"Let's give it five more minutes."

They waited five minutes, then ten more minutes after that. The Solid Hour of Sinatra was over.

The Kelly brothers entered the Ambrose together. The boy wasn't at the counter. Ed Kelly checked the men's room. Jimbo even went back into the kitchen. The punk had vanished. When the staff and the customers were later questioned, nobody saw anything. He would never be seen alive again. Kelly Brothers Inc. Had fucked up again apparently. The young man had been like a chicken walking into Colonel Sanders, and he never even knew it.

CHAPTER 11

I t was Wednesday afternoon when the body of Ricky Pasquariello was found in a densely wooded area in the New Jersey Pinelands. The boy had had his ears pierced, a bullet behind each one. A Philadelphia detective was quoted in the paper saying that the corpse was "a little too neat." He said that Pasquariello was no doubt killed elsewhere. Philadelphia, they suspected, then dumped in New Jersey. The actual location of the remains was in a spot directly across the river from South Philadelphia. He was not the first or the last to be killed in Philadelphia, then relocated to or buried in New Jersey. It was why they said the tomatoes tasted so much better just across the river. The young man had been identified by his tattoo's including one of a small red devil. The article stated that Pasquariello had a long record including an extensive juvenile record. He was known to traffic in firearms and allegedly could fill big orders.

When Torch called in the work that Thursday, he and Bah-Bah talked about the murder. Bah-Bah told Torch that the killers had used two different guns of two different calibers. That prevented one shooter from blaming it entirely on the other one, he explained. That was how it was usually done — two guns, two different calibers, at least, according to Bah-Bah.

"It's like on Kojak or one of those shows. If two shooters are involved, and there almost always are, they'll get one guy along and make him a deal. They'll say they'll pin it all on the other shooter if he agrees to testify, and he can plead out to a lesser charge. It doesn't really make a lot of sense, but the suspect is scared and probably not that bright to begin with, so he goes along with it to save himself. The detectives will tell him they know he was probably just along for the ride, and they'll testify that the other guy was the actual shooter. But if two guns are used, it's impossible to say he wasn't the actual shooter. It deters somebody from informing, because, once a man makes that decision, it isn't a long jump for him to start tell other stories to improve his personal deal with law enforcement. That's why if it's two shooters, they'll use different caliber guns."

Torch wondered if Bah-Bah knew for sure or was just assuming that they used two different types of guns. He never read anything about it one way or the other in the paper. He assumed that ballistics probably was sophisticated enough to determine if two different guns were used. He didn't see what different calibers really had to do with it. Then again, he didn't know for sure. He would have to ask Maria because she was the one who hung around cops and knew all about different ammunitions, calibers, and all that. She had two guns. One was a cheap one she kept in the house. She had a better one in her locker at the diner. She said the gun was "homemade," whatever that was. She said, if you carried a gun, to make sure it was a good or expensive one. That way, she said, if a cop caught you with it, he wouldn't arrest you because he'd want the gun for himself. If he arrested you, he'd have to turn the gun in. She said that you were going to lose the gun anyway, whether he turned it in or not. That was both the beginning and end of what Torch knew about firearms. The only time he ever fired a gun was one day up on the tracks with Felix.

Bah-Bah arranged to meet Torch at Maria's house at three o'clock. That would give him time to meet a few people he had to see up in the northeast. He drove his white 1966 Cadillac along 1-95, past Center City, up into the Northeast. He would have to see about a half-dozen customers today. He called these people his "Jewish Contingent," and he would do a lot more business with them during the basketball season this winter. Bah-Bah didn't have a lot of cash on him at the moment, so he mapped out a strategy in his head where he would first meet with the losers for the week, then rendezvous with the guys he had to pay off. Then he planned to ride down Roosevelt Boulevard to Logan and pick up the deed to the house, the one that Torch kept referring to, for some reason, as Caesar's Palace.

"Hot Rod Lincoln" by Commander Cody was on the radio.

Bah-Bah made his exit off 1-95 directly across from Holmesburg Prison. It looked like an old-fashioned, dungeon-like place in which James Cagney, George Raft, or one of those guys in the old movies would be jailed. The place gave Bah-Bah the chills just driving by it. He had himself spent few days in the detention center one time. He had been caught with a gun which he obtained from his crazy brother. His brother made a few losing bets and couldn't pay, so Bah-Bah took his firearm. It turned out that the gun had a history to it, though Bah-Bah never learned what it was exactly. He had to wait a few days until Constantine, as a favor to Gino, had the detainer lifted.

Early that morning, Torch had driven Maria to Einstein Hospital. Lee Oskar had stayed, once again, over at his grandmother's house last night. Then apparently, in the middle of the night, the boy developed breathing problems and had been driven to the hospital by one of Maria's brothers. The situation was stable after a few hours. The boy had been through worse than this in the past. His asthma attacks seemed to come less frequently as he got older. These days, they came only in the summer. The doctor told Maria that the climate and smog of Philadelphia contributed to the problem. Torch stayed with Maria at the hospital at Broad and Olney in Logan until about ten o'clock when he drove her to the North Star Diner where she was working the lunch shift starting at eleven o'clock.

At 12:45, Torch and his boys were playing pinochle on Maria's enclosed porch at her house. It was Torch and Frenchie against Felix and Jackie. They all drank iced tea that Torch served, and they ate soft pretzels purchased by somebody from a blind vendor who worked under the bridge on Broad Street. Torch found a jar of cheap yellow mustard for the pretzels. When it came to soft pretzels, the cheaper and more yellow the mustard was, the better.

Torch and Frenchie had gone ahead temporarily, but Torch reneged and Felix caught him. After each hand there was the usual conversation or discussion, sort of a synopsis of the previous hand. Somebody would always say why they led an ace or a certain card, or what their strategy had been.

Team Frenchie stole a bid from Jackie's team and got closer to them. The next hand, Torch gave Frenchie a meld bid, and Frenchie had a powerful hand but no meld, so he took the bid. Frenchie expertly played out all the trump cards, which were clubs, and made his double ace and ten of diamonds unbeatable. Frenchie threw out the only two trump cards remaining, and his double ace and ten of diamonds and said, "Rub it on your chest. I got the rest."

Jerry Blavat was the disk jockey on the radio at that time. He was in the middle of a set of blue-eyed soul music. He played "Soul and Inspiration" by the Righteous Brothers and "Expressway to Your Heart" by Philadelphia's Soul Survivors.

* * *

Maria fed the cat that lived outside the diner. He was arguably the best fed stray in the world. Today Maria gave the feline tuna fish salad left over from the lunch rush. The cat was orange and named Scorpio. Another waitress, Roslyn, had found the cat and gave it that name. That was two Novembers ago. Roslyn's boyfriend Derrick, by the way, was a hard hitter in the Logan nation gang and, in fact, was in jail for a shooting at the moment. Torch believed that Maria and Roslyn's friendship was a key reason why nobody bothered him right here in Logan Nation country, even though everybody knew he was from Ben's. Roslyn had been fired about a year ago, and Maria had taken over the job of caring for the cat.

She kept the name (Scorpio), even though she didn't like it. It made her think of the maniac serial killer in the movie *Dirty Harry*, who was also called Scorpio. Maria usually fed the cat chicken salad, fish, and steak. The quality food was wasted on the animal who would eat virtually anything. Maria never saw a cat that liked

French fries for example. Not only did this one eat them, but like a dog, she snatched them out of the air when Maria threw them to her. Tossing one past her was like trying to hit a ground ball past Phillies shortstop Larry Bowa. Maria would have taken the cat home, but the doctor said it would aggravate Lee Oskar's breathing problems. In the winter, on the coldest of nights, the owner of the diner let Scorpio sleep in a back room near the kitchen. Maria thought the cat couldn't care less one way or the other.

During his tenure as mayor, Jimmy Cerrone had instituted what was known as "Code Blue" on the coldest of winter nights. The police in Center City, on these nights, were to round up all of the homeless on the streets and take them to shelters. The problem was that many of the homeless didn't want to go into the shelters. They said, or their advocates, said that Code Blue was unconstitutional. Maria believed Scorpio probably felt the same way and really was not bothered by sleeping outside. Nevertheless, Maria convinced the owner of the diner, a man named Gus, to allow Scorpio to remain inside on cold nights. It was a rule incidentally, that if you owned a diner or luncheonette in North Philadelphia, you had to be named Gus.

Maria had fought with Torch all day yesterday. His financial situation wasn't looking very good right now, and he seemed unconcerned about it, as if he were on a paid vacation. Maria wished sometimes that Torch had his steady job back with the City of Philadelphia again. Yet she had never nagged him before about the numbers business.

Now it appeared that, by Torch's own admission, the cash flow had diminished for a while. He still booked the steadies and had some other phone business, but that was less than half of his usual, overall ribbon. All he was doing these days was hanging around with his friends, playing pinochle or whatever it was, and going swimming over in New Jersey at some lake they had founded when they were kids. Maria assured Torch that he wasn't going to lounge around for long while she worked fulltime at the diner. She hadn't meant to sound like a nag, but it did come off that way. She was just trying to make Torch understand life a little bit and not to be so short-sighted. Maria said that, when Torch was forty-five years old, he would want to be able to say that he had twenty or twenty-five years in someplace and had a dependable pension.

Then she showed him *The Daily News* article written by Larry McMullen. He wrote about five or six middle-aged Philadelphia gangsters who used to fly under Constantine's flag. These were men who probably hadn't done an honest day's work in thirty years; nevertheless, they had nice houses and cars and fancy clothes and ate frequently in top-notch restaurants. These were men who were on top of their world. Now these same men were holed up in a basement apartment near the U.S. Mint in Center City, and there was no money coming in. They were unable to move about the city freely because they were worried about Moscariello's men. The story was brought to McMullen's attention by a cop he knew in that district. The cop said that a hot dog vendor working in that neighborhood had been extending this crew credit. The vendor, a Greek who once had a sandwich shop in South Philadelphia, had known the mobsters in the good times, and they had been good customers of his. The problem was that now the gang had run up a collective tab of $600 which they couldn't pay.

The way McMullen wrote the story was strong. He underlined the irony of the whole situation. McMullen made it clear that there was more to honest work than a steady paycheck. It was like Maria's father always said to her brothers: "An honest job with long hours keeps you grounded. It has the tendency to keep you out of trouble." Maria thought the column was an exaggerated example of precisely what her father was talking about. Torch tried to act like he failed to see the connection between the two things but he did. It bothered him, and he knew she had a point.

As for herself, Maria didn't see being a waitress as a permanent position. She understood she wasn't going to be a teacher or a doctor, but she was looking at other careers. During one summer, while in high school, she worked for Peltz Boxing Promotions, doing advertising, and publicizing fight cards to local promoters. It was the kind of unique job that she saw herself doing one day, probably in another city. Hopefully, when Lee Oskar's health problems, improved she would make her move and take Scorpio along, too, with or without Torch.

Torch didn't like thinking about the future, so it followed that her forcing him to be realistic and think about it would be bothersome to him. After that argument was over, Maria brought up the new problem of the TV sets. That caused the second round of the fight.

Felix and the others wanted to move the TV sets from Grant's house to Maria's house. Torch said it was logical because it could be done so easily. Felix's father used to work construction for the railroad. When he eventually went to work at Schmidt's Brewery, he, Felix and Felix's brother stole a hand cart which was used by railroad workers to transport them and their tools to various sections along the tracks. The hand cart was manipulated by two men operating a crank. They had used the hand cart in the first place to take the TV sets from behind Nate's Reliable to the back of Grant's house.

It was precisely the type of stupid and immature scheme Torch would bring up once in a while. Normally Maria let Torch have his way, but this was ridiculous. She told him again about her father. He used to tell her brothers that stolen goods were something you just didn't touch — period. You certainly didn't bring them into your house, not under any circumstances.

Torch was starting to get tired of hearing wisdom from Maria's father, and he said, "Who is your father? Confucius or somebody like that?" Maria let it go. She had made her point. If it was important to Torch to act like the boss or some tough guy, that was one thing, but he wasn't going to bring those TV sets into the house, and that was all there was to it. She didn't know who Confucius was or what he had to do with anything.

★ ★ ★

Bah-Bah arrived at two o'clock that afternoon and Torch made the introductions to everybody. Jackie had already met Bah-Bah once at Oscar's. Torch had told Jackie on that occasion, "Bah–Bah can do things for you. He put me on Front Street; he can do the same for you."

Of course, that was nostalgia. Torch didn't think getting Jackie involved with Bah–Bah was doing him any favors at this point. As far as the other two were concerned, Torch didn't trust them enough. He personally didn't worry about Felix, but he couldn't trust Felix enough not to burn Bah–Bah somehow, some way down the road maybe. Then he (Torch) would feel responsible if not libel in some way, and he didn't want to stick his neck out. As for Frenchie, Torch didn't trust him, period.

As always, when Bah–Bah was around, the first thing that came up was where they were going to eat. Frenchie had to see his probation officer who had a subdivision, the Northwest Division, right next to the Astor Diner where Maria worked. The plan was to swing by there, drop Frenchie off for a couple of minutes to see his P.O. to report in. Then they would go to Jericho Beef on Ogontz Avenue, where they would get the best chicken, ribs and potato salad not only in Logan, but anywhere in North Philadelphia. The specialty was these little rotisserie chickens that you could get with this red sauce slapped on with a paint brush. Then they would continue over to Caesar's Palace and have a feast. A part of Torch felt a little guilty because these weevils were already moving in on Bah–Bah's house. It was clear that the former inhabitants of Caesar's Palace were going to move in again, just like before, whether Bah–Bah owned the house or not. Somehow Torch thought that Bah–Bah was walking into a buzz saw, and it was partially Torch's fault. The truth was that Bah–Bah didn't want to live in that house or any other house around here anyway. That being the case, Torch didn't see why it had to be a problem for anybody. Also, Torch hoped to talk Bah–Bah into allowing them to transfer the TV sets that were now in Grant's house just next door to Caesar's Palace. Torch also hoped that Bah–Bah would sell some of the TV sets for them. Bah–Bah surely could do something like that. They would only have to give him maybe $100 for every TV he sold, and Bah–Bah would know how to get rid of them. Best of all, this would be done outside of the neighborhood and Washington would never know anything about it. This had all been discussed among them before BahBah arrived that afternoon. Torch figured that Bah-Bah wouldn't fully be settled in until early next week at the soonest, and they agreed to give Grant another TV, just for keeping the sets in his house until that time.

The five of them piled into Bah-Bah's Cadillac. Torch, being the only one that really knew Bah-Bah, sat in the front seat. They drove out to Lindley Avenue and made a left turn. They drove by Wakefield Park at 16th and Lindley. Bah-Bah could see that it wasn't a park like the ones in South Philly. This one had trees, squirrels, birds, valleys, and hills. Torch explained to Bah-Bah that this was the "countryside" of Logan, compared to the other side of Broad Street where the Warnock and Caesar's Palace were. When school was canceled because of snow, there would be fifty or sixty kids around here sledding down the giant hill at the far end of the park.

When Jimmy Cerrone left office, the following administrations made drastic cutbacks in the city's budget. They initially targeted the areas of recreation and park maintenance. Cerrone had paid a lot of attention to and always prided himself on allocating funds for recreation, wildlife, and that sort of thing. It had always been a strong suit of his. It was why many people in Logan — at least, this part of Logan — really missed Cerrone when he was gone, even though sometimes they were reluctant to admit it. Maybe in the long run, it didn't matter much, but when Cerrone finally ended his tenure, it seemed to be the beginning of the end in West Logan.

Immediately after the Cerrone administration, there were drastic cutbacks to city services. In the sixties and seventies, when Torch was growing up, giant street cleaning trucks would come by frequently. If you asked people who live here now about those trucks, nobody would even remember them. To them, such city services were sort of an urban myth. In the summer, when Logan School was closed, the giant schoolyard, which was the biggest in the city, was alive with activity. Softballs, bats, and gloves were provided for softball games in the schoolyard. Kids played on the swings, the small ones on the mini-swings, monkey bars, and the Maypole. Two or three games of chink (a handball game) went on simultaneously in the schoolyard, some with as many as a dozen kids in the game. Inside the school, arts and crafts and shop were taught. When it rained, everybody went inside the school where the gymnasium was, and everybody played basketball. All of that ended after the Cerrone administration.

The absence of the activities in the schoolyard at Logan School foreshadowed the pending doom which would soon envelop Logan. Yet it was Wakefield Park that typified the neglect by the ensuing mayoral administrations.

Torch remembered a neighbor of his named Gee-Gee, a Ukrainian immigrant, telling Torch as a boy that a lion lived in that park. Torch told Lee-Oskar the same story once. Lee-Oskar's eyes looked like saucers, Torch remembered. All during Torch's childhood, during the summers, he woke to the sound of buzz saws. City workers would be trimming the trees in the park across the street. There was a shack in the park that had tractors and electric mowers that the city workers stored there. Beyond the shack, about one hundred yards or so, was a mansion. In the mansion lived the head of the park guards, a man named Loftus and his family.

The house also served as a type of mini-police station for park guards. There seemed to be a handful of them around this park or the one across Ogontz Avenue, where they played football in the winter and baseball in the summer. The overwhelming burden that these "free-loading" families caused the city would be relieved by the new mayor. They were displaced not only from Wakefield Park, but other such homes in city parks which were collectively known as Fairmount Park throughout Philadelphia. Maybe it seemed like a good idea at the time, but you could pinpoint the exact time that part of West Logan began its downhill fall. It happened, or at least it started to happen, the day the park guards left. Without their presence, the park was turned over to drug dealers and hookers. First it was the abandoned work shed that burned down. The mansion became a hotel of drugs and prostitution and squatters until it also eventually burned down. There were still hills in the park, but there were no valleys because they had been filled in by weeds and garbage. A path ran through the park. This path became invisible as it, too, was overrun by weeds. The trees, not only in the park, but also the ones that lined most of the streets in Logan, were also neglected and died in the 1980s.

"What parish is this?" Bah-Bah asked.

"Holy Child," somebody replied.

"That's what I thought," Bah-Bah continued. "Man, that's a cathedral, that place, isn't it? We used to play them in basketball."

"Wait a second. You played basketball?" Torch said. "I find that hard to believe."

"I was a good athlete. We played all around here. Holy Child, Inky, Saint Ambrose, Saint Henry's, all over. I remember Holy Child had this one player who was outstanding. A white kid. I saw him about ten years later when I got caught with a gun once and spent a few days in the Detention Center until Constantine had the detainer lifted. He remembered me, and we became friends after that. He bet a few football games with me. The games lost and I never saw him again."

"What was his name, this person? Torch asked.

"Red ... did you guys know him?"

An uncomfortable silence took over the car. Torch gave Bah-Bah a brief rundown of Reds's fate, the drugs, his death at Danny Parker's, everything. Then he talked about Reds's brother, Shine, and what happened to him.

"Wow!" Bah-Bah said. Jesus Christ, he was sorry he'd brought it up now. He gracefully changed the subject, looking at the scenery.

"You know, growing up in South Philly, you get this image of North Philly ... the jungle. You never think of it as looking like this."

"This is Logan," Torch said. "I mean, it's North Philadelphia, but you're thinking about what ... Connie Mack Stadium and Temple University?"

"Right, where is that, Connie Mack?"

"That's about twenty-five blocks south of here. That's what you're thinking of, where the riots were, I'll bet."

Torch turned and faced the others in the back seat and said, "People in South Philadelphia just know about the riots. They think that's the only thing that ever happened there."

Just then Frenchie gave Torch a sign with his hand.

"Pull over here," Torch said to Bah-Bah. They were one block short of the probation office and about a half block past the infamous candy store, Dunn's. They were right across the street from the Logan schoolyard which had two full court basketball games going on simultaneously. All twenty of the basketball players and the twenty-or-so spectators on the sidelines were black.

Torch explained, "North Philadelphia isn't pretty like this neighborhood. This is the suburbs of North Philadelphia. They say Philadelphia was one of the world's breadbaskets in the decades after the war and North Philadelphia was one of the most productive parts of the city. Philadelphia had 300,000 jobs, and a lot of the manufacturing and retail was done down there. Now the city has about 50,000 jobs and hardly any of them are in North Philadelphia. Stetson Hats was down there. That was probably the most productive company. They left around the time of the riots, around 1964, I think it was."

"President Eisenhower signed the Expressway Act in the late fifties, and soon the expressways and the boulevards were in place, and that's when I think retail and manufacturing left North Philadelphia. When Stetson Hats left, I guess there was a feeling that, if they couldn't make it, nobody could make it in North Philadelphia."

"My father had a few of those Stetsons," Felix said.

"Everybody's father had a few of those Stetsons," Torch said. "Man, you don't see those kinds of hats anymore. Some were made of felt, and some had a little feather on the side. Put one of those on, and you're automatically a Rat Packer. They started going downhill when JFK became president in the early sixties. See, he made a big thing about disliking hats. And he sort of set the tone for fashion back then. Really, that's what I heard. So they were already going downhill when the riots occurred."

On the car radio a song was playing. The song was the "Boll Weevil Song" by Brook Benton. Bah-Bah was familiar with the song; he'd heard it before but had never paid much attention to it. It was a strange song about an insect called the boll weevil who, with his family, was looking to "take a home." Apparently, the family confronted a farmer, and they told him,

"You better sell your old machine
Because when I get through with your cotton
You can't even buy gasoline."

One day a few of us were hanging out here turning on the fireplug. This was in the summer of 1971. This black guy came jogging by. He was wearing a shirt that read: Joe Frazier, World Champion. Somebody said,

"Look at this clown. He thinks he's Joe Frazier." Then somebody said, "That is Joe Frazier." That's right, Joe Frazier used to live somewhere near here. Germantown, I think. And he used to jog down here. It was in the summer of 1971, I think. No, it had to be the summer of 1970 because he was training for his fight with Ali in March of 1971. At that time, the neighborhood was roughly half-white and half-black. All the white kids liked Frazier, and all the black kids were rooting for Ali. Ten years ago, this whole neighborhood was still white. Then Martin Luther King was assassinated, and this whole place went haywire.

Torch looked at Bah-Bah and said, "You know what 'block-busting' is? That's what happened around here. The summer after Martin Luther King was killed, nearly every house had a For Sale sign in front of it. It was bizarre. See, what happened is, real estate agents tried to turn the neighborhood over, get the whites to sell cheap, and then they'd sell the houses to blacks and rip them off. For one thing, black people, generally speaking, didn't have access to traditional loans. They had to pay these high-risk, high interest loans in order to buy the houses. A lot of white people wanted to move to the suburbs or the northeast anyway at that time. But blacks who lived in North Philly would pay top dollar to live in Logan. This was the suburbs to them, and that's all that is around here, former residents of North Philadelphia. It's sinister the way it works. It's really devious. It's called 'panic peddlin''.

"Say, for argument's sake, your house is worth $25,000. Now, a black family moves on your block. Pretty soon, you have a real estate person knocking on your door, calling your house. Then you get flyers in the mail telling you that your house is soon going to be worth about half that much. So in order to get value, you put your house up for sale then. Now, it's a case of supply and demand. You have to lower your asking price. You put your house up for $22,500.

The guy down the street, he's thinking the same way. He wants to get out while he can still get some value for his house. So he sells his for $20,000. More and more black families move in. There is a greater panic. There is a greater need to leave. Pretty soon a guy put his house up for $18,000. That is the going price now, $18,000. Now another neighbor is panicking. He puts his house up for $15,000. See, just like that, the value of the neighborhood just decreased $10,000. And the real estate agents were relentless. They used to call the house and even come over on Saturday. They didn't advertise in the other white neighborhoods around here, like Olney or Feltonville. Essentially, it was part of the plan to rip everybody off, black and white."

Torch's explanation was very crude at best. There was a lot more to it. In a book called *Block-Busting in Baltimore* by W. Edward Orser in 1984, Orser described it all in greater detail, and gave better explanations. A synopsis on the back cover of the book read: "Like many suburbs, Edmondson Village, a post-World War I row house development with 20,000 residents saw a dramatic shift in its population between 1955 and 1965.Behind this change lay block-busting techniques adopted by realtors in which scare tactics were used to encourage white owners to sell cheap, followed by a drastic mark-up for a potential black buyer who lacked access to conventional bank mortgages."

Despite the model in the book (Edmondson Village), being a suburb as opposed to Logan, which was in the city, the characteristics of both neighborhoods seemed about the same. They even looked remarkably alike. The Christmas lights, the church, the way the community was laid out, all seemed familiar to anybody from Logan that ever saw the book. In the preface of the book, the author wrote:

"The range of feelings was wide. Among whites, they ranged from anger and bitterness to bewilderment and a sense of loss. Among African Americans, there often were measures of satisfaction with new opportunities, but also feelings of disappointment and frustration the interpretations differed, particularly for those on the two sides of the racial dividing experience, as did assignments of responsibility and blame. But common to all was a sense of social dynamics that seemed beyond individual control and a sense of disjunction, as if their lives had been marked at this one key point by a dramatic experience that still seemed unresolved and a legacy that was uncertain."

On the first page, the author interviewed two women. One was black and the other was white, and their comments were very telling. Wrote the author: "The recent reflections of two women illustrate the poignancy and the complexity of their experience in the West Baltimore neighborhood of Edmondson Village when racial change began to occur on a massive scale in the late fifties and early sixties. In an interview, I conducted with a white former resident, Marilyn Simpkins, she gave an explanation for the response of whites who panicked and fled the neighborhood. 'They saw a very secure world changing drastically,' she said. "And they couldn't accept it. This was a peaceful place, and in some respects, it was forced down their throats. They felt they had no other choice, I guess.'

In a separate interview, Margaret Johnson, a pioneer from the era of initial African-American settlement in the same neighborhood, described her own feelings about the flight of her white neighbors. 'They weren't friendly; they were prejudiced. They didn't want to live where colored people did … they didn't have to say it … they didn't tell you why they moved. They just moved.'"

When Torch talked to people about that time during his young life, he said he saw one time on *60 Minutes* about a town near a river that was contaminated with toxic poisoning from a nearby chemical plant. The water they were drinking and bathing with was contaminated, and of course, the houses all went up for sale at the same time. Torch said it was similar to what happened in that part of Logan around 1968 to 1971. In this book, *Blockbusting in Baltimore*, a former resident said, "I think the only thing that might be similar to it would be the three Mile Island Thing-something that could create such a fear."

Another quote in the book that people in Logan who saw that situation could identify with was the one that went, "It wasn't integration.

In the early stages, it was an evacuation."

The change in Logan was very rapid and dramatic. In the case of what happened in Logan, much of it was aided by the facts that the races were at the boiling point during much of late sixties anyway. The assassination of Martin Luther King was clearly, by far, the main factor in kicking off "the Panic" and, of course, the riots that followed his death. Obviously, the Vietnam War with its unfair draft was probably a factor as well. It was, on many levels, simply a fucked-up time in the country, and there were people there to take advantage. It has been said that racism and economics are often linked. Logan provided a perfect model for how and why that was often true. Bah-Bah saw Frenchie in his rearview mirror. As he walked to the phone booth, Bah-Bah noticed, for the first time, that Frenchie limped. Not only did Frenchie have a slight limp due to a bad knee, he also had a receding hairline and a gut. After a stretch in the army, the brig, and later the county jail, Frenchie seemed to have reached middle age while still in his twenties. It was almost as if God were preparing him for an early death. Bah-Bah noticed that Frenchie was talking on the phone but hadn't deposited any coins. He was doing something unclear to the phone.

"What the hell is he doing?" Bah-Bah said. He was uncomfortable here. He wanted to get the spare ribs or whatever they ate around here and split.

"He stuffed the phone," Torch said matter of factly.

184

"What do you mean, 'stuffed the phone'?" Bah-Bah asked.

"I don't know how he does it exactly, but he somehow stuffs the coin return slot with a pipe reamer. Then, when someone's call doesn't go through or if they are supposed to be getting change from a quarter, the return money doesn't come back to them. You hear the change being released by the phone, but the change just won't make it to the coin return slot because it is stuffed up. Then after a week or so, when Frenchie goes to see his probation officer, he pulls out that pipe reamer and all the change from the week comes crashing down. He used to do it with five or six different phones around here, but the phone company changed the model of the pay phones, and now you can only do it with a few of the old ones."

Bah-Bah smiled at that and saw Frenchie exit the phone booth, then walk toward the probation office. Torch continued talking about Joe Frazier.

"Yeah, like I said, the Ali-Frazier fight wasn't responsible for any riots or anything. It was just sort of a symbol of all the stuff that was going on just then, all the tension."

As the first fight between Ali and Frazier neared its thirtieth anniversary in the year 2000, Wallace Matthews, the boxing writer from *The New York Post* wrote: *"It became a small reflection of what was going on in the United States at that time, a symbol of the racial, religious, and ideological divide that was threatening to tear the country in two."* Matthews wrote that the fight *"also represented the ongoing struggle between black and white, between hawk and dove, between Christianity and the Nation of Islam.*

"Ali, of course, willingly carried the banner of the counterculture, and as a result, Frazier was forced to assume a burden he neither wanted or desired, the black boxer fighting for white America."

Matthews also wrote that *"Ali was the standard bearer for everything white America feared ... Black Power, Islam, hippies, the anti-war movement. Frazier became the unwitting and temporary hero of the establishment, the hard hats, and Nixon's so-called 'silent majority.'"*

Logan seemed to be a tiny, but accurate, reflection of the entire country just then because of block-busting, paranoia, fear, and mistrust. The excitement was heightened in Logan because Joe Frazier trained there.

Torch said, "After Frazier won the fight, there weren't any riots or anything like that. In fact, for a few years, there was this uneasy truce between the blacks and the whites. We didn't go in the school yard, and they didn't come in the park. And that's just how it was.

"Then this black kid named Fat Eddie was shot on his mini-bike. He wasn't hurt too bad, just got banged up. Some say that Frenchie was the one that shot him, and he did live on that street, but he never talks about it. Anyway, the riots started up again. I guess this was about 1973, but those riots didn't last very long because, by that point, blacks ruled this neighborhood. There wasn't very much resistance at all."

"See this neighborhood?" Torch said to Bah-Bah. "This could be South Philadelphia in five years. It happens fast, baby ... fast. One Saturday morning, pretty soon, you'll hear somebody knocking on your door. You'll try to ignore them because you'll think it isn't anything very important, but the knocking will continue until you finally get up and answer the door. And do you know who it will be? It will be Jehovah's Witnesses, a gang of them. From that day on, your life will never be the same, my friend."

"That's right," Jackie said. "And the first thing that happens is the poster with the Marlboro Man will come down, and they'll put up one with a black guy smoking a Kool."

There was a big line of people waiting around tables in the middle of the school yard. "What's goin' on there?" Bah-Bah asked.

"That's a free lunch program they have. It started in the sixties. One morning, I didn't eat breakfast. It was during the summer. I went over there and got a sandwich. Man, that food was nasty. It was a sandwich, cheese, and salami. The roll wasn't that bad."

It make you mean

That surplus bean

Pointing to the crowd, Bah-Bah asked, "Who are those people?"

In the crowd, there were nearly fifty black kids over in one corner of the schoolyard. "That's Logan Nation," Torch answered.

Bah-Bah nodded his head like that was an acceptable answer, as though he knew what Torch was talking about. They were watching as a few of the black kids started slap-boxing. Then another pair squared off and started boxing.

"That's like a ritual they go through. It means they're getting ready to fight."

Bah-Bah looked over at them. Torch laughed at the way his face looked. Six or seven black kids came out of the schoolyard, crossing Ogontz Avenue in front of the Cadillac. Bah-Bah slid a holster with his gun from under his seat.

"They won't bother us. They're fighting with Nicetown. That's their rival ... the Nicetown gang. Don't worry, Bah-Bah. As long as I'm here, you'll be OK. I walk over to Dunn's and have a soda. Then I'm not so sure," Torch said.

Bah-Bah and the others looked at two kids slap-boxing in the schoolyard. The one brother was clearly in a time warp with a big Dr. J. afro and a huge afro comb sticking out of his back pocket. He was obviously imitating Muhammad Ali, boxing much of the time with his hands down by his side.

Suddenly a middle-aged white man walked through the schoolyard on crutches with five or six little black kids following him.

"Look at this guy," Bah-Bah said.

"He owns a store around here. Jericho Beef, the place we're goin'. He coaches their football team. I don't know how much a coach he is, considering the way they play. We play them in the winter sometimes."

Frenchie returned and got into the back seat of the car. He displayed a handful of nickels and dimes that he got out of the pay phone.

"My P.O. is out in the field today. I was talking to my cousin in there. You know, the one from Inky."

Bah-Bah started the car and pulled out into the traffic on Ogontz Avenue. They were heading straight toward Jericho Beef. Bah-Bah took one last look over at the black kids slap-boxing. He couldn't get over that "ritual" which was what Torch called it.

A disco song was playing on the radio then. Torch drummed his fingers on the dashboard: *"Livin' it up*

Livin' it up, oh yeah

Livin' it up

Livin' it up at last"

Logan Nation, Ben's Inky, Nicetown, Block-Busting, even though this was only the other side of the city from South Philadelphia, it clearly was an entirely different culture here with an entirely different history and ground rules. And so it was on that hot July day, that Bah-Bah began his North Philadelphia adventure.

CHAPTER 12

The White Tower was a small hamburger chain with a handful of spots dotted throughout North Philadelphia. Physically, all of the restaurants were exactly the same in these neat little white buildings. One of the locations was at the corner of Broad and Olney, on Logan's northern border, across from the Einstein Hospital. Torch and Maria were eating a late breakfast there after visiting Lee Oskar.

The doctors had put a plastic cover over his bed and had been pumping fresh oxygen into him. They told Maria that Lee Oskar was responding well and improving. Despite that good news, the boy looked so tiny, helpless, and alone in that sealed bed. Torch could tell that Maria was frightened a little bit by the sight of him. Even though she knew he had been in worse shape in the past and had recovered, it really was worse than it looked. However, the ordeal, combined with Maria's hours at the diner, was beginning to wear on her, and it had started to show under her eyes. It had been a tough couple of days on top of a tough couple of years for her.

Torch and Maria ate in one of the four or five booths. The staple of the White Tower was oblong hamburgers (the W.T. Burger) served on these unique, specially-made oblong rolls and, as every cop in Philadelphia knew, the best coffee in the city. That's what Torch ordered, a W.T. Burger with cheese and coffee. Maria had eggs with a side of fried potatoes and, of course, coffee.

"It's too early for cheeseburgers," Maria said.

"Too early?" Torch responded. Then, mimicking a skit he'd seen John Belushi do on *Saturday Night Live*, he pointed to the plates of the other patrons at the in the crowded restaurant and said, "Cheeseburger, cheeseburger, cheeseburger." Then he added, "I already ate cereal before, I was up early."

"Damn! You went to sleep at six o'clock last night. I guess you were up early," Maria said.

The night before last, Torch had been at Caesar's Palace playing cards, and he'd been up about $200 or $300, so he didn't feel right about leaving until the others decided to break up the game. The money came in handy. He had bet three baseball games that night, which all lost, including the New York Mets who lost to the Phillies 1-0 in a game he and three of his boys attended.

He had been losing betting baseball in the last few weeks. It was untimely since he was writing fewer numbers these days, and not one of his customers had hit the number since long before Chick-a-dee was killed. However, Bah–Bah had it on good authority from his sources in Center City that the coast was clear. Other bookies unconnected to Moscariello were working down there, including Blue Eyes and a numbers writer named Eddie, a bartender at Bookbinder's. They were acting like they had a license, and nobody was bothering them. It wasn't as though Torch wasn't enjoying his semi–retirement, but the longer he was away, the more customers he was likely to lose. It took Alex twenty years to build up that book, and it bothered Torch that he was letting it be taken away from him. Torch planned to check it out himself later today.

"These are the best hamburgers," Torch remarked.

"For fast food," Maria retorted.

"White Tower isn't fast food. White Tower is a restaurant. McDonald's is fast food. I don't eat it."

"You eat Gino's food."

"That's different. They have Colonel Sanders' Fried Chicken."

"I saw you eat the Gino Giant."

Torch wiped some grease from his red moustache. "That's true. I did eat the Gino Giants sometimes."

"Well, the Big Mac is the same as the Gino Giant. The Gino Giant was created to compete with the Big Mac."

"The Gino Giant is *not* the same as the Big Mac. The Big Mac couldn't *hang* with the Gino Giant."

Just then, Torch saw Maria smile for the first time since this latest ordeal involving Lee Oskar began. Maria too noticed in Torch a positive change today. Since Chick-a-dee had been killed, Torch was much more subdued it seemed, not acting so confident at all lately. He had been humbled by the incident, scared shitless "in plain English," a term her mother used. He even made love different since then ... not better ... just different.

"Roy Rogers — they had some good chicken."

"They had the best coleslaw, creamy coleslaw ... remember it?" Maria asked.

"I'll give them that. They had the best coleslaw in the city. But as good as their chicken was, and it was good, when it came to that, the Colonel kicked Roy Rogers's ass. You can't beat them eleven herbs and spices."

When they left the diner, they got in Torch's car. They rolled down the windows, and Torch lit them both a cigarette. Normally, Maria smoked more than Torch, but he had been smoking more that summer ever since he bought this new lighter at Oceanwood the night Shine was killed. The lighter looked like a tiny pistol, and when the trigger was pulled, a flame appeared at the top. Torch planned to drive Maria to work at the diner, and he hoped to be on the phones by twelve o'clock. On the car radio, "I'll See You When I Get There," the 1978 song by Lou Rawls, was playing. The song started out with him talking.

"Man, I hope this woman don't put me through some changes today because I had a hard day today, ya' know?" Then he sang.

"How Ya' Doin'?

I hope you're fine.

Did your day put you through changes

And mess up your mind?"

Maria asked about Bah-Bah and the situation involving his new house. Torch explained that Bah-Bah had been moving little by little into the house and would be officially moved in inside of a day or two. Torch made sure to tell her that he was only going to be there a few hours a day. Torch didn't want Maria to think that things were so bad that Bah-Bah was abandoning his family because he was being shaken down. He told her that Bah-Bah was having problems with his wife which really wasn't true. He said that this Caesar's Palace was a place for him to go to and get away if he needed it, if she threw him out. With Bah-Bah in the new house now, Felix, Frenchie, Doc, and Billy had their home back. In fact, they had already moved in, and it was working out well for everybody. Torch also told her that he was going into Center City that day and things were improving on that front as well.

"I just hope you know what you're doing, Torch," Maria said.

Torch noticed that his car sounded even worse than normal. The red oil light appeared, once again, on the dashboard, and he had just filled it with oil a week ago. Pretty soon, he would be pulling into a gas station and saying to the guy, "Fill it with oil and check the gas."

Cars such as this one ran in the summer, but anything ran in the summer. In the winter, it was a different story. Torch didn't think his car would make it through this year. It did have a good stereo system though, and the speakers in the back, provided by Shine himself, were state-ofthe-art. The background speakers were especially good on certain songs such as this one. Lou Rawls's voice came out from the front speakers:

"I just called to say
That I'm on my way."
Then from the back speakers.
"And I'll see you when I get there
I'll see you when I get there
I'll see you when I get there
I'll see you when I get there."

Just then, they were driving past the U.S. Armory on Ogontz Avenue, a mile up from where they were yesterday in Bah-Bah's car talking about Joe Frazier and all the excitement. Torch thought about yesterday and that look Bah-Bah had on his face when he saw those kids slap-boxing. Torch chuckled the same way he did then.

Logan always had a certain mystery or stigma attached to it. When Torch was growing up, people used to always ask him about block-busting from his up-close viewpoint. In more recent years, people had forgotten about the block-busting that went on there; instead they would ask him questions about the sinking homes, such as, Did he live in one? Did he know anybody who lives in one? Was he ever inside one of those homes?

In the book *In Cold Blood*, Truman Capote wrote quite a bit about the village where the multiple murders occurred. Holcomb, Kansas, would always have that stigma and would always have a certain mysterious quality. According to a pamphlet, a report of the book by Clifton Fadiman in the Book-of-the-Month Club News, "Holcomb became a community filled with fear and suspicion." Capote wrote about the way the neighbors interacted suspiciously among each other.

To a lesser degree, this fear and suspicion had been present in Logan. A good example was the way certain white neighbors fled the neighborhood in the middle of the night so that their homes wouldn't be vandalized by their neighbors. The U.S. Armory played a role, at least allegedly, in the story that was Logan. People outside of Logan didn't even know the armory existed. Even some in Logan never knew it existed.

In the late sixties, Torch would occasionally see a procession of monster-sized United States issue tanks, Army Jeeps, and khaki-colored buses designed to transport troops all riding down Ogontz Avenue. The vehicles had white stars on the doors and some had American flags on them. The procession drove right by the Logan schoolyard, and Torch could see it from his kitchen window. He never knew exactly how many vehicles there were, just that it took about twenty or thirty minutes for all of them to go by. The whole neighborhood vibrated when those tanks came by. It was never something that was advertised beforehand. Torch never really thought about it except that, for a kid that young, it was kind of exciting just seeing those tanks and Jeeps and knowing they were only a half mile from his house.

Maria was the one who told him about a man named Phil Yanella who used to come into the diner. He was a sociology professor at Temple University and had been studying Logan and planning to write about the block-busting that went on there. According to him the procession was designed to scare the hell out of the blacks who lived in Logan, particularly the Logan Nation Gang. He said the tanks only came out on nice, warm days when the schoolyard was full of people (black people). According to this professor, the procession was "a show of strength," meant to be a deterrent to any thought of an inner-neighborhood type of revolution.

Despite Torch being as suspicious as the next guy and reluctant to dismiss any wild, mysterious conspiracy theory, whether it made sense or not, he laughed about what the professor had told Maria. Torch was sure that the only conspiracy here or sinister plan was his own. It was a devious plan to get into Maria's pants by acting like he was so smart and that he was some important government spy. Torch didn't see how scarring the black kids in the schoolyard benefited or profited anybody. Not that they would be afraid, even if this had occurred to them which it didn't.

Nevertheless, considering that the Vietnam War was going on, Torch had to ask himself what exactly those tanks and Jeeps and army buses were doing there in the first place. As the years went on, Torch had to wonder why very few people seemed to remember that, as if tanks being driven down residential streets was something you might forget. It was mysterious to Torch the way the adults didn't seem to want to talk about it.

One of the cooks in the diner was a small customer of Torch's who owed him a fishcake, so Torch went in to have a cup of coffee and check him out. He sat at the counter, and two black guys about Torch's age were in line to pay their check. Torch was certain that he went to school with one of the kids in the first or second grade. There were two brothers that he knew named Eric and Brian, and

Torch was sure that the guy in line had one of those names, although he wasn't sure which.

Torch got out of his chair and shook his hand. "It's either Eric or Brian, I forget which." "Eric," he said.

Those two had spent many hours together in the schoolyard playing basketball, pivots, twenty-one, pig, around-the-world, and rough house.

"Why did you stop coming around?" Eric asked.

The question surprised Torch, as if the guy didn't understand.

"Well, you know how it was back then."

They didn't come in the park. We didn't go in the schoolyard.

There was a certain embarrassment that showed on each of their faces, but that was too bad. It's just how it was in Logan for a while, and they both knew it.

In the summer of 1978, the entire city of Philadelphia was threatening to be torn apart by race. Logan itself, on the other hand, despite what experts such as Sergeant Harry Quinn and Ken Washington said or thought or feared, had remained relatively peaceful. It had already gone through racial problems in the late sixties and early seventies before other parts of the city. Logan really didn't have a racial problem of any note in recent years.

Torch had a recurring thought just then. Guys like this one here kept popping back into his life over the years. They seemed to follow him wherever he went. The white kids that he had been in grade school with were long gone, never to be seen again. These black kids that he vaguely remembered, on the other hand, seemed to follow him. When he played basketball up in Germantown, they were there. When he first went up to Maria's house deep in the southwest corner of Logan, a place white kids generally didn't go and some didn't even know about, they were there. When Torch had to go to the Youth Study Center, they were there also. It probably served him well that he knew them, had gone to school with them, and had the good sense not to get on their bad side, now that he thought about it.

Also they were there with him at Parkway High School in Center City. It was a magnet school as opposed to a neighborhood school.

Actually it wasn't a magnet school in the normal sense. Parkway was a satellite school so named because according to John Blocks, much of the student body was often in a marijuana haze. It was an experiment in education, unique to Philadelphia. There was no other high school anywhere exactly likes it with such a format. It was labeled "the school without walls." It had sections or headquarters in six different parts of the city where you had homeroom. The majority of classes though were held at mainly various institutions such as the University of Pennsylvania, Temple University, South Philadelphia High School, the Franklin Institute, And the Academy of Natural Sciences. Other classes may have been held in the basement of a church in Center City. The students were given subway and bus tokens to get from one place to the other if the classes weren't within walking distance. It was possible to be in North Philly, West Philly, South Philly and Center City all in the same day. It probably wasn't the greatest high school when it came to preparing for higher education. It did lead the city in the mid-seventies in graduates of graffiti writers however. It certainly gave each student a sense of the city which was positive and valuable. If you are old enough to remember *Welcome Back, Kotter* or perhaps unlucky enough to have seen the show on reruns, then you can imagine what Parkway was like. And by the way, the show really didn't seem that bad the first time around. It was the show that launched John Travolta's career. He played Vinnie Barbarino, a student and a main character. His classmates included Juan Epstein, Arnold Horshack, and Boom-Boom Washington. Parkway kids were similar. There was a certain joy for them in going to school every day just like the characters from *Welcome Back, Kotter,* collectively known as The Sweathogs.

Then Torch worked for the city which was to work what Parkway was to high school. It seemed like a natural progression. It was similar; he again ran into kids he had met somewhere along the line. There were black girls from Logan or girls from North Philly who had cousins from Logan. Working for the city was similar to going to Parkway because for one thing it drew from every corner of the city. It was like a magnet school all over again. It was a little like Logan schoolyard all over again.

When Torch left the diner, he stood for a second in the parking lot before he got in the car. The usual smell of hamburgers and fried onions from the exhaust fan was on him. It made him think of his old dog Rex. Whenever the dog got out of the house and ran away, he always made a beeline for this diner. No doubt he was drawn here by the smells from the same exhaust fan. Torch always knew to drive to the diner and find the dog. When the dog saw him, he had this stunned look on his face as if asking, "How did you find me so fast?"

While standing in that lot, Torch also vaguely recalled that he had a dream the night before. Right now it was only a distant flash, but it had something to do with this diner. It wasn't anything he would suddenly recall, so he thought about something else instead. He looked across the street into the wide concrete schoolyard. One time he was supposed to meet Alex in Center City, and he drove to the diner and parked there. He ate breakfast, then went outside, and started to walk home, forgetting that his car was in the lot. It was in the middle of winter on a school day. The schoolyard was deserted. It wasn't like people were suddenly going to start chasing him with weapons and spears in their hands, so he walked through the schoolyard. But twenty feet into the schoolyard, he started running. At first he was just jogging, then he was at full speed. Running, at that point, was a decision made by his legs. It seemed like his mind had nothing to do with it. He wasn't thinking; he just bolted.

When he reached the 17th Street exit, he saw his house and the empty spot in the street where he parked. He was out of breath by then, so he couldn't run back even if he wanted to. He just walked all the way back to the diner, and of course, it was all right. It was as though he had been preprogrammed to think his life was in danger just because he was there in enemy territory. It was just a tiny example of how stupid everybody had been acting. Torch now smiled at the memory of that, although at the time it didn't seem funny as much as foolish. He was embarrassed by it, frankly.

This day, Torch drove from his mother's where he ate dinner and stayed over last night Maria's house. He answered the phone and called in a few numbers and horses. He incorporated last night's box scores into his books and read Jack Kiser in the *Daily News*. Finally, at about 1:30, he went out of the back door of the house, crossed the tracks, walked down into the Logan subway stop, then rode into Center City.

* * *

Jim Kelly arrived at the North Star Diner a few minutes past twelve o'clock. He bought the *Daily News* in the vestibule. Then he sat at what was his usual spot at the counter in the old days. He and his partner Ed Kelly had worked in Germantown's 14th District for three years, and this place had been a hangout, of sorts, for them.

The waitresses he knew from back then were mostly all gone now. One that did recognize him was a short and sassy blonde girl named Donna who was the sister of one of Torch's boys. She kissed Jimmy on the cheek and was all smiles as usual.

"You look good ... relaxed," Donna said.

He did look relaxed. In fact, Donna had never seen him before in civilian clothes. Today Kelly was wearing dungarees, sneakers, a '76ers jersey with the name George McGinnis and the number 30 on his back.

He wore a white M.A.B. paint cap.

"How about Ed? Is he still with you?"

"Of course, still partners. He had to work today. I had off."

"What brings you up here, to Logan, I mean?"

Kelly took a second before he answered. He hadn't thought of a response to that question beforehand. "Had to testify at the 14th, an old case I was involved in." It was a bad lie. Would he really testify in a '76er jersey, dungarees, and an M.A.B. paint cap? Donna seemed to buy it.

"Maria's here," Donna said.

"Where?" Jimbo squealed, revealing more enthusiasm than he would have liked.

"In the back," Donna said.

Just then, Maria, his old flame, stepped from the kitchen into the dining area. She gave Kelly a reserved look and purposefully took her time before walking around the counter, also kissing him on the cheek.

Kelly's mouth went dry. He froze. Maria was a sexual athlete, and they had had a great time together. He knew about Torch, but so what? Torch had been on the lowest rung of city government, and he wasn't even that now. All Torch had was money from the lawsuit, and when that was gone, what could he offer Maria? He was too young to even really appreciate a girl like Maria. He didn't know Torch personally, but sources had filled him in on a plan to use him. It was why Kelly had come up to Logan in the first place. He had spent the morning walking around 10th and 11th Streets between Windrim and Lindley Avenue, just poking around, hoping that he would get lucky and discover the underground meth lab that they had information was around there. The Kelly Brothers were back in business. They knew who owned the methamphetamine lab, and they knew who protected it. They just didn't care. They knew that a man named Glenn Miller, a Scorpion, and one of the original members of Ben's, was a top-notch methamphetamine cook. They knew that the Scorpions ran the methamphetamine lab — all of the meth business — for Constantine in the City of Philadelphia, which was sort of a meth capitol in the east.

They planned to pressure Torch into convincing Glenn to betray his employers. This was Constantine's last hurrah anyway. They were planning to deliver one last blow to his organization. Surely Glenn could see that Constantine would soon be out of business entirely in any case. Glenn, on the other hand, could survive. He could go on to be with Moscariello, they figured. Of course, Glenn had plans of his own, and if his scheme worked out, he would be rich.

Torch, the theory was, would help the Kellys out in their handling of Glenn because he would have no choice. They were going to threaten him with opening up that old murder case against him. The murder of John Base had been swept under the rug by the 53ʳᵈ District cops because there were insinuating circumstances, including that an officer's son had been a participant in the murder. Torch still had worries or fears about it all though. Kelly understood that Torch was the nervous type and was certain that he would cooperate with them.

Maria was waiting on a black couple, a couple of stools down from Kelly. The man's name was Ernie and Kelly recognized him from years before. Maria set two coffees in front of them and took their order. Then she sent their order through a tiny window into the kitchen. Kelly said to her, "What's up, buttercup?" "Not a thing, chicken wing," Maria said.

Kelly picked up something in her joyful tone. Right then, he believed that Maria was giving him a play. He was certain now that something could be rekindled here.

"I'll be off in ten minutes," Maria informed him.

Kelly sipped some coffee and opened his *Daily News*. He went to the back section and read about the Phillies' victory the previous night. On the front page of the paper, the big story was the ongoing racial tension in Southwest Philly. It had started during the spring and continued until now, halfway into the summer. Apparently, the previous night, a mob of black neighbors had beat up and hospitalized a white resident. It was in retaliation for the shooting death of a thirteen-year-old black youth which also occurred a week earlier in Southwest Philadelphia. Kelly went to the column written by John Chapman next. Chapman's column today dealt with Jimmy Cerrone (surprise!). Specifically, the column addressed the progress of the registration drive which he supported and championed.

Chapman wrote: "Four major polls have the black vote between 83 percent and 95 percent against the Charter change. Yet a bare majority of black war leaders polled (11of 20) were against the Charter change. Behind this display of black ward disunity in the face of black voter unity are efforts by the team of Cerrone's roughnecks to hold down a large black vote. One tactic is simple, and the other is more complicated. According to several authoritative sources to report this same story, the Cerrone people candidly accept a crushing black electoral as an undeniable, inevitable fact. What the recreants are counting on is the traditional low black turnout. To help history repeat itself, the Democratic Committee has devised two strategies for suppressing the black vote. First there will be an attempt to hold back Election Day 'street money' to the black wards where a large and uncontrollable black vote is likely. Gene Harris, a top Cerrone aid, denied this and said that 'street money was never a factor.' However, an unnamed 'prominent' black politician was quoted as saying that as much as $10,000 was being offered to black ward leaders if they can hold down the vote to 25 percent in their district. 'If these black ward leaders, who say they oppose the Charter change,' said the black politician, 'can bring out 24, 25 and 26 percent of the vote, then they can claim, 'Hey, I did my best.' That will mean they took Cerrone's money.'"

Chapman wrote that the registration drive was going fine but added that there were still a small number of already registered black people who planned to vote for Cerrone. Chapman stated that this was "outrageous" and that he should receive zero support from black Philadelphians. Chapman touched on Cerrone's ill-advised speech at Whitman Park section in South Philadelphia in March. Whitman Park was a major can of worms in itself. Whiteman Park was a low-income development that the Federal Government was planning to build. The neighbors were frantically opposed to this project, and Cerrone had promised to represent this group as they were always had been staunch supporters of him. In March, at a rally there in opposition to the construction, Cerrone said that the Charter change vote was coming down to simply a black/white issue. Cerrone said, "In the black community, they're saying, 'Vote black,' (against the Charge change). So I'm saying simply, 'Vote white.'"

The media jumped all over Cerrone for saying that. It was Chapman himself who pointed out the coincidence of the speech taking place on March 15th ... the Ides of March. Chapman pointed out that it was the anniversary of Julius Caesar's death.

"And now his ancestor, Philadelphia's own J.C. had committed what amounted to political suicide on that same date. Jimmy Cerrone was too smart a politician not to realize that saying 'vote white' would open the flood gates. For the local media to print even more bad press about him. Yet, here it was. Four months later and Cerrone was only slightly behind in the pre-election polls. Clearly, however, the self-confidence that Cerrone always displayed in the past didn't seem to be here now. In the last election (1975), Cerrone had bluntly said, "This election was over the day I announced. In fact, some political analysts could say that Cerrone's 'Vote White' statement was a pain-induced act of desperation."

* * *

Watching Cerrone during the Charter change drive was like watching the latter rounds of the prize fight between Muhammad Ali and challenger Leon Spinks about six months before. Spinks carried the entire fight, but even in the late rounds when Ali was hopelessly behind on points, you still had the odd feeling Ali would shock the world again and find a way to pull it out. Even if you had no interest in politics or in Cerrone, in particular, there still was an interest in seeing if the old guy could pull it off here, too.

Larry McMullen also wrote an article in that day's *Daily News*. McMullen was Kelly's favorite writer. He was the local Jimmy Breslin to Kelly. There was an economy in his writing style. Every paragraph was poignant. Almost every sentence was like a left-handed jab setting up a powerful right blow. An editor of *Brotherly Love Magazine* said that McMullen could "write about the history of the world in 800 words and do a good job." His columns had a certain flexibility to them. Three people could read his story, and all three would take something else away. They could argue, all three of them about what he was trying to say or the point he was making. Even an individual that read his column in the morning may have an entirely different take on it in the evening when he reread the story. Unlike some of the other *Daily News*'s columnists, including heavy hitters like John

Chapman and Pete Dexter, McMullen was born and raised in the city (South Philadelphia) and had a giant home-field advantage. He personally knew many of the local newsmakers that he wrote about, including both Jimmy Cerrone and Angelo Constantine. Jim Kelly liked his no-nonsense honesty and the way he didn't put in many flowery images. He appreciated the way McMullen never bad-mouthed anybody, even an adversary that he hotly disagreed with. He wrote (Kelly believed) with an old-school dignity. Finally Kelly loved the way McMullen didn't beat you over the head about how much smarter he was than you. He didn't refer over and over to some obscure painters from the fifteenth century or quote some homosexual poet who committed suicide one hundred years ago in Philadelphia. In late November 1963, following the Kennedy assassination, many reporters were looking for a new slant to give to the massive story. New York columnist Jimmy Breslin wisely and famously interviewed the presidents would-be-grave digger. McMullen in writing his stories, using his many connections would often seem to find a fresh angle like that. For example, in covering a murder case, instead of just talking to the lawyer and the prosecutor, he may interview the court psychologist or probation/parole officer. He had a knack, it seemed, for often finding "the grave digger."

McMullen, on this day, disagreed with the controversial story his college John Chapman wrote the other day. McMullen's column was titled "In Defense of Cerrone." McMullen wrote that what happened at Whitman Park really wasn't as bad as what the media was painting. McMullen talked about a hypocrisy that existed. He said it probably confused Cerrone. He said the world of politics was somehow separate from everything else. He stated that the people of Whiteman Park, the ethnics there (Polish and Irish), were not only Cerrone's constituents, they would walk through walls for Cerrone. It wasn't that they were racist. It was more that they didn't have a stage and never did have one. Cerrone was their only voice. McMullen wrote that "the pundits and the political experts missed the point quite a bit when it came to Cerrone." McMullen talked about an infamous time when a few years earlier Cerrone had been hooked up to a lie detector machine. He was then asked questions about a lofty and expensive political deal in Philadelphia which he claimed he knew nothing about. As it turned out, Cerrone failed the lie detector test. Cerrone's opponent in the next election, in 1975, was a black man. He made a big deal about Cerrone failing the test.

McMullen wrote about it and then quoted from a book called *The Cop Who Would Be King* written by Daughten and Binzen which was about Jimmy Cerrone written in the mid-seventies: "So a machine had certified him a liar. He was still their man, their leader, their hope, and they would help him in any way they could." McMullen continued, "While the outlook in North and West Philadelphia may have been bleaker still, they at least had their champions during this period. Martin Luther King was only the most visible symbol of a coalescence of forces working to improve the lot for blacks. Congress, spurred by its liberal whites, produced massive amounts of legislation designed to aid blacks. Business and schools, often clouded by the courts, became laboratories to test methods whereby black children could be better prepared to meet the future. And every day, on the front pages of the newspaper and on the television news programs, the spotlight were trained on these developments. In the white ethnic neighborhoods though, things only seemed to get worse. It was their children who were shaken down for their lunch money. It was their taxes that were raised to pay increased welfare benefits. They were leaderless. When they did organize to protest, nobody listened. Worse yet, they came off looking like a bunch of redneck bigots."

Then McMullen wrote: "Working class whites in the inner city and whites of the middle class in or out of the cities have different concerns particularly with crime. The working-class is much more vulnerable to it and therefore have a much greater, personal interest in it. In a poll published this year by the FBI, Philadelphia has the lowest crime rate in the United States's top eleven cities."

McMullen quoted from an article written in a national magazine which discussed Cerrone. The article included a chairman of the Democratic Party in Minneapolis. His name was Woodrow Fryman. He originally lived and worked in politics in the Philadelphia area. In the article, Fryman said, "Even out here, people get the wrong idea about Cerrone. People ask me about him all the time." McMullen further quoted Fryman as saying, "Many people will only see Cerrone in negative terms, failing to see the improvements he's made downtown and to the city's security. They really don't know anything about the mayor." He also said, "It's the same problem conservative viewpoints have historically had in this city. They have a hard time cracking through the media."

McMullen, later in the article, quoted Fryman talking about more of the "eastern media myth" which was what Fryman called it. People out here see the Whitman Park residents on TV. They see Cerrone getting them worked up, and they don't understand how Cerrone could have been a two-term mayor. In particular, people out here are curious about the Whitman Parkers and Cerrone's other staunch supporters.

I explained that there was a large body of people who identify with a lot of Cerrone's views. It was generally a class of people who felt as though they themselves had been put down, alienated, or short-changed.

Mr. McMullen admitted that while an "eastern media myth" may have existed, still the negativity expressed toward Cerrone was more extreme. McMullen quoted Jimmy Cerrone himself who said, "I never saw a media so aggressive and so determined to do a candidate in."

Continuing, McMullen wrote: "My colleague, John Chapman, wants to turn this election into a pissing contest between blacks and whites. His recent column titled 'Vote as if Your Life Depends on It, Cuz It Does' was overly dramatic, even for Chapman. If a black dog and a white dog were fighting in the street, Chapman could make it a racial issue out of it. He could write a column about it, saying that the black dog was somehow at a disadvantage because of his color. Politics should never take on such a low form as simply "Vote White" or "Vote Black." And elections should be determined by where each individual candidate stands on certain important issues. Cerrone probably, in a very earnest fashion, believed that mindless white voters who vote white, are only negating certain black voters who may be voting solely because a candidate looks like him or her. Furthermore, Cerrone is a leader. He has always shown leadership qualities. The honest truth is that even if Cerrone was believed to be leading the City of Philadelphia down the drain, he was, at least, leading it. Italians will vote for Cerrone in any case, and you can't blame them for that. I grew up in an Irish parish in South Philadelphia. We were surrounded by Italians. The people of my parish were similar to the Whitman Parkers that you see on the news. We were surrounded by Italians and a cradle to grave type of rivalry grew out of that. Economics, jealousy, and competitiveness contributed to this bitterness. Also, there seemed to be a need for us Irish to finally have somebody we could look down upon. Italians filled that void and naturally some hostility grew out of that. When Irish immigrants first came to this country in the mid-to-late nineteenth century, they were met with similar hostility. The Irish were the new kids on the block. Economics was a big factor then, too. Irish immigrants would gladly work for cheaper wages. Everybody knows about the signs that read: "Irish need not apply." Those signs, a piece of America's tradition of prejudice, are legendary now. Nevertheless, at least, Irish immigrants could speak English. That, of course, gave them a big leg up on their immigrant counterparts from all over Europe. Irish people speaking English could fulfill civil jobs such as policemen and firemen. Naturally, Irish pulled way ahead of their immigrant counterparts in obtaining political power also. Even in Italian strongholds like South Philadelphia, the Irish had the upper hand. For one thing, the Italians were fiercely religious and loyal to the Catholic Church. But here in America the Italian Roman Catholics were second-class citizens, even among immigrants, and even in the Catholic Church. The key positions in the parishes, even the ones that were almost entirely Italian, were held by Irish people. They had a leg up on priests and nuns and bishops, for example.

It was Jimmy Cerrone who broke the door down and allowed ItalianAmericans to hold important jobs and to obtain the political power that they have now at City Hall. It wasn't easy for them.

Jimmy Cerrone was the first Italian-American police commissioner and the second Italian mayor of a major city. In a strange case of "the more things change, the more they stay the same," twenty years ago in the 1950s, there was a different sort of housing problem in South Philadelphia. Then, Italians had protested the city's planning for housing in South Philadelphia. The unsympathetic mayor who was Irish said, "What do those Dagos know about housing?"

McMullen talked more about Cerrone's belief in the ethnics of Philadelphia, such as the Irish, Italians, Poles, and Jews. McMullen wrote that, with Cerrone in charge, Philadelphia would be a better, safer place. Again McMullen quoted from *The Cop Who Would Be King*: "The women in the row house neighborhoods will continue to scrub the front steps in the morning. On summer evenings, the men will continue to sit on folding chairs on the sidewalk. The kids will continue to play on Lighthouse Field. Jimmy Cerrone would be their protector, their father figure, their *'padrone.'*"

Then McMullen himself wrote: "Right now the polls have Jimmy Cerrone slightly behind. However, no politician that I ever knew or heard of holds a light up to how inaccurate polls can be. It's always been that way with Cerrone. If you don't understand why, then you haven't been paying attention. To white people, who are still the majority of voters in the city, being anti-Cerrone is somehow 'hip.' Not voting for Cerrone is perceived as being progressive. It means that you have climbed into the middle-class. It's hip sort of like the way it was hip or fashionable to root for Muhammad Ali over Joe Frazier. Therefore, pre-election polls and pre-election rhetoric are almost entirely antiCerrone. It follows, therefore, that you will not hear people around the water cooler at work talking about how they support Cerrone. When that curtain is drawn in the election booth, however, then it becomes a different story. Then they'll be thinking about crime and criminals.

They'll be thinking about security. They will vote for their leader."

Jim Kelly and Maria had a private conversation at a booth in the back of the diner. It was Maria's coffee break, and she told Kelly about Lee Oskar and his being in the hospital. Kelly asked Maria about Torch.

Then he asked her about Glenn Miller.

"What about Glenn Miller?" Maria asked.

"Do you know him?"

"I know *of* Glenn Miller. He was a bandleader. Him, Benny Goodman, the whole gang. He died in a plane crash."

"And they wrote a song about it. It was called 'The Day the Music Died.'" "That was Buddy Holly," Maria said with a straight face.

"Well, anyway, did you know him?"

"Buddy Holly? Didn't he sing 'Peggy Sue'?" Maria said, visibly disappointed in Kelly. *This* was why he came to see her?

"I'm talking about Glenn Miller," Kelly said, all serious. "Not the bandleader. Glenn Miller, the Scorpion."

Maria's attitude toward Kelly wasn't exactly flirtatious. She seemed friendly and willing to answer Kelly questions, but she really couldn't. He kept asking her about Glenn. She told him she didn't know anything about Glenn, and that was the truth. She wondered what, if anything, Torch had to do with this. This Kelly had a lot of nerve. Did he really think that she would help him get Torch into trouble somehow with Glenn Miller? The man was a Scorpion. She had enough problems.

Kelly left after their conversation. He made a mental note to spend more time around Logan and, in particular, the North Star Diner.

That night Torch booked the numbers up until 6:30. Then Torch and Maria had dinner at the Asia Chinese Restaurant on Broad Street. The Asia was one of the two top-notch restaurants in Logan. The other was an over-priced Portuguese restaurant on 13th and Rockland called Pedella, whose claim to fame was that Jacqueline Kennedy ate there a few years ago. Torch personally preferred the Asia, and they ate there about twice a month. Torch told Maria that everything had been fine down on Sansom Street that day. A man named Dave Ming who owned a seafood restaurant down there hit the number 409 for $500. Torch couldn't get over that. Ming had a reputation in Philadelphia as being both a top-notch restaurateur and businessman. He was also revered for his very hard work ethic. He, for one thing, was personally on the docks at five in the morning assuring to get the freshest and best catch of the day. Essentially, everything he touched turned to gold, certainly in his case luck was the residue of hard work. Now, the first number he ever plays in his life comes out straight. Torch would see Bah-Bah tomorrow morning and then pay off. Torch was happy because he made $100 off the top.

Maria ordered what she almost always ordered when they went to the Asia. It was an egg roll, shrimp fried rice, and shrimp with lobster sauce. Torch, on the other hand, at the Asia almost always ordered oilbasted chicken. It was a dish Torch had never heard of before. It was chicken in an oily, hot, inky-black, soy sauce-like gravy. It was dynamite. Torch told Maria about the Phillies game two nights ago that he and his friends attended at Veterans Stadium. He said that it was exciting because Steve Carlton took a no-hitter into the eighth inning. The no-hitter was eventually broken up by the Mets' light-hitting second baseman, Felix Millian.

Torch told Maria that, while they were at the game, the scoreboard out in centerfield as it did every night flashed the names of different groups in attendance. For example, it might say up there "Cisco's bar" or "Olney Lanes" or "Mary Horton's 16th birthday party" or "Mike Rose's bachelor party." Among the groups mentioned on that particular night was "the 53rd Philadelphia Police District." Maria didn't see the irony in that at all. Everybody else did though. Logan had been a key neighborhood, it seemed, not just lately because of the election but in general. The 53rd district was the busiest and largest district in the city. There were mounted police, K-9 police, police in unmarked cars, cops dressed as old ladies (the granny squad), police in helicopters, police on the beat; the railroads had their own police, there were transit cops in the subway, there were park guards (at least, while Cerrone was mayor). They patrolled not only in cars but also two different-sized vans or "wagons." Under Cerrone, they even had a greyhound-sized bus to move around in. Torch and his friends knew half of them on a first name basis. They were almost like the tree-lined streets, part of the overall scenery. There was Washington with his "hands-on" style of police work. He would routinely frisk them four or five times a week. He would spy on them, sneak up on them, stalk them, and hide from them. One time, he even jumped out of an ambulance in order to catch them doing something. He could hear the zip-top of a beer can five blocks away. When it came to lighting a joint, he was right there, too, like he could hear the match being struck. Soon he would be on the scene like an urban Smokey the Bear warning about forest fires. When they were younger and spent more hours in the neighborhood and too young to be in bars, it was a continuous cat and mouse game. In those days, when Torch went to bed at night he used to roll over and say "Good night, Ken." *That* was why it was remarkable that the 53rd cops would be there that night. But even after Torch explained all this to Maria, she didn't see the poetry in it. It went right over her head.

"Did you know Glenn Miller?" she finally asked.

"A little. Why?"

"There was a cop in the diner today asking about him. He mentioned your name, too."

Torch really hated that diner and wished Maria worked anywhere else. "He worked in the fourteenth district; now he's in South Philly."

"What's his name?"

"Kelly ... Jim Kelly. I used to go out with him." That was great. "I don't know him," Torch said.

"Well, he knows you. He kept asking about you and Glenn Miller. He's a Scorpion, isn't he? Why did he put you together like that?" "I don't know." Torch was visibly upset. "See. This is what happens. This is what happens when you have 8,000 cops in a city that can be policed by 4,000, especially these cops. That's what all the tension in the city is over. It isn't Jimmy Cerrone as much as it is your friends ... the cops."

"I just worry. I don't worry about Chick-a-dee and what happened down there and those others that were killed. I worry about what you're doing here in Logan, over Caesar's Palace. I don't know what you're into over there."

Torch was mad that the cops got her started.

"Don't worry," Torch said. "Jane home, Tarzan come home."

"What do you think he wanted with Glenn Miller?" Maria asked again.

"I don't know. I only see Glenn once in awhile. He was friendly with Charlie Tuna when we were all younger. But I never really knew him that well," he told her.

"Did you hear about Felix?" Maria asked.

"What about him?" Torch replied.

"He got moved on last night, down on Fifth Street. Kelly told me he got jumped," Maria said.

Torch was shocked that he didn't know about this. Then again, he had been downtown all day. He hadn't been around Ben's on Warnock or Caesar's Palace all day, so it was understandable.

"Kelly told me," Maria said. "He said Felix wasn't sure who it was. Kelly said it might have been Inky. He was in the Einstein, but he wasn't hurt too bad or anything, so they let him go."

Torch had been so preoccupied with Chick-a-dee's murder and the effect it would have on his business that he had not been thinking about neighborhood events. He wasn't exactly sure what the implications of this latest development would be, but he was sure there would be some. As predicted, it had already been a had been a very dramatic summer ... and they were still one week shy of the All-Star break.

CHAPTER 13

Every policeman in the City of Philadelphia was on his toes. They had been alerted to reports that residents were arming themselves in the event of an all-out, city-wide race riot. The rumors had been reinforced by several anonymous letters to *The Philadelphia Daily News*, as well as to *News* columnists John Chapman and Larry McMullen. There were also a number of disturbing phone calls to local talk radio shows.

On this particular morning, 53rd District Captain Harry Quinn called Ken Washington into his office as he did every two weeks or so for an update. It made Quinn feel good to see Washington out of his pretty suit and in the police uniform again. On the flip side of that, Washington was astonished to see that the Irish sunburn on the tip of Quinn's nose seemed to be getting brighter and brighter.

Quinn was proud that no racial problems had developed between Ben's and Logan Nation or the blacks around the Warnock Tavern, specifically a small corner there called "The Warnock Street Gang." Quinn gave Washington most of the credit for that, but it had been his idea, after all, to bring Washington back to Logan in the first place. Quinn was also pleased that there had been no new violence of any note between Logan Nation and the Nicetown gang since the end of the school year. Washington told Quinn about Felix getting jumped on Fifth Street, probably by Inky. That was small change to them. White boys fighting each other simply did not figure to have the same detrimental effect on Cerrone's campaign as a racial conflict would have, and it wasn't as embarrassing as the continuation of a gang war which had already claimed six young lives as the Logan Nation-Nicetown conflict had.

Quinn had bigger fish to fry now; specifically, the methamphetamine lab that he'd heard about a few months ago was now taking a bigger role in things. It had become more important, and it frustrated Quinn that nobody, not even Washington, could come up with the precise location of this lab.

Once Washington was seated in Quinn's office, he was given a document to read. It was an ordinary police report from the Atlantic City Police Department. The reported stated: "An underground narcotics industry is flourishing in the boomtown atmosphere that gambling will bring to Atlantic City. Federal, state, and local drug investigators acknowledge a dramatic increase in the volume of illegal drugs that flow through Philadelphia and into Atlantic City. These officials say methamphetamine, commonly called "speed" is still the drug preference.

But more expensive drugs may soon surpass speed as the favorite among the well-to-do casino crowd. Barbiturates such as Quaaludes also are commonly abused drugs."

"More and more drug dealers see this as an area to see their wares," said Atlantic City's Police Sergeant Frank McCrory of the Office of Special Investigations. "We have problems pertaining to drugs because the casinos draw a lot of people and money. And money draws drugs." We aren't talking about any penny-ante stuff going on around Atlantic City," said John Brooks, Executive Director of NARCO, a drug rehabilitation program. "We have some major suppliers in this area and the connections are unbelievable."

In an effort to identify some of these suppliers and their connection, the *Daily News* interviewed numerous drug investigators on all government levels and examined county, state, and federal court records. Those interviews and records revealed that "The Scorpions Motorcycle Club," despite numerous prosecutions of many of its members on drug and other charges, is still heavily involved in the manufacturing and distribution of methamphetamines in and around the Southern Jersey area. Philadelphia's crime family, formerly headed by the late Angelo Constantine, has always had close ties with the Scorpions."

A state grand jury took notice of the Scorpions' involvement in 1976 when it indicted thirty-one people, mostly Scorpions. The indictment alleged that the Scorpions were trying to corner the methamphetamine market. "Organized crime is involved in drugs, both in and out of Philadelphia," said Joel Stark, a cop DEA agent, scoffing at the theory that the crime family of the late Angelo Constantine does not and did not deal in narcotics.

"If anybody tells you organized crime is not in drugs, they're out of their minds," said another law enforcement source. "With the profit margin, everybody is in the act with narcotics. It's unbelievable."

"That's interesting, I guess," Washington said. "What does that have to do with us, though?"

"Now take a look at this," Quinn said. He handed Washington an official court transcript displaying the testimony of a former admitted Scorpion. Attached to the official document was a *Daily News* article which Washington was reading that stated:

"A man wearing a concealed bulletproof vest across his chest and a blue hood over his head, told a congressional committee here today that black market manufacturers of methamphetamine — known on the street as 'Speed' — have created a multimillion dollar business controlled in a large part by an unholy marriage between the Scorpions, an outlaw motorcycle group, and organized crime. Testifying before the U.S. House Select Committee on narcotics abuse and control, which conducted a day-long hearing on the spread of illegal drugs in the Philadelphia area are, the anonymous witness said he manufactured speed for two and a half years and earned 'well over' $100,000 a year for turning out the potentially deadly product. The witness had previously served time for his role in making the meth."

"Anyone can make speed," the witness told the panel, sitting at the Federal Building at Sixth and Market Streets in Center City Philadelphia. "But to make good speed is something else."

The committee convened at the request of Pennsylvania Senator Richard Francisco, a Republican from Montgomery County, zeroed in on the Philadelphia area because Francisco stated it was one of the centers for the illicit production of methamphetamine. The committee was anxious to learn why methamphetamine production and use were so prevalent in the Philadelphia area.

Later on in the article, the hooded witness noted that the murders of Constantine and Chick-a-dee had to do with their opposition to expanding their drug business. The witness said that, with Moscariello running things, he expected Philadelphia's organized crime family would be producing and dealing speed to an even greater extent.

"While organized crime is involved in the manufacturing end," the witness said, "outlaw motorcycle gangs are definitely distributing and possibly also involved partially in the manufacturing of speed." He stated the gangs, specifically the Scorpions, provide most the equipment, chemicals, and financing.

Washington still wasn't sure what this had to do with him. He really didn't care about Atlantic City or gangsters. His world was his beat in Logan. His thing was working with juvenile gangs.

"Read the transcript," Quinn directed.

Finally Washington saw what this had to do with him. The witness stated in the transcript that, as far as he knew, Chick-a-dee was not killed by Moscariello or any New York crime family like everybody was saying. He stated that he believed the Scorpions were directly or indirectly involved with the reckless and dangerous bombing of Chick-a-dee's house in South Philadelphia. The witness further testified that he worked at two of the biggest labs in Philadelphia. These labs were in North Philadelphia. One of which, the witness testified, was in the Kensington section of Philadelphia, the other in the Logan section, further north.

Also, in two separate places, the name of Glenn Miller was mentioned in the transcript. He went on to state, "Apparently Miller, who has not been charged with anything officially, is a topnotch methamphetamine cook who runs the underground laboratory in Logan."

Washington, armed with this new information, was furious. Apparently it was true. There was a meth lab in his part of Logan, and he didn't even know where it was. The inability to locate this lab angered Quinn, but it embarrassed Washington.

When Washington left the 53rd District, he caught a ride going south and got off at Broad and Lindley, above the Logan subway stop. Washington had always been on the heavy side. It seemed as though he had been in a lifelong battle with his weight. It was another reason why he always welcomed the job of walking the beat. Ordinarily, he would have walked the ten blocks from the 53rd to Broad and Lindley, but the city was in the middle of a heatwave just then and Philadelphia police cars had great air-conditioning. Cerrone even made sure that the kennels, where the police dogs were housed, were kept comfortably cool. During his first administration, the high cost of doing this caused a lot of criticism from his enemies. When the anti-Cerrone people had nothing else to complain about, they would complain about air-conditioning for the dogs. The complaints went on for years in Philadelphia.

Washington walked one block to Ben's Candy Store, sat at the counter, and drank a black and white milkshake. Then he bought the *Daily News* and read an article by news reporter Juan Gonzalez. Parts of the article summed up a lot of what was going on in Philadelphia that summer. The caption of the article read "Tensions among Ethnic Groups Heighten." The article stated:"Almost everything in Philadelphia lately has been couched in terms of black and white, especially by some in the press, politicians, religious leaders, and academics. Racial tension in Southwest Philadelphia is hardly new. But the sniper killing of thirteenyear-old Tracy Chambers last week is the most serious incident in a series of events that began escalating with Mayor Cerrone's 'White Rights' call last March. The chain of events has continued through the Charter Change movement, the Whitman Park controversies, the All-Black March in Center City to protest the lack of minority hiring and contract, for 'the Gallery,' and now the conflicts in southwest. Racial antagonists have taken us to possible widespread armed conflicts between blacks and whites."

The excellent article captured the tension. It talked of the citizens arming themselves.

"There is probably not a street in Philadelphia where some people are not already armed. The poorer the community, the more widespread the possession of guns because people often arm themselves to defend against the growing number of criminals who may attack them or their children.

The city is about half-white which also means it is half non-white. As long as blacks and Puerto Ricans are pitted against whites by this system, all will lose. While we fight among ourselves, our city falls apart before our eyes. It's our choice, fellow Philadelphians. Go the old American route of racial conflict or see all nationalities join together, not out of any idealistic love for each other, but because of a common need to survive against the problems we all face."

That night, Torch and Maria visited Lee Oskar at the hospital for the last time. He was going to be released in the morning. When they arrived at Lee Oskar's room on the sixth floor, Maria's mother and younger brother were already there. Maria's ex-sister-in-law, Rose Durie, had apparently just left,

Maria saw that Lee Oskar had company and seemed to be in a good mood, and then she asked Torch to come with her downstairs to the cafeteria in the lobby. When they got there, Maria bought a pack of Marlboros from a machine, and they sat at a booth. They both ordered only coffee. They lit up cigarettes, and Maria asked Torch about Felix, who had gotten beat up worse than was originally thought but still had not spent a night in the hospital. Torch simply said that he hadn't seen Felix yet. Maria also asked about Bah-Bah, who was moving most of his furniture into Caesar's Palace tomorrow.

While they waited for their coffee to arrive, Torch excused himself, saying he had to go to the men's room. Instead, when he slipped away, he called Bah-Bah. He bet a hundred dollars on the Boston Red Sox who were playing at Yankee Stadium. He really wasn't crazy about the game or any other of the games on the card that night. However, he planned to be in the house all that night and would listen to the game on the radio broadcasted by the

Yankees' network. The Red Sox pitcher that night was right-hander Louis Tiant, who was in the unusual underdog role. The Yankee's pitcher that night was Ed Figueroa. Figueroa was a big eight-to five choice over Tiant. Despite the fact that, according to Torch's records, Figueroa had shut out the Red Sox last September, the line here seemed very high. It was a bet made strictly on general principles. Plus, Torch wanted to give moral support to the old guy (Tiant) who was on the downside of a great, long career.

At the moment, Torch was feeling pretty good about things. Lee Oskar would be coming home and that would make Maria happy. Also, Bah–Bah had sold a few of the TV sets and, most importantly, Torch's book was returning to normal. Torch was also pleased that Bah–Bah was helping them get rid of the TV sets. Bah–Bah would know what to do with them. He could sell more TV sets in a few weeks than Torch and his friends could sell in a few months, and the best part about it was that, since the sales would take place elsewhere, Washington would never know anything about it.

Torch half–listened and sipped his coffee while Maria was telling him about the medications that the doctors prescribed for Lee Oskar. Maria finished her coffee, stubbed out her cigarette, and suddenly stood up from the table. She said, "I'll be waiting upstairs." Then she walked out of the cafeteria.

Torch didn't understand her abrupt departure until he turned around and saw Ken Washington standing there in full uniform. Torch, except for once or twice, had successfully avoided Washington all that summer. Now for the first time, he and Washington were one–on–one. Torch, for some reason rose, from his seat. Washington walked over and sat in the seat across from Torch that Maria had just vacated. The two men shook hands.

Torch was wearing a white muscle shirt with a picture of two boxers in a ring on the front of it, and with the words "Blue Horizon" which was a boxing club in North Philadelphia.

Washington said, "A guy like you should never wear a shirt like that."

Torch realized that Washington was using psychology on him. Washington almost always, in one form or another, found a way to belittle Torch. If Torch had to explain it to somebody, it would be difficult. Washington just always had something to say. After all these years, it had become almost an involuntary habit Washington had. Torch, on the other hand, had grown used to it, and it didn't even bother him anymore. It was so predictable; it was humorous.

On the flip side, Washington seemed smaller to Torch than he usually did. Torch would always think of Washington walking the beat in the winter. During those months, he wore his big police coat and carried a big black notebook that he kept under the lapel in which he kept addresses and phone numbers. Despite still having the gun and belt, Washington appeared smaller.

The waitress came over to the table, and they both ordered black coffee.

"So what's going on, Torch?" Washington asked.

"Nothing. Everything is fine, I guess," Torch responded.

"Sure. Everything is great. First Reds gets killed. Then Shine got killed, and now you have a major problem with these other white kids. Everything seems like it's going great for you guys." Washington then asked, "Can you tell me anything, Torch?"

"Tell you anything about what?" Torch asked.

"About anything. We hear reports of citizens stockpiling guns all over the city. Did you hear anything like that?" Washington asked.

"I never heard anything about that," Torch said, thinking now about the Yankees' game on the radio, which must have been starting around then.

"If a race riot ever broke out in Logan, you guys would be like a one-legged man in an ass-kicking contest," Washington said.

Torch smiled at that old expression. His father used to say that.

"This isn't a game, Torch. I don't know why you're laughing. I guess you figured out why I'm back here in the first place."

"I think it has something to do with Logan Nation and Ben's, probably connected to this election coming up."

"That's right. I'm back here to ensure that Ben's and your neighbors from Warnock Street don't start fighting. I'm back here to ensure that Ben's and Logan Nation don't start fighting again because everybody knows that would be a massacre. I heard about Felix, but that was Inky, wasn't it? That's true. It was Inky, right?"

"I talked to Felix's brother. It was probably Inky. I think it was over some girl from over there."

"A girl named Dottie?" Washington said.

Torch wasn't surprised that Washington knew the girl's name. It occurred to him once again that somebody, one of them was talking to him … it had to be that. "Well, if it was her, I'm sure Felix would tell you getting beat up was worth it."

"Felix's brother said it could be these other guys from Germantown. They aren't as big as Inky, but they're crazy. I hope it was Inky because, at least, they won't come into Logan. At least, I don't think. They have as much interest in coming around the Warnock as I do of going to 126th Street in Harlem."

"It wasn't those guys from Germantown. I know the ones you mean. What would guys from Germantown be doing on 5th Street anyway? It was Inky. So now you have your black enemies to the west of you, and your white enemies east of you, and they're the ones that will probably wipe you out before Logan Nation or Warnock Street even get a chance. Don't misunderstand me, Torch. If I sound concerned, it isn't because I really care. I have worked with gangs all over the city. I have come to realize that the black gangs only exist in the first place simply because of a pre-existing problem we have as blacks in America. With white gangs, it's a different story. They usually exist only for certain specific evil purposes. See, there's a natural tendency that people have to gravitate to those with a similar bond. It's fine for white ethnics to join clubs such as the Sons of Italy, for example. When an Irishman runs for a political office, he can count on votes, and he can count on fundraisers, support from the city's Irish population, and that's fine. The Jews, too, are famous for helping each other out … right? Those white ethnics have a strong natural bond already in place. A black man can't look at a map, point to some country in Europe or someplace and say, 'I'm from here.' The blacks don't have that, given the malicious way they were brought here. As a result, the only thing left for a lot of these youngsters is 'I'm from Nicetown,' or 'I'm from 12th and Poplar,' or 'I'm from 15th and Venango,' or 'Somerville,' or 'Brick Yard,' or 'Logan Nation,' 'The Moon Gang,' 'The Clang,' the 'Valley Gang,' etc.

"So, in the black community, a gang situation amounts to more or less a cultural problem. Given that, you can see why it is important to them. At least, you can see why they think it is important to them. Also, you have to factor in that many are less educated and generally more misguided to begin with. Then the gangs only serve to bring them down more. In the final analysis, unfortunately, there is a higher premium placed on street-gang-culture. And that is why, when you talk about the gang-related deaths in Philadelphia, hundreds of them, virtually all of the murders and most of the violence is black on black."

Torch could agree with Washington to a point. White ethnic groups often helped each other out. He thought it was overrated, however. He couldn't see, for example, how a Ukrainian Club on Broad Street in Nicetown was doing any good for its members when all they did in there was drink, play darts, and eat sausages.

"Nobody gives anybody anything just because they're a certain ethnic type. You could argue just as strongly that ethnicities and religions divide, or alienate people more than it does anybody any good. Just look around the world. Look at Ireland or Germans and Jews and all that. What good did ever it do me? For example, I mean, most everybody I ever interacted with here in Logan growing up was mostly Irish. My background never did me any good, not here and definitely not when I worked for the city. "That's what I'm saying, Torch," Washington said. "That's exactly it. Right now, you're isolated in this neighborhood, and your being Jewish isn't doing you any good. You're out here alone exactly like the black kids I was talking about. For you, there is no ethnic group of any note to which you can gravitate. For you, there is only Ben's. It's something that you think can help you, or in your case, protect you. That is why a guy like you, who can't fight a little bit, can walk around and act like the king of the jungle and not worry about anything."

Torch figured that Washington had a point. He had never really thought about it before. Charlie Tuna, Torch's brother, wasn't a corner boy. He was an easy target, just like the other handful of Jews in West Logan. He fit in with the girls though better than Torch. That was for sure and was more or less accepted because he was a good athlete. Nevertheless, Charlie Tuna experienced much more racism than Torch ever did. To be honest, Torch could only remember one or two bad experiences growing up as a little Jewish kid in Logan. Then he started hanging around Ben's, and there was a certain respect that grew out of that, even though he was only twelve years old. Then nobody minded that he went to the Catholic Youth Organization (C.Y.O.) dances. Nobody said anything like they did about Charlie tuna when Torch was in the C.Y.O. basketball league or that he played basketball at Holy Child gym. Then Torch never even thought about somebody fucking with him.

Washington advised, "The sooner you become a man and learn to walk on your own, the better off you'll be. Then you'll see. You'll receive the support and you'll kick ass. Right now, you are an accident waiting to happen. That goes for all your friends. You guys are at a funny age right now. Everybody wants to fit in. Nobody wants to look like a pussy. That is a recipe for disaster. You have to grasp the very real concept of life after twenty-five or thirty. The trick is to get to that point and to reach there in one piece. Listen to me now. It's a shame because you have a lot of glue in your head; you could achieve something. That corner-boy stuff is more detrimental than you realize. It's an old story, but it still is true. I mean, you get labeled. It's guilt by association. First the teachers label you. Then the adults in the neighborhood, the neighbors, label you. Pretty soon, this negative reputation develops. You start only interacting with the worst kids in the neighborhood because the others want to stay clear of you, and that includes girls, too, by the way. Eventually, you get labeled by the cops, probation officers, and even judges. It's a never-ending vicious cycle. Eventually you get in serious trouble, not just because of shit you may have done, but you'll start getting blamed for shit you didn't do ... that's labeling. You will suffer from something somebody else does. Keeping your own nose clean isn't good enough anymore because you can't control what the others in your circle are responsible for.

"Take Frenchie for example. He is a guy that single-handedly can get everybody hurt or get everybody in trouble. He may not want to do it intentionally, but with guys like that, it tends to happen anyway. He nearly did it before. I'm right about that, don't you think?" "What do you mean?" Torch asked.

"I mean, when he shot Fat Eddie."

"Do you really think he did that?" Torch said.

"Don't you?"

"I'm not sure. I don't know. All I know for sure is that the guy they arrested was innocent. I knew him. David Hoffman."

"You *knew* him?" Washington said it like Torch just told him that he knew Lee Harvey Oswald. It made Torch smile.

"I knew him. He used to play basketball every day in the schoolyard. He got along fine with the black kids over there. Everybody knew he was innocent. I haven't seen him since then, but I saw his sister a few years ago. Her name was Susan. She was good friends with Leo's sister. Their family and Frenchie's family had to vacate the neighborhood that same day with just the clothes on their backs. They ransacked their houses. Don't get me wrong. Frenchie is a boll weevil and a thief, but I don't have him as a sniper."

"How about Fat Eddie, did you know him? "Washington asked.

"I didn't know him at the time. I guess I saw him in the schoolyard, something like that. Then a few years after the incident, I was with these three white kids, the Reynolds brothers, I grew up with them. They lived down there in the heart of Smedley Valley, and when there was that Civil War, they just stayed there with their neighbors, the black kids. Anyway, I was with them one day, and there must have been twenty or thirty of us down there, drinking wine, smoking reefer. I never felt uncomfortable down there ... Smedley Valley, I mean. Fat Eddie was there that day. He didn't seem to hold a grudge about what happened to him. He never was comfortable from what I heard about how they made him this martyr and used his getting shot as a kick-off for them riots. That's really my only memory of him."

"Well, Frenchie did that, Torch. There is no doubt in my mind. It was during the summer, and the windows were open. His mother was ill at the time. She was on the couch but couldn't sleep because Fat Eddie was riding his mini-bike up and down the street. Frenchie went out and told him to stop. Fat Eddie told him to go fuck himself. Then Frenchie called the police from a phone booth from the candy store there on the corner … Chester's, but there was no response. Then he called them about fifteen minutes later. They still didn't respond. So, he shot Fat Eddie. Later, he told some girl, and she told me."

Torch shook his head. "It doesn't prove anything. Maybe you're right. Maybe there was more to it, a grudge or something between them, how do you know? Plus, that part of Logan you know, there was a lot of tension back then. You have to put it in context."

"*In context?*"

When Washington started talking about Frenchie, Torch suddenly remembered his dream that he couldn't recall the other day outside the diner. He and all his friends were in the back of a pick-up truck. The truck was red, sort of like the one Fred Sanford owned, and Frenchie was driving. He made a sharp left turn, so sharp that everybody flew out of the back. Torch went sailing through the air and landed right in the bushes that surrounded the North Star Diner. Then he woke up.

"It's in the past. That was years ago. Now the kid stuff is over, Torch. You guys have reached the turning point in your lives. The writing's on the wall. Either get married and get a job, or you'll be in some bar in Logan ten years from now, the only white guys around, and saying to each other, 'Do you remember we did this?' and 'Do you remember we did that?' As for right now, I'm losing my patience with you guys. Things are going on right under my nose, and I'm the

only one that doesn't know about them. It makes me look foolish."
"What things?" Torch asked.

"For one thing, what about those TV sets that were stolen?"

"TV sets?"

"The ones stolen from Nate's Reliable about six or eight weeks ago."

"You know, this is the third time I heard about those TV sets," Torch said. "What is so important about them, and why does everybody think I know about them? Some cop was asking Maria about those TV sets at the diner. That was the *first* time I heard about those TV sets."

"The TV sets aren't important to me. It is my boss. He's obsessed with you guys for some reason. I tried to tell him nothing is less significant than what you guys are doing. The Scorpions are making a move to run a lot of organized crime in Philadelphia and Atlantic City, and my boss thinks you guys have something to do with the Scorpions. He overestimates you. He's convinced that, because the TV sets were stolen on a Sunday night, the offenders had to be white. He said that if the thieves were black, the crime would have been committed on a Friday night." "What?" Torch said.

"It has something to do with the idea that white offenders would be afraid of getting caught and having to spend the whole weekend in jail, whereas black offenders wouldn't necessarily worry about it."

"I don't know about all that," Torch said. "That sounds crazy."

"You're right Torch. It is crazy; criminals don't go into an enterprise thinking of the consequences. In large part, that's what makes them criminals in the first place, and I think that applies especially to young offenders because the crime is generally more spontaneous. I still think that you know where those TV sets are. It has nothing to do with them being stolen on a Sunday night."

"Like I told Maria two months ago, on that particular Sunday night, we all went to the movies. We go to the movies a lot on Sunday nights," Torch said.

"What movie?" Washington said.

"I don't remember the name of the movie. It wasn't a movie like *Jaws* or *Gone with the Wind*. We go to the drive-in movies on Sunday night. It's called the perversion-excursion. Even all the girls go. The movie was probably called *The Swinging Cheerleaders* or *The Naughty Nurses* or something like that," Torch explained.

Washington grinned at that. He had told Quinn that these guys were only kids.

"Like I said, I personally don't care about those TV sets," Washington said. "I'm concerned about something else right now. Do you know Glenn Miller?"

Torch wondered to himself what Glenn Miller must have done that would suddenly make him so important to everybody. "I know him vaguely. That is, I *knew* him. I haven't seen him in a few years," Torch offered. Torch pictured Glenn ... brown hair, wiry strong. He looked like one of the Rolling Stones on the pamphlet of one of their .45s in the 1960s. Torch always thought of him like that for some reason. He looked like one of the Stones.

"There is a meth lab in Logan. It is somewhere right around the Warnock. Glenn Miller is involved in it. We want him to come in and finger the place for us, and we'll take it down at a time he isn't there. Otherwise, we will eventually find the place on our own. Then we will nail him to the cross. We'll hit him with the R.I.C.O. law, and he'll do a *minimum* of twenty years. I'm looking for some cooperation from you, Torch. I never forgot about that murder case."

"What murder case?" Torch asked, although he knew exactly what Washington was talking about.

"That guy you called 'Spit Upon John.' You know what I mean, up on the railroad tracks," Washington said. "I know exactly who was up there when it happened."

"You said you know, huh?"

"It was simple police work. The murder was committed in the afternoon during a school day. I knew you guys used to cut school up there."

Washington was right about that. In those days, it was dangerous for white kids to go to public schools in Logan. That was especially true if they thought you were from Ben's or any white corner for that matter, but particularly Ben's, and that could be virtually anybody. Most of the white kids in Logan went to Catholic school, but some went to public school. They solved the problem in their own way. They simply didn't attend. It was why Logan had one of the highest truancy rates in the city during that era. It was comical; there were more kids on the tracks playing hooky on the weekdays than there were out on a Saturday night.

"You, Felix, Jackie, and Teddy all cut school that day. I never thought you had the balls to do it yourself. I'm certain it was Felix or Teddy, probably Teddy since he left the neighborhood the next day. But all of you were there, so it doesn't matter. What was that all about, Torch, some deep hatred of homosexuals?"

"First of all," Torch said, "being a faggot is one thing. Walking around in a security guard uniform, paying corner boys to spit on you and punch you is something else. Personally, I never talked to the man. Bad things happen to guys like that. What can I say? I'm surprised he lasted as long as he did, if you want to know the truth. Shit, I can remember him crawling around the floor in the Logan movies and us stomping on him, spitting on him, throwing popcorn on him, laughing our asses off. As for homosexuals, the answer is no. I don't particularly like them. Just don't put your hands on me, and I don't care what you are."

"Torch, the guy Base, he was sick. We all understand that. But you just described some sick, bizarre behavior on your behalf, too, you and your buddies."

"Fuck him," said Torch. "What am I? Phil Donahue? Besides, that was a long time ago. I think the movie was *Bonnie* and *Clyde*. That shows you how long ago that was. I'm not saying he deserved to get his head cracked by a railroad spike."

"How did you know it was a railroad spike? And what the hell do you know about homosexuals?"

"I heard it was a railroad spike. Maybe it was something else. What difference does it make. I knew a few homosexuals from high school and I worked with a few of them. Like I said, I'm not

Phil Donahue or somebody. I admit, I'm not an expert on them. Basically the men are bitches and the girls are ball-breakers. I'd say from the little that I *do* know of them. I went to high school with a transsexual." "You mean a transvestite," Washington said.

"A transvestite is a cross-dresser. This was a transsexual. It was originally a boy named Terry who actually went through the operation. Isn't that a great name? Terry? It's as if his mother named him that saying, 'I'm going to name this child Terry, so in case he ever becomes a girl, he won't have to change his name.' Since I knew he was really a boy, there was no fire there as far as I was concerned, no electricity, but she was beautiful. She looked like a young Marilyn McCoo of the Fifth Dimension."

"Marilyn McCoo, that redbone was the love of my life," Washington said. The statement threw Torch off guard for some reason. He'd never heard Washington say something like that before ... sentimental, you might say. He wasn't very generous when it came to compliments in the second place.

"I saw her sing 'One Less Bell to Answer,'" Torch was saying. "I'll never get that image completely out of my mind. I think it was on *The Ed Sullivan Show.* That was a high-water mark in my life, seeing her on that show."

Washington remembered in his interviews with Torch that he was infatuated with black women. The fact that Torch was never with a black woman no doubt added to the mystery or allure for him. He never knew until now that it was connected to him seeing Marilyn McCoo on Ed Sullivan way back in the 1960s.

"Them black girls really turn you on, don't they, Torch?" Washington remarked.

"Ain't it all pink on the inside?" Torch replied.

"I don't know," was all Washington answered. But then he said, "Let's not get off the subject. That particular murder means nothing to me, except it was on my beat. It makes me look bad ... an unsolved murder. All I want to know is about this meth lab. I know you guys have nothing to do with it. I know you have nothing to do with the Scorpions. You wouldn't be hurting anybody you know by helping me out. Besides, you'd be doing Glenn a big favor. Plus, I will never bring up all that murder again. It will be closed as far as I'm concerned. There is no statute of limitations for murder, and I'm the only thing that stands between you getting away with it. I know you know or heard about this meth lab. Things figure to get tough in the near future, given the climate in the neighborhood and in the city in general, and it would be in your interest to have somebody like me as a friend. I know you write numbers, ya know? All of us know. But out of respect to Maria, we leave you alone. At least, so far, we left you alone. Don't worry, Torch. You're too small for anybody to care. Your strength is in your lack of strength.

The meth lab, that's a different story."

"You mean a speed lab? I never heard of anything like that."

"All right. Keep your eyes and ears open for me, it will benefit you somewhere down the line."

The meeting was apparently over. Washington got up from his seat. Then he said: "Remember what I said, Torch. It is time to make the transition, man. You need to separate yourself from your boys. Shape up and be a man, little Jewish kid."

"I knew those guys all my life," Torch said.

"Hey! You knew shit all your life, too," Washington retorted.

Torch didn't respond to that. Washington let that settle in for a second, and then he added, "Remember when you used to do all those imitations? You used to talk like Edward G. Robinson and Johnny Carson?"

"Right."

"Well, try being yourself sometime."

Torch wasn't shocked that Washington made that statement. He had said the same thing before to him years ago. Then he came up with a new one.

"Do you remember that movie with Humphrey Bogart, *Casablanca*?" "Right ... *Casablanca*."

"Well, remember when that cop says, 'Round up the usual suspects'?" "Right, of course, I remember that," Torch said.

"Did you ever think about what he meant by that?" Washington asked. Then he walked out of the cafeteria.

At home, Torch listened to the Yankee's game on the radio. Yankee sluggers Craig Nettles and Chris Chambliss hit home runs off Louis Tiant sealing a 7-2 victory over the Red Sox. Torch knew it was a bad bet.

CHAPTER 14

On the last Saturday in July, *The Daily News* printed an anonymous Letter to the Editor. This letter was typical of five or six letters that sparked rumors of certain Philadelphia residents arming themselves in anticipation of a race riot.

Re: Whitman Park

"This is clearly a racial issue. The blacks are for it and the whites are against it. If it should all result in violence, terrorizing, bombing but is contained in that area, federal troops could very well keep it under control. On the other hand, should the majority of Philadelphians throughout the city become involved, the project could start a revolution."

The heat wave continued in Philadelphia through that weekend. It was type of mid-summer weekend when it seemed that every white person in the city was down the shore. Torch thought about going into Center City, but he figured there would be little, if any, action down there. Maria was working at the diner that weekend, and Lee Oskar was at his grandmother's.

Torch, Pin, and Frenchie visited Felix, who was still recuperating at Danny Parker's house. Felix said he couldn't wait to move back into Caesar's Palace in a few days and that he never felt comfortable at Danny Parker's since the day Reds was killed there.

The four of them bought a case of beer and played pinochle. They watched two major televised prize fights which frequently came on TV on Saturday afternoons in those days. One fight featured Torch's hero, featherweight Danny "Little Red" Lopez. Lopez was a fan favorite and was on TV a handful of times. He was improving with every fight, and this was a stepping-stone toward his title chance in 1979 which he would win.

The other bout featured South Philadelphia's Matthew Saad Muhammad. He was a light heavyweight, and like Danny Lopez, he was a favorite of the networks and of all boxing fans. In addition to his skill, Matthew Saad Muhammad displayed incredible heart. The light heavyweight division was the most exciting and competitive of all in the late seventies, and Saad Muhammad was right in the middle of it. To Philadelphia boxing fans who were numerous and knowledgeable, Saad symbolized the era, and the eventual World Champion did not disappoint today, winning the bout in five rounds. At the top or almost at the top of every weight class in the sport of boxing there was a Philadelphian representing. Philadelphia, at that time, was still a big city with a provincial outlook and an inferiority complex. As Peter Binzen pointed out in his book, *Whitetown U.S.A.*, about Kensington (an Irish section in the lower northeast of Philly), "This was the city where even the head of organized crime lived in a simple row home." In a way, the city was like an adult who still bought his clothes at the Junior Bazaar. Since nothing major was going on, Philadelphians learned to embrace the small local treasures available to them. These small things included cheesesteaks, Friday with Frank/Sunday with Sinatra, watching Julius Erving in the winter, and Steve Carlton pitch every fourth day in the spring and summer. In the sixties and seventies, Philadelphia was still a top-notch boxing town, just as it had been in the days of Jack Dempsey. They talked about boxing as much as any other major sport. A lot of the joy locals had was connected to the rich local boxing lore and history. Nineteen-seventy-eight was a changing point for Philadelphia in many respects, for better or worse. Boxing sort of typified that overall change and indeed seemed like the perfect metaphor. This one boxer was in right in the middle of it. Thirty years after the fact, a website, phillyboxinghistory.com would reflect of this era:

"Matthew Saad Muhammad left the nest and moved to the budding world of casino boxing and fame on national TV. Saad's battles at the Philadelphia Spectrum were among the last of their kind in Philly's great history. Furthermore, 1978, the best year in spectrum history, was really the beginning of the end for old-time boxing in the city. Before long, all the major bouts would be staged in Atlantic City or Las Vegas, and the golden age of Philly boxing would be a thing of the past."

Also that day, Torch and his boys watched a televised exhibition match between pool legends Willie Mosconi and Minnesota Fats. The contest was televised from Resorts International Hotel and Casino, the first casino in Atlantic City. According to an article in *Forbes Magazine*, Bally Corporation, which had a near-monopoly on the manufacturing of slot machines, reported that Resorts this year bought 1500 of their machines or roughly $3 million or about $2300 a piece.

★ ★ ★

On Sunday, Bah–Bah brought some things from his house up to Caesar's Palace. Mac, Turkey, and another guy named Kevin were on his steps, and they all went inside the house with him. Bah–Bah had a deck of cards, rice paper, a calculator, a box of chocolate doughnuts, and a carton of chocolate milk. He showed them a card game, an Italian card game called *Sette Mezzo*.

At one point that afternoon, the four of them walked to Ben's Candy Store. On the way back, Washington snuck up behind them and had them spread eagle against a garage door. Turkey, who was thinking that Washington was off that day, unfortunately had a small canister of marijuana on him.

"What's this?" Washington asked when he found the pot in Turkey's pocket.

"Spices for my mother," Turkey said.

There were certain guys that, for no good reason, Washington didn't like, and Turkey was one of them. Pin was another. There were a few like that.

Washington withdrew his police radio from his belt. He barked in some numbers, gave their location (13th and Windrim), and requested a wagon.

Bah–Bah wanted to turn around and say to Washington, "Wait a second. I don't even know these guys. I don't know anything about that pot."

He managed, instead, not to say anything. What he did do next was pretty amazing. Washington was going through Mac's and Kevin's pockets. Bah–Bah, then, took his hands off the wall, straightened up, and started walking away toward Caesar's Palace. He acted as if this matter had nothing to do with him, which, as far as he was concerned, it didn't. Washington, seeing this, quickly withdrew his nightstick. He grabbed Bah–Bah by the back of the neck and led him back to his place against the garage door.

Then Washington said, "I don't know where you're from or what cops you've dealt with, but when I put you against a wall, you don't get off that wall until I say so. And you never ever walk behind a police officer like that." Washington spilled out the contents of the canister in the street and then resumed frisking everybody. He started with the biggest one there — Kevin, who was wearing dungarees and a wife beater T-shirt. which exposed his bare arms and a tattoo of a boxer with the word *Southpaw* written under it. He said to Kevin, "What's your name?" "Kevin Walton," he answered.

"Do you have a brother named John Boy?" Washington asked.

Turkey and Mac laughed at Washington's very rare attempt at humor. They knew he was going to let them slide the minute he spilled out the evidence.

Washington then withdrew the radio again and called in some numbers and said, "Disregard that request for a wagon." Turning to the others, he growled, "You three get out of my sight, and don't say I never gave you a break. I want to talk to Fred Flintstone here."

Turkey turned back around and said, "Hey! Thanks, Washington. Thanks a lot, man." Washington could see then, from the way Turkey was slurring, that he was already a little high. "I'm not giving you a break, Turkey. I'm giving Mac a break. Mac, get him out of my face."

About twenty feet away, Turkey turned around again and said, "Really, Washington, I appreciate it."

"I'm not going to say it again," Washington said. Bah-Bah was still spread eagle against the garage door. Washington walked over and stood behind him. He had Bah-Bah face him and then Washington asked, "Do I know you?"

"I don't think so," Bah-Bah said.

"Did you ever do time?" Washington asked.

"No," Bah-Bah answered.

"Do you want to?" Washington said. Then he added, "South Philly, right?" Bah-Bah was startled.

"Originally, yes. I work up in the northeast now, so I bought a house over there on Windrim Avenue," Bah-Bah said.

"I already know where you live," Washington said. "Where do you work?"

"Paramount Auto. It's on State Road." Bah-Bah knew the owner of Paramount Auto Supply. He was officially on their payroll as a sort of phantom employee. Bah-Bah thought it was a good idea in case anybody started asking questions.

"Ask your new friends about me. See, I just gave them a break because I like Mac. If it weren't for Mac, I would have busted Turkey right there. See, it's a good idea to get on my good side. As for you, to tell you the truth, I haven't made my mind up about you yet. That's up to you."

"They aren't my friends," Bah-Bah said. "I don't want any trouble up here."

"Well, it doesn't look that way," Washington replied.

"I haven't broken any laws. Those guys are always on my front steps. Naturally they were the first ones I met. To tell you the truth, I'm not really looking for any friends or anything like that. I'm a married man. I got a son."

"All right," Washington said. "Go join your friends and just keep your nose clean. Don't let them talk you into anything stupid. A crime is a crime. It doesn't matter if you were coerced into it or whether or not you originally planned it. Keep that in mind. Those guys are no good, man. They are boll weevils. Do you know what a boll weevil is?"

Bah–Bah had heard that term used a few times up here. "It's an insect," Bah–Bah replied.

"Right," Washington said. "A boll weevil is an insect that doesn't do anybody any good and takes everything. A boll weevil will take your house, eat your cotton, eat your food, and won't leave until you have nothing left. That's what those guys are. I'll be watching … now go."

★ ★ ★

That Monday Torch booked pretty good. It reminded him of when business was better and things were in full swing. Mickey, the bartender from Center City, played the number 3–7 box for $50. It was worth $3,000 if he connected. He had been playing that 3–7 box occasionally for the past two weeks. Mickey, in addition to being a bartender, was also into real estate and would occasionally go crazy with these numbers. He said that he'd had a dream about two weeks ago where he saw Paul Newman playing *Cool Hand Luke* running through the swamp. In the dream, just like in the movie, Paul Newman was wearing a blue work shirt with the number 3–7 on the back of it. That story cracked up Torch.

A waitress from Oscar's named Kay bet a number with Torch for three dollars. The number was 514. She said she had a dream with the number 415 in it. She said she reversed it because, "When you dream, it's like a mirror image, so you see everything backwards. Didn't you know that?" She said it like Torch was supposed to know that somehow. Torch was thinking to himself, how the hell would I know something like that?

Lee Oskar was home and seemed to have made a complete recovery. In fact, he looked better than he had just two days ago. Maria was noticeably happy about it all. She was grateful and appreciative of Torch's support and apparent concern during the illness. It made it harder, therefore, to do what she was going to do. She had fallen in love with Jim Kelly again who kept visiting her at the diner. She figured that she probably had never stopped loving him in the first place. Kelly didn't like Torch, and Maria wasn't about to let him keep writing numbers from her house. She was waiting for the right moment to spring the bad news on him. She had thought it over thoroughly. Jim Kelly was simply a more practical choice, although she had feelings for both men. There was a certain security in being the wife of a policeman. Also, Jim Kelly would be a real father figure for her son. She was an adult and a parent and had to have thick skin about this.

Bah-Bah's phone wasn't hooked up yet, but he called Torch from a phone booth in Big Jim's Luncheonette next to the Warnock. Bah-Bah told him what happened Saturday and his run-in with Washington. It disturbed Bah-Bah that Washington already knew him.

"I told you about him, so what? You didn't do anything up here. He's letting you know you're on his radar that's all. Everything's games with that guy. I told you about him."

* * *

There were no games on the baseball schedule that night, and Bah-Bah was going to drive up to New York later in the day. He told Torch he had won big playing cards the previous night and now he was taking the Kennedy family out to have breakfast. That was what Bah-Bah had started calling Torch's friends — The Kennedy Family. He called them that because he couldn't remember all their names, mainly because he didn't care enough to. The only thing he was certain about was that most of them were Irish, so that was what he called them — The Kennedy Family.

Torch was listening to WHAT, a talk-radio station in Philadelphia geared toward the black community. It had an all-black staff and the overwhelming majority of callers and listeners were black as well. On this day, the topic of conversation was the registration drive. The host of the show at the moment was talk-radio veteran named Gary Snowden. He was saying that the numbers in recent weeks had been relatively sluggish. He noted that it possibly had to do with the extremely hot weather in the past few weeks, but that was no excuse. He pointed out that, to blacks in Philadelphia, registering and voting in this special election was no less important than the Civil Rights marches in the sixties.

Then he even played a song that Torch remembered from the 1960s. Torch hadn't heard the song in ten years and had only heard it once. It was the day Martin Luther King was assassinated, and they brought all of the children into the gymnasium of Logan Public School. Each child was given a sheet of paper with the lyrics of two songs on it. The first song they sang was "We Shall Overcome." The other song was the one Gary Snowden was playing right now. It was called "Won't Turn Me 'Round."

* * *

That afternoon, Bah-Bah stood on the steps of his new house with a half dozen of his new friends, including Frenchie, Felix, and Doc, who also lived at Caesar's Palace.

Doc was older than everybody else. He was in his late forties or maybe in his fifties. For all anybody knew, he could have been in his sixties. It was hard to tell with him. He was an ex-Marine, who was discharged before the Vietnam War. Despite that, he came home extremely troubled anyhow since his mother had died while he was over there. Torch didn't know Doc before, but from what people told him, he had been extremely close to his mother. He apparently was a classy guy and had dressed always well before that happened. Now he was an alcoholic, a meth user, and part-time heroin user, in that order. He had a red beard and ponytail and looked a little like a cross between singer Willie Nelson and actor Barry Fitzgerald in the movie *The Sea Wolf.* Until he set up housekeeping at Caesar's Palace, Doc had lived on the street. From time to time, he would find an abandoned house to squat in, but mostly he lived in abandoned cars. He played football or stickball and drank in the Warnock, just like everybody else. He had aged dramatically in the past five years due to the booze, drugs, and a few extremely cold winters in the mid-seventies. Everybody, from the old ladies to the little children, knew him. He was a favorite among the kids who called him "Dippy Doc." They really did love him, probably for the same reason they loved Big Bird or Fat Albert. The kids, no doubt, saw him as simply a harmless, almost animated character. He spoke in a raspy voice and moved almost always in a herky-jerky kind of fashion. He walked with an exaggerated stroll, frequently with a quart of Schmidt's in his right hand. He walked almost always with his eyes scanning the street for discarded change, jewelry, lighters, watches, or whatever treasure he might find. Occasionally, you would ride down the street and see Doc acting like a jeweler examining something that he found in the gutter. Doc was friendlier than the others with the blacks in the neighborhood. That turned out to be a very smart move because in a few years, the neighborhood would become entirely black, except for Doc, and they (the blacks) more or less took care of him. He was a survivor, and Torch used to think that, if he didn't die in his sleep from the cold one night, he would outlive all of them.

While it was true that children loved him, dogs, on the other hand, hated him. Even the most timid dog wanted a piece of him. It could have been because of their acute sense of smell that was offended by an odor that he usually emitted. He didn't hurt anybody though and was, generally speaking, a kind sort with a pleasant disposition. He knew just about every diet pill doctor in North Philadelphia. He was the one that overweight people saw to set up appointments for them. Then they took advantage, buying a $10 or $12 prescription which enabled them to obtain around eighty Schoobies which they sold for $1 apiece. Of course, Doc always received a gratuity for that.

In the final analysis, Doc was no more or less a boll weevil than the rest of them were.

While they were standing on the steps, they heard a tremendous noise from around the corner. Apparently, an abandoned house on 11th Street had an explosion and subsequently a small fire started in the basement. Soon the narrow street was filled with police cars and fire engines.

Philadelphia police vehicles, until the 1970s, had always been red. Beginning in 1973, the old police cars and vans were being replaced with new blue vehicles. That had been Jimmy Cerrone's idea. He said that he wanted the police vehicles to be blue to distinguish them from the fire department so that his brother, who was the fire commissioner of Philadelphia, would know the difference. By now, the summer of 1978, most of the police vehicles were blue. Although there were still a few of the red police cars left at that point in time. Anyway, on this occasion, both blue cars and a few old red cars were on the scene.

Bah–Bah and the others watched as the firemen fought the blaze that ensued and eventually got it under control. Then Bah–Bah left to go into Center City to see a big customer, a lawyer who drank in Oscar's.

★ ★ ★

It had rained hard the previous night, and now everything seemed fresh and cleansed and cool. Torch crossed the tracks on his way to Ben's. He noticed the cucumbers in Maria's garden were almost ready to be picked, along with the lettuce she planted. The tomatoes were full already, but still green and inedible. It was going to be a great year for tomatoes later in August. Torch exited the tracks by Ben's as usual. Inside an old guy named Izzy, who used to take orders when the Penn Fruit across the street was still open and later worked at the fruit stand with Torch and his friends, was playing pinball. Izzy went to every 76ers home game as well as to the Palestra where he watched the Philadelphia College basketball games. He was drinking a large bottle of Coke. The Staple Singers were on Ben's radio singing "I'll Take You There." Torch sat at the counter and drank a black and white milkshake with a package of Cheese Nips. He looked at the girlie magazines and read the letters to the "Happy Hooker" in *Penthouse Magazine*. All was well with the world.

In the *Daily News*, there was a report of Jimmy Cerrone at a press conference. Cerrone was quoted as saying, "We are living in awful times and the press has done more than its share to make them awful. I have never seen such viciousness as that being done now by the press." Cerrone complained of "a new type of reporter, who is a stranger to Philadelphia, unfamiliar with its ways and is not accountable to anyone. With paper and ink, they destroy people, families, and cities." Cerrone said that, contrary to media reports, Whitman Park was not populated by racists. "The people who live there are good, decent, hard-working people who are afraid of having their neighborhood ruined by low-income projects. Those people aren't racists, and I agree with them."

Torch then walked across the busy intersection outside of Ben's to the delicatessen on Old York Road. As always, Ben wanted salami on a Kaiser roll with mustard. On the way back, Torch saw Washington out of the corner of his eye and tried to ignore him. Washington confronted him and said something like, "What's in the bag, Torch?" "It's a sandwich for Ben," replied Torch.

"It seems like every time I see you, you're holding a bag. I have a theory about guys like you." Washington said.

"What's this now?" Torch asked.

"You see these homeless guys always walking around with bags and stuff, even in the summer. Do you know why?" Washington asked.

Torch couldn't wait to hear this one.

"I think they think that they're carrying their mothers around with them," Washington said.

That was typical of the type of thing Washington would say. Torch remembered a few times seeing Washington downtown at City Hall when he was testifying there in court. Torch had a customer who worked in a bagel shop. He sometimes paid Torch off with a huge bag of bagels, and once or twice, he may have been carrying a bag. Now there was this time, which was possibly the third time Washington saw Torch with a bag. In none of those instances, however, was Torch carrying his mother around with him. At least, he didn't think he was.

"How about that explosion the other day?" Washington said.

"I heard about it," Torch replied.

"It was a meth lab."

"You don't say."

"You knew about it," Washington said.

"I heard about it last night for the first time. At first, I thought it was just a rumor about the meth, I mean, but I put it side by side with what you told me at the hospital and guessed that was the lab you were referring to. Like I told you before, I knew nothing about it."

"I'll tell you a secret," Washington said. "That explosion was intentional. It wasn't an accident like everybody is saying. They found chemicals in there used to make a type of bomb." Torch flashed on Glenn Miller.

"See, I tell you things, Torch. You need to throw me a bone one in a while. That's only fair," Washington said.

"All right, I'll tell you something. I'll tell you a secret. Two or three guys were down the shore on vacation, staying with some girls at a house down in Oceanwood. Apparently the police down there found out that they were from Logan. At the crack of dawn one morning, the police raided the house with shotguns and everything from the front and the back. They searched the house. Apparently they thought there was going to be some retaliation for what happened to Shine, which is ridiculous. Then the next day two, secret service type guys walked into the Warnock and asked all these questions about Shine's friends. They had suits on with the dark sunglasses and the whole bit. They wanted to know what Ben's was. I swear, that's exactly what they said. 'Ben's.'"

"I'm ahead of you on that, Torch," Washington said. "There is more to it than that. See, after Shine was killed, those cops down there received death threats. They traced one threatening call to the Warnock. That's why they were on their toes and a little paranoid. Those cops took the threats seriously, and they don't fool around down there ... obviously." Then Washington added, "I never understood exactly what happened down there that day. What? Did he try to jump over a drawn drawbridge? Who did he think he was, Burt Reynolds or somebody?"

"No, it wasn't anything like that. He never saw that they had raised the drawbridge. That's what everybody thinks ... what you're saying, I mean," Torch replied. "See apparently these guys —" "Who were they?" Washington asked.

"Frank, Louie, Sean, them guys. You know Frank, the roofer with the black hair, him, and Mouse. You know him."

"Eugene," Washington said. "I know him."

"Well, they were asking questions about the incident for a lawyer that is looking into the case. They found out seven years ago the same thing happened down there. One lady saw them do the whole thing this time. She said they turned out the lights and drew the bridge open. She claims she saw everything. But apparently from what this lawyer said, her testimony wouldn't be credible because her son was killed in the same type of accident down there seven years ago. They said her testimony would be thrown out. I don't know how much sense that makes, but that's what I heard."

"Well, what really happened down there was this," Washington said. "Frank and Mouse were down there; you're right. And also, Frenchie was there. Frenchie was sick; he was throwing up. They were on the Boardwalk, I think."

Torch knew that Frenchie had ulcers so that sounded possible.

"Some cops down there saw that Frenchie was sick and asked if they could help him somehow. Then they started talking, and somebody mentioned Shine and that he was a friend of theirs. That was why the cops were concerned about it. Don't tell me Shine's family is going to have a lawyer look into that?"

"Where is the money gonna come from?" Torch said.

"That's what I thought," Washington said. "It's probably just as well. Nothing good would ever result from a lawsuit like that. Down there, it's a different story. New Jersey is a different world from Philadelphia."

"That's true, but the Scorpions' lawyer is looking into it. And he is one of the top lawyers in the city. Did you ever hear of Malcolm Jokelson?" Torch asked.

"I'm a cop. He is the Scorpions' lawyer. What do you think?"

"That's the rumor I heard. I don't know if it's true," answered Torch.

"That's pretty hard to believe," Washington said. "There's nothing Shine's family can do about that; it's over. It's a real shame. The boy couldn't help himself. He was a classic car thief. I mean, most of the time, when Shine was arrested for car theft, he was just out joy-riding. It wasn't necessarily economic. Look at the time down the shore; look at that sports car he was driving. He could never afford a car like that in his wildest dreams. That's why he stole cars, I think. It was more or less connected to an inferiority complex he had. As I said, he was a classic car thief. That's all that was. It's like he had an illness, and stealing cars was his way of self-medicating. It was like some use drugs. Stealing cars gave him a rush. It was a speed high of sorts. In fact, that's exactly what it was."

"Whatever it was, that was dirty pool what happened down there. That wasn't nice," Torch said.

"Torch, in some ways I agree with you. As a criminal psychologist, I could make a sympathetic case for Shine. As a police officer though, I would have to take a hard line. I mean, hard-edged criminals have a saying, 'A cop is a cop is a cop'. Well, there's a flipside to that as well which is: 'A criminal is a criminal is a criminal.' And I'll tell you something else. I don't care if they get F. Lee Bailey, they are never going to get anything out of that case. For one thing, Shine didn't even have a job, so how can they sue somebody? Are they going to prorate how many Schoobies he would have sold over the next forty years?"

When Washington said, it was like a speed high, he really hit the nail on the head as it applied to Shine. He remembered Shine playing that game in Ben's store, an addiction; yeah … that's exactly what it was. It all didn't make it any better, though. If anything, it made it worse.

"I got to take this sandwich over to Ben's now," Torch said.

"Oh, yeah, that reminds me. I wanted to ask you something. Why is it that you guys don't hang outside Ben's anymore? Why it is that you originally hung at Ben's, then you went two blocks east to the Mr. Grocer's, then you went three more blocks east to 10th Street and the Warnock? Why is that?" Washington asked. "You keep going further east all the time. Why did you move from outside Ben's in the first place?"

Washington knew the answer to that, and Torch knew that he did. It basically boiled down to the natural progression of the neighborhood: blacks in Logan started moving in on the west side of Broad Street and gradually moved more and more east. As a result, the white kids who remained moved further and further east themselves. They were like a middle-aged guy's receding hairline, going back and back and back. Torch didn't need to explain that though, and instead addressed the other specific question: why didn't they hang outside of Ben's anymore? "I don't mean this as a racial slur or nothin', but somebody from Logan Nation could sneak up there on that catwalk with a rifle, and it would be a dead aim to Ben's store. That's why we don't hang outside there."

Washington turned around and looked up at the bridge. Then he looked at the distance toward Ben's. Torch was right. It was about half the distance that Oswald had been from Kennedy.

★ ★ ★

That night they planned to go to Liberty Bell Harness Racetrack. It had been Torch's idea. Moshannon Express was entered tonight. It was his first race back since that Saturday night when he and Maria watched him lose narrowly and finish second. That night, the horse had a tough trip. He wasted a lot of energy going from side to side, and he was "parked" on the outside for quite a while, never finding a "seat." He was in a softer spot tonight and would probably be the post-time favorite. Jack Kiser had him picked second, at 2-1 odds. Kiser's comment was *"Took scenic route last."*

It was still light out about 7:15 when Torch met Bah-Bah, Felix, and Billy Young on the steps of Caesar's Palace. The first post at Liberty Bell was at eight o'clock, but Moshannon Express didn't run until the finale which wouldn't go off until about 10:30. Torch told Billy and Felix that he would come back and get them in an hour. Then he and Bah-Bah walked down to the Warnock Tavern. On the way to the bar, Torch explained that the others were going to transfer the TV sets from Grant's house to Caesar's Palace.

Bah-Bah stopped suddenly and said to Torch, "I locked the door before I left."

"Don't worry about it. Let's just go down to the bar, have a few drinks, and they will be on your back porch in an hour."

When they got to the Warnock, there were two police cars parked outside the furniture store across the street. A helicopter circled high above them, directly over the railroad tracks. Torch told Bah-Bah that the helicopter was a railroad-police helicopter that occasionally would ride above the railroad tracks looking for vandals or trespassers. Another police vehicle, one van with the numbers 5301 on the side pulled up outside of the Warnock. The cops, four or five of them from the three vehicles, were continually looking skyward toward the roofs or toward the helicopter. Bah-Bah noticed that about a dozen people were outside the bar now looking up toward the roofs.

"What happened? Bah-Bah asked somebody.

A neighbor, who had been in the bar, explained that a few kids from the neighborhood were up on the roofs drinking a case of beer; it was no big deal. Torch remarked that maybe those same kids were breaking into one of the stores. There was a moving company there called Fagan's, Mark's Beer Distributor, and an auto body shop.

"They got them, though. The railroad detectives got them. They're not going anywhere," the man said.

The scene made Bah-Bah think of the movie *Dog Day Afternoon* with the helicopter and all the people and the hot weather and everything.

Evidently one of the suspects was fourteen-year-old Henry Taimanglo. Four of his seven brothers were outside of the bar now. They stood in a line all together with their arms crossed and kept looking up at the roofs. Finally a railroad detective, who was familiar to Torch, appeared on the roof about fifteen feet up. He was talking to the officers down the street. From the body language of the police on the street, the unmarked cop on the roof was saying something that irritated them. Now about twenty curious spectators were outside the bar, looking up. Eventually a fire truck with a hook and ladder pulled up right outside the furniture store on the sidewalk. A mobile stainless steel ladder was placed against the wall, making a stairway up to the roof. The plainclothes officer on the roof led the four boys to the ladder, and they started climbing down. The first one was Mitchell Briggs, who hung around with Henry Taimanglo. Although this was an unusually peculiar thing going on, Torch thought he understood part of it.

He explained to Bah-Bah, "See, Philadelphia police don't generally go up on the railroad tracks. I guess it has something to do with private property or something. The police on the roofs are just railroad detectives. I guess they didn't want to walk all the way down to Logan Station with the perpetrators in handcuffs. On the other hand, they probably didn't want to bring them off the tracks, climbing over some wall or in between some hole in a fence or something like we do, because if somebody got hurt and the police weren't authorized or something, you know it might involve insurance or something like that. It's the only thing I can think of for why they would do something like that."

It was true, Philadelphia police, for whatever reason, rarely went on the railroad tracks. It was, after all, why kids used to cut school up there in the first place and why generations of kids used to drink up there. It was a virtual sanctuary from both police and adults Over the years, Torch could only remember three instances when regular Philadelphia police came on the railroad tracks. The first time was in 1973 after a policeman on the beat walked into Kane's Bar next to the Asia Restaurant on Broad Street while a robbery was in progress. The officer was shot and killed, and the police pursued the killer who ran up on the tracks and was eventually shot and killed himself. The second time was a few years later when a policeman saw Torch and his friends on the tracks. He jammed on his brakes, jumped out of the car, and made a futile attempt to try to catch them. Torch always laughed thinking about that occasion. The cop was a heavyset sort with one of those big red W.C. Fields noses. Then there was the time when Washington himself surprised Torch and his friends coming up there on those very same roofs. It was in the afternoon, and they were minding their own business, joyfully passing around the Boone's Farm Apple. Everybody jumped off the edge of the roof except Torch. It wasn't that he was unafraid. He simply didn't have the guts to jump off the roofs like everybody else. Washington, for whatever reason, let Torch slide. He seemed much angrier at the ones who ran in the first place. It didn't seem to Torch to make much sense anyway, running from Washington, since he knew everybody's names and addresses.

Along with Jackie, the three of them walked into the Warnock. "Victim" by Candi Staton was on the jukebox in the bar:

Wasn't hardly worried about tomorrow
You were my future
As long as I was being satisfied
I didn't need nothin' else nah, nah, baby

Grant was bartending and placed a bottle of Miller in front of each of them. Torch was updating Jackie on what Washington had told him the other night at the hospital. He told Jackie about how Washington said he knew it was them on the tracks that day and that now Washington was asking about the TV sets. Torch said he was certain somebody was giving Washington first-hand information.

Torch said he knew because he used terms or words like "Caesar's Palace" or "Schoobies" or "spit upon John," and those were things only they said. How else would Washington, who was just a cop after all, know all these terms unless somebody was talking to him?

Then Jackie said, "You know, I was just thinking about something. One time I was talking to Connell." (He was the former I.R.A. member who now lived with his cousins nearby in Olney). "Connell told me that, in the Catholic neighborhoods in Northern Ireland, the I.R.A. discourages crime. Connell said it's because, if a Catholic boy gets arrested by the Protestant police, he's going to be put in a situation where they might offer him a deal where he'll have to infiltrate the I.R.A. That's why it benefits the I.R.A. to deter crime. Connell told me, if they catch you stealing or anything like that, do you know what they do? They shoot you in the kneecap, not with a real bullet, but with this hard plastic type of bullet. They shoot you right in the kneecap."

Torch flashed again on that dream that he had, the one where Frenchie was driving that truck. Jackie didn't need to spell it out. He was talking about Frenchie. Frenchie was a guy, after all, who always had one foot in jail.

Bah-Bah got up and walked to the men's room. Another customer was at the urinal, so he walked to the middle stall with a toilet. This was really strange. Life was really strange. It was like there was a giant explosion in South Philadelphia, and he'd gotten blown up with it and suddenly found himself here in North Philadelphia, right in the middle of the cast of *West Side Story.* This was a strange place. He didn't like the way everybody used his house as a hangout. What irritated him more was the way everybody automatically assumed that it was all right with him and also the way they made themselves feel comfortable there. Aside from all that, though, Torch was right about him being safe up here. It was a little similar to being in a foreign country. That was how different it was to him. It was strange the way they had all of these ground rules up here, like that thing across the street just now. And then there was that explosion on 11th Street. What was that all about? It was also strange, too, the way these guys talked, including the cops. Everything was a joke or a fable or a story. Everything had a moral or a hidden message, and they always used chickens or roosters or pigs or boll weevils to illustrate their point, like they were in kindergarten. Then there were those nicknames including Pig, Worm, Squirrel, Mouse, Charlie Tuna, and Fat Dog.

There apparently was a speaker in the bathroom. The music was loud in the bathroom, just as it was in the bar outside. A song was playing that Bah–Bah had never heard before, but he recognized Jerry Butler's voice singing, "I'm Just Thinking 'bout Coolin' Out."

I need a break from this routine
Tired of chasing this old, tired dream

I'm just thinkin' about coolin' out
I'm just thinkin' about coolin' out
I'm just thinkin' about coolin' out

Bah–Bah relieved himself. He looked up on the wall and saw something written in pen right above the toilet. It read: "Be like dad, not like sis. Lift the lid before you piss."

Above that message was another, this one written in Magic Marker. Bah-Bah had taken courses in poetry to fulfill an English requirement before he graduated from Pennsylvania University, therefore, he knew a little about poetry. This was one he never saw in an anthology.

I had a little rooster, oh yeah ... and
I put him on a fence ... and
He said he was from Ben's, oh, yeah ... because
He had good sense

BOOK III

Caesar's Palace

CHAPTER 15

Torch didn't understand women. He probably knew less about them than most of his friends, and that's saying something. All his life, he never could grasp it. He knocked his head against the wall. He never understood why a woman wanted a tuna that tasted good and not a tuna with good taste. They wanted a real man, one who worked and had his shit together. Didn't they know that he was developing and perfecting the perfect baseball-betting formula? Didn't they appreciate that he would be making several hundred thousand per season? They weren't impressed by his gangster-in-training-act. Woman didn't buy into his bullshit at all. They didn't appreciate or care about his knowledge of Sinatra or Humphrey Bogart or Roberto Duran. Torch only knew Maria at the moment, and that was enough for him. In the last week or so, Maria seemed more passionate to him both in and out of bed. Even Torch could pick up on it, and it both surprised and excited him. Of the two of them, however, only Maria knew that this was the end of something and not the beginning of something. It was tantamount to a grand finale, sort of like the one at the fireworks display on the Fourth of July in Olney.

It was one morning in the first week of August when Maria read Torch his rights. She explained the part about Jim Kelly and the drastic change that was going to take place. She talked a lot about Lee Oskar and said that she based much of her decision on her concern for him. She made decisions; some were right, but she made mistakes along the way, too. Right or wrong though, Lee Oskar always came first. She talked about Kelly's plan to move to Denver. She said that, on the very afternoon Kelly told her about that plan, she had spoken to Lee Oskar's doctor who told her that her son would do better someplace that was dryer and cleaner. A place like Colorado, she thought to herself.

Torch knew that Maria wanted to be a cop's wife. He knew all along that it probably was unrealistic for him to think he could ever change that.

Maria was in the kitchen making breakfast for them. Torch got a few phone calls from small bettors. Maria listened to Torch repeat the bets.

"Four, one, two, box a squirrel."

"Seven, three, three, fifty cents over a squirrel."

"You want seven, one, eight, straight a fish. That's three–fifty overall."

Maria figured that she had simply outgrown Torch. She thought of that girl Stephanie in *Saturday Night Fever* when she said to John Travolta, "You're nowhere. You're a cliché, man. You're nowhere, and you're headed no place."

Maria listened to the radio in the kitchen. A Philly group, the Delfonics, were singing:

So you think no one cares (oh, boy)
What a down thing to think of
And if you give me a chance I will give you a true love
And every day I watch you
I just can't do without you
You're so doggone pretty
I got to have you and I gotta sayyyy

Torch was arguing on the phone with some woman from a collection agency who had just called. She asked Torch to go to a neighbor's house up the street, knock on the door, and tell them to call a certain number. The woman on the phone said that the client had her phone disconnected. Torch yelled at her not to call him again and hung up on her.

Torch came in the kitchen and explained to Maria, "It was a collection agency. Beverly from up the street owes somebody money again. I told them before that I didn't want to get involved. Like I'm really going to go up there and knock on her door. The same people called about six months ago. In fact, I think it was the same lady."

"They called yesterday, too," Maria informed him. "I just told them that I knew her, but I wasn't really friendly with her, and I really didn't want to get involved."

"Of course, what gets me is, they probably call all the stupid honky neighbors on the block and ask them to go to her house. The probably don't even ask the black neighbors, you know what I mean?" Torch said.

The Delfonics and Maria sang:
And every day I watch you
I just can't do without you

Torch told Maria about going to Veterans Stadium again last night to see the Phillies against the Cincinnati Reds. The Reds won the game 8 to 6 on a grand slam hit by the Reds' George Foster.

John Chapman wrote an article the next day in the *Daily News* about the apparent suicide of a young man confined to a wheelchair. Chapman wrote that the youth had been paralyzed in a gang confrontation in 1974. He apparently had wheeled himself off the 30th Street Bridge near West Philadelphia into the Schuylkill River. Then Chapman wrote something about the young man, whose name was Calvin Hunter, being a spokesman for the anti-violence and anti-gang war movement in the 1970s.

Chapman, as he usually did when he wrote about gang wars in Philadelphia, added the poem by Gwendolyn Brooks:
We real cool
We quit school
We lurk late
We shoot straight

We sling sin
We thin gin
We jazz June We die soon.

Torch and Maria watched Channel 6's Action News at twelve o'clock. The lead story was about the back-to-nature group called MOVE whose headquarters were at a house in West Philadelphia. Several of the MOVE members, including one named Delbert Afrika, who held a rifle, were interviewed. For six months now, the Philadelphia police had continued a 24-hour surveillance at the house. Dozens of Philadelphia residents of all races spent time outside the house just hanging around. Everybody in the city knew that, at some point, the administration would have to deal with the MOVE members and that peaceful negotiations were not working out. The MOVE members represented a "clear and present danger" as one report put it. Several of the MOVE members had outstanding warrants against them for minor infractions. The MOVE members pointed out that they were a peaceful organization and had a right to be left alone. They talked about Cerrone's police state. They protested Cerrone and particularly the Philadelphia police. In one incident, a female MOVE member allegedly had a harsh confrontation with the police resulting in a miscarriage. The MOVE story, like the Whitman Park story, was another giant racially charged situation that Cerrone had to deal with that summer.

The next story concerned a police raid on a house in North Philly where cockfighting was going on. The news anchor tried to make it sound real important and shit. "The successful raid," he said, "was a coordinated, joint effort between the Philadelphia police and the S.P.C.A." "Looks like somebody didn't get paid off." Torch said.

"You think so?"

"Just guessing. Who knows? Did you ever see one, a cock fight?"

"I saw them in P.R. Of course, it's legal there. It's kind of cool at first. The birds look like little boxers in a ring. I mean, they are bobbing and weaving." As Maria said this, her head went from side to side, imitating the birds.

"Why don't they leave them people alone?"

"Because it's barbaric. I mean, birds can get killed or permanently injured. The owner sees this and wants to pull his bird out, ya know, rest him, put him in a lighter spot in the future. But the bettors, the men, they are like animals. They don't give a shit about the bird's health. A bird could have his eye-hanging out of its socket, and they are yelling for the manager to keep his bird in the fight. I mean, I seen some nasty shit. But it's what you don't see that's worse. My uncle raised them to fight. He had two of the toughest birds on the island. They were full brothers. One was named Carlos Zarate, and the other was named Carlos Monzone, after the boxers. Carlos Monzone, he was the better of the two … Monzone. I was around it, and from him, I knew a little about the business. When a female would give birth, they would take one of the babies, and they'd put him in with a champion fighter. They know the baby has no chance of winning, and he'll probably get killed. They just want to see if he shows some heart. If he does, if he puts up any kind of fight, then they'll let his siblings live. If the baby shows no interest and tries to escape or fly away, then they'll kill his siblings. You don't know anything about that racket. Believe me, that shouldn't be legal anywhere. You don't know what you're talking about. Stick to baseball, *gringo*."

When Maria was talking about the birds fighting, it made Torch think of something. "I remember you fighting that girl in the schoolyard.

Man, that was a battle."

"Which time? There were a few times."

"The famous one. 'The Thrilla in Manilla.' You know which one."

"Valentina, I remember it," Maria said. "She was tough, but I got the best of her. I think I won. Well, really she won. It was over some guy.

He was a dope fiend."

"Was it Lee Oskar's dad?"

"Some other guy, he made Lee Oskar's dad seem like Mr. Rodgers. We became friends after that, me and Valentina. She lives in Maryland, but she has a son up here someplace. She was in the diner a year or two ago."

Maria asked Torch about his conversation with Washington the other night in the hospital.

"He was just asking me some stuff about the tests he used to give us," Torch replied. And really, that wasn't too much of a lie. It was his usual games anyway.

"What were those tests anyway, Torch?" Maria inquired.

"Just some questions dealing with the environment and other things like drugs and slang and things like that."

"I never understood what all of that meant, when you told me about it before."

"I don't understand it myself, Maria. I think it has something to do with how people are restricted by their environment, something like that. I mean, you could have a virtual genius, a person who can obtain and retain all this information, but he could be walking around not knowing how to get a job, how to act when he gets that job. He could maybe not know the capital of the state or who the vice president is. Instead, he might know all this stuff that will never do him any good. That doesn't mean he isn't smart. I think that's what Washington was getting at," Torch said.

"Did you tell me that he was writing a book about you and your friends?"

"It wasn't a book. It was more or less a study that he was doing. He said that he gave the same test to black kids and white kids in Logan. He said they scored the same, but in spite of that, the black kids were more at risk for dying early or going to prison."

"Give me an example of the kind of things he would ask you," Maria said.

"I forget most of it. I remember one set of questions. They had to do with drugs. One of them was 'What is second generation pot?'"

"That's when you have a handful of roaches, and you unwrap the roaches and then make a joint out of it. That's second-generation pot," Maria said.

"That's right. Another one was, "What is pancakes and syrup?"

"I never heard of that one."

"It's Robitussin and Doridins. Anyway, those are examples of the drug part of the survey. Then he had a cultural test that had to do with prison terms and slang and things like that. Another thing he asked us was what 'to take him off the count' meant."

"Doesn't that mean to kill somebody, take them off the count?" Maria asked.

"You're pretty good at this."

"Ask me another one." Maria was enjoying herself and felt that Torch seemed to be in an all right mood considering that not only had he just been kicked out of his house and office but he also had his guts ripped out like Ingrid Bergman did Humphrey Bogart in *Casablanca*.

"Another one was 'what are wolf tickets?'"

"Do you mean like he's selling wolf tickets?"

"Another was 'what is *The Watchtower*?'"

"The newspaper? The Jehovah witnesses' pamphlet?"

"What are 100 aces?"

"I don't know that one."

"I knew you wouldn't get that one. It's a Pinochle term, meaning there's an ace in every suit — clubs, diamonds, hearts, spades."

"What does pinochle have to do with crime?"

"I didn't say it had anything to do with crime. That's not what Washington was trying to say," Torch responded.

"What exactly was he trying to say?"

"It is simply an intelligence test, but it's a different kind of intelligence test. I don't know. Ask Washington the next time you see him."

Torch wasn't angry with Maria. She was doing what she had to do. On the other hand, he wasn't interested in remaining friends. He didn't even know what he was still doing there playing these games with Maria.

At one o'clock, Torch went out the back door and across the tracks to Ben's. He drank a Cherry Coke and then went on to Caesar's Palace where everybody was sitting on the steps, including Bah-Bah.

One of them called Navy was talking about one time when they were up in the mountains. Another one of them called Butch had a cabin there. Navy was saying that, one night, they were outside cooking and two bears came to the campsite. Everybody ran to their parked station wagon, locked the doors, and watched while the two bears began to demolish the campsite. They knocked over the chairs and the food that was being cooked. They were in the process of destroying everything when a much smaller bear came upon the scene. The smaller bear was on all fours, unlike the others who stood up like humans, which only made him look even smaller. Despite that, when the other bears saw the new bear, they broke camp, related Navy. "See, it didn't matter that the other bears were bigger or that there were two of them. This other bear was a grizzly."

Before Navy could say anything else, a car pulled up, across the street from Caesar's Palace. The occupants of the car were white teenagers. They didn't get out of the car at first though. They were just sitting in the car talking, as if debating the issue. Finally, a guy and a girl got out of the car. Yet another of Jackie's brothers, Chucky, apparently had gone to Holy Child with them, so he walked over to them. Bah–Bah watched as Chucky talked to the occupants of the car and saw him shaking his head. Eventually Chucky came back across the street by himself and explained that apparently Shine had taken money from them, about $50, to buy them Schoobies, and they had some idea that they would be reimbursed.

"That is the most ridiculous thing I ever heard," Felix said. "Shine is dead. What did they expect us to do about it? This isn't Sears. Tell them they're burnt."

"Right," Jackie said. "Tell them there's an old saying, 'He who pays in advance is poorly served.'"

Just then Bah–Bah noticed Felix whispering to a guy named Polski whom Bah–Bah saw around Caesar's Palace before a few times. Polski ran into Caesar's Palace. Chucky walked back to the car and began talking to the driver. Polski came out of Caesar's Palace with something wrapped in a towel, which he hid under the tire of a car. Then he sat on the steps again.

As much as Bah-Bah wanted to see what happened, he had many things to do that day. First he had to go up to his office in the northeast. Then he had to go downtown to his newsstand. Torch also was busy that day. He had to go into Center City which he only did once a week these days. They decided to eat first. They were going to Porky's Point in North Philly about ten blocks away. Torch and Jackie got in Bah-Bah's Cadillac.

Bah-Bah handed Torch $345 that he'd won betting the previous week. Torch had won twice on a pitcher that had been gold for him all summer. His name was Ross Grimsley, now of the Montréal Expos in the National League. Grimsley was a left-hander traded to the Expos by the Baltimore Orioles of the American League. It was a tactic Torch used whenever the situation presented itself; he would bet on lefthanders switching leagues. It worked like a charm; at least, in the case of Grimsley, it did. He won twenty games in the 1978 season, usually as an underdog. It was, by far, the best season Grimsley had had in a fourteen-year career. Torch removed the cash, stuffed it in his pocket without counting it, and threw the envelope out of the window.

They all had money just then. Moshannon Express didn't disappoint the other night at Liberty Bell. He ha changed tactics and stayed close to the lead throughout. Then in the stretch, he pulled away easy for a two-length victory. The Logan contingent hammered him at the betting windows. He went off slightly better that two-one and paid $6.40 which wasn't too bad, considering the weak company and the fact that Jack Kiser had picked him near the top.

Jackie sat up front and worked the dashboard radio. The Rolling Stones were singing their song entitled "Miss You." Bah-Bah didn't say anything, even when Jackie turned it up. The truth was, though, that he didn't like the Stones. Like many his age from South Philly, he was still into Three Dog Night or Chicago, even after they adopted that soft, pussy, "Saturday Here in the Park" sound. Like many of them, though, for the most part, "the Day the Music Died" (the day Buddy Holly died) really *was* the day the music died.

Porky's Point had a wide assortment of food. They had chicken sandwiches, egg rolls, shrimp fried rice, cheese steaks, and their specialty, roast pork. They also had things like Pig's ears and blood sausages. Torch knew of only two other places where 'blood sausages 'were sold. One was at a spot in The Italian Market in south Philly. The other was in The Reading Terminal Market in Center City. Porky's Point was the only place in North Philly that sold 'blood sausages'. Bah-Bah and Torch ordered roast pork. Jackie was wearing dungarees and a green shirt with white writing on it. The inscription read, *American by birth, Irish by God*." He ordered two cheesesteaks.

When the food came, they went to one of the outdoor tables. They all drank sodas.

Bah-Bah said, "This isn't roast pork. I don't know what to call this. It looks like veal scaloppini."

"That's roast pork. It's just different from what you're used to. That's pulled pork, unlike the South Philly-style pork. You guys crack me up. It's like nothing ever existed, except South Philly. It's usually made with a gravy that's too sweet, but it's all right here. Generally though the South Philly-style with the raab and provolone is better, I admit. Nobody ever even heard of veal scaloppini up here. Forget it. It doesn't exist."

Bah-Bah said that he had been fighting with his wife. He had been staying at Caesar's Palace, instead of going home at night. Bah-Bah was curious about what had happened outside of Caesar's Palace that afternoon. Torch told Bah-Bah that it was too early in the game for him to start asking about the Schoobie business. He told Bah-Bah that the less he knew about that, the better. He said that everybody got touchy when an outsider started asking about that and "outsider" included him.

Then Jackie said to Bah-Bah, "A chubby guy like you could make out pretty well."

"It's true," Torch said with a straight face. "You could clean up, especially since Shine's death created a vacuum. He sold between two and three hundred Schoobies a week."

Bah-Bah remembered how Washington warned him about getting sucked in by these guys. Apparently he was talking about this very thing. They already had him working by selling TV sets. Bah-Bah wasn't sure if Torch was serious about him going to the doctors to get diet pills. He was sure that it wasn't going to happen. Torch, with his baseball winnings in his pocket, picked up the check.

Jackie kept Bah-Bah company that day. They drove Torch to Broad Street, where he caught the soul train going south into Center City.

It was while on the subway that Torch thought about the column Chapman had written that morning. It suddenly, finally, just then dawned on him who Chapman was talking about. He remembered that, when he was in Parkway High School, a film had been circulated and shown throughout the city's public schools which featured a young man talking to his brother about the senselessness of the gang-related violence in Philadelphia. The speaker had been shot and was then in a wheelchair. Torch was certain that this was the same man that Chapman had written about that morning and his suicide.

When Torch was on the phone doing his work that morning, then reading the paper in Ben's and then being with his friends, he hadn't thought about his situation with Maria. It was lonely on the subway, though. The impact of it all hit him just then. There was some graffiti written with a magic marker on the door of the subway operator's car. It was lyrics from a Rolling Stones' song:

You can't always get what you want
You can't always get what you want
But if you try, sometimes, you just might find
You get what you need

CHAPTER 16

For the past week, Torch had been writing numbers out of Caesar's Palace. All his customers were calling him at that number. Torch spent some nights there, sleeping on the couch downstairs. Other nights he slept at his parents' house in the northeast and drove back to Logan in the morning.

In Philadelphia, the deadline for the revolutionary group known as MOVE was approaching. It was now only no more than a few days away. Jill Porter, a columnist for the *Daily News*, wrote during the first week in August: "There has been some indication recently that MOVE members might refuse to abide by the court order which gave them ninety days to evacuate their headquarters at 307–309 North 33rd Street."

The DA from Philadelphia, Ed Rendell, said, "If they do not vacate by midnight of the ninetieth day, they will be in violation of an outstanding order of the court." Another city official said, "I don't anticipate anyone violating the order."

The big issue throughout the whole affair had been that there were children in the house. There were rumors that many of the children had been sent off as a potential confrontation with the police neared.

Once again the district attorney from Philadelphia stated in the article that it was his understanding that there were no children in the MOVE residence at the present time, but even if there were, police would still go in and make arrests. "No one is to blame if the children get hurt but the MOVE members. Make no mistake about that."

Mayor Cerrone warned that MOVE members would "be put down with legal force" if they ignored a clear-out-immediately court order that the city would seek tomorrow morning. "Sufficient force will be used," he asserted in a meeting with reporters outside his office. "They name the game. Whatever force they use, we'll use more."

The article reported that Cerrone had stated repeatedly during the long stand-off, that began in May 1977 when the city tried to make health code checks in the vermin-infested house, that the presence of children was all that stopped a police invasion of the group's barricades.

"But now," the mayor said, "there will be no more negotiating, no more meetings. It's been a circus long enough. We've been tolerant. We can't prolong it anymore."

"We want to end this peacefully without giving up any of the community's rights. MOVE members have broken the law, and they'll have to stand trial," added Rendell.

The *Daily News* reported that sixty-nine police officers, ranging from a chief inspector to detectives, had been on patrol daily outside the MOVE house since May, waiting to serve warrants on the eighteen members believed to be inside. The salaries over that time had amounted to $1.2 million. Rendell stated, "The city may have waited a bit too long. There is a need for action. Anytime eighteen individuals can tie up a major city ... it's not a good result. But remember, the DA can't order the police to execute warrants."

Police had ringed MOVE headquarters since the May 20th incident when members appeared on an outdoor platform of the house pointing firearms and making threats, demanding that three of their members be freed from prison. Many MOVE members were slated for common pleas trials on felony charges, including rioting and weapons violations.

Jill Porter of *The Daily News* also wrote that: *"Insiders say Jimmy Cerrone would like to avoid a potentially bloody confrontation at MOVE* since it could make for an uncomfortable campaign issue if he runs for a third term." (Of course, Cerrone would have to be victorious in the charter change election this fall for that to even be possible.)

Asked yesterday if he believed politics was involved in the inaction so far, D.A. Ed Rendell replied that he had reached a point where he believed "politics is involved in choosing between vanilla and chocolate ice cream."

★ ★ ★

On Friday night at ten o'clock, Bah-Bah sat at the kitchen table of Caesar's Palace with four or five others, playing a poker game called guts. There were about eight or nine of the regulars either in the kitchen with them or out in the living room watching TV. Then there were about four or five other kids that Bah-Bah didn't recognize. A few of the people there were drinking bottles of beer, but some were not drinking at all except for cups of coffee made from a Mr. Coffee machine that had been in the kitchen since Bah-Bah moved in. An eight-track player was playing the 1978 nasty Rolling Stones Album *Some Girls* off of which were big cuts like "Shattered" and "Miss You." Then there was an 8-track of a live concert by the local outfit, The Magnificent Men. The blue-eyed soul group was from Harrisburg, Pennsylvania, but played all around Philadelphia in the 1960s. This particular 8-track was of a live concert they did at the Uptown Theater on North Broad Street in the sixties.

During the entire night, the doorbell kept ringing. Strangers would come in the house. They were all young, in their late teens or early twenties. They would go upstairs for a few minutes with one of the regulars, and then they would leave. Bah-Bah assumed it had something to do with purchasing marijuana or schoobies. At least the ones Bah-Bah didn't know would ask him politely when they wanted to go upstairs to use the bathroom. Except Bah-Bah noticed that up here though, most of them pronounced it "baffroom." The ones that he knew, the ones from Ben's never even extended him the courtesy of asking. That was how he knew the difference. They acted like it was their house since the beginning. Bah-Bah himself started to think that it was pretty funny. Bah-Bah had not expected this at all. Torch explained that there were a few squatters there. And frankly it didn't bother him, at least initially. He didn't have friends up here, and the company was welcomed. Somehow having people around made him feel better, a little more secure. He thought he was buying an abandoned house, a "haunted house" they used to call them. Instead he discovered the place was already partially furnished with a sofa, chairs, tables, and even conveniences like the Mister Coffee, a working oven, a refrigerator and a stereo. It was like buying a built-in den of inequity. Having company was one thing, but he didn't think he would come home like the other night at three or four in the morning and find various speed freaks playing cards or doing crossword puzzles and drinking coffee. And they were never embarrassed at all. You couldn't embarrass them. He worried about what they were using his house for and all these teenagers especially on the weekends. Many of the youngsters were strangers to him. There were a lot of girls on the weekends, some from the neighborhood and others from the northeast. They made him more than a little nervous because they weren't shy or embarrassed at all.

Bah-Bah mentioned that he had seen the infamous "sinking homes of Logan" for the first time that day. He said Torch had told him that, in twenty years, the sinking homes would have to be demolished.

Fancy Frank was drinking coffee and sitting directly across from Bah-Bah. Frank was often at Caesar's Palace late at night, playing cards until morning. At the moment, he lived at his mother's house around the corner but spent more time here. He had worked as a bouncer at a club in Center City, formerly controlled by Constantine. At that time, he had an apartment in South Philadelphia. The disco was now run by Moscariello, and Frank lost both his job and his apartment. He had curly brown hair and was darker than most of the others. A year or so ago, he started to add a vowel to the end of his last name and out of nowhere claimed that he was half-Italian. Bah-Bah never saw him drink anything other than coffee. He spoke in rhymes and riddles, but on this night, he had been quiet. When Bah–Bah started talking about the sinking homes, it seemed to open the floodgates, and Fancy Frank didn't shut up after that.

"They've been saying the sinking homes would be demolished ever since I was a kid. They probably were saying it ever since my father was a kid. They were saying it in the thirties.

"When I was about twelve, we used to thumb over to Jersey to swim. There was a place there called Holiday Lake. Sometimes we would hitchhike to Oceanwood. The first few times I was with older guys, and I was scared. It was the first time I had been away from the neighborhood. Seeing all of them New Jersey license plates, that kind of bothered me. It was like I was in another country. We'd come home over the TaconyPalmyra Bridge, and then come down the Roosevelt Boulevard to Logan. The first thing you would see was those crooked sinking homes, and then I knew I was home."

The eight-track player blasted the signature song by the Magnificent Men.

All the things a man could suffer from
I've suffered from
All the things that I've overcome
I got tougher from

Frank continued his lecture. "Same as when I got back from Vietnam in 1972. Man, that was a trip. They not only didn't know why we were over there, they didn't even know where Vietnam was. It was like, 'Yeah, Vietnam, it's over there some place."

"I got sent home, and we were flown into the North Philadelphia Airport up in the northeast. I thumbed down the Boulevard just like when I was a kid. I got a ride right down to 9th Street, and you could see those slanted sinking homes. Until then I didn't cry or anything, but when I saw those houses, man, I just broke up. The thing I thought about was all those other guys I had been there with, who wouldn't have this experience.

"There was a Pat's Steaks right there off the Boulevard. The whole time I was over there, all I thought about were those cheesesteaks. They were lousy cheese steaks, but they were still cheesesteaks. This

Pat's Steaks had a sign on the side that read 'Of South Philadelphia Fame,' but I don't think it was. Anyway, the first thing I did was eat two cheese steaks. It's funny. Everybody from Philadelphia that was over there said they were going to do the same thing. 'Man, the first thing I'm gonna do when I get home is go right to South Philly and Pat's Steaks and get me two wit onions.'"

Bah-Bah was about the same age as Fancy Frank. Like him, Bah-Bah was a Vietnam veteran, and he could relate to everything Frank was talking about. The Magnificent Men sang,

"I know it's just a matter of time. I'm gonna find peace of mind."

"Yeah," Frank continued. "That food over there wasn't exactly like Bugs cooking. That food was nasty. The navy had better food."

Bugs was the official cook at Caesar's Palace. Frank often spoke in a type of rhyming pattern, especially when he was doing speed: "G.I. beans, G.I. gravy. Gee! I wish I joined the navy."

They continued to play cards. Fancy Frank had lost several hands in a row. At one point, he got up and walked into the living room, opened a closet door, and went inside and stayed there for about three seconds. The he got out of the closet and walked back to the table and sat down.

Bah-Bah was amazed by that behavior. He was more amazed that nobody else seemed to think there was anything out of the ordinary about it. Nobody even seemed to pay any mind to it.

A new eight-track was playing now. It was a live version of a concert Billy Paul in England. *Thanks for saving my life*

For picking me up

For dusting me off

hanks for saving my life

Felix's brother Johnny or J.R.B. was talking to Bah-Bah, pointing to his little half-pint bottle of gin that he was drinking with orange juice. The bottle of gin had the brand name Gordon's on it. Then Johnny said: "Little Leon with a grin, drank a bottle of Gordon's Gin. Leon said, after he got plastered, go to hell, you shitty-assed bastard." The eight-track played and Billy Paul sang:

I can live

I can live
Now that I found you baby
I can live
I can live

A new song came on the live album. It apparently was from England. Bah–Bah had heard this particular song a million times. It was all you ever heard in Philadelphia around 1973, but he never heard this particular version before.

Billy Paul was talking now, and he said, "I'd like to thank my English audience because if it wasn't for you, I'd have never won the Grammy Award for this particular song in 1972."

His voice was half-singing and half-talking now. "We're giving you the Philadelphia sound. Coming from Philadelphia pool rooms and Philadelphia back alleys, the Philadelphia ghetto and back streets. That's where we hooked up and started a thing. That's where they started talking about …"

Then he sang:
Me and Mrs. Jones, we got a thing goin' onnnnnn
We both know that it's wrooonnnng
But it's much too strong
To let it go now
We meet every day at the same café,
Six-thirty, and no one knows she'll be there. Holding hands, making all kinds of plans,
While the jukebox plays her favorite song

Fancy Frank was talking a mile a minute now about the Leaning Tower of Pisa. Frank said it was the same problem as with the sinking homes. He said the tower was built on unstable ground and by the year 2040, the tower would topple over, unless something is done to straighten it. The thing was the Italian government didn't want to straighten the tower because the bottom line was that the slant gave the tower its charm. He went on to explain that, if the tower were straight, it really wouldn't be the tourist attraction the way it was now. Frank said the unstable foundation that the building was on was similar to the cinder and ash foundation that the sinking homes in Logan were built on.

★ ★ ★

On Monday, Bah-Bah met his best friend, Bob Santore, at the Logan Restaurant on Broad Street. Bah-Bah was complaining about his situation. He told Bobby about how these guys thought nothing of eating breakfast, lunch, or dinner at his house. He went on to tell Bobby about Bugs and all the cooking that he did. Recently, somebody had shot a deer, and Bugs had cooked that. He told Bobby they were always eating something. They either had chicken or spare ribs or food like that.

"These are white guys?" Bobby asked Bah-Bah.

"Yeah, this is Torch and his boys. Yeah, they're white," Bah-Bah said. Then he rubbed his chin like he was in deep thought about it. Finally he said, "Sometimes it's hard to tell, to be honest with you. They don't realize it, but they got like a black accent. It confused me at first, but a lot of them sound a little like Richard Pryor. Not Richard Pryor exactly but a few of the characters he does in his act. They played an eight track of his, and when I first heard it, it hit me. Then they got a few up there like this one cat Bryon. You close your eyes, you would swear he was black. Torch said he was from Somerville, about ten blocks away from Logan. It is all black over there, he said. Torch said, when Byron first came around there, you couldn't understand him which is kind of funny because I still can't understand him. He was a graffiti artist Torch said. His name was *Bstarr*. He had been living on the street, there at the house, or in abandoned cars for years. Only up here, they pronounce it 'abandit.'"

"Bryon's like an artist," Bah-Bah said "He showed me these sketches he did. He had about twenty-five of them. Most were of these graffiti writers. Some depict these ghostly figures; they were comic-like with these weird, funny noses. The figures, he said, represented the writers, and you only see their heads looking over the walls. The walls had things spray painted on them. The figures were the writer, and the wall was his because, see, he defaced it, and he was looking over the wall for cops or neighbors. He said he got caught earlier this summer writing things in a schoolyard. He had to whitewash the entire place. He said he was drunk when it happened and it was such a poor job. He was embarrassed. He wasn't embarrassed about getting caught spray-painting on the walls, he was embarrassed about how sloppy it turned out."

"The other day," Bah–Bah continued, "this guy Bugs was making 'elk balls.' He does all the cooking over there, this guy Bugs. Yeah they are a strange people."

"Elk balls?" Bobby asked Bah–Bah.

"Right, I actually thought they meant testicles from an elk. I mean, you don't know with that crew. It's sort of like meatballs, but really, they were better than meat balls. But anyway, these guys, they just seemed to move in. There's nothing I can do. I lock the doors; they come in through the windows. I lock the windows; they're in there anyway. Torch told me they have a tunnel from the house next door. You believe that?" "Well, if you want to, we could talk to my uncle Paco," Bobby said.

"I know you could. I thought about that," Bah–Bah said. "I just don't want to embarrass Torch. Besides, don't want to start fighting up here. I don't really mind them; it's just that I'm afraid of getting in trouble. Torch told me not to worry about it, and I trust him. I have to trust him. I have no other choice. I worry because there are kids in there and everything, minors even, sometimes. Even though I'm not there, I'm still responsible."

"Even when you're not there?"

"Right. I mean, I come in the afternoon, and they're watching *Let's Make a Deal* or *The Gong Show*. That's their favorite show, *The Gong Show*. Christ, they remind me of my son when they're watching that. And it's funny … their whole life is sort of like *The Gong Show*. I mean, you know how *The Gong Show* has characters that come and go every few days? Well, that's what it's like up there." "Don't they work?" Bobby asked.

Bah-Bah was smiling now. "They all work, but it's mostly in pieces here and there. There's always different ones around; some are from Ben's but mostly they're just from around there. They have their hustles, or they sell this or collect that. I don't think they take it all very seriously, to be honest."

★ ★ ★

On Monday, John Chapman, in the *Daily News*, responded to Jimmy Cerrone's claim the previous week that the residents of Whitman Park weren't racists. The column was titled "What Exactly Is This Thing

Called Racism?"

The column started out by stating:

"Whitman Parker's don't hate blacks. They simply don't want them living next door, and that's not racist. Organizing to prevent blacks from moving next door is racist. If you want to distinguish between bigotry and racism, remember this phrase: 'Bigotry hates; racism subjugates.' Why Whitman Park residents don't understand that their opposition to the housing project is motivated primarily, if not solely by racism, bewilders me. In no way does this suggestion impinge their dignity, their decency, their loyalty to family or commitment to God. They just don't want blacks living in their whiteenvelope habitat. If you'll forgive a metaphor, that's known as calling a spade a spade."

Chapman went on to say that the word "racism" was frequently misused and abused.

"The most distressing aspect of the Whitman Park controversy is the vacuum in communication. The English language is being abused. Racism has a very precise meaning with historical and sociological context. Racism is not bigotry or racialism. Racism is an attitude, an activity peculiar to Western civilization going back to the fourteenth century, which subjugates the meaning and denies a group of people upward mobility, solely because of their skin color. It has absolutely nothing to do with hatred, yet somehow, well-meaning people, who are racist, get uptight when you gently reveal their blatant racism. Expressed in contemporary terms, racism is disproportional disparity in the

condition between blacks and whites. Whitman Parkers' perpetuate it, and their allies reinforce it.

Let's talk about racial disparities for a moment. But first parity. Blacks are 12 percent of the population. In a recent national poll, two-thirds of blacks surveyed believe they do not have access to economics, educational and political equality.

'Nonsense,' respond many Americans. 'Look at all the jobs blacks are getting. Preferential treatment, quotas, affirmative action.' Dig it, but explain to this fragile mind what the following means. Black teenage unemployment, 39 percent, white teenage unemployment, 10 percent. Black median family income, $9,500. White median family income, $16,000. Black unemployment, 11.8 percent. White unemployment, 5 percent. Twice as many blacks are unemployed today as they were ten years ago. Blacks constitute only 2 percent of the nation's doctors, 2 percent of its dentists, 1.5 percent of its lawyers, and 2 percent of its PhDs.

In the criminal justice system, 74 percent of all blacks convicted of larceny in state courts received a penal sentence, compared to 49 percent of all convicted whites, and finally, for the Whitman Parkers', 74 percent of all dilapidated housing in America is inhabited by blacks. Maybe that disparity in the condition between white and black is not due to racism. If not, what do you call it? Unfortunately, 'racism' has become a chic word. Cerebral clowns like Jimmy Cerrone tosses the word around at any black who disagrees with them."

Also, in the first week of August, there was the funeral of Calvin Hunter in West Philadelphia, who had committed suicide. Elmer Smith of the *Daily News* wrote about the anti-violence advocate. He pointed out the strange coincidence of the funeral being on this day, the third anniversary of a big "Stop the Violence" march in North Philadelphia in 1975, a deadly year in the saga of the juvenile gang wars in Philadelphia. Smith's column stated in part:

"We kept a running death toll in little boxes near the front of the paper in those days. You could call it a gang-war digest. Those with more time could read the full stories of the gang deaths with pictures of anguished family members with the chalk outlines of the latest fallen warrior. By the mid-seventies, the body count had risen to almost one-a-day in a war whose origins and objectives were unclear even to the combatants."

Smith talked about a group called the Concerned Black Men, whose origins grew out of that march. They had hoped it would be a turning point, the beginning of the end of the major juvenile gang violence. And for a while, it seemed to be.

* * *

That Sunday night at the Rockland, they all sat around the horseshoe-shaped bar and listened to the music and played pool. The Rockland was a long bar, much bigger than the Warnock. It had these mirrors strategically lining one wall. The mirrors allowed the bartender to see the customers at the far end, even if his back was turned. Nice Ray, an ex-Scorpion, was bartending that night. He was middle-aged but had a body structure that reflected the high-school defensive tackle he had been. He had jet-black hair, suspiciously black since he was in his late forties. He had sideburns in the style of his hero Elvis Presley. Ray had already served last call. It was just shy about twenty minutes before two in the morning. The television news was on as they all wanted to see the Great Wallenda, a fearless tightrope walker who had fallen walking a tightrope between two buildings in Puerto Rico that afternoon. Torch had caught his act at Veterans Stadium in 1976. It was because of Wallenda probably that the news just happened to be on at that time. Pecky Lynch, the best pool shooter in Logan, known as the "Mayor of Logan" was holding court at the Rockland's small pool table. He was running the table, and Torch was his opponent just then. Torch looked up at the TV set on the wall, chalking his pool stick in the off-chance he would get to shoot. Felix just happened to be standing next to Torch. He was next in line to play Pecky. Felix, too, was chalking a pool stick while looking up at the TV set. Before they talked about the Great Wallenda, they had a story where they brought a police officer from South Philadelphia out in handcuffs. The policeman was covering his face from the reporters' cameras. Apparently this particular policeman, whose name was Ed Kelly, had been arrested for shaking down drug dealers in South Philadelphia.

Felix said, "Do they expect people to be upset about drug dealers? They should give this guy a medal."

Just then, Torch noticed a mask of terror seemed to come over Felix's face. "Jesus Christ!" Felix said as he turned and whispered to Torch and then lowered his voice. "Torch, he's the one who shot Reds."

Torch's head snapped over to Felix, and he looked at him in amazement. "I thought you said that you didn't see the guy who shot Reds."

"I just told everybody that. Why should I stick my neck out? I'm telling you now. He's the one that shot Reds. I can't say for sure it was him, but I'm sure he was there the day it happened. I told you it was cops," Felix said.

Then it struck Torch, that last name ... Kelly, but he was sure that Maria's boyfriend was named Jim Kelly. This must be a different Kelly. Surely there was more than one cop in Philadelphia named Kelly. Torch hadn't seen the policeman on TV very well, but he seemed familiar. He was digesting what Felix told him. He wondered if Maria knew this one.

The bar was closed. The doors were locked and the lights were out. Ray was wiping down the bar. Most of the customers were gone, except for three or four of Torch's boys. Occasionally they would stay and help Ray close up. Some were putting the chairs up on the bar, so the floor could be cleaned.

Somebody changed the channel. A replay of that days

"soooooouuuuulll Train" was on now. Torch looked up at the black kids dancing. They had colorful clothes ... red, yellow, orange. They had these wide lapels and apple-jack hats. A black girl, the lead singer from the group First Choice, another kick-ass 1970s Philly group, was up there singing. She was moving her shoulders and hips back and forth. Plus, her arms never stopped. She sang a song produced by famous award-winning Philadelphia producer Bobby Eli.

Said he's dangerous, armed and extremely dangerous
Said he's dangerous, armed and extremely dangerous

The day that I gave into his charms who would think that he would succeed

Then go on his way leaving me here with another mouth to feed

So, girls, if you see him, you might think that you need him

He may look like the average guy, but he's wanted by the F.B.I.

Nice Ray was yelling now, trying to get the few left to leave the bar. It was time. Ray had to be careful; the bars in Pennsylvania, according to the liquor control board, had to be closed by two o'clock, and when they said two o'clock, they meant it. Three weeks ago, cops had come in the Rockland at two o'clock on the nose. The place was still half-full, and there were as many minors as Western Pennsylvania. The cops gave Ray a break, though; they didn't violate him at all. He just had to buy about a dozen tickets, tickets he would never get rid of, to the Philadelphia Police sponsored Thrill Show. He turned off *Soul Train* on the TV set and told somebody to unplug the jukebox. He said it a moment too late. In that the instant, a new song came on. Rose Royce was singing her 1978 song "Love Don't Live Here Anymore."

CHAPTER 17

O n August 8, 1978, the entire City of Philadelphia had its eyes on the MOVE situation out in Powelton Village in West Philadelphia. It was the deadline for MOVE. Right up until the end, there was a feeling that a last minute agreement would be worked out between the administration and the radical group members and a confrontation would be avoided. That was what everybody called it "the confrontation." However, the front page of the *Daily News* said it all. The headline was simply two words: MOVE DOESN'T.

And just like that, everything else was on hold: the Whitman Park story, the police brutality charges, the scandal involving police shaking down drug dealers, the registration drive, the charter change drive, the underground war between the Scorpions and Moscariello, the racial strife in Southwest Philly, a fear that the juvenile gang wars of the midseventies might return.

The Philadelphia police and MOVE engaged in a shootout at the crack of dawn that morning. One police officer, James Ramp, was shot and killed. Several other police officers were shot as well, in addition to a few firemen. The media had highlighted police picking up a MOVE member and taking him into custody. There was a great deal of footage of the shootout on national news, as well as the subsequent bulldozing of the "compound," but there was very little on what had led up to the confrontation. It was the lead story, in fact, on the national news. As bad as the publicity had been for Cerrone, it, at least, knocked the latest police drug scandal involving the lead suspect, Officer Ed Kelly, off the front pages of the local papers.

With regard to the police scandal, Torch had been correct; Maria's boyfriend was named Jim Kelly. He wasn't this Ed Kelly who was in trouble now. Nevertheless, Torch understood that the two were partners. Since this was a conspiracy involving as many as a dozen police officers, according to the papers, it was doubtful, if not impossible, that Jim Kelly had no knowledge of it.

Leaving no doubt as to his guilt, Jim Kelly didn't wait for Internal Affairs to come after him. Jim Kelly took whatever money he had and disappeared with Maria and Lee Oskar.

★ ★ ★

The City of Philadelphia was more concerned than ever about race riots. The MOVE situation, particularly police brutality charges that resulted from it, as well as the latest police scandal, were both racial in nature and were obviously extremely damaging to Cerrone. Both were precisely the type of things Cerrone wanted to avoid. By this point in the summer, with everything that happened, it really didn't look good for Cerrone, who was tumbling in the pre-election polls.

Again, city administration focused its attention on the city's interracial neighborhoods, such as Logan, in fear of possible racial disharmony. City workers had recently been visiting Logan and interviewing residents, going from door to door, trying to feel the pulse of any developing tensions and figuring out ways to diffuse them.

★ ★ ★

Bah-Bah wouldn't have believed it a month or two ago, but here he was, in mid-August, drinking al fresco on the corner of 11th and Duncannon in Logan. A whiffle-ball game was in progress. Torch parked the blue Buick Wildcat and joined them as they either played or sat on a ledge beside an apartment building. The apartment building was four stories and basically was a microcosm of the neighborhood, which is to say that it had once been classy but now was crumbling. All types of accents and foreign smells and music came from the building. In the summer, men from foreign lands who lived in the building frequently sat outside, drinking quarts of Schmidt's, and they were not embarrassed about wearing short pants, sandals with socks, and Panama hats. The corner typified Logan; it was an ordinary inner-city neighborhood, but places like this had so many trees around it, it almost felt like you were in the jungle in a King Kong movie.

Bah-Bah knew all of the eight or nine young men sitting on the ledge from around Caesar's Palace ... the Kennedy family. Two city workers, a male and a female, were talking to a trio of black brothers who lived on that block, Levi, Eddie, and Pete. The two city workers didn't look like they were employed by anybody. They had sandals, long hair, and the guy even wore a red bandanna.

A home run was over the hedges of the house directly across the street from where everybody was sitting. From what would be considered centerfield of the baseball diamond, the two city workers started walking toward home plate.

"Who are these people?" Felix asked.

"They've been around a few days talking to the neighbors, Felix. They are from the city, Urban Coalition, something like that. You know what that means."

The city workers headed toward the group sitting on the ledge.

Fancy Frank, who was out on the pitcher's mound in the middle of the intersection, gave them a dirty look, and said, "You're disrupting a game here. Can't you see that?"

The man kept walking; the woman stayed back.

Tony's family also lived on that block which was about a half-block away from the site of the meth lab explosion, and his nephew Kevin was playing with a Portuguese kid named Ramone.

The city worker started talking about a misunderstanding between the races that was causing turmoil in the city. He spoke directly to Felix, and he said that the problem almost always started with the whites.

"I don't know what you mean. Ain't no racial problems around here. I know one thing, you couldn't care less about blacks or whites in Logan, and definitely not whites," Felix said.

Just at that moment, Torch noticed Tony stand up, walk over to his nephew and whisper something in his ear. Kevin started walking toward his house. Then Torch noted that Frenchie, who was at bat hitting lefthanded as usual, was looking down the street. Torch suspected that he was looking for the Man to see if the coast was clear. He saw the eye contact between a few of the others. He suddenly saw people moving around like they were getting in position for something ... body language was what it was. Torch had seen this many times before. And whenever he saw it, something bad always happened.

Just then, as if on cue, a large family of Puerto Ricans walked by on Duncannon Avenue.

"How do you like America now that you're here?" Frenchie shouted, and everybody laughed. The Puerto Ricans didn't react.

"See what I mean? See what I mean? This is the type of thing I'm talking about," the hippy city worker said, gesturing with his hands, all excited.

The woman worker across the street apparently had seen the same danger signs that Torch did, and she called to her co-worker saying something about having to return downtown.

"Let's go," Torch whispered to Bah-Bah, who was sitting next to him on the ledge.

"What?" Bah-Bah said.

"Seriously," Torch said, "something's going to happen here."
"I don't know about that," Bah-Bah said. "I know about that ...
Andiamo."

★ ★ ★

The next day, Torch ate breakfast at the North Star Diner. It was the first time since he had been thrown out of the house and the first time since the police scandal broke that he had been in the diner. He had been to the house earlier where Maria's brother was now living and picked up the few worldly goods that he had left behind. This included his notebooks containing the pitching records and some rice paper which he'd never used. There were also a few books including two paperbacks, *The World of Jimmy Breslin*, *The Godfather*, and a hardback, *In Cold Blood*. He had a picture of Alydar and Affirmed in a photo finish at the Preakness, and a few eight-tracks: the Average White Band's *Pick up the Pieces*, *The Best of the Spinners*, *Saturday Night Fever*, Harold Melvin and the Blue Notes, *If You Don't Know Me by Now*, and *Johnny Cash Live at San Quentin Prison*. Donna waited on him and said that she hadn't heard anything about Maria, but she'd cleared out her locker at the diner, took Lee Oskar, and didn't show up that morning. She said police from Internal Affairs had been there asking questions about her and Kelly. She also said that other police were there who she heard were federal agents. She mentioned that Maria even took the stray cat who lived outside.

"Scorpio?" Torch said. "She mentioned that cat a few times."

"Well, the cat is gone, too. I guess she took him. She always said she would. He's a good cat, a boll weevil, but a good cat."

Donna didn't mention Denver, and Torch didn't say anything about it. He apparently was the only one who knew where she was or where she probably was. He thought about sharing it but decided he should keep it to himself instead. It might be valuable to somebody, so why should he give it away? This was a Monopoly game and that information was a Get out of Jail Free card that he could stash under the board. He wasn't exactly sure, now that Maria was gone, how he stood with the cops and specifically Washington. Washington was involved in some serious heavy things. What if he suspected Torch was on to him? Would Washington come to see Torch as a threat, a nemesis?

Torch had had a disturbing dream last night. He was working in an office; he thought it may have been at City Hall. He was sitting at a desk doing paperwork. It was during the winter, and there was a radiator in the corner. The radiator was making a hissing sound, the way they ordinarily do. But the hissing got louder and louder. When

Torch walked over to inspect the radiator, he saw that the hissing wasn't coming from the radiator but from three of four snakes that all suddenly popped out of it. It made Torch uneasy. He had a teacher in high school who had told him about how certain biblical stories featured snakes or serpents. He said a snake or serpent telegraphed that something bad was on the horizon. It might be a flood or a plague or famine or some other disaster.

While Torch was there, he overheard a white girl at the counter talking to Donna. The girl said she was originally from Logan and had moved away. She said she had just recently run into a boy she went to Logan School with. She recognized him and asked what happened to him. He had suddenly dropped out of school, and she never saw him again. He was a Jewish kid, the real McCoy; his parents were from Russia, she said. The girl told the boy that she used to see his sister sometimes playing outside the house, but she never saw him. Then the boy said he didn't have a sister.

Torch thought he understood where the story was headed. It was possible that he'd heard this story or a variation of this tale before. Maybe it was years ago, long forgotten but still in the back of his head. Whatever it was, Torch was not surprised when the girl said, "You see, the girl was really this boy."

It wasn't the type of story that you hear every day, and Logan was probably one of the few places you would ever hear something like that.

While the girl talked, the miniature juke box in front of her on the counter was playing Philly songs — Blue Magic, the Stylistics, "Darlin', Darlin'"," Baby" by the O'Jays, and at the moment, a song "Too Much Heaven," originally by the Bee Gee's, was playing, done here by the Three Tenors Of Soul from their album *All the way from Philadelphia*. That album by the way, Torch thought was produced by Philadelphia's award winning, world famous, Bobby Eli.

"The parents were so paranoid about Nazis that they disguised the boy. That paranoia or fear never leaves. Not if you're an immigrant like his mom was. My mother was from the Ukraine. She never did anything that extreme, but I could almost envision her doing something like that."

Until this girl mentioned that her own mother was from the Ukraine, Torch didn't realize who she was. For one thing, she was so much bigger than he was when they were kids; now he was taller. She had short hair now, too ...Valentina.

★ ★ ★

The media pounded away as the police scandal had taken on a life of its own. The media hinted that the allegations of wrongly convicted drug dealers coming forward were only the tip of the iceberg. It said others had remained silent because of a certain climate of fear that existed in the city. But now drug dealers were on the news, coming forward, claiming through their attorneys that they had been framed and set up by Ed Kelly and his partners. They said they had proof, and at the very least, they deserved a new trial. Many, of course, were in the process of filing lawsuits for false arrest and, in some cases, even for false incarceration.

On August 19th, John Chapman wrote probably the most hurtful of all his anti-Cerrone articles. The column included this passage:

"Across the nation, Philadelphia has become synonymous with the country's worse police brutality, a political thug for a mayor, a declining quality of life, and, most tragic of all, a new bottom in race relations. Hate that has polarized people, built invisible Berlin walls around neighborhoods as if they were foreign countries."

That night, they were playing poker at Caesar's Palace. During the night, Torch lost about $175, but still was hanging in there as the early morning hours came along. Then the number of players grew smaller, and the pots grew bigger. It was during those hours that you could get even real fast; however, Torch continued to lose. In one hand alone, he lost $60. Torch eventually lost everything that was supposed to be his ribbon, which he had to get together for Bah-Bah the next day. But they all still had money because Bah-Bah had sold more TV sets for them, and now there were now only twelve or so remaining on the back porch of the house.

Somebody had obtained an entire case of Tastykake Butterscotch Krimpets. They all ate them and drank from a jug of homemade wine. Bah-Bah recognized the taste of the wine since it came from South Philadelphia. Torch originally bought the wine when he had gone to school with a girl from downtown. Her father sold 1,000 cases of wine a year. Unfortunately, he had gone out of business, alleging that the Liquor Control Board of Pennsylvania had shut him down. This homemade wine, which they called "grog," was a popular drink around here.

Bah-Bah was enjoying himself. He was up about $150 in the game and had said at one point, "These Tastykakes are better than I remembered them."

"Food always tastes better when it is stolen," Efrem said.

A Richard Pryor tape had been playing; Bah-Bah now, like everybody else it seemed, knew the routine by heart. Pryor right now was imitating a preacher.

"We are gathered here today, ta celebrate in this year of bicenteniality. In hope of freedom and dignithhy. We are celebrating 200 years of white folks kicking ass. Now white folks have had the advantage of disunderstanding on their side for quite a whillle. How essen ever we offer this prayer, and the prayer is 'how long will this bullshit go on? How long? How long? How long will this bullshit go on? That is the eternal question. Man, has always asked, 'How long?' When man first got here, he asked, 'How long will these animals kick me in the ass? How long will it be before I discover fire and stop freezing to death? We always here at the church of Understanding and Unity have tried to figure out how long?' Now it says in the Bible, we will know 'how long' when an angel comes up out the sea. He will have seven heads and the face of a serpent and the body of a lion. I don't know about you, but I don't want to see no motherfucker like that. I see him come out the water, I'm going to shoot him in the ass.

We are only making on collection this year, and we ask that you donate five or six hundred. We won't be fucking with you no more. We won't be coming around your house asking for shit or nothing like that."

Richard Pryor, in the short term, was arguably the funniest goddamn standup comedian of all. Of course, he didn't transcend the decades like Rodney or George Carlin or Don Rickles. Pryor was a staple of the 1970s. He was around as far back as the sixties. Hell, he was on Ed Sullivan in 1966. He, of course, was much more subdued on that stage and at that time, and he just wasn't funny. He was still Richard Pryor in the eighties, but by then, his act seemed stale. His prime, his era was in the seventies. He probably could never have gotten away with his shit in subsequent decades. It wasn't just his making fun of whites and blacks which he did equally. It wasn't that he was a pioneer in his very liberal use of the now commonplace N-word. It was also his (what now would seem to be outrageous) making fun of handicapped people. Imagine his act in the touchy-feely nineties or the politically correct twenty-first century.

"And to the crippled people of the congregation, could you find another place to go to? Goddamn! You come in here bustin' up furniture, knockin' shit over … and you deaf-dumb motherfuckers, we don't need you here. They got schoools for you motherfuckers to learn to speak."

But instead of getting all serious and righteous and going "That crap isn't funny" or "He shouldn't say those awful things," you instead reacted by laughing your head off. So in a sense, you were laughing at yourself, too. He seemed to be the perfect comedian for these youngsters at that precise moment in time who gathered in places like Caesar's Palace or the Rockland or Warnock to party and generally act like pigs. Imagine a comic in the subsequent touchy-feely decades saying that shit. It would never happen.

Pryor's act was a little shocking or, at least, surprising even back then. He was a staple of that era, of that decade to be sure, never would another be quite like him … period. It would be impossible.

The Richard Pryor tape came out and music from the stereo blasted out. Fancy Frank started doing a dance, gyrating his hips. He raised his right hand to his forehead and wiped the imaginary perspiration from his brow. Barry White was singing:

There you were out there on the floor
The way you moved, girl, only made me want you more

The card game in the kitchen stopped. Some went into the living room to watch the show. They were yelling now. Some were yelling now,

"Do that! Do that!"

Even Bah-Bah was laughing at this strange sight. Others started coming in from the kitchen. The living room TV was on, but nobody was watching it. Barry White continued …

Oh, ecstasy when you lay down next to me

Oh, ecstasy when you lay down next to me

Bah-Bah half-wished Bobby could see this scene. It typified what was bothering him. It wasn't any one specific thing. It was more that he simply didn't care anymore to be around all this overall craziness. It was all, he was sure, the shoobies, the booze, the TV sets in the back, these young girls, all a fuse looking for a match.

He was a little surprised that Fancy Frank was such a good dancer and displayed such energy since he was in his forties and didn't seem to be in good physical shape at all.

Oh, ecstasy, when you're layin' down next to me

Oh, ecstasy, when you're layin' down next to me

★ ★ ★

The next night police officers from the 53rd District raided Caesar's Palace. Two police cars with three officers pulled up outside and knocked on the door. Roughly ten people were in the house at the time, and they ran out of the back door. They ran down the driveway, which was adjacent to the railroad tracks right into the arms of more police who were waiting at the end of the driveway with a van. Bah-Bah noticed how everybody, except him, seemed to be anxious to get into the wagon. He understood why later. He was the last one, sitting on the edge of the tiny bench inside when the policeman who Bah-Bah didn't recognize was about to close the door. The last thing he did was whack Bah-Bah on the left knee with his nightstick. Felix explained to him later that the idea was to not be the last guy placed in the van because cops had a habit of doing that.

The van drove up Old York Road toward the 53rd District. The ride was bumpy as Old York Road had cobblestones, as well as trolley tracks. Felix further explained to Bah-Bah that this was another little game cops liked to play. He said it was much worse when you were handcuffed and the van went speeding around and you could do nothing except bounce around in the back of the truck. Felix said they placed you on the seat where you first went in, and that was the last time you were sitting down 'til you arrived at the police station.

Ostensibly, they had all been charged with "disorderly conduct." In actuality, the brass at the 53rd District was concerned about a city worker who had gotten beat up yesterday afternoon at the Warnock Tavern.

Washington was at the station house when the van arrived. Each of the suspects was interviewed individually. Bah-Bah was interviewed by Ken Washington himself, who explained the situation. Washington said that the city worker was also a writer who did feature articles for the *Daily News*. That being the case, the incident was more of a priority to them. Washington explained that, as far as he knew, the city worker, thus far, had expressed no interest in filing any kind of official charges.

Washington asked Bah-Bah a number of questions then, none of which concerned the city worker. He asked him about methamphetamines, Chick-a-Dee, Moscariello, the Scorpions, all kinds of things.

Originally, they were all to be arraigned via closed circuit television from the Police Administration Building in Center City where a magistrate was sitting. As it turned out, however, the monitor was out of order. They were going to have to be driven down to the police administration building or the Roundhouse in Center City, but Washington was instrumental in providing their release with no charges. They walked back together from the 53rd District and arrived home at 3:00 a.m. at Caesar's Palace.

CHAPTER 18

The longest day of Torch's life started in an ordinary way with him booking numbers and horses at Caesar's Palace on Monday morning. Bobby Santore and Bah-Bah were going to Little Italy that day, and since Torch had never been to New York, they offered to take him as well.

Bah-Bah and Torch had donuts and coffee at Big Jim's Luncheonette and waited for Bobby to pick them up. Bah-Bah explained how expensive it was up in New York. He said, "I'm taking a Gee-Whiz myself." Bah-Bah was telling Torch about the raid on Caesar's Palace the other night. The swelling on Bah-Bah's knee had subsided, but he was still limping slightly.

Bobby drove a Cadillac. It was a few years newer than Bah-Bah's. It was brown with a white top. The car radio was tuned to an A.M. oldies station, W.I.P. They played Sinatra, Sammy, Tony Bennett, Bobby Darin, Johnny Mathis, that kind of thing. Torch continued the conversation regarding the writer.

"Until last night, I didn't even know about that guy getting beat up," Torch said. "I had a feeling that was going to happen." Torch continued. "That was why I pulled you out of there the other day. I knew you didn't want to have anything to do with that, especially now with you up living here and everything. I told you it was going to happen."

"You were right. You were right," Bah-Bah said, shaking his head. "Felix said the cops were just covering their asses and going through the motions of an investigation. He said they probably didn't really care about some hippy writer from the *Daily News* who had no business being around here in the first place."

"Were you there when it happened?" Torch asked.

"I was in the northeast seeing somebody, and when I came back to the house, the front door was locked. I got out my key and tried to get in, but it was bolted from the inside. Now I was pissed off already, then I hear the bolt open and the door opens about four inches, but the chain lock was still on. Then this blond kid finally opens the door and says to me, 'Ring the bell. Always ring the bell. A cop will always knock.' Do you believe that? In my own house. Now I'm furious. I wanted to kill this little prick, some blond Irish kid. There were six or seven of them sitting around my living room like it was group therapy. That's when they told me what happened. They thought I was going to let them stay there and hide. I kicked them out. Then they were all saying, 'Lame dude, Bah-Bah, lame dude man.'"

"Listen, man, I'm getting tired of them guys. It's all right having them around for laughs, but I don't want them in there when something like that is going on, and it seems like something like that is always going on."

"Bah-Bah loves it up there, Bobby," Torch said from the backseat. "He's a real corner hopper. You should see him. They had to lock his ass up the other night. Threw him right in the back of the paddy wagon with all the other kids."

"I'm serious about this, Torch," Bah-Bah said.

"There is an advantage to having them there. It's the same reason Grant always took care of them, so he could sleep at night. He knows everybody is right next door; it makes him feel better. It's probably why nobody ever bothered Grant. You're under our protection, think of it that way."

Torch regretted saying that last part before Bah-Bah even had a chance to respond. When Bah-Bah got really mad, his nostrils actually flared like a bull. He was doing that now. He had turned his neck and shoulders around and was facing Torch.

"Under your *protection*? Who are they going to protect me from … Moscariello? Do those guys know who I am? I could ask his uncle to come up here," Bah-Bah said, jabbing his thumb toward Bobby.

Torch didn't intend to get Bah-Bah this fired up.

"Take it easy. I just always wanted to say that," Torch said. "You're right." Torch tried to sound as diplomatic as possible. He certainly didn't want to be responsible for Bobby's uncle, who had been one of Constantine's craziest guys in the old days, coming around.

"Moscariello isn't Constantine. The cops are all over him, and now they have those R.I.C.O. laws in place. In a year or so, he may not even be around, and you can go back downtown."

"Hopefully," Bah-Bah said, "and as far as Grant is concerned, I hear you on that point." "There is arguably a built-in advantage, and Grant understands that. But living next door is a completely different story. If anything happens, then I'm the one responsible, not Grant. There are stolen goods in the back of the house. You have guys selling schoobies. You have the numbers going in the morning, then I have the sports betting at night. Then on the weekends, all those kids, them girls from the northeast, and I don't even know what they're doing. I'm the one that's responsible if anything happens, and nobody there seems to appreciate that. They think it's a big joke."

"You're right, Bah-Bah. They have to respect that."

"The regular ones who live there, Frenchie, Felix, Efrem, Doc, Billy Young, Bryon, and them guys, they respect it. It's all the other kids I worry about. After what happened the other night, I started thinking about the television sets in the back especially."

"Did they come in the house?" Torch asked.

"No, but that was this time. Like you said before, once cops come to a certain place, it becomes a habit." "That's true," Torch said.

"The other night was the last straw. I don't want to press my luck. I was interrogated at the police station by Washington himself, and it got me thinking."

"Washington?" Torch said.

"Everybody was questioned by plainclothes detectives except me. But the funny thing was, he didn't even seem to care about the guy who got beat up. He started asking me again about what I was doing up here.

He asked me about Maria and that Jim Kelly guy she's with. He wanted to know where they were."

"Yeah?" Torch was all ears now.

"I know that guy, Washington," Bah–Bah said. "I didn't realize who he was until the other night. I told you he recognized me the first day I moved around there. I didn't figure it out until the other night."

Bah–Bah didn't finish that story. Torch knew that Bah–Bah was letting the suspense build. He had to know that Torch was on the edge of his seat. Torch knew Bah–Bah would get around to telling him the story in his own time. Torch just sat back and looked out of the window at the acres of cornfields. They were in New Jersey now. Nat King Cole was singing "Nature Boy."

★ ★ ★

Ken Washington sat at Ben's counter. He was drinking a blend; it was a lemon drink that Ben made with water as opposed to seltzer. Three weeks after the MOVE shoot-out, it was still a prominent story in the papers. Washington was reading a story that day written by John Chapman. Chapman talked about riding bikes with his son the other night. He wrote that he started thinking about the son of the slain officer James Ramp. His article continued:

"It brought me back to the horror and sadness of that gruesome day. It would be so comforting if the MOVE crisis were a clear-cut issue, a gravellyassed bunch of unwashed revolutionaries desecrating a neighborhood, breaking the law and defying all limits of civility.

In such a situation, the police become a logical extension of us all. They take on the nasty job of trying to get the MOVE purveyors of filth to obey laws we have accepted all our lives. The police are the champions of our tranquility. But Mayor Jimmy Cerrone has changed the rules. He has turned what should have been an ordinary down-the-line enforcement of the law into a re-election crusade with such shameful and racial overtones; the black community is tottering on the brink of open conflict. There is nothing racial about MOVE, yet last night almost half of the city's black elected officials gathered in City Hall to discuss the MOVE-police battle's racial implications. Their somber restrained statement warned of a racial crisis of such magnitude as to demand a federal investigation by the attorney general of the United States. The statement was mild. Walk around North and West Philadelphia and talk to some residents. They are seething. The tragic pattern of events in Philadelphia has only underscored the recent warning by the U.S. Department of Justice Community Relations Service Director, Gilbert G. Pompa, that 'there is an undeclared war between police and minorities that we're committed to prevent.' In Philadelphia that undeclared war is especially unfortunate because Cerrone takes the position that the police can do no wrong, have never done any wrong, and will never do any wrong. for the black community. This amounts to an open-sesame abrogation of their rights. For the rest of the citizens, their freedom is cheapened, their lives diminished. Delbert Africa shouting the most vile obscenities and threatening violence under the cowardly cover of children falls easily outside the pale of civilized behavior. But a belligerent Jimmy Cerrone, accusing the press of being responsible for the environment of hate has done as much as any one single person to create this hate and thrust us all into the cesspool of aggression. The air is heavy-laden with tension. People are still uptight."

★ ★ ★

Bah-Bah, Torch, and Bobby walked around Little Italy. Bah-Bah bought a case of Fox's-U-Bet chocolate syrup. They ate at Umberto's Clam House, the landmark in Little Italy where Crazy Joe Gallo got iced. Torch ordered a scungilli salad.

"That's real scungilli salad," Bobby said. "That stuff is a rumor in South Philadelphia."

Bah-Bah ate spaghetti with mussels and clam sauce. He was twirling a large forkful of it when he began re-telling the story of how he knew Washington.

"Remember I told you I used to work the Zigonette games at my house?" "A million times," Torch said.

293

"Well, I didn't pull all this together until the other night when we all got locked up. It started a few days before, though, when I first saw that Ed Kelly on the news getting arrested. I thought he looked familiar, but I couldn't place him. Then after the other night, after talking to Washington, I remembered."

Bah-Bah explained to Torch all over again how it was his job to "take care" of the police to make sure everything went smoothly, the customers weren't bothered, and everything was alright. He, sometimes, worked in the kitchen, or sometimes, he worked at the front door. He also had the responsibility to make sure everybody had enough to eat and drink. Part of his job was to, sometimes, drive up to Chinatown. Bah-Bah's house was on the northern end of South Philly, only ten blocks from Chinatown. Bah-Bah explained that Chick-a-Dee had an arrangement with a certain restaurant up there, and all Bah-Bah had to do was place the order and then pick up the food. He never paid for any of it. A typical order, he said, might have been seventy-five egg rolls or fifty bags of spare ribs, something like that.

"One night," Bah-Bah said, "we ran out of sodas. I didn't know what to do. There were no all-night convenience stores or anything like that back then. So I had one of those old-fashioned red wagons in my basement from when I was a kid. I went around to a soda machine at 10th and Federal. I had about $50 in change up in my room. I bought every soda I could from the machine and put it in the wagon. It was about three o'clock in the morning, and I'm walking through South Philly with this squeaky wagon full of sodas. I got to the corner of my street, and this police car pulls up beside me. The cop in the driver's seat was white. The window was down; it was summer. And he said to me, 'That sodas for the game, isn't it?' What could I say? I just kind of smiled at him. The passenger was a black cop who I didn't get a very good look at. Most of the cops were white; in fact, they were Irish … young guys. Anyway, that was the night we got raided. Yeah, they got us for about $70,000, we figured."

"*Seventy thousand dollars?*" Torch asked skeptically. South Philadelphians, especially *this* South Philadelphian, often had a tendency to exaggerate.

"That really wasn't one of our bigger nights. I saw a guy win $60,000 in just one hand. If I told you who it was, you would recognize the name," Bah-Bah continued. "I saw a guy, an undertaker, lose his entire business. He actually threw the deed to his business in the pot. Then he borrowed money, and in a few hours, he won his business back. I'm sure you would know the name of the undertaker if I told you. It's one of the big ones on Broad Street, I'll just say that. We had bigger nights there, but that night we figured we lost about $70,000. That's what we figured the cops got us for. Anyway, this guy Kelly was the cop in the car. I recognized him when I saw him on the news the other night. He was the one driving the car, and he was there when they came in the house. The black cop in the passenger seat I think was your boy ...

Washington. I didn't realize it at first. I should have. He recognized me the first day."

For some reason, Torch was not shocked by this news. It had been in the back of his head ever since Felix told him that Ed Kelly was one of the cops who ripped them off at Danny Parker's house when Reds was killed. According to Maria, Washington knew the one Kelly which had to mean he knew the other Kelly. It followed; therefore, Washington had to have, at least, suspected that these two were playing dirty pool. Washington was simply too smart not to know. Now it made sense why Washington was so obsessed with who was selling drugs.

* * *

To Ken Washington, walking the beat was the most practical form of police work. It served many positive functions. For one thing, it deterred crime. It was also an excellent information-gathering tool. A good beat cop blended into the community and knew the people. A good beat cop always noticed when something was missing. By the same token, a good beat cop also noticed when something was there that shouldn't be.

Washington left Ben's store and walked down Windrim Avenue. He passed Caesar's Palace and walked toward the Warnock Bar. He saw the professor pushing a shopping cart. He had just come from the beer distributor. He had a case of beer in cans and a case of soda in bottles in the shopping cart. Washington's eyes followed the professor walking down the sidewalk. That was when he saw what was wrong. Washington zeroed in on a crate of orange soda that was about twenty feet away from the front of the beer distributor. Then Washington looked at the group of young black youngsters who were outside of the Warnock Bar doing nothing in particular. Washington caught them stealing glances at the case of sodas. It was a strange place for the sodas to be. There was something besides the mere presence of the sodas that made Washington focus on them. He wasn't sure exactly what it was. Maybe it was the way the orange soda glowed, like a piece of the sun had broken off and dropped right there. The sodas were covered with ice which was sweating down the sides of them, and the bottles gleamed. Also, it was a very hot day after all, Washington was thirsty, and perhaps the sodas had a type of mirage effect on him, too. He didn't know exactly what it was, but the way the sodas were looking, they just invited somebody to steal them. Washington seemed to have a sixth sense about these kinds of things, and once again, he looked at the black kids outside of the Warnock. He put it all together and concluded that those sodas were trouble. Somehow he knew that he would be hearing about those sodas later.

* * *

Bah-Bah drove Bobby's car on the ride home. Torch sat in the front seat, and Bobby was lying down in the backseat. At one point, Torch broke off a piece of chocolate cannoli and handed it back to Bobby. Bobby took the cannoli and said, "Torch, man, you are a credit to your race."

They were riding now past the swamplands of New Jersey. At one point, Torch lowered the window.

"I got the air condition on," Bah -Bah complained.

"I need some fresh air, from that wop-water you guys wear. You take a bath in that? What is that anyway, Hai Karate?"

Bah-Bah then said he had been talking to Gino's son the day before. "I mentioned your name. He's not very fond of you, you know?"

Torch wasn't quite sure who Bah-Bah was talking about. Gino had a few sons. "He said, 'Yeah, that guy Torch is a 'ball breaker.'"

Now Torch knew who Bah-Bah meant. His name was Frankie.

"What did he mean by that, Torch?" Bah-Bah asked. "I was surprised to hear him say that."

"He was booking baseball for Gino, and I used to bet games, and I'd ask for all the lines on all the games. Or I'd ask for ten different games. I mean, that's just the way I used to do it. I had a system. I was knocking him dead. I'd make up my own line. Then if Gino's line was off, I would automatically bet accordingly. I wasn't really picking the games. It worked for a little while anyway. It had to do with the pitchers. I'd almost always specify my pitcher. Sometimes I'd specify both pitchers. Like for instance, I'd say, 'I want the Dodgers (Sutton) over the Mets (Espinosa).' Then I'd only end up betting one game for a quarter or something. I could tell that it was getting him mad. Eventually he told me I had to bet $50 a game if I wanted to specify the pitchers. He said it wasn't worth all that writing and everything for only a $25 bet. He really just didn't want me to call him, period. I told him that was bullshit. Gino agreed with me. It was just a few months he was on the phone. I know who you're talking about now."

"Something else he mentioned," Bah-Bah said. "Didn't you work for Gino and you screwed up and they replaced you or something ... what happened?" "I didn't screw up. He made a big deal out of some bullshit. Frankie flat-out didn't like me, and he got Gino all worked up." "But what was it?" Bah-Bah asked.

"It was one summer. Gino was on vacation. I was booking baseball for him. It was really light action, and I didn't have to worry about collecting or anything like that. I just took the action and I called it in. I was in Center City one Saturday. There was nobody around. I was playing pinochle in the cutlery store with Sam the Blade. Roberto Duran was fighting that afternoon at the Spectrum."

"Right, Duran, he mentioned something about that," Bah-Bah said.

"I still don't see what the big deal was." "What happened?" Bah-Bah asked.

"Somebody from the shoe store next to Sam the Blade's store, well, one of the salesmen named Jose, was going to the fight that day. He said one of the owners of the store wanted to bet the fight, this guy named Bud. The line on the fight had Duran as a 3-1 favorite. The guy he was fighting was named Edwin Viruet. He was out of New York, I think. If you took him, you only got 2-1. I told Jose that Bud could bet the fight with me. Anyway, Bud ended up betting $200 on Duran, laying $600." "You sat on the bet," Bah-Bah said knowingly.

"Right, it was worth a shot at those odds. They fought a year or two before and Duran won, but this Viruet gave a good account of himself. Anyway, Viruet was really tough. Howard Cosell announced the fight. It was on national T.V. Duran beat him in a decision. But this guy Viruet, he really gave Duran a tough fight. He was tall, and he looked like Doug Collins. I got my money's worth; it was fine. Then on Monday or Tuesday, I paid Bud, and I thought that was the end of it. A day or two later, Gino started yelling at me and saying I used his good name to solicit bets and all this stuff. Then two days after that, I saw Gino in Oscar's, and he was still talking about it.

"I didn't twist Bud's arm to bet the fight. If he wanted to lay that ridiculous price, then I was glad to take his action. It was just between me and him. Anyway, Gino kept on and on about it. That was the first time I saw that the boss was cracking up. And that was before Atlantic City and Constantine getting killed and everything else that happened. He was always high-strung. I mean, I remember once I went around Oscar's on a Thursday. I ordinarily went there on Friday, not Thursday, and he saw me and was up there. 'Hey, Torch!

What are you doin' here on Thursday?' and I could almost hear the alarm bells going off in his head. I told him, 'Take it easy, Gino. I'm off tomorrow, That's all'. I remember a few times being in the bar with him, having a conversation, turn my head, turn back, and he'd be gone just like that; he'd see something or sense something. I had a cat like that named Zorro. When he got old, I'd watch him. He would be sitting on the floor. Then he's stand up, walk four feet, and sit down again and I would wonder what he was thinking. Gino reminded me of that cat a little. Once I came around and I had to stop at the Hair Loft on top of Oscar's. I had customers there, Henri, Pete, and them. They used to play numbers and horses. Anyway, the door was locked. I knew Gino was up there getting his haircut. Gino thought somebody would shoot him in the barber chair, ya' know, like old what's-his-name up in New York. The only time I saw him at peace was at his viewing. I'll tell you another story. That football season, two guys from my neighborhood were betting the games with Gino, $500 a rattle, or something like that. One Sunday, one of them called Gino and bet a $500 reverse. Then fifteen minutes later, the other one bet a $500 reverse, but using the opposite sides. Gino called me right away and asked me what was going on. I told Gino they were doing him a favor. I mean, if one of them won, the other had to lose or possibly both could lose. I would love to take two bets like that. What was the problem?

"Gino said, 'I seen guys do this before. They're taking a shot at me.' I guess Gino thought that one of them would win and collect, they'd split the money down the middle, and the other would obviously lose, but he just wouldn't pay. That's what Gino meant by 'They're taking shots at me', I guess."

"Yeah, that sounds like something Gino would say. It's like one time I loaned that guy Charlie, the sandwich shop guy on Sansom Street, $1000. I loaned it to him because Gino didn't trust him and never lent him money. I was glad to lend Charlie money; he was a successful business man expanding his place. I told Gino about it, and he said I would never get all my money back. Then the first week Charlie paid me two payments. Gino said, 'He's setting you up.'"

Bah–Bah sought out Bobby's eyes in the rearview mirror.

"Do you know what Gino meant by that 'He's setting you up?' See, in this business, guys will try to set you up. They'll borrow $500 and pay you back real fast. Then they'll borrow $1000 and pay you back real fast. Then they'll borrow $2000, and you won't ever see them again. See, they were setting you up from the beginning. That's the kind of thing I was talking about. That's the kind of thing Gino had to deal with for thirty years. Parasites, you know, tried to use him."

"You really had to be on your guard in South Philly," Bah-bah continued, "especially an independent guy like Gino. People down there, ya' know, a lot of guys, they play position. For example, remember the other night when we were drinking that homemade wine?" "Grog," Torch said.

"Right. 'Grog'. Well, that isn't exclusively homemade wine. That is mixed with commercial wines. I mean, the guy sells between 1,000 and 2,000 *cases* a year, so it can't all be homemade wine. Anyway, that was a cottage industry in South Philadelphia. They had guys running all around the city in other neighborhoods, where they didn't know any better, selling cheap state store wine in unmarked bottles, telling everybody that 'My Uncle Vito made this in his cellar,' with the dirt floor and all that, ya know? Moscariello put a street-tax on them. That's what I heard. That's why those guys are out of business now."

Torch had heard that the Pennsylvania Liquor Control Board put the grog men out of business, but he leaned toward Bah–Bah's explanation now that he thought about it.

"I mean, guys would borrow money at 20 percent and then lend it out again at 30 percent. Gino was the last one to lend money out at 20 percent. Now it is 30 percent everywhere. Moscariello made it like that."

"Torch, did you know that your first loan sharks were Jewish? That's right. See, usury is counter to Christianity, so that was why Jews were the first loan sharks." Then Bah–Bah continued, "Did you know that they're going to make a sequel to the movie *Jaws*?"

"You don't say."

"Right, it's going to be called *Jews*; it's about a loan shark."

★ ★ ★

The ride back from New York took two hours. Bobby and Bah-Bah dropped Torch off at his car which was parked near Caesar's Palace. Torch drove around for about twenty minutes until he found the rest of his boys. They were drinking from a keg of beer in a driveway next to the railroad tracks by Fleers bubblegum in back of Poodle Head's cousin's house. Connell was talking in an Irish accent about some black kids and a crate of orange soda that was stolen that day.

Drinking draft beer was dangerous. It had a tendency to sneak up on you. One reason probably was that you had no way of really keeping track of how much you consumed. Torch also suspected that the foam or something made it stronger. Whatever it was, it seemed like you got drunk faster when you drank from a keg. It snuck up on you. It was safe to say that that afternoon they were all drinking too much. Somebody mentioned seeing bantamweight Carlos Zarate, a knockout artist from Mexico on TV that Saturday. Last year (1977) *Ring Magazine* named Zarate as their Fighter of the Year.

Another topic of conversation was the end of baseball's Pete Rose's long-consecutive-game hitting streak. Rose had batted safely in fortyfour straight games until the other day in Atlanta. The streak was ended by a combination of two Atlanta Brave pitchers. The starter was Larry McWilliams and the reliever was Gene "Gino" Garber. It was Garber who struck rose out in the final at-bat to end both the game and the streak. Garber had played in Philadelphia for four seasons until he was traded to Atlanta just two months ago. During his time with the Philadelphia Phillies, he had become a fan favorite. He featured this unique windup and delivery that everybody imitated when they played stick ball. Garber's best pitches were a dazzling assortment of off-speed pitches and change-ups. It was with this so-called junk that Garber finally got rose out. First Rose complained about the selection of pitches that he was offered.

Rose said that Garber should have "challenged him" with fastballs, especially since it was the very end of the game and Atlanta had a huge 12-run lead at the time, and Rose had said something like "I could have hit the ball 500 feet, and they still would have had an 11-run lead." Then Rose was pissed off about how Garber celebrated by jumping off the mound. "Like he had just won the World Series," Rose said.

It was possible that Garber had violated some sort of big-league etiquette or code here, but frankly Rose, who Torch never liked anyway, came off looking like a baby about the whole thing, especially since "he was still crying out loud about it days later," according to Stan Hochman, a sportswriter from the *Philadelphia Daily News.*

Torch first heard about the end of the streak that night on the eleven o'clock news. It was the top story as it had gained the interest and attention of so many people, even those who didn't ordinarily care about baseball. The remarkable streak developed a strange national curiosity. In Las Vegas, for example, the casinos offered odds to bettors on how long the streak would last. Pete Rose's team (the Cincinnati Reds) played to large crowds in National League Cities all over the country. Even at the all-star game that summer, 30,000 people came before the game just to watch Rose take batting practice. The streak had come through Philadelphia, too. In fact, it had nearly ended here. In one game, several weeks ago, Phillies pitchers had shut down Rose all night. Then in his final at-bat, Rose surprised everybody by laying down a perfect bunt and narrowly beating out the throw by Phillies Golden Glove third baseman Mike Schmidt. The streak represented the closest anybody ever came to catching Joe DiMaggio's majestic fifty-six consecutive-game-hittingstreak in 1941. It was the same year that thirty-seven-year-old Pete Rose was born. The following morning, Torch had stopped in Ben's to buy a pack of smokes. While he was there, he read the sports section of the *New York Daily News.* He only paid attention to this newspaper during baseball season because they did a good job of listing starting pitchers, betting odds for that day's games even selections for three or four games. A typical comment might be something like, "Guidry lost two weeks ago at Boston. Look for turnaround tonight and go with Pinstrippers over Red Sox." On the next page, Torch saw a cartoon in the sports section. It was a caricature of Joe DiMaggio drinking a cup of coffee. To Torch's generation, DiMaggio *was* Mr. Coffee. The cartoon was the work of the famous artist/ sportswriter Bill Gallo. Underneath the illustration was a caption that read, "I'm glad that's over. I was up to forty-four cups."

★ ★ ★

Grant pulled up in a station wagon and brought out a box which contained shirts with each person's name on the back and distributed them. They were in a softball league sponsored by the Warnock Tavern that played other bars around in the northeast. The shirts, besides having their names on the back, had white letters spelling out "Warnock Tavern" on the back. The shirts were red with blue trim. About six of them were back there and they walked from the driveway under the railroad bridge toward the Warnock Tavern. Torch, however, went across the street to a Chinese restaurant called Sonny's and ordered a shrimp fried rice. Then he walked toward the bar, eating from the container of shrimp fried rice with a plastic fork. He was wearing his new Warnock shirt, and he had left his old white undershirt back in the driveway. When he got in front of the Warnock, he paused to finish because he didn't want to go in the bar while he was still eating. He leaned against the wall across the street from the bar and ate from the container. The door to the bar was open, and Elvis Presley was singing "One Night with You." Torch watched Connell come out of the bar and walk ten or fifteen feet toward Warnock Street, a little street just to the west of the bar. Two black kids that seemed to be completely unsuspecting were standing there talking. Connell grabbed one by the back of the neck. He was shouting at him, something about the sodas.

Two black teenagers were also walking east right by the altercation. One was wearing a baseball cap backwards. His name was Chops; the other one was named Snake. He was from Nicetown. Torch wasn't sure what happened then, but one of them exchanged words with Connell. Torch heard Connell say, "Mind your own business."

The next thing Torch knew Connell was boxing with one of them. In fact, Connell punched one black kid's face so fiercely that he knocked him backwards and to the ground. The other one pulled a knife out from somewhere and swung it at Connell, who ducked and ran into the bar. The black kid with the knife turned and saw Torch across the street and ran directly at him. Torch ran behind the car he was leaning on, around in a circle, and made a beeline for the Warnock Tavern door. Just then, the bar emptied out, and it was either Big Blocks or Connell that struck Chops with a baseball bat. Chops dropped the knife and was quickly smothered by the others. There must have been six or eight of them now. Torch himself, was drawn into the fight, fueled by both alcohol and fright. He had his belt off and also hit Chops, who was on the ground now. The other one had disappeared. Torch heard Chops moan and yell. Then Torch heard Chops get hit with the baseball bat, and the moaning and yelling stopped. Then he heard the bat slam down into the street. The bat bounced and vibrated. They all ran up Warnock Street. Felix was in the lead, and he turned into a narrow alley in the middle of the block. When he got into the alley, Felix peeled off the Warnock shirt and stuffed it in his back pocket. Everybody else did the same thing. Torch understood the reasoning behind it. The cops would be all over the place now looking for guys in red shirts. Torch pulled his shirt off, too. The others all turned left into another alley, but Torch went straight and came out on Eleventh Street, Torch threw his shirt down in the sewer right there. Then he crossed Windrim Avenue and ran into a driveway which led him onto the railroad tracks. He then climbed onto the roofs of the little shopping district there, which included an auto mechanic, a beer distributor, and the furniture moving outfit.

The roof there looked like the roofs in the movie *On the Waterfront*, where Terry kept his pigeons. Torch, thinking about the other day and the incident with Henry Cordero and Mitchell and the other ones, was now checking the sky for police helicopters. He didn't see any, and he crawled to the edge of the roof. He stuck his head over for a peek at what was happening below him in front of the Warnock Tavern. Four or five police vehicles were now outside the bar, as well as an ambulance. The bar was empty now, but the sound of the jukebox was still blasting out of the open front door.

I'm just thinkin' about coolin' out
I'm just thinkin' about coolin' out
I'm just thinkin' about coolin' out
I'm just thinkin' about coolin' out

From where Torch was right now, he could look south and see the City Hall tower which was about fifty blocks away. Torch walked back to the railroad tracks and proceeded east across the railroad bridge, over Tenth Street, passing Fleers bubblegum, and periodically he would turn around and look behind him and up in the sky, too. His heart was beating fast, and suddenly he became very tired. The railroad tracks to them, among other things, had been like a huge super-highway. That was especially true when they were all young and walked everyplace. From the railroad tracks, you could get to the swimming hole in the northeast where they went during the summer. From the tracks, you could go right to the bowling alley, where they used to go to all night bowling up in the northeast. The railroad tracks could take you to Barrett Playground. The railroad tracks passed Inky, Seventh and Rockland, Ben's, and even Logan Nation and Nicetown. At what was really Seventh Street, the tracks met another set of tracks which went north and south. Kids called this "over-under." Torch took the tracks underneath and walked south now. These tracks would take him right to the Rockland Bar where he knew Nice Ray was working. The Rockland was far enough away so police, not even Washington, would be looking for them there.

Neighborhoods in North Philadelphia were, oftentimes, framed by railroad tracks. Logan was that way. These tracks which he was on now were basically the unofficial eastern border of Logan. East of here was Olney. The railroad tracks that ran by Maria's mother's house, which would be about 20th Street, ran by Fisher's Station which was the western border. West of that was Germantown. Torch walked by the busy basketball courts filled with white kids who didn't seem to notice him. He felt stupid wearing no shirt, but walking past there gave him an idea. If anybody asked why he wasn't wearing a shirt, he would just say that he was playing basketball and had taken off his shirt, then had forgotten the retrieve it when he left.

Torch was always one of those guys who traveled in a group. He didn't intentionally try for that, but it just always seemed to turn out that way; that was how it had been for as long as he could remember. He was never one of those "I Walk Alone" guys. It was another thing Washington had been on the money about. And right now, walking by those unfamiliar white kids, in what was basically enemy territory, he felt very lonely. He crossed the tracks over by Maria's to Ben's every day, and it never bothered him. But the truth was he didn't walk on the tracks by himself very often. It was just something he didn't do. He walked about ten blocks on these tracks and then exited down at Seventh and Rockland. Then he walked two blocks east to the Rockland Bar. It was only about seven o'clock, but the bar was already crowded and noisy. The jukebox was playing, and Teddy Pendergrass was singing "The Whole Town's Laughing at Me":

Maybe if I spent more time with you
Maybe then, maybe then you'd still be mine
Ohhh, and only if I had been more kind to you
There'd be no need for this man to be cryin'

The whole town's laughin' at me
Silly fool, how'd you lose such a good thing?

The place was packed already. A woman, Rose Durie who had been married to Maria's brother was there. She was with two of her brothers including the youngest of that family, Michael. Michael himself had hung at Ben's for a while and in fact, he had done two tours of duty there. He was there when Torch first hung around Ben's then he was away for a bit, then he was back a few years ago. These days Michael hung at a small corner at seventh & Rockland, an ally of Ben's. There was an Asian at the bar called Togi. Torch knew his cousin's Jay & Fugi from Dunn's back in the 60's. Togi was eating a small box of pretzels. A canister of mustard sitting was sitting on the bar. This was not an uncommon sight in Philadelphia bars. A few from Inky parish were there, including Walt and Sharkey, horse –players who torch knew from Keystone racetrack and Jimmy Holland, a bartender from 'the Seaport' bar on rising Sun avenue in Lawncrest (northeast of Logan & Olney). A black man, a good pool shooter named Charley was there. for a long time, torch thought that Charley was a construction worker by the way he dressed most of the time. Torch came to understand that Charley was probably just a hustler (pool hustlers often dressed as construction workers).

The beautiful, blond girl from Inky was also there. In the weeks since Felix was jumped on fifth street, it had been determined that Inky was responsible.. the reason, at least to torch was never clear. It could have been because of his girlfriend Dottie who was married to an Inky boy but that was never made official. The truth was that felix and his brother Johnny or 'J.R.B.' had a beef that went back for a long time. hen J.R.B. got married he bought a house behind enemy lines on a small street called Delphine, between Fourth and Fifth. when he got separated from his wife, this became a sort of party house with a few corner b boys living there on and off. they called the house 'the ranch' and it became sort of like Ceases Palace /East. One summer night boys from Inky drove by and with a shotgun blew out the front windows of The Ranch and a light that was next to the front door. torch hears about this from B Starr who was sleeping on the living room floor at the time. Nobody was hurt but a point had been made for sure. felix getting beat up might have had something to do with Dottie but it was never written in stone.

When Nice Ray saw Torch, he gave him a sarcastic look and said, "What are you, macho man or something?" Then Ray turned and said to everybody, "Look, Torch is macho man." Then Ray pointed to the sign on the wall which simply read: *No shoes. No shirt. No service.*

Torch was afraid Nice Ray would say that. He turned around and started to walk out. The telephone rang behind the bar just then, and Ray picked it up and answered, "Nice Rockland."

Torch had reached the front door on the Fifth Street side of the bar when Ray called him and told him that the call was for him and to pick it up on the wall extension. Torch had a feeling that the phone call had something to do with what had just happened outside the Warnock twenty minutes ago. He almost didn't want to answer. Efrem was on the line. He told Torch that somebody had gotten beat up outside the Warnock. Apparently, from the way, Efrem spoke, he didn't know that Torch had been present when it happened. Torch went along with it, too, like he was shocked.

"Cops are all over the place. They locked everybody up at Caesar's Palace."

He also mentioned they were holding Connell. Efrem said that they were going to go bowling up at Adam's Lanes in the northeast and they would be driving by the Rockland in fifteen minutes, so Torch should be standing outside. Torch waited on the corner of Fifth and Rockland inside a phone booth. Efrem had said Joseph Taimanglo was driving. He had a '67 Wildcat, similar to Torch's, only with more power and a few years newer. Torch figured that he would be able to get a shirt up at the Adam's Mall where the bowling alley was. Torch ate a slice of pizza from Crown Pizza next to the Rockland and waited. They were there in fifteen minutes. Efrem and Joseph Taimanglo were in the front seat, and Jamie, Leo Reilly, Tommy, and Michael Taimanglo were in the back seat. Torch got in the front seat in the middle and said that he'd lost his shirt playing basketball at Barrett, just as he had planned to say. They filled Torch in on what happened. They explained that it had started originally with a case of soda being stolen by some kids earlier that day. Somebody said that, in addition to Connell, two others, Eddie or *Butch* and some old guy from the bar, were in custody.

Torch liked going bowling. That was always a good time. This would be the first time they went during regular hours. Normally they went late at night and stayed for all-night bowling. The speed freaks would be up there bowling at three or four o'clock in the morning.

Joseph took the Roosevelt Boulevard up into the northeast. He made a left turn on Adams Lane and a police car fell in behind him. The police car followed him for about ten seconds, and then put on his flashers and siren.

"Shit," Joseph said.

"Joseph, you are a non-driving motherfucker," Michael said.

"I didn't do anything," Joseph said. "He thinks I'm Puerto Rican. That's the problem."

The Taimanglos' were of an Irish mother, but most of them were dark like Big Jim, who was born in Guam. They were darker, most of them, than Maria.

The policeman walked over to Joseph and asked him for his license and registration. Then he said, "You guys smell like a brewery."

The boys were asked to get out of the car. It was only then that Torch realized that the car that stopped them was from the 53rd District, which was nowhere near here. Torch started getting paranoid, thinking somebody had tipped them off or something like that.

Within seconds, two more cars and a wagon arrived on the scene. These vehicles were from the 25th District. All seven of them were frisked and put in the wagon. No explanation was given, except that they were under suspicion for something. One officer explained that they would be questioned and then released. Torch had momentarily forgotten, but now he was very conscious again of the fact that he didn't have a shirt on.

The police vans went from Adams Avenue to the Boulevard. Soon they were on 1-95, heading south. This meant they were going to the Roundhouse in Center City and not to the local District. It was a twenty-five-minute ride to the Roundhouse. When they got there, they were placed in two cells. Three went in one cell and four in another. The cell Torch shared with Jamie and Michael had a toilet in it which flushed with the sound of an explosion every fifteen minutes whether it needed it or not. Torch, imitating Jimmy Stewart in *It's a Wonderful Life*, said, "Clarence, every time you hear that sound, it means an angel just got his wings." Clearly, to that point, Torch was not alarmed about his situation, although he was a little curious.

Of the three in the cell, Michael was released first, and he was joined by his brothers, Joseph and Tommy, who were in the other cell. They waited in the lobby of the Roundhouse until first Leo, Jamie, and then Efrem were also released. Torch was the only one of the seven that was held. Torch started thinking about the incident outside the Warnock, about Connell and the others, and if they said anything about him.

Two hours later, Torch was brought into the basement of the Roundhouse. There he was placed in what they called "the tank." Torch had worked in a clerical capacity at the Roundhouse one summer, so he was familiar with the tank. It was basically a large holding cell. Torch had worked days, and he didn't recognize any of the people that were there now. The room was covered with writing done in magic marker. Metal benches were on one side, inmates had carved their names in them using keys. There were even words written on the ceiling that somebody with iron balls wrote with a lighter.

The boys upstairs had long since left. There was nothing they could do. Nobody had told them anything about Torch's situation. When Torch first got in the tank, which was about 20 feet by 20 feet, it was still relatively early in the evening. It held about ten or twelve men at that point. Most of them were black, but a few were white. In the next few hours, every twenty or so minutes, more people would be released while some new faces arrived. By twelve o'clock, there were still about twelve people in there, but they were all new faces. Torch was the only one that remained in there. He was very aware of that. The police and clerical staff outside of the tank were clearly visible through the bulletproof glass that surrounded it; however, they seemed oblivious to whatever was going on in the tank at any moment. Somebody told Torch they heard the police here were waiting to see if the one who got beat up would pull through. It was exactly what Torch had been thinking about, worrying about. Was this why he wasn't released with the others? These were the longest and scariest hours. He kept thinking of that Rolling Stones' song.

I killed a man I'm prison bound the hand of fate is on me now.

At two o'clock in the morning, the 76ers' reserve forward James "Jellybean" Owens was brought into the tank. He had been, in addition to a 76er, a local college standout. By three in the morning, the place had, at least, twenty-five customers in it. Most of them were simply "driving under the influence" cases. Torch heard that Jellybean had been brought in for a cocaine possession charge.

At one point, in the middle of the night, Torch couldn't help but fall asleep right on the floor of the tank. He tried to stay awake because he was afraid that he would miss his name being called or something like that. When Torch did wake up, it was to the voice of a black man yelling in the pay phone that was in the tank. He was yelling at a woman, and he was saying, "What's the matter with you? This is important. I don't want to talk to some little kid. When the phone rings, you answer it. You answer your own phone. What's the matter with you?"

Two black guys were there in similar jumpsuits. One was talking to Torch, and he was showing pictures of him in poses outside the Coliseum in Rome. He must have had fifty pictures, all similar. They each had him in different poses, flexing his muscles with the Coliseum visible in the background. When the other went to use the pay phone, Torch looked at the red writing on the back of his black jumpsuit. There was a map on the back of it with green as countries, black as water, and there was writing in red letters. The stitching on the back of the jumpsuit had the name of their outfit. They were called "Morocco's." Underneath, there was a list of places such as Cambodia, Pakistan, Vietnam, Taiwan, North Philly.

Then the other one, the one with the pictures of him outside of the Coliseum, also got up to use the phone. It was then that Torch could read the writing on the back of his jumpsuit. The writing was a little different. In red letters on his jumpsuit, it read:

There is no afterlife

You create your own
Heaven and Hell
Right here on earth

It was dawn by the time Torch was finally called out of the tank. You could tell it was dawn because there were TV sets all over the inside of the basement that showed the parking lot outside. Also, you could tell that it was drizzling. Torch was then fingerprinted and taken for a mug shot. Torch was handcuffed to a young black man about the same age as him. The two of them were brought down together to see the judge in a makeshift courtroom in the bowels of the Roundhouse.

Charlie Tuna was sitting on one of the benches with about ten other family members of those being held, bail bondsmen, and lawyers. The black kid with Torch apparently had been there for some sort of vandalism charge and was held on $300 bail. Then Torch went before the judge. The judge said, "Why isn't this prisoner wearing a shirt?"

A bailiff explained that Torch had been brought in last night in an apparent sweep of a neighborhood. The bailiff reminded the judge that it had been very hot the previous night.

The judge said that Torch had been arrested for aggravated assault, and he was released on $3000 bail, of which he had to post only 10 percent. It was only then that Torch realized that Chops or Snake, whichever one it was, had pulled through and there was no murder charge. Charlie Tuna paid in cash, and Torch was given a subpoena for court in two weeks and then was released. On the ride home, Charlie Tuna talked about what happened. He drove a white Volvo.

"This is only the beginning. I hope you realize that. This isn't going to end now, not from what I heard."

"Jellybean Owens was in there," Torch said.

"I heard something about that on the radio. They said he was arrested for possession of cocaine. Hey, you can always say that you were locked up with Jellybean Owens."

"That's great," Torch said.

Charlie Tuna turned onto 1-95 and headed north. Philadelphia's Soul Survivors were singing their big song, "Expressway to Your Heart." Charlie Tuna was saying that he was around Caesar's Palace that morning, but nobody was around. He said he heard the one who got beat up was from Nicetown.

Torch listened to the song and to the squeaking of the windshield wipers, and halfway home, he was asleep.

BOOK IV

Answer

CHAPTER 19

Nothing had ever scared Torch as much as being locked up and not knowing if the charge was murder. He figured he would rather kill somebody for real than go through that again. This was the second time in his short life that he had brushed up against a murder rap. Washington was right — he should grow up and start moving in another direction before it was too late.

Even though the victim was now on the way to recovery, there was a feeling in the neighborhood on all sides that there would be some form of retaliation. This was the first time Torch looked forward to the summer ending. He promised himself that he would fly under the radar for the next week or so, and, except for the morning hours, he avoided Caesar's Palace.

Connell and two others were still being held at the detention center, but there was no indication that police were pursuing others that may have been involved in the assault. There was a rumor that friends of Chops from the Nicetown gang had been seen riding through Logan and around the Warnock with shotguns. This was only a rumor with no credibility attached to it. It was almost predictable that a story like that would start circulating. Nevertheless, the rumors at least initially, alarmed Torch. It was one reason why he didn't want to be around there for a while. Stories like that would inevitably pop up and scare the hell out of Torch whether they were true or not.

Washington was concerned about the fight and situations that might occur because of it. A few days following the incident, Washington talked to several black neighbors. The consensus was that they were not very happy with the police reaction or with the subsequent investigation. The fact that Chops wasn't from the neighborhood or that he was ultimately going to recover from his wounds were both beside the point. They were flat-out angry about the whole incident. It was around this time, during these unofficial interviews, that Washington picked up on a very real tension surrounding the incident. It clearly was a situation that he (Washington) needed to get on top of.

Torch really didn't want to talk to anybody for a while. He did his work in the morning, and then went back to the northeast. He went to harness races at the Brandywine Racetrack in Delaware most every night, and that was how he planned to spend the rest of the summer.

* * *

Glenn Miller parked his motorcycle and sat at a table outside Porky's Point. As usual, he ate the specialty, roast pork. He ate a side order of *tostones*, which was a sort of a Puerto Rican version of French Fries. They were formed into patties, deep-fried, and brushed with garlic oil. He washed it all down with a large Pepsi from a blue cup. After he ate, he remounted his chopper, the nicest bike around, and proceeded north on Fifth Street.

Through another Scorpion, Glenn had made arrangements to possibly unload the quantity of meth that he had been sitting on. The buyers were a "big outfit" in New Jersey. These people were allegedly willing to pay a reasonable price and, more importantly, would buy the meth with no questions asked. A meeting was to take place at the Lord Cheltenham Bar, which was located at the very northern end of Fifth Street.

Heading north from Porky's Point, Glenn drove through the "golden mile" which was predominantly Hispanic. There were restaurants, grocery stores, clothing stores, most of the products you could purchase from outdoor stands. Glenn rode under the overpass of the Roosevelt Extension at the Schuylkill Expressway. He continued to ride north into Olney, which was still a lot German at that point. He rode past the Rockland Bar, Italian restaurants, pizzerias, and bakeries. Then he passed Incarnation Church and the Schwarzwald Inn, a famous German restaurant. He rode past Ukrainian bakeries and a fish stand where you could buy *baccala* (the only place in North Philadelphia that sold it.). He rode past an Indian grocery store, a Korean restaurant, and he waited for a light at Fifth and Tabor. The light changed, and he proceeded north.

Just then a brown Cadillac turned left onto Fifth Street and remained about forty or fifty yards behind Glenn. Glenn went through a green light. The Cadillac sped up and made it through the yellow light behind him. The Cadillac continued to stalk Glenn, about twenty-five yards behind him now. Neither Glenn nor the Cadillac seemed to be in a hurry. Glenn passed a Philadelphia reservoir on his right and waited for a light at Fifth and Champlost Street. The brown Cadillac, driven by Bobby Santore, with his uncle Paco in the passenger seat, was behind him in the right lane, still about twenty yards back.

Suddenly Fifth Street turned into a primarily residential section with fewer pedestrians. The Cadillac sped up. At one point, they were only five yards behind Glenn. Out of nowhere, they were, once again, in a busy business district. On Glenn's left was Fishers Park. On his right was a block that featured a few bars, the Fern Rock Movie and a pizzeria.

After that, Fifth Street was residential and quiet once again. He was only about five blocks away from the end of Fifth Street when Glenn, once again, pulled to a red light. The Cadillac pulled up beside Glenn. Paco kept his face straight ahead as he struggled to bring his shotgun up from the floor. At first, Glenn didn't pay any attention, but from out of the corner of his eye became aware of the old man in the car next to him struggling with something. Glenn kept his face straight ahead. Then the shotgun came out of the window, and Glenn heard the man shout something to him, something like "Hey, Wisenheimer!"

The shotgun blast ripped into Glenn's Scorpion colors on his chest. The blast was so strong that it sent Glenn flying off the bike and to the curb where his body in the gutter and his back upright leaning against an abandoned newsstand. His eyes remained open, and Paco looked at him as they sped off. Glenn's eyes seemed to follow him and had this weird half-smile on his face. He didn't appear to be in shock or afraid or angry. The look on his face freaked Paco out a little. It was like Glen was sharing a little private joke with himself. It was like he was thinking, "Boy, now, I know why they call it the shotgun seat."

* * *

Bah-Bah headed toward Logan from the northeast, where he had made several payoffs and collections that afternoon. It was about 4:45 when he got on the Roosevelt Boulevard. He would have plenty of time to set up for tonight's baseball games.

At 4:58 in the afternoon, with the sun still burning brightly, a Molotov cocktail was thrown into the back shed of Caesar's Palace. A fireman said the shed was obviously the first thing destroyed and suspected that gasoline made it into the living room, the center of the old row-house, which went up rapidly in flames.

Firemen claimed that they were at a disadvantage fighting the fire. It had been a hot day, and the fire hydrant across the street had been on for much of the day. Therefore, the pressure was low, and the firemen said they were lucky just to contain the blaze to one house. A crowd made up of several different nationalities was growing across the street, watching the fire from Sal's Auto Body Shop. Police cars were on the scene as well as the fire truck. One uniformed police officer was talking to neighbors in the crowd.

Grant was standing out in the middle of the street watching in agony with his hands on his head like a pitcher who had just beaned a batter unintentionally. The firemen were smashing his windows with axes. The smoke poured out of the second story of Caesar's Palace next door.

"I don't understand that," Grant was saying over and over. "I paid $400 a piece for those windows."

Of course, Grant wasn't a fireman. Bah-Bah, who had just arrived, had seen this before; they always broke windows, whether it looked like it made sense or not.

Looking up at a window that the firemen's hose was hitting, Bah-Bah couldn't tell the difference between the shards of glass and the droplets of water. A rainbow from the hose's spray could be seen through the smoke pouring out of the house. Bah-Bah turned his eyes to the gathered spectators and figured there were probably representatives from every continent in the group. Then he noticed several young girls talking excitedly on the steps of a nearby house. One of them was saying, "They came after Torch; that's how all this started."

Bah-Bah overheard someone say, "It doesn't make sense. They have houses, too."

Bah-Bah stayed around until the firemen got the blaze under control. Then he rode back to his house in South Philadelphia. The first thing he did was call Torch, who already had heard about Caesar's Palace. BahBah asked Torch if he was going to be all right. Torch said it wouldn't be a problem and that he could book out of his parents' house for a while.

"What about all your work?" Bah-Bah asked. "All that stuff is lost. It isn't going to be a problem, is it?"

Torch replied, "I called in my steadies, and that's about it. I didn't lose anything important."

Bah-Bah then went about calling the few baseball bettors he had and told them that he was back at the South Philadelphia number. For some reason, Bah-Bah wasn't worried about Moscariello at the moment. The boll weevils hadn't run him out, and he just felt relieved that his short North Philadelphia adventure was over.

CHAPTER 20

At 6:40 the next night, Torch and Charlie Tuna were getting ready to go to the Brandywine Racetrack. One of Torch's favorite horses was entered that night. His name was Town Drunk, and he was ridden by Verne Crank. The horse loved to win but had been overmatched his last few races at the Liberty Bell Racetrack back in the winter and spring. That night, he was entered in with lighter company at Brandywine, his real home, where Verne Crank was usually a leading rider.

Torch was still booking the night number when the phone rang.

It was Freddy, a bartender from the Little Pub in Center City, who made a small bet on a horse at Brandywine that night. Torch asked him where they stood, and Freddy said he thought they were even.

"Don't you still owe me forty dollars for two horses that you bet at Oceanport?"

"I already paid you that. I gave it to you outside of Oscar's that day."

"Oh, that's right. That's right, I'm sorry, Freddie. I don't keep that work around. Christ, I've had three offices since then."

At five minutes after seven, Torch and Charlie Tuna were leaving the house. Just then, the phone rang again. This time, it was Donna from the diner. She told him that Washington had been there that day and told her to get in touch with him. She said that Washington wanted to talk to him about what happened outside the Warnock and the best thing Torch could do was to talk to him. He wasn't after Torch, but other cops wouldn't look at it the same way. He told Donna that he could have locked Torch up in the past but always let him go, and it wasn't just for the numbers either.

Torch was scared. He tried to put that night out of his mind. Washington would understand, though, what happened. He knew Torch was a nervous wreck, and he probably would be better off explaining it to Washington than somebody who didn't know him. Besides that, Torch had cards to play himself.

"Is Washington going to be in the diner tomorrow?" Torch asked.

"He comes here every morning," Donna said.

"Tell him if he wants to talk to me. I'll be at Ben's between one and two."

At the racetrack, Torch's mind was elsewhere, and he lost a hundred dollars.

* * *

At 1:15 the next day, Torch sat at Ben's counter reading *Ring* magazine's article about Philadelphia boxers. The trainer of then heavyweight champion Larry Holmes was quoted in the story. He said, "I would never take a fighter to train in Philadelphia. All Philly fighters want to take your head off."

The article talked about the overall tradition and marriage that existed between the city and boxing. Clearly the writer had spent time in the city. He had seen fights at the Blue Horizon and the Spectrum. He quoted *Daily News* columnist Pete Dexter in the story. Dexter had said,

"Philadelphia is the only place where two bums would be fighting in an alley and they would both be feigning and throwing double jabs."

The author of the magazine article also interviewed *Daily News* writer Larry McMullen who said, "I think Philadelphians have a sense of history instilled in them. I'm talking about American history. In some respects, Philadelphia is the quintessential American city. Boxing appeals to the people here because, on a certain level, it is the quintessential American game, more so than even baseball. If you look at boxing, you can trace the upper-mobility of groups of people. That almost selfevidently is America. I mean, first it was the white ethnics. They made their mark on boxing. Most notably there was Jack Dempsey, a larger than life American hero. He was arguably bigger and more popular than even Babe Ruth. Boxing historian Bert Sugar even said that. Between the First World War and the Second World War, Jews dominated boxing and, at one point, held six of the eight weight-class title belts. Italians made their mark also along with the Jews. They dominated the lighter weight divisions. These groups had their heavyweight champions, too, like Max Baer, Primo Canero, and eventually Rocky Marciano. In the middle of them was the long reign of heavy-weight champion Joe Louis. In my house, my father's heroes were Irishmen, namely heavyweight champion James Braddock and even more, Irish Billy Conn, the light heavyweight champion of the world. Billy Conn stepped up in 1941 and nearly upset the great Joe Louis and, in fact, had the fight won until the thirteenth round when Louis knocked him out. I remember listening to the Louis/ Conn fight with my father. I remember listening to the blow-by-blow broadcast of the first Ali-Joe Frazier fight with my daughter Lauren (then a baby). And at the risk of sounding overly dramatic, it seems to me that those two events, those two fights, bookmarked my life, or, at least, the important part. Joe Louis's reign foreshadowed the dominance we see up to this day of the black fighter and his dominance of the heavyweight division, as another ethnic group rose up. For a short time, Sweden's Ingemar Johansson held the heavyweight championship belt when he beat Floyd Patterson, adding to the international flavor of the prestigious heavyweight division. Twelve months later, Floyd Patterson avenged the fight. I can remember the names since Floyd Patterson. There was Sonny Liston, Cassius Clay/Muhammad Ali, Jimmy Ellis, Joe Frazier, George Foreman, and so on. I can rattle the names off easier than I can the names of the presidents in this century. Anyway, it is, I think, the sense of history attached to the sport that tends to appeal to the average Philadelphian. As for the fighters themselves, I think, there has always been an advantage because of the competition here in the gyms. There are also the teachers here and the best trainers such as Yank Durham, Hank Cisco, Georgie Benton, Slim Jim Robinson or those who specialize in developing and working with young talent like my friend Charlie Sgrillo in Kensington. I also think Philadelphia boxers are avoided somewhat. As a result, they may have missed out on bigger purses. This unfortunate state of affairs was a bonanza for local fans. I mean, we as local fans got to see the very best here in Philadelphia when they really should have been in Vegas or New York. My favorite local fighter, for example, was middle-weight Willie 'The Worm' Monroe from North Philadelphia. He should have been an international, world- class champion, on a stage and with the exposure like Sugar Ray Leonard. He was so good. He even once upset 'Marvelous' Marvin Hagler."

The article settled Torch for a few minutes. It took his mind off his situation. He had been more than a little nervous about his meeting today with Washington. Torch knew what he had to do. One way or the other, Washington, even if he didn't know already, would figure out that Torch was present when that individual got beat up outside the Warnock.

Washington was like Deacon Jones, the defensive end from the Los Angeles Rams. You were better off running at him than trying to run away from him. Torch just had to not be a pussy and explain to Washington that even, if he could prove Torch was around when Chops got beat up, he would bring Washington down with him. That was the right move — stand up and be a man. Unfortunately, that was something Torch wasn't good at.

Torch looked at the other magazines on the shelves in Ben's store. He thought back to the day when Reds was killed. He was certain, by now, that Washington had set that whole thing up. He remembered that day clearly because it was a week or two before Valentine's Day. There were all kinds of heart-shaped boxes of chocolates on the wall in the store. Most were already paid for or partially paid for. The names of families were on many of them — Reilly, Walton, McCrory, Pritts, Dolan ... Torch remembered because Washington glanced over and smiled when he saw the hearts. Torch and Shine were playing pinball. Washington came in and said that a purse had been snatched. Two people fitting Torch's and Shine's descriptions had been identified by a witness, Washington said. A police car was outside the store, and Washington escorted Shine and Torch to the 53rd where they sat in a cell. It was complete bullshit. Washington knew that they weren't purse snatchers. Furthermore, there probably weren't two guys in the world together that matched Torch's and Shine's description ... and two white kids ... in Logan? They had been questioned, then held for three or four hours. It was after they had been released that they heard about Reds getting killed. Torch, thinking about it in recent months, came to believe that Washington probably anticipated trouble. He had had Shine and Torch locked up as a precaution. They were both regulars at Danny Parker's house, and Washington didn't need them showing up when the shakedown was taking place. As it turned out, Torch had been accurate on this theory of his.

At 1:30, Washington came in the store.

"Hey, Torch. Where are the mighty Ben's now?"

Torch knew what Washington meant. Torch had driven through the neighborhood, and there was barely a white face to be seen now that Caesar's Palace was destroyed. There was also a rumor that Grant had sold the Warnock Bar. That, by the way, turned out to be true, and in October, the Warnock reopened as a black night club called Uncle Bill's Timeout.

"Donna says that you want to see me?" Torch said.

Washington glanced over at Ben who was behind the counter acting like he wasn't listening. Washington led Torch out of the store.

"It is about the other night," Washington said when they were outside. "The neighborhood is about to explode. There were more than three people involved in that boy getting jumped outside the bar. Two black neighbors put you at the scene of the crime, Torch. One said he saw you hitting the guy on the ground with your belt. Then another said that he saw you running behind his house in the back alleys with Felix and a few others minutes after the incident. He said that you weren't wearing a shirt."

"Was I ever the kind of guy to run around without a shirt?"

"Not under normal circumstances maybe, but there is more to it than that. I saw Connell and them at the detention center. I read the transcripts. They all said the same thing. They all said that they took off their shirts because they were wearing these red and blue Warnock

Tavern baseball shirts, and they didn't want to be identified."

"Did anybody mention my name?"

"The neighbors did. One that said he saw you with your belt off. Another just described you as 'the one with the red hair.'" "That could be a few people," Torch said.

"He said 'the one with the red hair and the big mouth.'"

"I heard that Chops is going to be all right. Three guys are in custody for it, so I don't see what the big deal is."

Washington shook his head. "It is exactly like what happened when Fat Eddie was shot off his mini-bike. The people in the community didn't care necessarily about him getting shot. They understood what was going on. Besides that, three white boys had been stabbed that I know about. There was that kid Burk from 1-5-D, Billy Velez from Dunn's, and Turk from Ben's, plus who knows who or what else. My point is, even counting Fat Eddie, Logan Nation got the best of the white boys. So there was no reason to get angry about it. It's like you said to me up in the hospital that night, you have to look at the whole picture. You had to put it in context. The community wasn't angry about Fat Eddie getting shot. They were angry about how the police didn't care enough to conduct a thorough investigation. They seemed to just grab the first white boy they could find and blame it on him. It was someone, it turned out, that everyone knew was innocent. That's where the anger and trouble came from. This is just history repeating itself. That's why it's important now that everybody involved with what happened is held accountable. I mean, these people are very upset. One neighbor described a big guy. He had a beard. It sounded like Johnny Thunder. He was there, wasn't he? Johnny Thunder?"

It was ironic that Washington mentioned Johnny Thunder at that moment. Torch was just replaying the scene in his mind. He remembered, for some reason, that Elvis song playing on the jukebox in the Warnock. That always meant or almost always meant that Johnny Thunder was there.

Washington sounded like a nut to Torch, talking about those people getting *moved on* and where each one was from and all that. Torch was surprised Washington remembered that bullshit, surprised he knew about all that in the first place. Now was the time for Torch to explain that he had the goods on Washington. It was time to appear strong or tough; however, when he spoke again, it was only to offer Washington a gift.

"That guy Kelly, the one with Maria, the one that everybody's looking for. I know where he is … Denver." "Denver?" Washington said.

"I think Kelly has family out there or something. Maria told me they were going to Denver. She said that the air in Denver would be better for Lee Oskar. The doctor told her that his asthma condition would improve."

"Why are you telling me this?"

"Why not? You said I never tell you anything. There you are. I don't give a damn. Go get 'em."

"Still, Torch, if you had anything to do with what happened outside of the bar, you'll be locked up for it. The whole thing is too big, too important. It's out of my hands. It isn't an ordinary bar fight. It was a racial thing, and this is an election year. And after what already just happened, ya' know, with MOVE and the problems in southwest, it becomes important. The captain is on my ass about this. Even the commissioner has an interest in this, and it probably goes higher than that. It's a good thing Chops pulled through, or they would have nailed you to the cross. Where were you when that happened?"

"We went bowling," Torch said. "On the way there, we were stopped by the police. They took us all down the Roundhouse. I was there all night. I don't even know why."

"You were held for suspicion of what might have very well been a murder case had that youngster died. You never would have been released … believe me. There were people monitoring the situation, just waiting to snatch you up. Efrem told me about that night, and you guys getting locked up."

Washington had personally checked out the story Efrem told him. At first, Washington didn't believe him and that "all-night bowling" stuff, but it turned out it was true. They had been intercepted by a police cruiser in the northeast, just a few blocks from the bowling alley. Washington had called down to the Roundhouse himself and talked to the intake people who were on duty that night. They confirmed it; Torch was in jail all night. Washington even had intake send him Torch's mug shot to show around, in case Torch tried to hide out somewhere in the Northeast or South Philly or some other white neighborhood. Washington also cleared up the mystery of why they were stopped and locked up in the first place. Apparently, a jewelry store had been robbed on Fifth Street in Olney that afternoon. A 53rd district cruiser went up to the northeast to the home of the owner for a routine interview or report. On the way back, something about the fight outside the Warnock came over the police radio. The names of three suspects were mentioned. One was Torch's name, and the others were Dave "Slant" Zerwick and Jimmy Taimanglo. The latter two had simply been in the bar when the fight broke out. They had been detained briefly at the 53rd but were released. Just seconds after hearing the name Taimanglo, one of the officers spotted Joey's Buick. When the police stopped them, and saw the car full of people, including not only Torch but *three* Taimanglos, he didn't know what to do. He thought the best thing was to run them all down to the Roundhouse. Then, when it was determined that none of them were suspects, they were all released. That is, they were all released except for Torch, who *was* a suspect.

"Like I was saying, I talked to Connell and the others at the detention center, I think they're going to crucify them, especially Connell, and they can, given the climate in the city right now. We *might* have to deport his ass."

"I hope not," Torch said. "It's ironic, right? I mean Connell comes from Northern Ireland where he's in prison. That was politics, him being I.R.A. and all. President Carter helps to get him released, and that was politics. Then he gets caught up here in 'the land of the free and the brave,' and the politics here and gets locked up anyway. Maybe, since Chops is going to be all right and with Caesar's Palace being firebombed and all that, maybe it will blow over."

"What do you mean? What's your point?"

"I mean, ya know, they got their pint of blood," Torch said.

Washington was grinning now and he said, "You guys still don't get it, do you?"

"Get what?" Torch said.

"Torch, tell me something," Washington said. "Those TV sets that were stolen earlier in the summer were in the back of Caesar's Palace, weren't they?"

Torch didn't respond. He didn't even know what Washington was talking about. What did the TVs have to do with it? he wondered. Torch noticed now that the grin was gone from Washington's face. He seemed pissed off about something.

Then he said, "This is insulting if you want to know the truth. This here is fucked up. You guys got fooled by the oldest trick in the book, ya' know, 'blame the niggers.'"

"What do you mean?"

"What do I mean? I mean, I have an eyewitness that saw the person throwing the Molotov cocktail in the back of Caesar's Palace. It wasn't a black person from around the Warnock or somebody from Nicetown or Logan Nation. The person that threw the Molotov cocktail was white. Now, I don't know for sure who threw that device, but I have a good idea of who it was. Mannnnnn, I tried to warn you about Frenchie, didn't I?" Now Torch knew what the TV sets had to do with it.

* * *

Torch drove to Bah-Bah's house in South Philly the next night. He had won a few dollars with a glorious late season winning streak. The succession of the consecutive victories was spearheaded by one of Torch's favorite pitchers, soft-throwing, left-hander Doug Rau of the Los Angeles Dodgers.

After they conducted their business, Torch told Bah-Bah about Washington and his insinuation that Frenchie had betrayed them. Bah-Bah's face was a mask of apathy with no expression at all. In reality though, he (Bah-Bah) was processing the information. He was thinking about something he'd heard outside Caesar's Palace the night of the fire. Somebody had said, "It doesn't make sense. They have houses, too."

It didn't mean anything to him at the time, but now it did. Yet instead of reacting one way or the other to this startling accusation, BahBah just shifted gears and changed the subject.

"Is Maria Italian?" was all Bah-Bah asked.

"Are you crazy? Her father's Puerto Rican, and her mom is Irish," Torch said.

"I mean, because of that name ... Maria," Bah-Bah said.

"Maria can be Spanish, too. Didn't you ever see *West Side Story... Daag"* Torch said.

CHAPTER 21

As for Glenn Miller, it was widely held that his murder was linked to a hundred thousand dollars' worth of methamphetamine which had been stolen from the old Philadelphia crime family. This group had been in hiding and had popped up one last time to take revenge on Glenn. At least, it seemed that way. It was as though this was their last official act as a powerful crime force in Philadelphia. Not much was heard of their business dealings after Glenn's murder. Most of Constantine's men either fell in line with Moscariello or were killed, including Chick-a-dee's immediate successor who was gunned down outside his home in South Philadelphia the following spring.

Glenn's murder was a big story on the local news. The media inadvertently implicated Moscariello by suggesting that Glenn's and Chick-a-dee's murders were related, which was not the case. Washington knew about it first-hand, told Torch, and they understood that the stolen drugs were from the lab on Eleventh Street in Logan, which had subsequently been blown up to conceal the robbery. That lab, without a doubt, belonged to Constantine.

* * *

Bah-Bah returned to Logan with his brother-in-law, John Taggs, who to Torch looked remarkably like Chef Boyardee, to sign papers relinquishing any connection to his house, which was now just a burned-out shell. After their business, Taggs who worked at City Hall, took the subway south to his office. Bah-Bah was wearing a suit in anticipation of Glenn's funeral that morning. It wasn't that he was friendly with Glenn. South Philadelphians liked to go to funerals, whether it made sense or not.

Doc, J.R.B., Efrem, Billy Young, and some others who had squatted at Caesar's Palace off and on for the last several years moved into another abandoned house down the street which they called the MGM Grand, and life, post-Caesar's Palace, went on.

Bah-Bah drove around until he caught up with Torch and several others on Wellens Street at Danny Parker's house where Felix was staying again. Bah-Bah shared a huge bag of soft pretzels he bought that morning from the factory near his house. They were standing on the porch talking while Frenchie showed off some tomatoes that he said he'd grown but which everyone knew he had stolen from some neighbor's garden.

"Nothing like growing your own produce," Frenchie said.

The tomatoes reminded Torch of the ones in Maria's yard. Right now, her brother occupied the house which was fine, but those tomatoes belonged to him. Torch was saying that even when they had a small yard in Logan, his mother grew tomatoes, cucumbers, eggplant, radishes, lettuce, and even corn, although the corn never quite matured to where it was edible. It was a practice Torch said that she kept up now in her larger garden in the northeast.

"Where did you say your mother lived again, Torch?" Frenchie asked.

Frenchie had the stereo in Danny Parker's living room at full blast. The singer was Wet Willie; he sounded a little like Van Morrison.

You say you got the blues
You got holes in both of your shoes
You're feelin' alone and confused
You gotta keep on smilin', keep on smilin'
You say you found a piece of land
Gonna change from city boy to country man
And you gotta keep on smilin' Keep on smilin'

There were six or seven of them. Most were going to the funeral. Some were dressed up; they wore nice pants and shoes with a wife beater T-shirt. It was a short-lived summertime- formal-wear-style around here. '*Look at the way these birds dress*' Bah-Bah was thinking. Felix wore a blue suit that looked equally ridiculous. It was too small for one thing, and it looked, in every way, like a suit from seventh grade at Holy Child.

They went in two cars. Bah-Bah drove one, and the other was driven by Steve Nick. He drove a '59 Dodge that everybody called the Batmobile. Steve grew up on Windrim Avenue, a few doors down from Caesar's Palace. Then he was in the navy, in the brig, too, and now was AWOL. He was tall and thin with green eyes and black hair. He had been around for years and was one of the thirty or so white boys that Washington had interviewed for his survey back in 1974. Bah-Bah thought he was a musician of some sort, and he wrote songs even. He had stayed on and off, sometimes for weeks at a time, at Caesar's Palace. His mother still lived in the neighborhood and bartended, working days at the Warnock.

Torch, Bah-Bah, Jackie, and Efrem talked about going to the Spectrum that night in South Philadelphia to see everybody's favorite middleweight, Bennie Briscoe, who still lived in North Philadelphia, battle against young lion Marvin Hagler.

* * *

The funeral was at Givnish Funeral Home on Fifth Street in Olney. It was, in fact, only a block or so away from the spot Glenn was killed. The business was on a block of Fifth Street that was usually very quiet. There was a circus-like atmosphere today however, and it sounded like the infield at Atco Raceway because of the many motorcycles and choppers. There was also a very noticeable police presence, starting with a uniformed cop in the middle of the street directing traffic. There were, at least, two marked police vehicles there. In addition, Bah-Bah pointed out a parked, unmarked van that he said was part of the Philadelphia police's' organized crime unit.

Both *Action News* and *Eyewitness News* had vans there as well. All of this or almost all of this was connected to this alleged war between Moscariello's people and the Scorpions over the meth trade. When the hearse left, and proceeded toward Holy Sepulcher Cemetery, it was followed by (according to the *Daily News)* between eighty and one hundred Scorpions on their bikes, wearing their colors.

On the ride home, they talked about Glenn a bit. Out of the corner of his eye, Torch caught a glimpse of Frenchie. He was quiet, just staring out of the window. Torch wondered what Frenchie was thinking. Both Frenchie and Glenn had pulled the same trick. Both robbed from a house, then blew up the house to cover their tracks. It was as simple as that. It was like Frenchie stole the idea right from Glenn's playbook. And Frenchie may have gotten away with it had it not been for Washington's secret witness. That is, he may have gotten away with it for a short time, just like Glenn had. But the truth was that things like this almost always came out in the wash. Frenchie had to know that. But like Washington liked to say "Criminals didn't often look at the possible consequences of their actions. It was largely what made them criminals in the first place." Now here they were returning from the funeral of Frenchie's idol. Torch liked to think that Frenchie was thinking of his own mortality just then.

As for the brazen, reckless, dangerous act itself, Torch had thought about how it all must have happened. Frenchie had cousins over in Olney who hung at Inky. They had probably helped him. They probably used a van or maybe a station wagon (there were only eight or ten sets left) and parked across the tracks from Caesar's Palace on Wagner Avenue. They crossed the tracks, then liberated the sets, and then firebombed the back shed. Torch couldn't remember where they were that day. It was a hot day, though, and those who weren't working were maybe over in Jersey, swimming.

* * *

Seven of them took the Soul Train to the Spectrum to the fights that night. The crew included several who attended the funeral, as well as John Blocks and Larry Green. Greenie was yet another off Windrim Avenue, who like Blocks lived only a few doors from Caesar's Palace. Greenie was younger than Torch and company. Torch thought that he was a combination of Irish and Jewish. He himself was a boxer fighting out of Joe Frazier's Cloverlay Gym in North Philadelphia. There, Greenie had sparred with some of the finest middleweights in the country, including Briscoe, Willie "The Worm" Monroe, Eddie Mustafa Muhammad, Bobby "Boogaloo" Watts, and Eugene "Cyclone" Hart.

In the main event, Bennie Briscoe fought for the seventy-ninth time. His opponent that night would become the best middleweight of the next decade. "Marvelous" Marvin Hagler was the best this crowd in Philadelphia had seen since South Philadelphia's own Joey Giardello in the early sixties. It appeared that night that this was Briscoe's last fight, although, as it turned out, he hung around until 1982, fighting professionally for an even twenty years. It was a fight that didn't promise surprises, and it lived up to the hype as Hagler dominated throughout.

Nevertheless, Torch had to be here, perhaps this would be his last chance to see this living legend in person. Briscoe had earned the right to fight for the championship of the world on three different occasions. In each case, he lost. Briscoe twice fought the greatest of them all, Carlos Monzone, once fighting him to a draw. His most recent title shot was last year (1977) against the tough Rodrigo Valdes, who already had been victorious over Briscoe twice. In the third fight on national TV, Torch didn't figure things would improve, and he was correct as Valdes won easily.

The first-time Torch went to the fights was in West Philly. He was with Charlie Tuna and some older guys from Dunn's in the mid-sixties. Briscoe's opponent that night was another Philadelphian, Stanley "Kitten" Hayward. It was a hard fight, and Kitten got the decision. Kitten had a style where he finished strong. He was known for that. He did it this time as well to narrowly get the decision. The Flamboyant Kitten had both experience and class advantage at that point. He had just knocked out a highly ranked opponent from New York at the Blue

Horizon on national television. The thing was that, after all these years, both men looked the same. Kitten worked at City Hall and looked like he could still fight in his fifties. The case of Briscoe and his ability to defy age was even more eerie. Briscoe was a famously hard worker and trainer. And with the shaved head, he never changed much.

In the novel *God's Pocket*, written by *Daily News* columnist Pete Dexter, a main character was a construction worker also from North Philadelphia. His name was Lucian or "old Lucy." He, too, was a black man, and he was bald. When many Philadelphians read the book, some probably pictured Briscoe in the role. In one passage, Dexter was describing Old Lucy's wife watching him walk to his job:

"She handed him his lunch at the door and watched him walk down the Lehigh Avenue toward Broad, where he caught the C bus for work. From behind, if he had his hat on like he did this morning, you would have thought he was thirty-five years old. In fact, he was nearly twice that, but there was nothing lame or old in his step.

Lucian had gone bald early, but she hadn't cared. His body was still hard, like a young man. She wondered at the way time passed him by. He never even wore out his shoes like other people did, and there wasn't a day in his life he went to work against his will."

Finally, even thirty years after Briscoe's last fight, he was paid the highest honor by the phillyboxinghistory.com website. They started a tradition of giving a statuette of Benny to the best Philly fighter of the year. The website said this of him:

"He is the very symbol of Philadelphia's great boxing history. He was one of hardest punching, toughest, most accomplished ring attractions. Briscoe is the inspiration for our award.

Now Bennie Briscoe's legacy is set. From now on, Philadelphia boxers will be awarded in the name of this great fighter. and his image will now rest upon the shelves of the very best of a new generation of fighters. Briscoe's skills and accomplishments have become the measuring stick for all fighters who do battle in the city of Philadelphia. They may be good, but are they Briscoe award winners?"

★ ★ ★

The next day Bah-Bah sat behind the wheel of the white Cadillac with Bobby Santore next to him. It was Bobby who drove when his uncle Paco blew Glenn away on Fifth Street. Paco had offered Bah-Bah the job first — $1,000 just to drive — but he refused. It wasn't that Bah-Bah was Glenn's friend; he had only seen him once or twice at Caesar's Palace and didn't care about him one way or the other. Also, unlike Bobby, Bah-Bah wasn't concerned about scoring points with a family that was now just about powerless. On the surface, he felt the same way about Frenchie. What good would it do to kill him? He wasn't even very angry that Frenchie had firebombed his house. He couldn't care less about Frenchie, and he knew he would never see any of those guys again. There was no money in this, but dollars and cents had nothing to do with it. Firebombing his house, Bah-Bah understood, was symptomatic of the sickness of the way they lived up here. They wanted to play games ... all right; Bah-Bah would play, too.

The car was parked fifty yards away from Dunn's Candy Store, under the shade of oak trees at the entrance to a city park. They had been waiting for slightly over thirty minutes.

"Where is this fuckin' guy?" Bah-Bah finally said. "I saw him last night in the bar."

"The bar? You go in these bars?"

"The bars are all right. You just can't go in the wrong one. I mean, they got Inky bars, Ben's bars, Logan Nation Bars, Puerto Rican bars; 1-5-D got their bar. There are Scorpion bars. Cops got their bars. Dykes got their bars. They got Nazi bars even. The bars are OK. You just can't go in the wrong ones, unless it says *chez* on the sign outside, like this place over here on Ogontz Avenue. *Chez Eva's.* Because Torch told me that *chez* means *house*, and that means anybody is welcome there. It's a different world up here, bro."

Bobby looked at him then. "Natzi bars?"

"Oh, yeah! Clubs, I mean. They got I.R.A. bars up here, too. They collect money, you know, for arms, shit like that. Torch showed me a few of those spots. Those places are over in Olney. It's a creepy neighborhood, Olney. Logan, too, creepy neighborhood. Have to speak all kinda different languages and shit up here, especially in Logan. Does Frenchie know who you are?"

"I met him once or twice," Bobby answered.

"Good. I want him to understand what this is."

"There he is. He's doing it just like you said he would."

"I saw him do this before."

Frenchie was hovering around outside the candy store.

"Wait until he gets in the phone booth."

Frenchie entered the phone booth and pretended to speak on the phone while he manipulated the pipe cleaner he used to stuff up the money slot. When it came loose, a treasure of quarters, dimes and nickels spilled out. The Cadillac pulled up to the curb near the phone booth. Frenchie sensed the car and heard its motor. He turned his back and pretended to talk. Bobby kicked the door open, and Frenchie's back went as deep into the booth as it could possibly go. He looked out and saw the white car at the curb and then saw the gun raised. It got his full attention. He vaguely recalled the face behind the gun. It was Bah-Bah's boy. The powerful gun unloaded in his chest and made him spin around. He managed to look again and saw Bah-Bah smiling at him from the car. It was a game after all. Then, a smaller caliber gun was pressed behind Frenchie's ear, and two shots were fired, making this murder look like a pro job with two gun men. That was the way Bah-Bah wanted it. He didn't want the others (Felix and them) to think Frenchie was killed because he stole loose change off somebody in a bar two years ago or something stupid like that. They would know that he (Bah-Bah) was behind this. They would know that he was nobody to fuck with after all. They would understand finally that he *allowed* them to live in his house as opposed to them running the place against his will. Bobby returned to the car, and they drove off on Ogontz Avenue, past *Chez Eva's*, past Jericho Beef, the spot where they bought those spare-ribs the first day he moved around here. Bah-Bah maneuvered the car through Nicetown, then onto the expressway, never to return to this place again. As the Intruders sang "Cowboys to Girls" on the radio, Bah-Bah thought about the upcoming Labor Day weekend. He looked forward to talking about his strange summer with his friends over sausage and peppers. As he listened to this song, the song actor Kevin Bacon claimed was the best song ever recorded, he realized that, at the very least, his taste in music had improved.

* * *

About an hour later, Torch crossed the tracks and walked over to Maria's house. He had brought a paper bag with him and picked what was left of the tomatoes she had grown. On his way back along the catwalk crossing the bridge over Broad Street, Torch noticed a railroad detective hiding about one hundred yards ahead of him. Hearing a noise, he turned around to see, out of the corner of his eye, another railroad detective twenty-five yards behind him. He was trapped. A freight train was heading east just then. Torch climbed over a steel barrier, dropping the tomatoes. Torch's only hope was to beat the train and cross the tracks. The detectives would have to wait for the slow-moving freight train to go by. Unfortunately, Torch slightly misjudged the speed of the train. His instincts and his timing were a little off. The top half of Torch's body did beat out the train; his legs didn't.

CHAPTER 22

In September, the Supreme Court of the United States proclaimed that it was unconstitutional to prevent the homes of Whitman Park in South Philadelphia from being built. Construction was to begin on the new houses in October. This foreshadowed Jimmy Cerrone's loss in the special election to change the Philadelphia Charter, so he could run for a third term.

A group of citizens maintained that keeping any mayor whose administration was more than eight years old was not conducive to good government and not in the best interest of the constituents. But that group was relatively small. It was the new voters, several hundred thousand of them who never even registered before and were simply voting against Cerrone, because he was Cerrone, who swung the election. Ninety-five percent of this group voted "No" or against the charter change.

On Friday, Felix and Jackie walked down Windrim Avenue on the other side of the now burnt-out Caesar's Palace. They were on the corner of 11th and Windrim, right by the ambulance station when a 1968 white Impala pulled up. The driver and the passenger in the front seat were both black. Another youth was crouched down in the back seat. They were from the Nicetown gang. The one in the passenger seat yelled out to Felix and Jackie, "Where you from?"

Jackie and Felix looked at each other for a second.

"Ben's," Jackie called out.

Just then the third youth, who was wearing a baseball cap backwards, popped up from the back seat, and a shotgun materialized out of the open back window. The first blast caught Felix in the chest and spun him around. The second shot hit Jackie in the leg, and the third one caught Felix in the ribs. He was DOA at Einstein Hospital. Jackie arrived there in serious condition, but would be released in one or two weeks.

On the Tuesday after Labor Day, Washington went to Einstein Hospital. He stopped in to visit Jackie who was still there recovering from his wounds. Jackie didn't help him out with any information, just as Washington knew he wouldn't. It didn't matter anyway since Washington had a lot of connections within Nicetown and had learned the shooter's identity. It was the same guy who had killed Lil Rock, according to his information. Washington thought there was something very poetic about all of it. The same person who started the trouble which brought Washington here in the first place was part of the ending.

Before Washington went to see Torch, who was in intensive care, he stopped in the cafeteria and had a cup of coffee. Washington had already talked to an intern about Torch. His condition was grave. They had said he was very weak and had asked Washington to be brief in talking to him and not to expect very coherent answers. They told Washington that Torch had lost a lot of blood and that they'd almost lost him. They had managed to save everything except his legs. In a few weeks, Torch would be sent to the Moss Rehabilitation Center which was next to Einstein Hospital for physical therapy. He would first learn to walk on sticks and then legs would be fitted for him. The whole process would take between six and eight weeks. "Young people usually make good recoveries with this kind of injury," the doctor told Washington. But they were more concerned about Torch's mental state as the trauma was simply too much for him. He still was partially in mental shock over the incident. Washington thought back to what police who were on the scene told him. It had taken three policemen to take Torch's body from the railroad tracks.

Torch was obviously in shock and said to one of the officers, "Don't tell my mom."

Washington took a sip of his coffee and thought about the last time when he was here at this hospital. It was when Lee Oskar was here, and Torch and he had had that discussion. So much had changed since then. Not only Shine, but now Felix, Frenchie, and Glenn were gone. Jackie was badly injured, as was Torch himself. Connell and maybe others would be in jail because of the fight outside the Warnock. The testing was accurate, Washington thought. These two groups — one black and one white — whose members had scored alike in his testing and were from the same neighborhood had ended up the almost same. There was a difference here maybe, but it was much less dramatic than it appeared in June. He was right; the environment even trumped race when it came down to creating the person and determining his destiny.

Washington found an old *Daily News* and turned back to the sports section. There was an article about Briscoe's fight against Marvin Hagler. The writer of the article was named Thom Greer:

"Fourteen thousand, five hundred and thirty disappointed fans, the largest non-title fight crowd in Spectrum history witnessed Marvin Hagler's utter humiliation of their hero, Benny Briscoe. With this fight, Briscoe was totally outclassed by a man who may indeed be on a collision course with the middleweight championship of the world. The unanimous decision of the judges was a gross understatement. Nevertheless, old Briscoe hung in there.

'He's still got punching power,' Hagler said. 'Benny's still a strong man. This was the toughest fight I've had in a long time.'

Hagler's trainer said, 'Marvin's at the top of his game, coming to Philadelphia and beating what I believe to be one of the best middleweights in the world. You know whether you've got it or not, when you come to Philadelphia and win, what more do you have to prove?'"

Washington then sought out John Chapman's column. Every few weeks Chapman devoted his column to letters written by his readers. He printed a letter in which a reader referred to an article that Chapman had written about a month ago. The original article came after Chapman had gone to San Francisco for a vacation.

In Chapman's article, much was written about San Francisco's gay community. According to Chapman, unlike Philadelphia's gay community, they were politically focused and aware. At the time of Chapman's visit, they were in the process of removing a councilman that they had fallen out of favor with.

Chapman had long viewed Philadelphia's gay community as an ally in this battle against Cerrone. Cerrone and the gay population of Philadelphia had been adversaries for several decades, going back to when Cerrone was a cop in Center City and then a police commissioner.

In the column, Chapman went on and on about the gay activism. At least, one reader of the *Daily News* was not impressed:

Dear Mr. Chapman,

Your column about the gay community in San Francisco seemed to be a bit excessive. What happened out there, John? Somebody must have really taken good care of you.

Chapman responded this way: *"Your mother was fantastic."*

Washington then reached into his shirt pocket and removed the envelope containing Torch's mug shots from last week. Washington was a cop who loved mug shots. He used them in investigations all the time. It amazed him how frequently he recognized a suspect from his mug shot. Minus a brush, comb, or brylcreem, a mug-shot perhaps, in many cases, gave a truer picture of the suspect. It was why maybe he preferred a mugshot to an outdated prom picture or wedding photo. He thought you could see things in them, too. Sometimes he thought he could see remorse or guilt or indifference. He thought about doing a study, using thousands of mug shots and seeing if there was any consistency to how a guilty suspect looked or held their eyes or something like that. Ultimately, Washington abandoned the idea but, it had crossed his mind. Nevertheless, he saw a certain value in them. Washington saved certain mugshots, collected them not unlike a collector of baseball cards. He had at home, the mugshots of criminals like Joe Miami, Frankie Flowers, and Chick-a-Dee. They were all dead now, murdered in this gangster-war over Philadelphia and Atlantic City. He had these "special" ones protected in plastic.

He had the mug shot of Constantine, too. That was his prize one, his valuable Mickey Mantle Rookie Card, and he kept that one under glass. He also kept the mug shots of the hierarchy of Philadelphia's notorious Black Mafia of the early seventies in plastic as well. Also, he had the mug shots of the members of the infamous K&A burglary ring, who started out doing jobs in Northeast Philly but ripped off houses up and down the East Coast. There was now a book about this team called *Confessions of a Second Story Man*.

Generally, mug shots in Philadelphia were taken at one of two locations. They were either taken at the Roundhouse, or they were taken up there on the seventh floor of City Hall at intake of the probation/ parole department. Fortunately for Washington, he had gotten friendly over the years with clerks that worked at each place. When Washington had to be at City Hall for court, he usually dropped in the intake unit and spent an hour or so checking out dozens of mug shots.

Of all the mug shots that he saw over the years, thousands of them, Torch's mug shot was sort of unique. Rarely did a mug shot tell so many stories. First of all, the profile shot showed a young man clearly wasted and beat by his night in the slam. That was obvious from the one visible eye at half-mast. In the straight-on picture, Torch's eyes registered pure terror and shock. Electrical shock was what Washington actually thought of. Yet, despite all that, despite the fear, Torch still had his head cocked in that gangster, John Dillinger-fashion. Torch had to be a ball-breaker to the very end. It was amazing or, at least, interesting to Washington.

But there was something else here, too. It was something much more important. At first when Washington received Torch's mug shots in the mail, he didn't notice it. It wasn't until the second or third time he looked that he noticed that it was definitely there, right in this simple black and white photo. Torch wasn't wearing a shirt. Torch, in his own words, had even said that he wasn't the type of guy to run around with no shirt on. Torch, no doubt, had removed his shirt that night for the same reason Connell and the others had removed their shirts, which was so that they would not be identified. To Washington, knowing Torch as he did, this was concrete evidence. Of course, a judge wouldn't necessarily see it that way. He wondered what Torch would say about these pictures. What he needed, Washington knew, was a confession from Torch. Washington figured that Torch would recover enough to go to court. Hopefully another arrest or two would satisfy the neighbors around the Warnock Tavern. Ideally there would then be some closure that would bring an end to the rumors going around and the racial tension consuming Washington's beat in Logan. Washington had been waiting days to confront Torch with these pictures.

Washington went into Torch's section of the intensive care unit at Einstein Hospital. He had no problem recognizing him, and he was smiling. Washington was sort of spooked by that. He walked over to Torch's bed without saying anything. He reached inside his pocket and withdrew the mug shots, showing them to Torch. "You're not wearing a shirt in this picture, Torch," Washington said. It was what he said before "Hello."

Torch didn't react. He knew what Washington was showing him. There was no need to explain it, and it didn't make sense for Torch to act like he didn't understand. As weak as he was, this was the time for Torch to say something. What the hell was Washington going to do to him now anyway?

Torch's speech was labored, and he was breathing with difficulty. "You know, I always wondered why you were so concerned about drugs. When Reds got killed, I honestly didn't believe at first that cops had anything to do with it. I just figured it was some dope addicts Reds knew somewhere down the line. I knew a cocaine dealer, a Jewish kid from Germantown. One time his house was raided. They took his personal phone book. I remember him telling me about that. He told me they always do that. Cops always go right for the personal phonebook of a drug dealer. Then about three months after Reds was killed, Felix told me that he couldn't find his phone book. That was when I first started thinking about it. I found out later that you were partners with that guy Kelly, and Felix said that one of the Kellys was there when Reds was killed. I already knew you were involved with the Kelly Brothers from other things."

Although talking was difficult for him, Torch continued. "Maria told me that you were friends with them. Plus Bah-Bah told me that you and Kelly ripped off a card game in South Philadelphia years ago. I know that you didn't mean for Reds to be killed. I'm not saying that, but it doesn't matter. He was murdered anyway. Those guys were set up man, Reds, Danny, them, most certainly by you."

Torch paused for a few seconds to catch his breath. "OK, you have those mug shots. We both know what they mean. The truth is he came after me with a butcher knife, and I was scared to death. I'd have been killed if they didn't run out of the bar just then. They saved my ass, and yes, I hit him with my belt, but I was scared, man. That was what happened. You have those pictures, and I really don't care. I'd just think about what you do with them if I were you."

Now it was Washington who was smiling as he said, "I just thought you might want these mug shots for souvenirs or something. Are you in any pain?" he asked, slipping the mug shots into the drawer of the cabinet next to the bed.

Torch was proud of himself. "Are you in any pain?" In other words, Washington wanted to change the subject. He was happy to get that business over with. Washington wasn't going to do anything with those mug shots because he couldn't. Torch had him by the *coglioni* as well.

"They have me on a ton of pain killers. I always want to sleep and not think about anything. But when I do sleep I have these crazy dreams all the time."

Washington told Torch that he had to leave, but that he had just wanted to stop by to see him. He told Torch that he had also visited Jackie upstairs. By the time Washington had exited the room, Torch was asleep again. The conversation had tired him out. His blood pressure had dropped dramatically. He began to dream.

He dreamed that he was running through the Logan schoolyard, just like he had done so many times as a little boy. He was running back, he believed, from the North Star Diner, after having just visited Maria there. (He had been dreaming about her a lot since the incident.) The details were sharper in this dream than the other dreams he'd had. Everything was more vivid. Maybe it was because this was, indeed, the grand finale of dreams for him. As he ran, he could make out the painted lines on the ground. He ran over the basketball courts, over the foul lines and out-of-bounds lines. He ran also over the games painted there in the cement. He could see them clearly. There was the Bottle Cap Court and Hop-Scotch and Boiling Seas. He had made it almost to the other side and the 17th Street exit when he realized that he had to go back to the diner because he'd left his car back there in the lot.

Then the dream shifted like dreams tend to do, and the schoolyard now was a huge pool, more like a sea of water. Maria was in this part of the dream and that temporarily comforted him. It was as if he knew he was sliding away, and he wanted Maria, the only woman he ever loved, to be a part of his last subconscious thought. At first he and Maria, in the dream, were swimming together. Then he was alone. Somebody had his arms and was pulling him through the water. The water was cold, and he moved effortlessly through it. Somebody else had him by the ankles now, and he was being stretched out. He was moving faster and faster, and he felt peaceful, even though the water was getting colder and colder. Then suddenly, there was nothing … only darkness.

The End

ABOUT THE AUTHOR
– SAMMY LEVITT

S ammy Levitt was born and raised in Philadelphia. He graduated from Temple University. He is a former Philadelphia city employee. His articles have appeared in *Gambling Times*, *Win*, and *American Turf Monthly* magazines. He has been an officer in the Roxborough Lodge Son's of Italy for over 25 years.